The Prince

His mother stood over him, a short blade already in her right hand. She held her left hand to the shallow gash that his blade had put in her hip. Her eyes looked as cold as those of his goddess when Shar had come to him in dreams. Her lower lip trembled. He did not understand why.

"I killed fifty men before you uttered your first squall and you think to take me unaware with *that?*" She nodded at the dagger. "Are you enspelled? Mad? What are you doing?"

Rivalen looked at the dagger in his fist, the black poison on its blade, the smear of his mother's red blood. "Murdering you," he answered, and started to stand.

The Dwarf

A rock shuffled under his foot, but Thibbledorf Pwent didn't hear it. As he scrambled over the last rise along the cliff face, up onto the high ground from which the dwarves had made their stand before retreating into Mithral Hall, a small tumble of rocks cascaded down behind him—and again, he didn't hear it.

He heard the screams and cries, of glory and of pain, of determination against overwhelming odds, and of support for friends who were surely doomed.

He heard the ring of metal on metal, the crunch of a skull under the weight of his heavy, spiked gauntlets, and the sucking sound of his helmet spike driving through the belly of one more orc.

The Paladin

Horror and compassion warred within her. Without a doubt, this man was the seed from which atrocities were sewn. Much of the fallout of the Rotting War could be traced to him and him alone. And yet, this servant of Ilmater—a paladin, by his garb—has lost his god, his son, and his war. All that was left was for him to lose was his life. Jaeriko could sense Maze itching to relieve him of that burden, too, but the assassin managed to hold herself in check.

"He sounds like a man who's lost his faith," Jaeriko said, fingering her locket.

"He sounds like a man who's lost his mind," Maze said. "Never empathize with the enemy. If you do, you'll never make your kill."

THE TWILIGHT WAR
Paul S. Kemp

Book I
Shadowbred

Book II
Shadowstorm

Book III
Shadowrealm

Edited by Philip Athans

Realms of the Elves
Realms of the Dragons
Realms of the Dragons II

FORGOTTEN REALMS

REALMS OF WAR

THE TWILIGHT WAR ANTHOLOGY

EDITED BY PHILIP ATHANS

The Twilight War Anthology

REALMS OF WAR

©2008 Wizards of the Coast, Inc.

Cover art by Raymond Swanland
First Printing: January 2008

9 8 7 6 5 4 3 2 1

ISBN: 978-0-7869-4934-2
620-21623740-001-EN

U.S., CANADA,
ASIA, PACIFIC, & LATIN AMERICA
Wizards of the Coast, Inc.
P.O. Box 707
Renton, WA 98057-0707
+1-800-324-6496

EUROPEAN HEADQUARTERS
Hasbro UK Ltd
Caswell Way
Newport, Gwent NP9 0YH
GREAT BRITAIN
Save this address for your records.

Visit our web site at www.wizards.com

Contents

CONTINUUM

Paul S. Kemp

The Year of Seven Tines (-365 DR)

Rivalen stood beside his mother at the edge of a forest meadow filled with violet flowers, deep in the wooded realm that once was the abode of the Arnothoi elves. The wind, bearing the woody, floral fragrance of late spring, stirred the leaves to whispers. Twilight painted the meadow with golden light.

A false face masked Rivalen's intentions. Only his hands spoke truth. In his left fist he cupped the smooth black disc that served as his secret holy symbol of Shar. In his right hand, hidden under his cloak, he held the cool, wire-wrapped hilt of a poisoned dagger.

The patch of *avenorani* flowers, deep violet petals surrounding the black core of the stigma, stretched out before them. The fading light turned them into an iridescent violet sea. A breeze caused the flowers to sway as one. They undulated like waves and cast a cloud of sparkling pollen into the twilight air. The silver motes tinkled like faint bells as they rained down.

"It is wondrous, Rivalen," his mother said. She placed her hand on his arm. "Your father will be so pleased when I bring him here."

"Yes," Rivalen said, though he knew his father would never see the meadow.

His father, Telemont Tanthul, the most powerful arcanist in Shade Enclave, had taken an interest in botany in recent years. Rivalen had lured his mother to the meadow in secret, with the promise of a unique gift to commemorate his father's imminent ascendance to the office of Most High, ruler of Shade Enclave.

His mother walked ahead of him, into the patch, amid the pollen, letting her fingertips graze the tops of the flowers. They shivered under her touch and sent more pollen into the air. The meadow looked otherworldly, a fey land of silver rain, tinkling bells, and murder.

Rivalen stared at her back, at the space between her shoulder blades. His grip on the dagger tightened. He tensed as he thought of lunging at her, of driving the blade into her pale flesh, but he hesitated and the moment passed.

She turned and smiled at him. She did not suspect his motives.

He had taken precautions to ensure his crime would not be discovered. He had transported them to the meadow from Shade Enclave, utilizing the Shadow Weave revealed to him by Shar. After the murder he would move his mother's corpse back to the enclave. The poison that stained his dagger, painstakingly crafted by his own hand in the quiet of his own manse, would leave no trace on her body and would make revivification impossible. After he healed his mother's flesh of the dagger's bite, it would appear that she had died in her sleep. Only Rivalen and Shar would know the truth. It would be Rivalen's Own Secret, and he would bear its weight.

His goddess had ordered the matricide in a vision. He did not know Shar's purpose and dared not inquire. The Goddess of Loss kept her own secrets and promised Rivalen nothing.

He licked his lips and tried to slow his heart. The hair on his arms stood on end. He told himself it was the magic in the air.

His mother turned a circle, still graceful and strong even in her middle years, even after birthing twelve children. She drew a deep breath of magic-infused air and laughed. Silver motes coated her embroidered velvet cloak, her dark hair, her pale flesh.

"The pollen tickles my nose."

He smiled, another false gesture on a day of falseness.

She gestured him to join her. "Come, Rivalen. You'd stand in the shadows of the trees when this beckons? Come out of the darkness. Come."

He did not move. He preferred the darkness.

"I could lie here and sleep under the stars like an elf," she said, her wistful expression that of the young mother he remembered from his youth. "Your father will marvel." She looked away and smiled distantly, as if imagining the pleasure the meadow would bring his father. "The elves say that if you inhale enough pollen while standing in a field of *avenorani*, your wishes will come true. Your father scoffs at such tales but standing here now, I believe it to be so."

His father was right to scoff. The Art of the elves had only enhanced the beauty and heartiness of the flowers, not granted them the power to grant wishes. The blooms flourished even in winter, changed color with the seasons, chimed in the rain, but nothing more.

"A legend," he said.

Her expression fell, and she eyed him with concern. "You

are far too serious for so young a man. Have I raised so somber a son?"

"My studies require seriousness, Mother."

"So they do," she acknowledged with a nod. "Your father drives you. But do not be so driven that the joy of life passes you by."

He let his face offer the lie of another smile. Shar taught him that joy was fleeting, that love was a lie. "Do not worry for me, Mother."

She turned from him, and he began the murder.

He whispered the words to a powerful abjuration that nullified all magic out to a distance of five paces from his person. The wards and alarms that protected his mother would not operate within the area of his spell.

His mother seemed not to notice, but the tinkling of the pollen fell silent when he completed the incantation, as if the flowers had grown sullen.

"I have never seen so many," she said, looking out over the field of flowers. "Do you think the elves know of this meadow?"

"The *arnothoi* moved west," he said, tensing. "The meadow is long forgotten. We are alone here."

Possibly she heard something unusual in his tone. Possibly she noticed the silence of the flowers at last. She turned back and looked at him strangely.

"Are you all right?" she asked. "You look pale."

For a moment Rivalen could not speak. He stared at her while his heartbeat drummed in his ears and his mouth went dry.

Concern creased the skin around his mother's eyes and furrowed her brow. "Rivalen?"

She took a step toward him.

His hand tightened on the dagger hilt under his cloak. He swallowed.

"Rivalen?"

She neared him, one hand outstretched. His breath came fast. He readied himself.

She stopped two paces from him, and her expression changed, hardened.

She knew.

"Rivalen," she said, and the word was not a question.

He jerked the dagger free and lunged at her, blade held before him.

Her reflexes surprised him. She sidestepped his attack and kicked him in the knee, wrenching it. He shouted with pain and waved the dagger at her as he fell. He felt the blade bite flesh, heard his mother curse. He fell amid the flowers, amid a shower of silver pollen. He rolled over and looked up, the dagger held defensively before him.

His mother stood over him, a short blade already in her right hand. She held her left hand to the shallow gash that his blade had put in her hip. Her eyes looked as cold as those of his goddess when Shar had come to him in dreams. Her lower lip trembled. He did not understand why.

"I killed fifty men before you uttered your first squall and you think to take me unaware with *that?*" She nodded at the dagger. "Are you enspelled? Mad? What are you doing?"

Rivalen looked at the dagger in his fist, the black poison on its blade, the smear of his mother's red blood. "Murdering you," he answered, and started to stand.

She snarled and stepped toward him, blade ready, but staggered. Her eyes widened and she wobbled.

"Poison," she said, and slurred the word. "But. . ."

"None of your protective wards are functioning."

She swayed, backed up a step.

"Nor your alarm spells," Rivalen said, on his feet. "Nor the contingency spells placed on you by my father."

She tried to back off another step, but the poison had stolen her coordination. She fell amid the flowers and sent up a cloud of silver.

He stepped near her, stood over her, held his holy symbol for her to see.

She stared up at him through eyes turning glassy. "Why, Rivalen?"

"Because love is a lie. Only hate endures."

Shock widened her eyes. "I am your mother."

"Only of my flesh," he said. "Not of my soul."

Tears showed at the corners of her eyes.

"Your bitterness is sweet to the Lady, Mother."

He kneeled beside her to watch her die. The tinkling flowers sang a funeral dirge.

She swallowed rapidly, reflexively. Her breathing was shallow. Her fingers worked, clawed at the ground, and reached for him.

"Hold my. . . hand, Rivalen," she said in a whispered gasp.

He did not reach for her, merely stared into her wan face. "We all die alone, Mother."

She closed her eyes, and the tears leaked down her cheeks.

"Your father will learn of this."

"No. This will be known only to us. And to Shar."

To that, she said nothing. She stared at him for a moment, then closed her eyes and inhaled deeply.

When her intentions registered, he smiled.

"What did you wish for, Mother?"

She opened her eyes and the hurt in her gaze was gone, replaced by anger. "To be the instrument of your downfall."

He stood. "Good night, Mother. I answer to another mistress now."

She gagged, tried to speak, but failed. Her eyes turned distant. She stared up at the twilight sky, and he saw the awareness melt out of her eyes.

Looking upon her corpse, he felt nothing—emptiness, a

hole. He ran his fingertips over the edge of his holy symbol and supposed that was point.

Rivalen.

He looked around the *avenorani* patch, and noticed for the first time that many of the flowers were wilted, dead. How had he not noticed before?

Rivalen.

His mother was calling him from the next world.

Uktar, the Year of Lightning Storms (1374 DR)

Rivalen.

Brennus's mental voice, communicated to Rivalen through the magical rings each wore, pulled Rivalen from sleep. He sat up in his bed, still groggy, haunted by tinkling bells, the smell of flowers, and the dead eyes of his mother.

Brennus?

A pause, then, *Are you well? You sound different.*

Shadows churned around Rivalen. Moonlight leaked through the shutter slats of his room. He ran a hand through his black hair, tried to dislodge from his mind the dream of his mother, the memory of matricide.

I am well, he said. *What is it?*

Erevis Cale has a woman.

Rivalen grew alert. *A woman? A wife?*

No, Brennus answered. *But a woman he cares for. I am unable to scry Cale, but he may return to her.*

Where is she?

She lives alone in a cottage northwest of Ordulin.

The shadows around Rivalen spun, coiled as he considered possible courses. *Watch her.*

Just watch?

Yes. If Cale appears, inform me immediately.

Very well. Rivalen, she is pregnant.

With his *child?*

Yes. But she does not know it yet.

Rivalen blinked. *How do you know it, then?*

His brother spoke in the self-satisfied tone of one who has mastered his Art. Brennus was a diviner without peer. *Discovering things is my gift,* he said.

The magical connection ended.

Rivalen tried to turn his mind to Erevis Cale, to the events in Selgaunt, to his plans for all of Sembia, but the thoughts of his mother dominated his mind.

He had healed the dagger wound in her flesh, magically concealed his involvement with the murder, and returned the body to her bed in Shade Enclave. As expected, his father had despaired upon finding his beloved dead.

His despair, however, had quickly turned to rage. Rivalen's mother's body had been found without the inscribed platinum and jacinth necklace Telemont had given her the night of her death. He had put it upon her himself.

Suspicious of his wife's death and his inability to have her revivified, Telemont had obsessed over the missing necklace, had sought it for years. He knew for certain that it must have been taken, that she must have been murdered. He had driven Brennus to focus his magical studies on divinations to assist him in finding the culpable party.

Rivalen had lived in terror of his father's wrath and his brother's skill for years. But even Brennus's divinations proved unable to locate his mother's necklace or learn of Rivalen's involvement.

Shar had protected her priest.

Often Rivalen had returned to the scene of his crime in secret, had scoured the area for the necklace, but found nothing. He told himself that a servant had found the body and stolen the necklace before announcing the news to the rest of the staff.

The death of his wife drove a spike of bitterness into the soul of Telemont. The loss of his beloved drove him, at Rivalen's urging, to the worship of the Lady of Loss. Rivalen marveled at the subtlety of the Lady's plan, still did, though he wondered why his mother had returned to haunt his dreams just then. He had not dreamed of her in centuries.

"Why trouble my sleep now, Lady?" Rivalen asked Shar.

After all, the moment of her triumph, and his, was nearly at hand.

❧ ❧ ❧ ❧ ❧

A distant rumble pulled Varra from dreams of shadows. She opened her eyes and rolled over in the bed. Save for the soft glow of starlight, darkness shrouded the cottage.

The air felt strange, gauzy against her skin, wet in her lungs. The empty space in the bed beside her—the place where Erevis should have been—looked like a hole.

Blinking away sleep, she saw a figure of shadow standing in the far corner of the room. Surprise stole her voice. Her heart hammered.

"Erevis?"

She lurched out of bed, and the abrupt movement caused the room to spin, to close in on her. Her stomach turned. She reached frantically for the chamberpot on the floor, put her head over it, and vomited.

When she looked up again, the figure was gone and she realized that sleepiness and the darkness had summoned a phantom of her hopes. Erevis was not with her. She was alone.

Pulling the blanket around her shoulders, she walked to the shuttered window. Pre-dawn light leaked through them, ghostly, pale.

Thunder rumbled again, but Varra knew the sky to make

a poor prophet. Thunder rarely brought rain. Her garden was parched under the ungenerous sky.

The rumble continued, took an odd pitch, rose, fell. She pushed open the shutters and looked out on the meadow, the elm, her vegetable garden, the wildflowers, the rough chairs Erevis had crafted from dead wood, the chairs in which they had sat when they said good-bye.

The western sky was clear. Dawn lightened it to gray. But the lingering darkness felt odd, unwilling to depart, and the plants in the meadow looked hunched, braced against the coming storm.

The roll of thunder continued, and it settled on her that she was not hearing thunder.

Barefoot, she hurried out the door and into the meadow. She turned a circle under the sky, scanned it for the storm, for the source of the sound. When she looked south and saw the sky, she gasped.

Clouds as black as a pool of ink marred the southern horizon. They churned, swirled, and roiled purposefully, like living things. Veins of green lightning lit them from time to time. The bank of clouds expanded incrementally as she watched, devouring more and more of the pre-dawn sky. She stared, agape, unable to process what she was seeing. It was not natural. It was no storm. It was her nightmare made real. Shadows had swallowed the man she loved. Soon they would swallow the world.

Clouds of birds thronged the sky, riding the wind northward. Movement from the edge of the meadow drew her gaze, and a dozen animals streaked out of the trees, boiled around her, and through the meadow—bounding deer, chittering squirrels, a raccoon. She had no time to respond and froze as they flowed around and past her.

Looking at the sky, a primal part of her understood that the animals had it right. She must run, too. Everyone must. The storm was coming, and to be caught in it was to die.

Fear freed her to act. She ran back to the cottage and pulled a large sack from among her things. She filled it with turnips, carrots, string beans, and potatoes from her garden, nuts and wild pears from the forest. She had little meat, only a fistful of jerky. She threw on her cloak, pulled on her boots, rolled a blanket into a ball, and headed out the door.

Water. She'd forgotten water. She dashed back inside the cottage, located a water skin, and filled it from one of the buckets she had drawn the night before from the drying creek nearby.

She stepped out into the meadow, under the eye of the storm, and headed northwest, into the unknown, following the fleeing forest animals. She did not know Sembia, but she knew there was a north-south road not far away.

Only after the sun rose to make a losing war in the heavens with the darkness did she think of Erevis and wonder if he was safe.

◉ ◉ ◉ ◉ ◉

Brennus, standing before the enormous cube of smooth metal, the faces of which served as his scrying lenses, turned the focus of his divination to the magical storm that had frightened Cale's woman.

When the roiling, lightning-veined clouds took focus on the cube's face, the twin homunculi perched on his shoulders whistled. Their small claws dug into his flesh.

He recognized the storm immediately for what it was—a planar rift. The Plane of Shadow had been released onto the Prime. But how had it been done, and who had done it?

"What is it?" asked one of his homunculi in its high-pitched voice.

"Silence, now," he said, and intoned the words to a divination.

When he completed the spell, he focused it on the image of the storm, felt around the edge of the clouds, and learned what it could tell him. He cast another divination, another, forcing his magic to worm its way into the core of a tenebrous sea, to unearth its secrets. Undead shadows teemed in its depths. Shadow giants stomped through its murk.

Ordulin lay festering and twisted on the Sembian plains, its buildings, parks, and citizens transformed into places and creatures of darkness.

And the storm whispered two names.

"Shar," said one of his homunculi in a hushed tone.

"Volumvax," said the other.

Brennus tried to make sense of events. His brother was Shar's Nightseer, yet Brennus knew Rivalen did not cause the rift. There was no purpose in it. Shade Enclave wished to annex Sembia, not destroy it. But the creation of the rift could not have been an accident.

"Look," said one of his homunculi, clapping with delight as a cascade of green lightning ripped through the mass of clouds.

"Be silent and let me think," Brennus said.

The destruction of Ordulin changed the dynamic of the Sembian civil war, perhaps changed the dynamic of his brother's relationship to his goddess.

The homunculi giggled as a swarm of shadows flew before the scrying lens, their eyes like glowing coals.

"Enough," Brennus said, though he was speaking to himself as much as to his constructs.

Both homunculi, book ends to his ears, glared and stuck out their tongues.

Despite the seriousness of the moment, Brennus smiled at the audacity of his constructs. He endured their insolence with a father's patience and pride. While his own father had forced him to take the path of the diviner, his mother had nurtured his fascination with constructs, automata, golems, and clockworks. Some of his fondest memories of his childhood were of showing off to his delighted mother the crude mechanical toys he had fashioned. He still missed her sometimes. She would smile at how far his craft had progressed.

He wondered why he thought of that now, of her.

"Treat," one of the homunculi said, and the other turned it into a chant. "Treat. Treat."

Brennus pulled a sweetmeat from an inner pocket and unwrapped it while the homunculi clapped and smacked their lips. He offered it to them and they devoured it. While they ate, he triggered the magic of the communication ring he wore, felt the connection to Rivalen open.

Rivalen. I have news.

His brother's mental voice, fatigued, answered him. *Erevis Cale?*

No, Brennus answered, and related to Rivalen all that he had seen and learned. Rivalen answered him with silence.

It will have to be stopped or little of Sembia will remain to occupy, Brennus said.

Still Rivalen said nothing.

Rivalen? Are you unwell? Shall I inform the Most High?

The tension crackled through the magical connection. *No. I will inform our father. Continue to watch the woman. Erevis Cale will come.*

Erevis Cale seems hardly to be—

Watch the woman, his brother said. *I know the name Volumvax. He is an apostate. He once served Mask before turning to the Lady of Loss.*

Mask? Brennus said, and the shadows around him roiled. *Erevis Cale serves Mask.*

Watch the woman. There is more to this than we yet see.

Brennus did not doubt it.

Varra trudged the game trails, trusting that she was headed west, until at last the forest thinned and finally gave way to the sun-bleached grass of the Sembian plains. Wind stirred the tall grass. Copses of trees dotted the otherwise empty landscape in the distance, lonely sentries bending in the breeze, as if paying obeisance to the coming storm. The ribbon of a packed-earth road split the plains. Pleased to have gotten so far so fast, Varra put the expanding storm to her back and hurried to the road.

Hours passed. The landscape appeared empty, populated only by ghosts and the threats issuing from the rumbling sky. Either the famine or the magical storm had driven most from their homes already. The wind from the south, from the storm, pawed aggressively at her cloak. The darkness weighed on her, dogged her steps, gained on her. She pulled her cloak more tightly around her and hurried on.

Nervousness rooted in her stomach as the sun moved from east to west. She imagined herself asleep on the plain, exposed at nightfall, with the darkness closing the distance. Fighting down the panic, she resolved to walk through the night. She would not stop until she found someone else, anyone else.

The storm growled at her resolve.

An hour later, as the sun shot its final, defiant rays into the darkening sky, she heard the creak of wagons and the low murmur of distant voices from behind her. She turned, hopeful, to see a ragtag group of five wagons winding up the road toward her. Perhaps a dozen men and women walked beside the wagons. Most carried packs stuffed with blankets, pots, tools, the leftovers from a home abandoned.

Almost tearful at the realization that she would not have to face the night alone, she stopped and waited for them to approach.

Tired, fearful eyes looked out of faces creased with anxiety and caked with road dust. A few smiled and nodded greetings. Most simply looked away. All spoke in hushed tones, as if they feared someone would overhear.

"Keep moving, lassie," said an elderly man. "They say Ordulin is destroyed. That everyone's dead."

A woman made a protective sign with her fingers. "I heard Shar herself stepped out of the sky. It's the Time of Troubles all over again."

"The darkness is following us," said a middle-aged man with a pronounced limp. "It has eyes. The Dales and Elminster are our only hope."

Mutterings, nods, and muffled tears greeted the pronouncements.

Varra was too tired and afraid to try to make sense of the words.

"We know nothing for certain," said the heavyset driver of a mule-pulled wagon. Household furnishings were piled high in the wagon: furniture, blankets, buckets, hand tools . . . A leather hat capped the top of the driver's head, and his belly hung over a wide leather belt. Gray whiskers dotted his unremarkable face. "For now we just keep moving. There'll be safety in the Dales." He looked around the caravan, holding the eyes of any who looked at him, speaking loud enough for all to hear. "There'll be safety there."

His words quieted the murmurings, but fear hung over the group. The man halted the mule and looked down on Varra.

"You alone, little sister?"

The words struck her oddly, and a pit opened in her stomach.

"Yes."

"Where are you going?"

She gestured vaguely down the road. "I . . . I'm not sure."

"Where are you from?"

She waved vaguely back at the forest.

The man shared a glance with the elderly woman seated beside him in the wagon. She wore a homespun dress over a veined, age-spotted frame that made a scarecrow look hale. Thin gray hair poked unevenly out from under her shawl. A thin, dark-haired man in a black leather jack slept in the seat behind them.

"I am Denthim," the heavyset driver said. "This is my mum. That other is another wanderer like you." He extended a calloused hand to her. "Up you come, if you will it. You'll be safer with us, I think. And I'd wager a fivestar that there's naught but abandoned villages before us for miles."

"And darkness behind," said the old woman.

The sleeping man stirred, mumbling something incomprehensible.

Varra took his hand, smiled in gratitude, and climbed aboard the wagon. "Thank you, goodsir."

The elderly woman grinned at her, showing age-blackened teeth, and gestured her to sit. Varra squeezed into the wagon, amid the sleeping man and pans, blankets, and barrels.

She glanced back once at the storm. It was gaining on them.

The sleeping man chuckled in his dream.

Rivalen's room darkened, as did his mood. The shadows around him churned. He sat on a divan, wrapped in shadows, in questions, and turned in his fingers the burned silver and amethyst ring Elyril Hraven had left in his lockbox for him to find, to announce that she had stolen *The Leaves of One Night*. He took the ring between thumb and forefinger and crushed it.

A rap at his door jarred him.

"Speak," he called, too harshly.

The voice of the Hulorn's chamberlain, Thriistin, sounded through the wood.

"Prince Rivalen, the Hulorn requests your presence. There is news from Ordulin. Something. . . strange is afoot."

Strange, indeed, Rivalen thought. He inhaled deeply and adopted his false face.

"Inform the Hulorn that I will attend him apace. I have only a small matter to consider first."

"Yes, Prince Rivalen."

The moment Thriistin walked away, Rivalen snarled and flung Elyril's ring so hard into the door of his townhouse that it dented the wood. He jerked the enameled black disc that served as his holy symbol from around the chain at his throat and stared his rage into its black hole.

"Why, Lady?"

She had kept her secrets from him, led him to believe one thing while doing another.

"I am your Nightseer," he said to the shadows.

The darkness made no answer.

He engulfed the symbol in his palm and started to squeeze.

"It was I who was to summon the Shadowstorm in your name. *I.*"

The disc bit into his skin. Warm blood seeped between his fingers even as his regenerative flesh tried to repair the damage. Still he squeezed, his rage building, his blood flowing.

"Why?" he said, his voice rising. The shadows around him swirled through the room, mirroring in miniature the Shadowstorm over Ordulin.

"Why?" The disc snapped in his hand with a loud crack and the sound brought home the realization of what he had done. His rage abated. The shadows around him subsided. He opened his palm to look at the symbol of his faith, broken and bloody in his palm.

"I had hoped to be your instrument, Lady."

The words caused him to think of his mother. He did not know why. And they also brought him revelation. He realized, with a clarity born of pain, that hope had been his transgression.

Accepting what he had done, he composed himself, stood, placed the cloven holy symbol in his pocket, and walked out of the room to attend the Hulorn.

The caravan arranged the wagons into a circle at nightfall, on the road but near the edge of the forest. Denthim organized the able-bodied men into watches and tried to calm the rest of the group. He distributed thin brass rods to the watchmen. Varra did not know what they were.

Denthim's mother, assisted by a few other women in the caravan, cooked several kettles full of thin broth. Children cried and laughed and played around the fires. Men and women spoke softly, fearfully, and looked back on the storm.

Varra helped as she could but mostly tried to avoid getting underfoot. A wave of nausea prevented her from enjoying the broth.

"Feeling unwell?" said the man who had been sleeping in the wagon.

His voice startled her, and she disliked his smirk, the knowing look in his dark eyes, though something about him reminded her of Erevis. "I am fine."

"Something in your belly, no doubt," he said with a wink, and turned away from her. She decided to ignore him, and he seemed content to ignore her.

The camp eventually settled into sleep. When Denthim returned to the wagon, his mother and the dark man were already asleep in the wagon. Varra's nausea had kept her awake and she smiled a greeting. Denthim smiled in return, though he looked weary.

"Wind is picking up," he said. He grunted as he pulled his girth up onto the wagon.

"It is."

He patted her hand. "Try to get some sleep, little sister. Tomorrow we move quickly. That storm is closing on us."

She nodded and decided not to look south. Denthim took more of the brass rods from an inner pocket. Varra saw that each was tipped with a dollop of a translucent substance.

"Sunrods," Denthim explained, no doubt seeing her curious look. "Tap the end on something and it glows like a lantern. Bought them from a peddler once. Had them for years. Here."

He handed her three. They felt warm in her hand. Denthim settled into the bench, and soon his snores joined the hiss of the wind. Varra rolled up in a blanket that smelled like hay, and slept.

She awoke later to a howling wind and a roiling stomach. Denthim and his mother slept near her in the wagon, stirring fitfully. The dark man lay curled up in the far corner of the wagon, difficult to see in the darkness. She realized that she had not learned his name.

Her stomach grew worse, and she knew she would need to retch. Unwilling to wake the others with the sound of her vomiting, she climbed out of the wagon and hurried toward the forest. She patted the shoulder of one of the men maintaining a watch as she passed.

"Need privacy," she said, and he grunted in reply.

She made it into the darkness of the trees, put her hands on her knees, and vomited. When she was done, she wiped her mouth with the back of her hand.

A violent gust of wind rattled the trees, and sent them to whispering. Goose pimples rose on Varra's skin. She felt the air change, felt it cool, felt it grow heavy. Something was wrong. She dashed for the camp.

"Awaken! Awaken!"

Before she had taken five steps she tripped on an exposed root and fell. The impact knocked the breath from her, and her warning died in a painful wheeze. The wind picked up still more, a gale that tore leaves and limbs from trees, and it carried on its currents hateful moans that made Varra's bones ache.

Screams erupted from the camp—one, another, another. Lights flared to life in the watchmen's hands—Denthim's sunrods. Varra half-crawled, half-ran back to the edge of the forest.

The wind sent a fog of dirt and dust through the camp. She made out dark, roughly humanoid-shaped figures with eyes like burning coals whirling in the wind, whipping through the camp, a storm of clotted forms. There were three living shadows for every person in the caravan.

The shadows, perhaps attracted to the light, swarmed the watchmen with sunrods. Dozens of forms whipped around the men, blotting out the light, reaching into and through the watchmen's flesh with cold, black arms. In moments all of the watchmen were dead, all of the sunrods extinguished.

Children cried. Women and men shouted, screamed. Varra could barely hear them above the moans of the shadows, above the wail of the wind. The shadows flitted through the camp, reaching out for warm flesh. And where they touched, they killed.

The camp devolved into chaos. People scrambled from their wagons, panicked and desperate. Horses and mules bucked and kicked against their tethers. Shadows swarmed the site, moaning, killing.

Varra heard Denthim shouting orders. He stood near his

wagon, holding the bridle of his panicked mule, even as the creature sought to break free of its yoke.

"Here," he shouted. *"Here!"*

Others took up his call, and a pocket of fighting men and women—sheltering the children, elderly, and those who could not fight for themselves—formed a rough line and hurried toward Denthim.

A dozen corpses dotted the plain. Shadows wheeled everywhere.

Varra knew no one would escape, not unless the shadows could be drawn off.

She acted before she thought. Sheltered behind the bole of a tree, she struck one of her sunrods on the trunk and it burst into light. She hurled it into the forest away from her.

A dozen pairs of red eyes turned from the attack and darted for the light. Varra ran farther back into the forest and struck another sunrod, casting it in the opposite direction of the first. The shadows' moans chased after it.

Varra ran deeper into the trees and ducked behind a tree, breathing heavily. She poked out her head to see that the shadows had already extinguished the first light. As she watched, they squelched the second. She had not delayed them long. She could still hear shouts from the campsite.

She held the last sunrod in her hand, stared at it, considered, her heart bouncing around in her breast.

She made up her mind, closed her eyes, and struck it on the tree.

"Here!" she shouted. "Here I am!"

She held the sunrod aloft and ran for her life into the forest.

Bone-chilling moans chased her into the trees. The sounds from the beleaguered camp faded. She heard only her own breathing, only the threats on the wind, the moans of the shadows.

She resolved to hold onto the rod until she had gotten far from the camp.

Sweat dripped into her eyes, felt cool on her skin. Limbs slapped her face, snagged her cloak. She stumbled once, twice, and little exclamations of terror escaped her lips. Fatigue and terror drained her strength. She threw her legs one in front of the other but felt as if she had sacks hanging from her belt sash. The shadows were drawing nearer. The air grew chill, the moans more pronounced.

She could not go on. Casting the sunrod as far from her as she could, she staggered off in the other direction. She didn't make it far before she sagged against a tree and tried to catch her breath. She heard the shadows moaning behind her, around her, but dared not peek out.

A hand closed over her mouth, and panic caused her to utter a muffled scream. She went limp; her body had no strength left with which to fight.

"Quiet," said a voice, and she recognized it as that of the dark man from the caravan. He removed his hand from her mouth.

She could not understand his presence, but fear caused her mind to work slowly.

"What are you doing here?" she whispered at last.

"Fiddling around the edges."

He grinned, the smile of a madman, and touched his hand to her belly. A stabbing pain wracked her abdomen. She screamed, doubled over. The shadows heard and answered her scream with moans.

"Who is she speaking to?" one of Brennus's homunculi said and cocked its head.

The other homunculus leaned forward and peered into the

face of the scrying cube. "I thought I saw someone."

Brennus cast several divinations in rapid succession to determine if Erevis Cale, perhaps invisible and warded, had come to Varra's aid. He had not. But for the shadows, she was alone.

"She speaks to herself," Brennus answered. "She is terrified. And she may have just lost her child to the strain."

Rivalen waited for moonset, then pulled the shadows around him and flew into the cool night air high above Selgaunt. The city stretched out below him, its torchlit thoroughfares like glowing snakes. The Elzimmer River looked like a black gash in the plain, a jagged, open wound. A few ships floated in the harbor.

Rivalen looked northeast, toward Ordulin, toward the Shadowstorm. He could not see it but knew it was there, summoned by Volumvax the Mad.

Shar had not chosen him, and his dreams had died in the darkness of her secrets. He looked into the moonless sky and shouted his rage into the void.

Varra, still gasping from the memory of pain, said, "What did you do?"

The man nodded at her belly. "Mind that child."

Varra stared, dumbfounded. "Child?"

"Yes, child. Worry over it later. Go now. They are coming."

But Varra was too stunned to move. She was with child? How could she not have known? How could he, a stranger to her, have known? She stared into his handsome face.

"Who are you?"

The moment she asked the question, she felt a nervous flutter in her stomach, fear that he might answer her truthfully.

He looked down, smiling, and poked a finger through a hole in his leather jerkin. "Interesting question." He sighed and looked up. "I am an actor. And we have a mutual acquaintance. Let us leave it there."

The shadows moaned, and she felt the cold of their coming.

"Come with me," she said. "We can hide."

He shook his head. "I must leave this place. But you cannot come with me." He pointed over her shoulder. "There is safety there. Trust me. Do you?"

From his expression, she thought much depended on her answer. She nodded, and he smiled. There was sadness in it.

"Then run. Now."

She looked around the tree, and the shadows saw her. Their red eyes flared, and a dozen black forms streaked at her. She looked back at the man, and he wasn't there. She had no time to think about where he'd gone. She turned and pelted through the underbrush, cracking tree limbs, stumbling, cursing, but never stopping. The thought of her child, Erevis's child, pushed her. She felt the shadows on her heels, moaning, reaching with cold fingers to drain the life from her flesh and that of her child. They were right behind her, closing, haunting her steps.

She burst through the trees and into a meadow of flowers. She did not slow. The shadows moaned, the sound right behind her. She heard the tinkling of distant bells and thought herself going mad.

"Where? Where?"

Tears mixed with sweat on her face. She had trusted the dark man, but he was a liar. There was no safety, only flowers and death. Her legs gave out and she fell amid the blooms. A shower of silvery pollen floated into the night air.

The shadows swarmed over her. Menace and cold chilled her. She screamed at their touch, felt it pulling the life from her flesh, turning her cold. She curled up, placed her hands over her stomach, over her child, and wished that she were somewhere safe, anywhere where she could raise her child in peace and light.

Brennus stared into his scrying lens. Shadows leaked from his flesh.

"Where did she go?" one of his homunculi asked, peering into the scrying lens.

The other sagged with disappointment. "They were going to kill her."

"What happened to the flowers?" said the first.

Brennus shook his head and watched the meadow for a few moments more. Every flower in the glade was black, wilted, dead, and the woman was gone.

The shadows wheeled about in frustration, then darted off.

Puzzled, Brennus cast a series of divinations through his scrying lens, thinking that perhaps the woman had turned invisible or otherwise masked her presence. But no, she was gone. He tried to refocus the eye of his lens on Varra, wherever she'd gone, but the lens showed only gray.

"How?" he said.

Both homunculi shrugged.

Brennus turned the scrying lens back on the meadow and studied it for a moment. He pulled the darkness around him, let his mind feel the correspondence with the darkness in the meadow, and transported himself there.

He materialized at the edge of the meadow. The dead flowers crunched under his boots. Were the flowers somehow involved in the woman's escape, or were they killed as a side effect of whatever magic the woman had used? A divination revealed the residuum of powerful magic, but he could not determine its nature. He attempted a magical trace to determine where she might have fled, but the spell showed him nothing.

"Where are you, woman?"

He could not leave the question unanswered. He spent the next hour scouring the surrounding forest, the meadow, casting one divination after another. He found nothing until one of his minor spells showed the faint glow of—

"There is something buried there. Retrieve it."

His homunculi squealed, leaped from his shoulders, and fell over each in their effort to please him. Both tore through the dead flowers, the soft dirt, until they pulled something from the ground.

"Mine!"

"Mine!"

They pulled at the small, dirt-covered item—a chain perhaps, or a necklace.

"Enough," Brennus said, and took it from them.

The homunculi stuck their tongues out at each other.

Brennus saw that they had indeed unearthed a necklace, coated in the sediment of years, probably something dropped accidentally by some elf or traveler. He whispered the words to a minor cantrip to clean the piece, and when it lay exposed in his hand—a platinum necklace with a large jacinth charm—it chased from his mind all thoughts of Cale's woman.

"Pretty," one of his homunculi said, as it climbed back to its perch on his shoulder.

Shadows swirled around Brennus, his own personal Shadowstorm. He could hardly breathe. "It was my mother's."

He turned over the charm and saw there the inscription:
For Alashar, my love.

"How did it get here?" the homunculi asked in unison.

He closed his hand over the necklace. "I do not know."

But discovering things was his gift.

WEASEL'S RUN

Lisa Smedman

The Year of Monstrous Appetites (-65 DR)

Weasel was going to die. And he was going to die sniffling.

He hated that.

He stared his hatred at the yellow pollen that drifted in lazy circles below him as he hung, face down, a quick-pace above the ground. The stinktrees were in bloom again, filling the air with a stench sharp as cat urine. He wished he had a hand free to grind into his itchy, weeping eyes. The pollen dusted his beardlocks and tickled his nose like flung pepper, clogging it with a constant, snuffling drip.

At least he couldn't smell the blood.

A hand grabbed his forelock and wrenched his head up. The Ghostwise cleric known only as "The Beast," his face blotched white with skull paint, inspected the magic-negating symbol painted on

Weasel's forehead. The pelt of a dire wolf draped the cleric's head and shoulders; empty paws dangled against his scar-gnarled chest. Sweat trickled lines through the splashed blood that had congealed on his body.

The Beast gestured at the line of six trophy heads, impaled on stakes. "Your warriors have been winnowed. Malar has taken them."

Weasel almost laughed. His warriors? Weasel was a mere scout—the army's favorite boot-out boy. Barely a sword-slogger; nowhere near being a sergeant.

"'Taken' them, has he?" A dribble escaped one nostril; Weasel snuffled it back in, priming his nose for a shot. "Then he'd better give 'em back. The Stronghearts don't like thieves; if they catch Malar, they'll strip him and dip him."

He trumpeted air out his nostrils, sending a wad of snot flying at The Beast's blood-caked feet. It missed by more than a quick-step. Flies stirred lazily, then settled again.

The Beast's eyes narrowed. "Do not mock the Beastlord."

"Or what?" Weasel sneezed. Snuffled. He twisted to get a look at the thongs that stretched from his wrists and ankles. They held him suspended at the center of a ring of human-high, claw-shaped stones. His hands and feet felt hot and numb; the raw leather thongs had dried tight. "No, wait. Don't tell me. I'll be strung up in the jungle and left to dry, right?" He rolled his eyes. "No, silly me—you've already done that."

He snorted out another wad of snot; this time, it landed next to The Beast's broken-nailed toes.

The Beast shifted his foot aside. He squatted down, one hand still tight around Weasel's forelock. His fingertips bulged, nails turning to claws. His breath was rank, like a dog's. "Take a good long look at your warriors," he breathed. "Tonight, you'll join them. This is the evening of the High Hunt—the only reason you are still alive. Tonight, we hunt."

"'We?'" Weasel sneezed. "Why, I'm flattered. But if it's just the same to you, I won't stick around for supper."

The Beast bared file-point teeth in a snarl. He stood, releasing Weasel's forelock. "Try to please Malar; give us a good chase."

Weasel flipped the forelock out of his eyes. "How much of a head start should I give you?"

The Beast roared with laughter. Leaves quivered; a bird screeched and flew away with a burst of orange wings. "Well spoken! A jest worthy of the Trickster!"

"Cut me down, and I'll dig up a sapling for you."

The Beast laughed again—even he, it seemed, knew the tale of Kaldair and the Toppled Tree.

It was Weasel's favorite tale, the one that had always earned him a seat at the Stronghearts' ale tables. Kaldair the Trickster, disguised as a halfling, had challenged Vaprak, god of ogres, to remove a tree from the ground without tearing its roots. Vaprak had torn out one mighty ebon tree after another, damaging them all; Kaldair had dug the tiniest of saplings out of the ground. As a result of Kaldair's victory, the ogres had been banished to the Toadsquat Mountains ever after.

The Beast drew one of his bone-handled daggers from a wrist sheath. "You're strong, for a spriggan." Serrated steel winked red in the ruddy sunlight as dusk settled deeper upon the jungle. "Let's see how strong." The Beast stepped over a taut-stretched thong and walked to Weasel's feet. He teased the tip of the blade along the rough sole.

Weasel braced himself for the slice and the aching rush of blood that would follow. Steel flashed. Weasel involuntarily bucked. . .

The thong holding his left ankle parted with a snap, and his foot thudded against the ground. Tingling fire streaked into his toes as sensation returned.

The Beast moved to his other leg. "Survive the night. . ." *slice, twang, thud* "and I'll spare your life—I swear it, by Malar's blood." He moved to Weasel's right hand. "But if my Hunt runs you to ground before the sun has risen. . ."

Steel flashed, parted leather. Weasel fell.

". . . you're meat."

Weasel lay on the ground, one hand in the air. He twisted and fumble-grabbed the thong an arm's span away from where it was tied to his left wrist. He'd been taught the strangle-snap as a boy, he'd used the trick on the Ghostwise, the time or two he'd been circled-round during a range-ahead and been forced to fight his way out, quietlike. But against The Beast, high cleric of Malar? Weasel might as well try to take down the Beastlord himself.

He drew the cord taut between wrist and numb hand, and offered it up to The Beast.

The Beast rested his blade against it. "A wise choice."

The leather thong parted.

The Beast stepped back and growled a word. The pelt he wore melded with his body, hairs shivering erect along his arms and legs. Magic crackled like a raging fire across his chest. A snarl burst from his elongating muzzle, and ears perked erect atop his head. His eyes grew yellow-red. Panting, he ran his tongue along jagged canine teeth. The dire wolf he'd become held Weasel's eye with a glare fierce and hungry. "Until the sun has risen," he snarled. "Or meat."

The dire wolf bounded away, up the trail leading to the clearing where the Ghostwise trap had been sprung. To the Ghostwise village where Puffpipe and Swaggerstep, Flashblade and Stomper, Chucklebelly and Headsuplads the sergeant had been run to ground, slaughtered, and eaten. The Beast himself had taken the first bites, ceremonially tearing open their bellies and bolting down great chunks of flesh from each soldier, one after the other, while Weasel had watched in horror from his hiding place, immobilized by the magical trap that had caught him.

Weasel glanced at the heads staked in the blood-soaked soil and wiped his nose with the back of his hand. He glanced at the darkening jungle, wondering which way to run. Wondering if he *could* run. His feet were blocks of fire, as if he'd just stomped through a numberry bush. He clomped his instep against his leg, trying to bang sensation back into it. And sneezed.

He glanced again at what remained of his squad, and shook his head, thinking of all the close scrapes they'd been through together since he'd joined their army. He almost wished there was a seventh stake, with his head on it. Almost.

"Pray me some of Tymora's luck, fellas. I'm gonna need it."

The Year of Discordant Destinies (-68 DR)

Weasel yawned as the Stronghearts' warchief made his way slowly up and down the rows of pole-stiff soldiers. The halflings all looked the same, to Weasel's eyes, in their identical wax-stiffened leather vests and helms, wooden shields slung across their backs. Each had a sling tucked into his belt, next to his stone pouch and waterskin, and stood with short sword thrust out ahead of him.

Warchief Chand padded up and down the rows, peering intently at this and that. The sergeant—Weasel could tell he was a sergeant by the green bracers on his forearms—trotted along at Chand's side like a dog, nodding earnestly at each thing the warchief said.

"There's a spot of rust on that sword, soldier," Chand would comment. Or, "That vest is laced crosswise." Or, "Comb that foot, soldier."

Weasel hoped the inspection would end soon. It had begun with a long and boring speech by the warchief about how the halflings would put an end to the bloodletting of the Ghostwise. How the assembled soldiers "Strongheart and

Lightfoot, shoulder to shoulder," would purge Malar's worship from the Luiren. How they'd make their villages safe again. How proud Chand was of "this hin's army." And on and on and on. . .

Weasel snorted. Proud? Chand seemed to find something wrong with every other soldier he inspected. The halfling found more faults on his soldiers than a herder found fleas on his dogs.

Chand finally made his way to the last row—and halted like he'd been cudgel smacked when he came to Weasel.

"Sergeant Hewn!" the warchief snapped. "What is. . . this?"

The sergeant quivered to stiffer attention. "A spriggan, Warchief Chand."

"I can see *what* he is, Sergeant," Chand said. "I want to know *why* he is *where* he is."

Sweat trickled from the sergeant's temples. "He's the new scout for Wildroot Squad, Sir."

"New *scout*?" Chand echoed in a strained voice.

Weasel smiled. "Yup." He nodded down at the sword he was leaning on. "Even brought my own sticker."

Weasel could practically hear the eyes of the halflings next to him creaking as they strained to watch what was happening—while still pretending to stare straight ahead.

The sergeant cleared his throat nervously. "The lads caught the spriggan trying to lightfinger a jug from the mess. They had him stripped and upside down in a vat of ale by the time I got there."

Weasel grinned, remembering that. The ale had been tasty.

"The spriggan shoved the lads off with magical fear," the sergeant continued. "I was of a mind to just run him off, until he told me he'd just come from the Gloomthicket. He passed right through it while The Beast's Hunt were wilding there, and somehow lived to tell the tale. I convinced him that fighting held more honor than fleeing. That he could make a worthwhile contribution to our forces as a. . ."

The sergeant faltered to a halt under the warchief's stern glare.

Chand turned his attention back to Weasel but spoke to the sergeant. "I'm disappointed in your lack of judgment, Sergeant Hewn." Chand's nose flared. "A *spriggan*, in this hin's army? Just *look* at him. That sword—filthy with rust! No shield. Trousers, spotted with. . . something nasty, I'm sure. Non-regulation vest, unlaced. And that hair and beard! All those ridiculous tufts and ribbons—*and* greasy. Why, the very smell of the creature is enough to make my eyes water. I'm sure he hasn't washed in. . ."

Weasel didn't hear the rest. He was beyond listening. The warchief might say what he liked about his silk vest and sword, but insulting a spriggan's beardlocks warranted a swift fist in the face. Weasel glared back at the warchief, who stood no taller than he did. Weasel's eye fixed on the ridiculous collection of feathers pinned to the warchief's leather vest.

"Listen up, you beardless little Cockelfeather," Weasel growled. "You apologize right now for sayin' that about my locks, or I'll—"

The sergeant's hand shot backward and clapped over Weasel's mouth. "My apologies, Warchief Chand, for this man speaking out of turn. It won't happen again."

"No. It won't." Chand spat the words out from behind clenched teeth. He leaned forward until his face was a blade's thickness away from Hewn's. "Get. . . rid of him," he hissed.

Anger flared in Weasel. So did his magic. In the blink of an eye, his body enlarged to more than twice its normal size—big as an ogre's. His unlaced vest barely covered his muscle-rippled chest; his trousers stretched tight across powerful thighs. The sword grew with him—now it was longer than Chand was tall. Weasel leaned on it, driving the point deeper into the earth, and stared down at Chand.

Chand looked up.

Way up.

Weasel cupped a hand behind an enormous ear. "What was that, Cockelfeather? It's hard to hear you from up here."

The soldiers on either side of Weasel took a nervous step back, breaking ranks. The sergeant, still holding his hand out in the spot where Weasel's mouth had been a moment ago, went white as a bone-painted Ghostwise.

Chand paled. Then he drew himself up. "Sergeant Hewn," he snapped.

"Sir!"

"I've reconsidered. Maybe a spriggan *does* have its uses."

"Sir?"

"This soldier is going to need a uniform. See to it."

The sergeant snapped to attention. "Sir! Right away, Sir."

Chand spun on his heel and marched smartly away.

Weasel grinned.

The Year of Monstrous Appetites (-65 DR)

Weasel ran along the narrow path through the jungle, back the way his squad had come. He was gambling the spike-traps and snarefoots hadn't been reset, that the binge of blood drinking had kept the Ghostwise too busy to replace their defenses. He needed to put as much distance between himself and their village as possible before the hunt began.

Every few steps he staggered as a fit of sneezing struck. As he ran, he scrubbed at his forehead with a sweaty hand. The symbol they'd painted there in blood crumbled and smudged. He snapped his fingers, testing to see if his magic had returned; a dull yellow flame danced across the tip of his thumb. He waved it out.

He stopped, blew his nose clear, and spread his hands, drawing in the magic of the jungle. Magic filled him, boosting his size. His head brushed the leaves above, his shoulder forced a branch aside, and a twig snapped under his sudden weight.

He was taller now; more than twice the size he'd been a moment ago. Stronger. Faster.

Stinktree pollen tickled his nose, prompting an explosion. Even his sneezes were bigger.

He ran.

With luck, he would make it to the spot where the drop was scheduled to be made, and signal the griffon to carry him out of here. Behind him, he heard a horn blare: the Ghostwise, beginning their hunt.

"At least they gave me a head start," he panted.

The forest had grown dark, making it hard to see the trail. Something caught his foot, sending him heels over rump. When he stopped tumbling he scrambled to his feet. He spotted stakes on the trail that had held down a length of assassin vine, which now dangled in the air. Tendrils sprang out of it, blindly questing for the creature that had blundered into it. If Weasel had been smaller, the vine would have grabbed him and held him fast. Crept its way up to his neck and strangled him.

The trap was crude, obviously intended for discovery. Weasel would easily have spotted it if he hadn't been running, even in the dark. He shrank down to spriggan size again, moved a little closer to the vine, and cautiously parted the thick wall of vegetation that grew at the side of the trail. A snap of his fingers provided enough light to reveal sawfoot traps, steel jaws open. A simple ruse: step off the trail onto one of those, and they'd snip off a foot—or as near to it as to make no difference.

He heard wolves' howls: Malar's clerics, hot on his scent. He didn't have much time. He stayed low to avoid the vine, and broke a branch off a tree. He used it to ease three of the sawtooth traps onto the trail, and threw leaves over them. The shifted clerics would have four paws in contact with the ground, and would be coming fast. With luck, one or two of them would spring the traps and be put out of the chase.

The howls drew closer. Weasel wiped his nose. Better get moving. He turned—and startled when he saw a dryad, standing on the trail directly behind him. She was naked, with small breasts and skin the color of mahogany. Tiny leaves dappled her hair. She smelled like berry syrup.

"Love to taste those lips, pretty one, but I don't want slivers. And I've got to run."

He didn't, though.

She touched his arm with fingers rough as bark and moved closer, her footfalls like the crackle of twigs. She spoke words that shimmered into his mind like liquid moonlight.

Come. One hand rustled up to touch her breast. *Lay your head here. Rest.*

Weasel sighed. The howls drew closer. He wondered dreamily why he was still standing here. He leaned toward her and laid his cheek against her breast; it felt like the burl of a tree. The sounds of the approaching hunters faded to insignificance. He felt pressure around his hand: her fingers, twining tight as assassin vine around his. Then her hand twisted.

One of his fingers snapped; he screamed. The branch fell from his hand. The dryad scooped it up, cradled it to her breast, and glared at Weasel. Then she vanished.

Weasel held up his right hand; his middle finger was splayed out at an angle, like a broken twig. He heard excited yips on the trail: Malar's hunt, closing in! Too close to run. He looked wildly around for a place to hide, then remembered the sawtooth traps. Even if he could leave the trail, the Hunt would scent him out. A tendril of assassin vine brushed his scalp; he ducked, escaping it.

Suddenly changing his mind, he grabbed the vine with his left hand. He yanked. The vine yanked back, pulling him into the air. He crashed through branches and came to a halt just as the first pursuer flashed into view below. The wolf started to glance at a falling twig—then yelped. Weasel heard the dull crunch of a sawtooth trap snapping shut and the crack of splintering bone.

His broken finger throbbed in misplaced sympathy.

A second wolf pummeled into the first, knocking it down but unfortunately not springing either of the other two traps. The rest of the pack halted in time. The largest of the Hunt— The Beast, in dire wolf form—sniffed the spot where the traps were concealed and growled.

Weasel, hanging above, felt the assassin vine twine down his arm, toward his neck. He didn't dare peel it off; a rustling noise would betray where he'd gone. With luck, The Beast would figure he'd either doubled back or used magic to escape.

The assassin coiled around his throat. Before it could tighten, Weasel wedged his free hand under it—nearly crying aloud at the pain of his broken finger twisting—and called a dull red flame to his palm. The vine recoiled from the heat, loosening. Another tendril wound around his chest. He let that one be.

The dire wolf growled at the wolf caught in the trap. The lesser wolf cringed, then rolled over, exposing its belly. The Beast cocked a leg over it in disdain, then turned and ripped open its stomach with his teeth.

The others sat and watched in silence as the shamed wolf bled.

The Beast yipped at the others, then sprang over the spot where the traps were hidden. Half of the Hunt did the same. The rest raced back the way they'd just come.

Weasel sighed in relief. A few moments more, and the wolf below would be dead. Then Weasel could move off. But as he listened to the whines of the dying wolf, stinktree pollen tickled his nose. He fought the urge to sneeze, felt his eyes grow watery and hot, nose-wriggled the urge away, only to have it build up again. He choked it back, sweat beading on his temples from the effort.

The assassin vine squeezed it out of him.

Ah-choo!

The tiny flicker of flame he'd been maintaining in the hand nearest his neck exploded in a bright flare of light. Flames also shot from his other palm. The assassin vine unraveled, dropping him. He crashed down through the branches, frantically trying to grab them with his good hand. He thudded onto the trail, narrowly missing one of the concealed traps.

The dying wolf looked up, saw Weasel, and let out a blood-choked howl.

Howls answered from up and down the trail. Malar's Hunt, acknowledging the news their prey had been spotted.

Weasel swore.

The Year of Festivals (-67 DR)

Weasel stood outside the hill-house that served as the armory, sword in hand. He watched as the procession wound its way through the village, singing lustily. Most of the halflings stumbling after the priestess were addle-witted, minds and bodies reeling from the aftereffects of spring cheese. Weasel had nibbled a little of the hard white cheese a while back, out of curiosity, but it didn't seem to have the same effect on spriggans. Nor did he much care for the taste. He'd quaff a double hand of ales instead, when he cared to get fumble-mouthed.

Today, however, he needed to keep his wits about him. Reeling the halflings might be, but if Weasel wasn't quick in his doings, someone was sure to notice the armory door had been left unguarded.

He stared at the priestess leading the procession, wondering how much a person would have to eat to get that fat. The halfling's blonde hair was unbound—a sure sign of a wanton wench—and she was nearly as wide as she was tall, so broad she waddled as she led the procession. She held a wooden shield in one hand, a woven wicker cornucopia in the other. Every few steps she jerked the cornucopia into the air, releasing a spray of loose grapes. The halflings behind her cheered and laughed, trying to catch them in their mouths.

"Beautiful, isn't she?" a voice behind Weasel said.

Weasel turned and saw one of the members of his squad—he never could tell one from the next, let alone remember their names—walking toward him. Only when the halfling pulled a pipe out of his vest pocket did Weasel realize which of them it was. Puffpipe—the only one in the squad who didn't crinkle his nose and complain about the smell when Weasel was nearby. Weasel hoped he wouldn't linger too long.

Puffpipe gestured with the gnawed pipe stem at the priestess leading the procession. "I'm courting her," he confided.

Weasel glanced again at the priestess, trying to see the attraction.

Puffpipe stared longingly at her. "When the spring festival's over, I aim to ask Willametta to twine the branch with me."

Weasel grunted. "Make sure it ain't attached to a snare."

Puffpipe laughed.

Weasel remembered their first patrol—how Swaggerstep'd had a little of the bluster knocked out of him when he'd ignored the sergeant's warning and kicked aside a branch, only to be yanked feetfirst into the air. The others in the squad had a good laugh at his expense, catching the coins from his pockets—until Headsuplads had pointed out the sharpened stake lying nearby. By Tymora's luck, a woodrat had gnawed the lashings that had held it to a branch above; otherwise, Swaggerstep would have been impaled.

"You'd better ask her sooner, 'stead of later," Weasel continued, trying to nudge Puffpipe along. "You never know when they'll send us out on patrol again."

"Patrol? During spring festival? Not likely!" Puffpipe peered blearily into the stem of his pipe, and plucked a piece of burr grass to clean it. He tried to thread it through the stem, failed, and gave up. He pulled out a pouch and tamped tobacco into the bowl, which was carved in the shape of a cornucopia. Pipe stem between his teeth, he looked hopefully at Weasel.

Weasel snapped his fingers and lit the pipe. The halfling started to thank him, but Weasel interrupted. "Look there! They're bringing out the *bouqtha*."

Puffpipe whirled so fast he nearly fell over. His licked his lips at the sight of the trays heaped with fruit-filled pastry. Forgetting even to bid Weasel farewell, he hurried off, trailing puffs of sweet-smelling smoke.

Weasel shook his head. The way Puffpipe was eating, the soldier would be as fat as his intended by the end of the three-day festival.

Weasel wiped sweat from his forehead and resumed his guard stance. Now that the rainy season was done, the weather was heating up. Soon swollen rivers and mud-slippery slopes would give way to brain-baking heat and the annual month-long explosion of star-shaped stinktree flowers. And then Weasel's agony would begin. Healing potions would ease his snuffling, but only for so long; it would have taken the whole army's supply to get Weasel through pollen season.

At last, the procession disappeared from view. Weasel opened the door behind him and slipped quickly inside, then closed the door on the singing. The hill-house was refreshingly cool, but dark; he sheathed his sword and waited while his eyes adjusted.

He looked around. Weapons were everywhere: Slings and stone pouches hung from pegs on the walls, scabbarded swords stood upright in racks, daggers of all sizes were laid out in neat rows on tabletops. Shields had been lined up like dinner plates against the walls. Color-changing sniper's cloaks, visible only as shadows, were draped from the rafters.

Weasel headed for the three strongboxes at the back of the armory. A few quick twists of his pick opened the laughably simple lock on the first one. Weasel lifted the lid and saw dozens of finger-sized glass vials—the vile-tasting sneakabout potions issued to patrols—as well as tiny pouches of the magical dust used to conceal weapons caches. Valuable, but easy enough to filch while on patrol—and not a healing potion among 'em. No sense wasting his time on this lot. He closed and relocked the lid and tried the second strongbox.

This was more like it! The second strongbox contained a number of pouches that, judging by the clacking sound when he prodded them, contained gems.

The quartermaster must have been anticipating thievery: a black diamond lay on the uppermost bag. Weasel wasn't going to fall for that; he knew where the gem had come from. It had been Stomper who'd found it, on one of the squad's very first patrols—that's how he'd gotten his nickname. Stomper had spotted the diamond lying out in the open in the middle of an abandoned enemy village and praised Tymora high and low for his "luck."

The diamond turned out to be cursed. Heavy as a pony, it weighed Stomper down so he could barely lift his feet. He'd tried throwing it away, but it just kept appearing again in his pockets. It had taken a priestess' blessing to finally rid him of the thing.

Carefully avoiding the diamond, Weasel picked up a pouch. He was just about to peek inside it when he heard a commotion outside: shouts of alarm, which swiftly became screams. An alarm clanged: The village was under attack!

Weasel cursed his ill luck. He'd been waiting *months* for the spring festival—it was the one time when no one else wanted guard duty—and now the opportunity to fill his pockets was gone. In another moment, soldiers would rush in here to arm themselves. He gave the other pouches a longing look, then decided one bag of gems would have to be enough. He slammed the strongbox shut and ran for the door.

He opened it onto a scene of chaos. The enemy was everywhere. Ghostwise halflings, faces whited out for war, tore into the unarmed celebrants. Malar's clerics, roaring their bloodsong, were a terrifying blend of halfling and beast, their arms transformed into the limbs of jungle predators. They slashed a savage furrow through the villagers. A handful of soldiers tried to stand against them bare-handed, but were no match for the magically augmented Ghostwise. The surprise attack was rapidly turning into a slaughter.

Weasel hesitated, hand on his sheathed sword. These weren't his people. He'd hired on with the halflings as a scout, not a swordsman. The army provided a steady trickle of coins and the occasional opportunity to grab a fistful more. The Stronghearts didn't pay him enough for him to throw away his life in a futile—

Something struck him from behind. He slammed face-first into the ground. Tasted dirt. Claws raked his shoulder, drawing blood. Teeth snapped for his neck. He twisted and saw he'd been knocked down by a were-jaguar. It snarled, its breath hot with fresh blood.

He screamed.

Magic burst from him, equal in volume to the shriek that wailed from his lungs. The jaguar sprang back, ears flat, belly to the ground as Weasel's fear-magic struck it. Weasel scrambled to his feet and started to back away—then realized he'd dropped the pouch. It lay on the ground between him and the were-jaguar, which lashed its tail, trying to work up the courage to attack.

"Niiice kitty." Weasel scooped up the pouch. The claws had torn a hole; a gem tumbled out of the pouch as he lifted it. Weasel caught it as it fell, then realized his folly as he saw what it really was. He'd stolen a bag of oversized glass marbles. *Glowing* glass marbles—but marbles just the same. The halfling's trickster god had played him for a fool!

He hurled the marble at the jaguar, yelling a shatter-shout at it for good measure.

Suddenly, he was flying backward through the air, propelled by a tremendous blast. He slammed into the wall of a hill-house and slid to the ground, ears ringing. A villager ran past, screaming, but Weasel couldn't hear her. The spot where the were-jaguar had crouched was a smoking crater in the ground. A tuft of its tail—all that remained of the beast— landed on the ground nearby.

"Some marbles," Weasel croaked, barely able to hear his own voice. "A kid could lose a finger, playing with those."

He realized he still held the pouch in his hand—and that Malar's beasts and clerics were still attacking. A Ghostwise, wearing bloodied spike gauntlets on each hand, chased after a soldier. Weasel sprang to his feet and hurled a marble at him. A shatter-shout triggered the marble, and the Ghostwise disappeared in a terrific blast. Weasel whirled and threw again, and another enemy vanished in an explosion that left Weasel reeling.

A hand tapped his shoulder, startling him—a soldier from his squad. Chucklebelly held out a hand and shouted something Weasel couldn't hear, but Weasel guessed what was being asked by the sling in Chucklebelly's hand. Weasel held out the pouch; Chucklebelly plunged his hand into it. Armed with the marbles, the halfling scrambled atop the hill-house.

Weasel, realizing the marbles would remain inert without his shatter-shout, clambered up there too. Chucklebelly's first two shots went beyond the range of Weasel's shatter-shout, but after

Weasel's frantic explanation, they became an efficient team. Chucklebelly's sling whirred, released, whirred, released—while Weasel turned this way and that, shouting as each marble struck. Too soon, they were down to their last marble. But it didn't matter. Malar's clerics were beaten; those that hadn't been blown to pieces were fading back into the jungle.

Days later—when the wounded, including Weasel, had been tended at the healing house and the dead buried—Warchief Chand himself came to the village to congratulate Sergeant Headsuplads on the initiative his soldiers had shown. Both Chucklebelly and Weasel were presented with a red cock feather. As the warchief tucked this into the buttonhole of Weasel's vest, Chand leaned close and spoke in a low murmur. "One day you'll have to tell me, soldier, how you knew the command word of a weapon crafted by human wizards—a weapon that was supposed to be stored securely in a locked strongbox." Warchief Chand straightened and spoke a little louder. "That's quite the initiative you showed. I'll have to tell Sergeant Hewn to keep an eye on you."

Weasel—who a moment ago had been contemplating easing a hand into the warchief's vest pocket, just to see if he could get away with filching whatever was inside it—tugged his beardlocks nervously. "Yes, Sir, Warchief!"

When the brief ceremony was over, Headsuplads, exuding a near-visible glow of pride at having the foresight to take on a spriggan as a scout, clapped a hand on Weasel's and Chucklebelly's shoulders, dragged them off to the mess, and bought them the first of many ales. There, Weasel toasted the sergeant and capered a jest at his expense. He turned to Chucklebelly—who liked to joke he drank his belly so big on purpose, so he could keep extra sling stones tucked inside its folds. This, he boasted, gave him the "last laugh" when an enemy thought him unarmed. Weasel used a fast-hand trick to "pull" the last blast marble from

Chucklebelly's folds. The others all dived for cover when Weasel fumble-dropped it at the sergeant's feet. Afterward, even Headsuplads had laughed when Weasel explained that it wouldn't explode unless he shattered it.

Later that night, Weasel staggered back to the hill-house where his patrol was billeted, drunk as a halfling with a full cheese in his belly. On the way, he spotted Puffpipe sitting on a door stoop. The halfling's head was down; his pipe lay on the stoop beside him, unlit. He was either staring at something in his lap or he was asleep. Weasel staggered over, gave his shoulder a punch, and held out the mug of ale he'd just realized he was carrying. "Hey Puffpipe, want a quaff?"

Puffpipe shook his head. "She died," he whispered. "Earlier today. They couldn't heal her."

Weasel took a sloppy pull of his ale and wiped his mouth with the back of a hand. "Who are you—" Then he saw the cornucopia Puffpipe held in his lap. The wicker was torn, stained with dried blood.

"Oh." The pride drained out of Weasel in a rush. He set the ale mug on a window ledge and fell into a squat beside Puffpipe. He drummed his fingers against his thighs, for once, not quite knowing what to say. Flames flickered; he balled his fists, extinguishing them.

Puffpipe looked up. Tears glinted in the moonlight. "Willametta was too weak to heal herself. And the other clerics couldn't. . . " He sighed. A tear dripped from his jowly chin. "She was the reason I was fighting." He waved a hand. "This village. But now. . . "

Weasel squeezed his fists tighter. "Now you're gonna quit?" he guessed.

Puffpipe's jaw clenched. "No. Now I've even more reason to fight." One hand groped for his pipe; the stem trembled as he tamped tobacco into it. Weasel leaned forward and offered him a light.

Puffpipe sucked on the stem and exhaled a long, sad stream of smoke. Tear-puffy eyes met Weasel's. "Why are you in uniform?" he asked. "Did you. . . lose someone?"

Weasel bit back the retort that he *wasn't* in uniform—the trousers, armor vest, and helmet he'd been issued were too loose when in spriggan form, too tight when he enlarged. He wore his own clothes, instead. He glanced down at the feather in his vest. "I was doing it for the reward. But after today. . . " His gaze drifted to the blood-splattered wall beside Puffpipe.

The halfling nodded and took a deep draw on his pipe. Its ruddy glow illuminated his face. "You're one of us."

Weasel blinked in surprise. That hadn't been what he'd meant. His ale-bleary thinking had been more along the lines of his having blown his one chance at getting rich—that perhaps it was time to finally leave "this hin's army." To gather up all the swag he'd been able to filch and move along. But his feet weren't following orders. Instead of marching him smartly along the trail that led to the spriggans' highsummer Gather, they'd meandered him back to his billet.

Weasel stood, fumbled the feather out of his buttonhole, and handed it to Puffpipe.

The halfling looked up, startled. "What. . . But I didn't. . . "

"It's for Willametta. She should have something pretty on her grave."

The Year of Monstrous Appetites (-65 DR)

Weasel tore his way through the thick undergrowth, cursing each vine and fern and bush that got in his way. The Gloomthicket was tougher than any obstacle course he'd ever run in training. He leaped over logs, crawled through thorn bushes, ran teetering along fallen tree trunks, and scrambled up and down boulder-strewn slopes. He changed size more times than he could count, enlarging when he needed to make a leap, resuming his normal size in tight-squeeze spots.

All the while, he heard Malar's Hunt braying in pursuit. By the sound of it, they were sticking to animal form, to follow his scent. That meant they had to move along the ground. By climbing a tree and moving through branches, Weasel might have been able to lose them.

Unfortunately, he couldn't. Not with a broken finger.

Still, he managed a trick or two to slow them down.

He spotted sparks inside a hole in the ground: the underground den of a pair of shocker lizards. He laid a false scent-trail into it, first forcing the electric-sparking creatures deeper into their tunnel with a dose of magical fear, then backing out again. He backtracked away from the den to a stream he'd crossed earlier and waded up it, grinning at his trick. The shocker lizards were small, but they'd be defending their eggs; with luck, they'd combine their attacks to deliver a lethal shock to the first wolf that nosed into their hole.

Later, Weasel passed a large, leafy lump, only to realize, with a jolt of fear, that he'd just run right past a night-slumbering greenvise. He stopped just out of range and threw stones at its bulbous head to wake it up. The plant reared up on its tendril legs and creaked its mouth open, releasing a choking, acidic fog. When the clerics got a whiff of that, it wouldn't be pleasant. Hopefully, the sentient plant would stay awake long enough— and be angry enough—to swallow one of them whole.

Still later, Weasel nearly blundered into a gully of twigblights before he realized the "thorn bushes" filling the ravine were, in fact, a group of the treelike creatures huddled together. He took off his vest, tied it with a length of vine to one ankle, then used another vine to swing, left-handed, just above the twigblights, dragging the vest along the ground behind him. By the time he reached the other side of the gully, his vest was full of slivers that oozed poisonous sap. He yanked on the slip knot, releasing it.

Smeared with mud, sweat-wrung, beardlocks frazzled— and still sneezing—he staggered on through the jungle. He'd managed to crudely splint his broken finger—nearly passing out from the pain of pulling it true again—but the whole of his right hand was swollen now. He no longer cared if he lived or died; he just wanted to lie down and weep.

Just a little while longer, he told himself. The forest was lightening; it was almost dawn. He could do it.

If he did, would The Beast keep his word?

Then Weasel heard a sound that made his pulse quicken: the cry of a griffon—the signal a drop was about to be made! He crossed the fingers of his good hand to invoke Tymora's blessing. With luck, it would be the drop for his squad, and not a dump of blightdust or inferno cinders.

A moment later, he heard heavy wingbeats. He fought his way to a gap in the jungle. He looked up with bleary, watering eyes and caught a glimpse of the winged lion circling above. A tiny speck behind its eagle head was the halfling rider; another speck was the bundlebag in its two front paws. Weasel enlarged, and waved frantically, but the rider didn't see him.

The griffon released the bundlebag. The bag was as big as Weasel was tall and heavy, but it fell slowly—drifting like a feather with its marking streamer trailing behind it, thanks to a transmutation. Weasel estimated where it was about to land, and thrashed his way to the spot. Inside the bundlebag would be food, fresh water, sling stones, keenoil—and, most importantly, healing potions.

He could see the bundlebag just ahead. Its streamer had caught on the branch of a tree; the bundlebag hung, twisting, below it. The branch creaked as the transmutation wore off and the bundlebag resumed its normal weight. Strangely, there was more than one bundlebag caught in the tree—what were the odds of that?

A whole bunch to nothing at all.

Those weren't other bundlebags hanging from the tree,

but pods. The bundlebag had landed in an orcwort tree.

Weasel heard a splintering sound: one of the pods cracking open. A spriggan-sized wort tumbled out, arms and legs wildly flapping. It hit the ground with a thud and rose a moment later, wrinkly purple skin steaming in the morning heat. Another pod tore open, and another, releasing more worts. Within a matter of moments, fully a score of the shambling creatures stood swaying at the base of the tree. Hands pawed the tree they'd fallen from, leaving smears of sap. As they stroked it, a gaping mouth creaked open in the trunk.

Weasel cursed his ill luck. He was well and truly cogscraggled, now. Wortlings were too stupid to feel fear; he couldn't drive them off by frightening them. Nor could he sneak past them; the wortlings could sense him through whatever plants he touched. One scratch of their splinter-sharp fingers, and Weasel would be asleep. Then they'd feed him to the tree.

"Figures," Weasel muttered as the wortlings turned and shambled toward him through the steadily lightening jungle. "Breakfast time, and nothing but me on the menu."

He pulled back a branch and waited. As soon as the wortlings came within range, he let it go. The branch sprang from his hand and smacked into the nearest wortling, knocking it down.

Weasel sprinted through the gap in their line. Wortlings flailed blindly at him as he leaped over the one he'd knocked down. He headed for the orcwort tree, enlarging himself as he ran. He slammed a shoulder into the bundlebag, knocking it spinning. It slammed into the tree's splinter-fanged mouth as Weasel dodged behind the tree. This time, Tymora favored him: the tree chewed greedily at the bag, gulping it in—then spat it out again when it wasn't blood that flowed, but a mix of ale from ruptured waterskins and bitter-tasting potions from the vials it was crunching.

At least the bag was open now.

Weasel led the wortlings on a ring-a-rosy around the tree. Still on the run, he scooped up one of the white-corked vials the orcwort had spat out, yanked the cork from it with his teeth, and gulped it down. He gasped in relief as his broken finger mended—and grinned as his eyes stopped itching and his nose cleared. Still running, he tore off the splint.

On his second pass around the tree he searched desperately among the scattered equipment for a vial with a blue cork—a sneak potion that would have allowed him to run on without leaving either tracks or scent. If he downed it and bolted away, The Beast would think he'd been eaten by the orcwort.

Weasel spotted a flash of blue among the scattered skip-stones, scattered biscuits, and spare clothing. He scooped it up—only to curse as the broken vial sliced his hand. Empty!

A root thrust out of the ground, tripping him. Then another: the orcwort, trying to slow him up. Weasel danced out of the way, careful not to get too close to the wortlings. He looped around the tree a third time, hoping for another look at the scattered equipment. He heard the braying howl of a wolf: the Hunt, hot on his scent.

Close—too close.

"Hang on, twiggies," Weasel panted over his shoulder at the pursuing wortlings. "The main course will be here in just a moment."

There *had* to be another blue-corked vial; a bundlebag should have been packed with enough for a full patrol. Surely all six couldn't have been broken. Surely not!

Third time lucky: He spotted one. He dived for it, nearly weeping as his fingers closed around the intact vial. Three wortlings threw themselves at him; Weasel shrank and rolled at the same time, narrowly escaping their scratching fingers. He lunged back to his feet, but before he could uncork the vial and drink it, a root coiled around his ankle, jerking him to a halt. The vial flew from his hands and landed on the ground a couple of quick-paces away. He enlarged, then shrank, loosening the root, and wrenched his foot free. He scrambled to the vial on hands and knees.

Just before he reached it, a wortling stepped on it.

Crunch.

A slavering wolf streaked out of the jungle—the first of Malar's clerics! It snarled as it spotted the wortlings. It tried to twist away from them in mid-leap, but a wortling raked its flank. The wolf tumbled in a loose-limbed heap, reverting to halfling form as it lost consciousness. The wortlings swarmed the fallen halfling and lifted him into the air, then heaved him into the orcwort's mouth.

This time, there *was* blood.

Another howl sounded—close! The wortlings turned in that direction—not hearing the howl, but sensing the stirring of underbrush as the wolves pounded closer. Weasel glanced wildly around. The roots were dormant; the tree was busy feeding. The wortlings were, for the moment, intent on the approaching Hunt. He could run—but the wolves were fast. Faster than wortlings. Enough of them would streak past the shambling wortlings to run him down.

That decided it. The only way out was in. As the tree opened its maw, Weasel raced toward it. He sprang forward, jammed a foot against the orcwort's lower lip, and pushed off into the air. He caught hold of a pod, and, as it rocked wildly, crammed himself inside. Feet braced against one side of the pod, back against the other, he grabbed the pod's broken edges and drew them together. He peered out through the crack, hoping the Hunt wouldn't notice his fingers. There was a chance they wouldn't; his hands were filthy, pretty near the same color as the pod.

Another of Malar's clerics burst out of the jungle. The wortlings surged forward. The pod, still rocking slightly, turned in place, preventing Weasel from seeing what happened next. But the sounds told the story. He heard snarls, furious motion, a sharp yipe of pain—and the *snap-crunch-spurt* of the orcwort feeding on another victim. As the pod slowed to a gentle spin, he saw the wortlings shambling into the jungle in pursuit of the rest of the Hunt.

Just as Weasel was commending himself for his cunning, a dire wolf padded out of the underbrush. The Beast. Roots burst out of the ground and tangled a paw; The Beast growled, low in his throat. His fur sprang erect, and magical energy crackled across his body in waves. He tore the paw free, yanking the root out of the ground all the way to the base of the trunk. The trunk cracked, and sap flowed—quicker than it should have. The orcwort's mouth snapped shut.

Nose to the ground, The Beast sniffed a zigzag course up to the base of the tree, then sniffed the orcwort's closed mouth. The pod slowly turned, cutting off Weasel's view.

When it came round again, The Beast was in halfling form. He stood, clawed hands dangling at his sides, staring at the orcwort tree. Then he growled and turned away. As he walked back in the direction he'd come from, Weasel exulted. He'd done it! Tricked The Beast! Now all he had to do was stay inside the pod until The Beast was far enough away.

Weasel suddenly realized the footsteps had stopped—directly beneath him. He glanced down, and saw that a drop of blood from his cut hand had landed on The Beast's hair. The Beast glanced up at the pod—just as another drop of blood fell. This time, it landed on The Beast's lips. His whited-out face broke into an evil grin.

"Come out of your shell, spriggan," he said in a taunting voice. "You gave us a good chase, but now the hunt is over. You're mine." He clawed the air; the pod ripped open. Weasel fell at his feet.

"Wait!" Weasel cried. He pointed frantically at the blades

of sunlight slanting through the forest. "The sun's rising—it's morning! I met your challenge. I survived the night—you have to let me live!"

The Beast bared his teeth in a mocking smile. "You weren't listening closely enough. 'Before the sun *has risen*,' I said. And it's not fully risen yet."

Weasel swallowed hard. The Beast *was* going to eat him, after all. He looked desperately around, trying to remember what else The Beast had said. "Well. . . you didn't run me to *ground*, did you? I went up a tree. You can't kill me without breaking your oath to Malar."

The Beast snorted—but his eyes were wary.

"Tell you what," Weasel said. "Let's decide it by way of a contest. A contest of strength. Which I challenge you to in Malar's name—a challenge I know you'll have to accept, because if you don't, it means you're afraid, and that's something your god just won't stand for. If I win, you have to let me go. If you win. . . well, I'll break out the seasoning."

The Beast chuckled. "Does it involve pulling up saplings?" He sniffed. "I can smell the dryad on you; I won't be tricked into damaging one of their sacred trees."

Weasel feigned a frustrated sigh. He glanced around and pretended to notice the spilled sling stones for the first time. "I know—we'll have a throwing contest! Whoever can throw a stone the farthest wins." He pointed. "Go ahead, choose a stone."

The Beast strode over to the stones.

Weasel held his breath. Would his ruse work? For several patrols now, Chand's soldiers had been using stones that were ensorcelled to return to the slingers' hands upon command. When Weasel spoke the word, the stone The Beast had thrown would return, assuring it didn't travel as far as Weasel's stone. It took skill to catch an ensorcelled stone; only an experienced warslinger could do it. The stone would likely smack Weasel in the head when it returned. It would hurt, but Weasel would win the contest.

"You think you can best me, as Kaldair did Vaprak," The Beast said, his hand not quite touching the stones. "But I know circlestone when I see it."

His fingers closed around an ordinary pebble.

Weasel groaned, wishing the pouch had included one of the blast marbles. All it would take then was one quick shatter-shout and. . .

Just a moment.

He thought back to the spring festival and the Ghostwise attack. To his jest in the mess hall. After he'd pulled the fast-hand and fumble-drop, they hadn't been able to find the blast marble; they'd evacuated the mess to search for it. Had Chucklebelly been keeping the marble all this time "for luck"? Was that what the halfling had been frantically searching for as The Beast and his Hunt sprang their trap?

Weasel drew in a deep breath—nice, not to be sneezing—and shatter-shouted. The Beast whirled, a stricken look in his eyes—then exploded.

Weasel didn't mind when the explosion slammed him to the ground. Nor did he mind the ringing in his ears. He didn't even mind the blood running from his nose—it wasn't half as bad as being plugged up from pollen, nohow.

He stepped to the edge of the crater where The Beast had been, and *tsk-tsked* at the tooth-and-claw necklace that had somehow survived.

"You really ought to be more careful about what you eat."

Then, before Malar's clerics or the orcworts could return, he sprinted away.

The Year of the Tankard (1370 DR)

The halfling drained his ale and set it aside, then leaned back against the mahogany tree. "And that's how it happened," he told the younglings. "How The Beast was defeated, by Kaldair in the form of a spriggan."

The younglings looked up at the storyteller with wide eyes. "Is it true?"

The storyteller shrugged. "What do you think?" He waved a hand at the athletic contests taking place in the sun-dappled field a few paces away. "To this day, the hin of the Luiren compete in the stone toss, the obstacle course. . . even our Weasel in the Hole game comes from this tale."

The younglings murmured together excitedly. "Could it be true? A *spriggan?*"

The storyteller waved a hand, shooing them away. "Off with you, now. I need my nap."

As they departed, he leaned back against the tree. "Younglings," he chuckled. "They'll believe anything." He drifted off into contented slumber.

As he slept, a twig-shaped hand gently stroked a lock of hair that hung against the storyteller's temple. A lock of hair tied with a ribbon—one of the peculiarities of fashion observed by the halflings of the Luiren.

"It's true," her leaves whispered. She sighed as she looked out over the cultivated fields of the Strongheart and Lightfoot—the fields that had once been thick jungle.

"It's true."

THE LAST PALADIN OF ILMATER

Susan J. Morris

27 Eleint, The Year of Queen's Tears (902 DR)
The Chondalwood

How dare he," Maze said.

Jaeriko struggled to keep up with the angry woman as she tromped through the tangled undergrowth of the Chondalwood. It was obvious Maze had little regard or skill for the ways of the forest. If she had possessed even a modicum of respect, she wouldn't have been making such a racket. Predators and worse for miles around must have cocked an ear to the woman's infernal crashing. Not that such attention would vex Maze any—Jaeriko imagined the fierce woman would welcome the chance to wet her blades on anyone unfortunate enough to cross her path.

Jaeriko, in contrast, was uncannily adept—walking solely on roots and rocks, and making as little sound as a ripple moving through still waters.

What was more, the vines, grass, and leaves curled and popped back into place after their every step, at her bidding. Perhaps that was why the General of Reth had sent her along on a task that—on the surface—she seemed exceptionally ill-suited for: to cover the dark, scowling woman's tracks as she stormed toward their mutual goal.

Jaeriko shook her head at a particularly virulent curse that escaped the unhappy woman's mouth. She didn't even need eyes to follow the path Maze cut—following the stream of invectives was simple enough. And though it brought her some small delight to see her own proficiency by the light of her companion's deficit, she would have strongly preferred their trip pass in silence. After all, the forest they walked was far from welcoming.

Even for someone as in touch with nature as she, the thick, choking trees and hard-packed earth studded with harder stones made for slow and uncomfortable travel. Moss dripped like blood from every sharp-fingered twig, mushrooms spangled the trees like spent arrows, and vines and branches wove themselves with almost human intent into the path of the two travelers, tripping and cutting whenever they could. To make matters worse, a veil of moon-bright ash hung in the air like a cloud of spores, riding in on every breath and obscuring the dark shapes of the firs and oaks until the travelers stumbled nose-first upon them.

Jaeriko's eyes were sore from squinting through the perpetual haze, her lungs ragged from breathing in the fire-choked air, and her skin dusty as a moth's wing. To Maze, it must have meant the world had declared war.

"Sending an assassin to do a thief's job," Maze muttered in a rare stretch of language unbroken by profanity.

"A . . . what?" Jaeriko said, standing like a startled fawn. Maze backhanded a branch that crossed her path, and Jaeriko ducked just in time to see it hiss back into place. Maze looked back over her shoulder and arched an eyebrow at the flustered druid.

"An assassin. What, you just now figure that out?" Maze said. "Yes, I kill people for money." Maze faced forward again, missing Jaeriko's stricken expression. "You helped me, when I paid for your services. Does that bother you?"

Jaeriko wasn't sure it didn't, but she was too shocked by her former client's lack of trust to contemplate it. "You could have told me!" she protested.

"You didn't need to know," Maze said.

"Your partner 'didn't need to know'?" Jaeriko said, but the pieces fell into place. The dark alley, the herb garden, the smell of almonds. The spells of stealth and speed, the exotic collection of weaponry, the extra coin for discretion. She told herself she had never known what the jobs were for, but she had never asked either.

"You're not my partner!" Maze said, interrupting her thoughts. "And what the Hells did you think I did, anyway?"

"I thought you were a thief," Jaeriko said.

"And you were all right with *that?*" Maze said.

Jaeriko shrugged. "People have too much stuff anyway."

Maze laughed, and though the sound was pitched high with frustration, it was the first sign of amusement she'd seen from the dour woman. Just when Jaeriko was about to take advantage of the unexpected levity, Maze tripped on a root and had to swing her arms out to avoid falling. "Gods damn him! I hate forests, I hate children, and I hate everything to do with this blasted war—particularly the undead. By the Nine, who does he think I am?"

"Isn't the question normally 'Who does *he* think *he* is'?" Jaeriko asked. Maze glared at her and Jaeriko felt a surge of compassion for the angry assassin. Who could blame her for her angst? Maze hadn't asked for this job. She hadn't asked to be assaulted in her home or to be forced into service at sword point. It was good coin, but it was still unasked for.

"I know who he is," Maze muttered.

It was just, the general's sword had moved so fast. Jaeriko couldn't have stopped it had it crossed her mind to do so. One moment Maze was telling the General of Reth what he could do with his job; the next, her friend's body was bleeding on the kitchen floor, lying in a pool of blood and chicken soup.

"The coin I'm paying for this job is more than enough to cover your friend's resurrection," the general had said. "Just bring me the boy."

There had been no further arguments.

Dead blue eyes darkened to brown as she refocused on Maze. Then a branch snapped back into place and Maze continued on her way, the errant limb smacking Jaeriko across the face. That was going to leave a welt. She rubbed at her skin and felt the gummy sap work its way farther into the rising abrasion. Great—she didn't have time to clean it now, so she'd have to let it go until morning—until after the job. By then, it would be nice and sore.

"Why doesn't he just do it himself? He's obviously powerful enough," Jaeriko asked, rubbing at the rising bump on her cheek. Maze's scorn burned more than the welt, and she dropped her hand.

"If you'd asked that question yourself before you invited him into my home, we might not be in this mess," Maze snapped. When Jaeriko colored but did not rise to the bait, Maze sighed. "Do you know what they say about the good General of Reth, our beloved patron? They say he's more like the devils of Arrabar than us . . . Turned for some reason known only to him, and liable to turn back again just as soon as he gets what he wants." Maze turned back to the path and continued walking, but her assaults on the flora were half-hearted at best.

"Then why did we accept his help—why are we helping him now?"

Maze shrugged. "Who am I to question when one devil wants to kill another?"

"You're a strange woman," Jaeriko said.

"No, Druid—you're the strange one. Most people are running as fast as they can from the war. All of our best soldiers are dead, or in the case of Arrabar, dishonorably raised to kill and die again. The streets of formerly great cities are littered with corpses, victims of a war-spawned plague that kills indiscriminately. Poor divided Chondath is disintegrating under her own sickening mass. Most people want to get as far away from this catastrophe as possible, but you—you're heading down into its bloody heart to kidnap a diseased boy from his deranged father. And you're pulling me with you."

Jaeriko shrugged. "Some things are worth fighting for. With the General of Arrabar raising the fallen to fight again, Reth might never win her freedom. And if we have a chance to stop him—even at the cost of our own lives—we have a responsibility to try. This could end the war."

Maze groaned. "So could killing the bastard."

Jaeriko couldn't argue with that—or wouldn't, with a self-professed assassin. Though she thought killing the General of Arrabar might be just a little harder than all that. Maze fixed her with a glare.

"So how far to this river of yours?" Maze asked. "Let's get this over with." Jaeriko nearly took a mouth full of fir.

"I thought you were leading the way!" she protested, wincing at the wail that found its way into her voice. Maze's glare hardened but then cracked under the weight of her smirk.

"I am," Maze said. "It's a joke. Ha. See? I can be funny too."

Jaeriko was flooded with equal parts relief and irritation.

"That is not funny!" she insisted.

"Anyway, we're here," Maze said, sitting down on a fallen, moss-riddled tree.

With Maze's body out of the way, Jaeriko could see the river. While the waters might be raging farther north, by this point the river was silent and strong, pulling the whole watercourse deep underground. That was no excuse for her not hearing it in advance of almost stumbling upon it, but she'd give herself the very real distraction of trying to calm an irate assassin as reason enough.

"Your turn, Druid."

Jaeriko walked over to the water. It worried her to place so much stock in the word of a man who had tricked her into leading him to Maze's house so that he could force them both into his employment, but she had little else to go on. The general told them that this river fed the cistern in the ruined citadel the General of Arrabar had holed up in. Provided he was right, a simple spell and an uncomfortable, wet time later and they should find themselves both within the citadel and undetected. Getting out undetected with the boy in tow would prove more difficult—but they'd tackle that problem when they came to it.

Reaching inside her doeskin jerkin, Jaeriko pulled out a locket. Reverently, she kissed it; the gold was cool against her lips. Then her fingers worked the catch, and it sprang open to reveal a sprig of mistletoe—her conduit to the spirits of nature. She spun the green sprig between her fingers.

"This will not be pleasant," Jaeriko warned Maze.

"Get on with it," Maze said. It was not as though they had a choice.

"Get in the water."

Maze complied, twisting her face as the water seeped under her leather. She ducked her head under the water and came back up gasping with cold.

"Keep your eyes closed and your limbs close until you feel air on your skin," the druid instructed. "The river's bargain allows you to breathe underwater, but it doesn't protect you from the dangers of underground water travel."

"Right, right," Maze said, but her teeth were already chattering.

"See you on the other side," Jaeriko said. Rubbing the mistletoe between her fingers, Jaeriko closed her eyes. *Sister River, listen to me. . .* Words ripped through her and off her tongue like lightning, burning away the instant her mind touched them. A loud, rushing, siren song filled her ears, and the smell of salt filled her nostrils—then all was quiet. She opened her eyes to see five red gashes open on each side of Maze's neck like cuts from a tiger's claws. The woman fell into the water, the red gashes fluttered open and closed, and bubbles of air escaped Maze's nose. Jaeriko held her breath for Maze as the woman waved, then let the powerful undertow sweep her away.

Moments later, Jaeriko joined her.

Air washed across Jaeriko's face and she gulped in breath blindly. Searching for something to hold onto, her fingers swept up and closed around something slick and unforgiving. She opened her eyes—bars. The cistern had a grate covering its mouth, and the bars were encrusted with slime. The water was damn cold. Goose bumps rose along her exposed skin as the wind swept across again, raising a low moan from both her and the cistern. Already Jaeriko's arms ached from cold and forced use.

She heard a splash and a gasp and saw two eyes blink back at her in the darkness. Maze.

"Holy Hells," Maze panted. "I never want to have to do

that again." A frown furrowed the woman's brow, and her fingers searched along the bars. "Gods be damned. I could deal with a lock, but there isn't even a door. What in the Nine Hells am I supposed to do with this?" She grabbed the grate in both hands and shook it angrily. It didn't budge.

"Shhh!" Jaeriko said. "They'll hear you!" The last thing she wanted to see was a ghoul's ghastly, flesh-torn face glaring at them from the other side of that grate. She could well imagine the spears and arrows that would follow.

"Bring them on," Maze whispered, but then she gritted her teeth and held her tongue.

Jaeriko breathed out a sigh of relief. It was hard enough to think with the icy water muddying her thoughts—trying to come up with any sort of way out with an irate assassin screaming in her ear was too much. Her fingers traveled automatically to the locket at her neck. Fire of the heavens, what was she to do now?

Jaeriko's eyes traveled the breadth of the grate. The whole contraption was essentially a stone opening to an underground river that had a grate tacked over it, probably to prevent intrepid intruders such as themselves from entering. There had been little to no modification to the natural stone at all, in fact . . . The fingers of her free hand traced the unworked stone as the other hand held the grate. A wild thought took root in her head, and she prayed it wasn't the cold speaking.

"Maze, hold me up," Jaeriko demanded.

"What?"

"Just do it." What felt like a band of iron wrapped around her waist, and Jaeriko felt Maze's breath against the shell of her ear.

"Hurry—I can't hold you for long."

Furrowing her brow, Jaeriko clasped one hand to her locket. She brought it to her lips. She didn't dare open it over the water—she hoped she didn't need that strength. Fear ran through her mind scattering her thoughts. The cold was ruining her concentration. With her free hand, she massaged their prison's stone circumference. *Father stone, wake up, she thought, please listen.* Stone was not her first choice of a medium. It was hard to read, harder to please, and the hardest to keep up a conversation with.

Just as she thought the stone would never answer, just as she felt Maze's arms weaken around her waist and saw the assassin's head begin to loll, she felt the fire of the stone's answer tear through her. Her fingers pushed through the stone and pulled a dollop of it away to rub between her fingers like clay. She shuddered with relief, and hit Maze's shoulders with her palms. "Let me down! All we have to do is push the grate up—it should move easily, at least for now."

Maze fixed her with an appraising glance. "You're more useful than you let on."

Jaeriko was unable to fully appreciate Maze's comment as her body quavered and shook. It was as though all of her heat had been consumed in that one spell.

"Just get us out of here," Jaeriko managed, her teeth chattering and clashing on every syllable. Maze nodded and let the water close over her head as she sank to the bottom of the cistern. Then, with a powerful push of her legs, Maze slammed out of the water and into the grate. It resisted initially but then pulled free of the softened stone with a wet pop. Hand-over-hand, Maze pushed the grate to one side of the cistern.

Pumping her legs, Jaeriko pushed herself up to the opening of the cistern and dug her fingers into the clay. She felt the water rush by her legs as Maze did the same. With agonizing slowness, she pulled herself up just enough to see where they had landed themselves.

A single light smoldered like a fallen star stuck in a white fang of a tower. It struck her as strange—how were the general's soldiers to stand guard with so little illumination? Then her eyes adjusted, and she saw the broken and malformed shapes that hunched like gargoyles along the walls. The undead required no light—nor sustenance other than that which can be garnered from a battlefield. They were the perfect soldiers.

A hiss of breath stirred the hair on the back of Jaeriko's neck; then a hand pushed her under the icy water. She heard the clang of metal on stone as the grate was shoved back in place—or almost back in place. Kicking and pulling at the hand tangled in her hair, Jaeriko struggled to catch sight of her attacker. Dark eyes met hers with a warning, and she stopped fighting. The hand let go of her hair and together, Maze and Jaeriko looked up through the distortion of the water.

A pale shape skittered forward, its limbs moving with unnatural speed and a total absence of grace. When it came to the grate it jerked to a halt and stood as still as stone. Lungs burning, Jaeriko began to panic. If she couldn't get to the surface soon, she would not live long enough to be killed. Just as it seemed the creature would never move again, it shuddered, and its head snapped in their direction.

Jaeriko bit back a gasp. The flesh had rotted on the left side of its face, baring white jaws and missing teeth. A rip in the skin under its eye socket shone like a red tear over which stared dispassionate eyes the color of old milk. It stood stiller than life above the grate, its old armor hanging off it like fat off a bone, looking—expressionless—at them. If it had been alive, Jaeriko would have sworn it had seen them and that their death would shortly follow, but after another lung-searing moment it took off in the same swift, broken gait as before.

Surfacing again with a pain-racked breath, Jaeriko allowed herself to shudder. She turned to thank Maze but Maze's attention was elsewhere. In her element at last, Maze shrugged the grate aside as though she were shedding a cloak, then surged out of the water and over the edge of the cistern with a speed and silence that spoke of exceptional strength and control. All was still for a moment, and Jaeriko tried to determine if she were to follow, then Maze's hand appeared out of the darkness, and the deft woman helped pull her out of the water.

The stench hit her first, coursing over her in waves—the sweet bite of rot, the bitter tang of blood, and the animal musk of feathers and crow's leavings. Then she noticed the glint of copper on the ground. Her fingers closed around the flickering metallic light. A copper coin. Looking for the round shapes now, she saw the floor was littered with them and what appeared to be sheets of paper. Armor, weapons, and bodies were oddly absent. She could smell them, but she couldn't make any out in the darkness.

Maze tapped her on the shoulder and pointed. Following the line of her finger, Jaeriko saw the same pale figure that had stood over them moments before scrambling past the tower without pause.

"It's running a circuit—bound undead are as predictable as the stars. We probably have another thirty heartbeats before it starts heading back this way." Maze pulled at Jaeriko's arm. "Follow me."

The assassin uncoiled like a cat and stalked forward, her body held low and her eyes focused on the white tower. Jaeriko followed as best she could, but found her eyes drawn again and again to the carpet of coins, papers, buttons, and refuse. There was something eerie about what was left behind—what the dead and their general had decided they didn't need. She passed a dark ribbon tied around a lock of muddy hair, a half-eaten trail ration crawling with moon-white maggots, a silver heart-shaped locket with broken hinges and shattered glass, a much-folded sketch of a woman looking back over her shoulder. . . .

She forced her eyes up and almost ran into Maze, pressed against the outside of the white tower like a shadow. Maze scowled back at her, then motioned for Jaeriko to move up next to her. The tower wall was cut from a stone that left a sandpaper finish, and her clothes and hair caught and tugged at her as she sidled up next to Maze.

"Why didn't that thing try to kill us back there?" Jaeriko whispered. Maze snuck a furtive glance through the finger-wide crack between the door and the wall near where it locked, then stared out in the direction of the cistern as she answered.

"It's probably operating under strict rules," Maze whispered back. "If we don't technically violate the conditions of its binding, it doesn't have to do anything. I was betting that it hadn't been given instructions as to what to do to people found underneath the citadel—as we were when we were submerged in the cistern."

"How do you know it wasn't given instructions to just tell the general?" asked Jaeriko.

"I don't," Maze said. Jaeriko's mouth formed an O. "That's why we have to move fast." Tension was visible in every line of Maze's body—from the tendons standing out on her neck to the stiff arch in her back. Tilting her head skyward, Maze closed her eyes and pulled what looked like a prayer necklace from her pocket. Fingering the long strand set with a bead in the center, she whispered something Jaeriko couldn't catch. Just then, the door to the tower swung wide, and another pale figure emerged, this one hung with brass metal plates with a soot-blackened blade slung through its belt. The metal of the blade made a quiet hiss as it rasped along the stone.

The moment it strode past them, Maze leaped at its back, knee first, and whipped the cord around its neck, the bead centered beautifully on the center of its throat. Her knee planted itself mid-spine. Jaeriko watched in horror as Maze yanked back on the cord and shoved down with her knee, riding the flailing creature to the ground.

"Destroy it!" Maze said, and Jaeriko stared at her.

The flesh on the creature Maze had mounted sagged as though it wanted to flee the bone, but the lack of living muscle seemed to have no effect on its strength as it set a yellow-clawed hand down on each side of it.

"Now!" Maze said, a note of panic entering her voice.

But Jaeriko stood, frozen, as the rotting creature pushed up and spun under Maze's hold till it faced her and the bridle she'd improvised proved useless.

Maze cursed and dropped the strand, the bead forgotten. Her arms crossed and she withdrew a knife like a thorn from a sheath on her upper arm—then she fell backward as yellow claws filthy with decay snapped up at her, rolling out of harm's way. The pale monstrosity, liberated from its rider, climbed to its feet seemingly uninjured, but in the light from the tower above, Jaeriko could see the shadow where its windpipe used to be.

The creature opened its mouth as though to shriek, but a wet gurgle was all that found its way out. Then its dead eyes found hers. In two quick jerks it turned to face her, like a badly strung marionette. Jaeriko knew she should run, duck, strike, something, but in terror's grip she stood transfixed by its impassive gaze. Gathering its limbs under it, the ghoul sprang at Jaeriko—and she could not even find the breath to scream. It stopped a hand's breadth from her nose as a sloppy red line tore across its throat in a flash of silver. Then its head slipped backward and its body tumbled to the side, hitting the open door and sending it swinging.

Maze caught the door with the still-bloody blade and glared at Jaeriko, panting. "Next time I tell you to do something, you do it. You hear me?"

"I . . . I can't do this," Jaeriko whispered, staring at the crumpled, headless corpse. A corpse that had been someone's son. That had just tried to kill her. That could still try to kill her for all she knew. Fear rose in her gullet, and it tasted like bile.

"You don't have a choice, Druid," Maze said, her eyes glittering. "And if you don't do what I say, you don't have a chance, either."

"You don't understand," Jaeriko said. "You kill people all the time. I can't do this." Maze sighed and motioned her through the door into the white tower.

"I do understand," Maze said. "More than you know. But I also know that they're already dead, and that if you don't help me put them down, you'll end up dead too. Besides, you gave your word, Jaeriko. Where are all your brave words about ending the war?"

"I didn't know it would be like this," Jaeriko said, but Maze had already moved into the corridor, so her words were for her ears alone.

Swallowing her tongue and her misgivings, Jaeriko followed. She shut the heavy wood door, revealing a painting of broken hands wrapped in and clasping a red ribbon on its back—the symbol of Ilmater, god of mercy. It appeared the tower had once been a temple. The ground could hardly remain consecrated, though, if it held the clawing undead within its walls.

Putting the matter out of mind, Jaeriko turned to see Maze motioning for her to hurry at the end of the hallway, and she nearly tripped over the uneven floor catching up. The corridor was short, as could be expected for the first level of a tower, and was made of the same ghostly stone on the inside as out. The walls were bare, but there were clean shadows where pictures once hung. The most terrifying aspect of the former temple was its utter silence. Walking in that hallway was like walking in a tomb—the sounds of life as alien as its concept within those stone walls.

When the silence came to an end as Jaeriko joined Maze, she thought she would be pleased, but what she heard haunted her more than the absence of life before. Sobs echoed in the corridor, soft at first, but louder as the pair slinked toward their source. At the end of the passage was an open archway that led into a room, and from that room spilled light and sound—the first human sounds they'd heard outside of each other. As they crept closer Jaeriko could make out a kneeling figure—misshapen in which she assumed was armor—backlit in the light of the room. Words formed in the weeping.

"Ilmater forgive me." The man's voice was deep and thick with tears. "He suffers so that others may live. Please." Jaeriko could see his hands clasped in imitation of Ilmater's on the tower door. "I would gladly have given my body to this corruption, had you not prevented it." The man's voice was bitter, almost accusatory in its grief. "It was the only way. Were he older, he would pay her price willingly—the sacrifice of one for the good of many. You must see that." His voice grew desperate. "Why have you forsaken me?"

Horror and compassion warred within her. Without a doubt, this man was the seed from which atrocities were sewn. Much of the fallout of the Rotting War could be traced to him and him alone. And yet, this servant of Ilmater—a paladin, by his garb—had lost his god, his son, and his war. All that was left was for him to lose was his life. Jaeriko could sense Maze itching to relieve him of that burden, too, but the assassin managed to hold herself in check.

"He sounds like a man who's lost his faith," Jaeriko said, fingering her locket.

"He sounds like a man who's lost his mind," Maze said. "Never empathize with the enemy. If you do, you'll never make your kill."

"I don't want to make a kill," Jaeriko said.

But Maze had already moved on, motioning for Jaeriko to move with her. Turning the corner, they went up a staircase and emerged in a narrow hall with a door some twenty paces distant, lit by a single torch. The door was old wood, and the hinges were dull with wear, but the lock gleamed bright brass in the flickering torchlight. Jaeriko was grateful that the general's pleas to his god could not be heard through the floor and the twisting stone of the staircase.

"Perfect," Maze murmured. "This is what we came for."

"How do you know?" Jaeriko asked.

"What else does the general have worth locking up?" Maze padded up to the door and traced her fingers around the metal of the lock.

"Are you going to pick the lock?"

"Hells, no." Maze looked up, irritated. "I'm not a godsdamned thief. Why won't you listen to me?" The question was rhetorical, as the assassin turned, scowling, back to the mechanical device on the door.

"Then—"

"Just sit down and shut up." Maze pulled a vial out of the pouch on her belt and uncorked it—pointing it away from her. The stopper of the vial had a long glasslike needle attached to its bottom, and a drip of clear liquid hung off its tip. It glistened iridescent in the torchlight, then fell to the floor, drilling deep into the white stone. With great care, Maze dipped the needle into the vial and applied the point to one side of the lock.

The door burst open, banging against the wall, and a broken, pale figure in armor stood backlit in the doorway.

"Damn it!" Maze shouted, splashing the contents of her vial up into her attacker's face. Steam and the acid stench of boiling flesh flooded the hallway, accompanied by the most hideous hissing and popping sounds. Moments later, the pale figure in the doorway crumpled to the ground, faceless. Maze nudged it with her foot. It was another one of the general's ghouls. What it was doing coming through that door was beyond Jaeriko—possibly standing guard?—but it confirmed her suspicions about the fallen temple.

"Well, that's one way to open a door," Maze panted. With a mock bow, Maze motioned Jaeriko in.

It was obvious upon entering that the room was the source of the light that shone from the white tower. Alone among all the rooms in the tower, it was well lit. A red carpet graced the floor, pictures hung on every available section of wall, and candles burned on every horizontal surface, bathing the room in flickering light. An open window on the far side of the room let in a cool breeze and let out the room's startling radiance.

In the center of the room was a plain bed on a steel frame made up with white linen. Twisted in those sheets was as poor a boy as Jaeriko had ever laid eyes on. Boils peppered his fair skin like freckles, his fingers were blackened and bone-thin, and his skin glistened with sweat in the cool air. His eyes were closed and his lips were cracked and covered in dried blood. Moaning, the boy turned and thrashed in his covers, deep in the thrall of fevered dreams.

A hissing intake of breath alerted Jaeriko to another presence in the room. She snapped her head to the side and caught sight of a red-haired woman with frightened gray eyes holding a mallet inches from its gong.

"Maze!" Jaeriko cried.

Silver streaked through the air and blood blossomed in the woman's hand from the knife pinning it to the wall. The mallet fell to the carpeted floor without a sound. The woman opened her mouth to shriek but Maze's hand found its way into her mouth.

"Gods, Maze. You could have pinned the mallet!" Jaeriko rushed to Maze's side and examined the knife and the wound it had created. The woman's fingers were white with tension, and the dark red blood that pumped down it to drip on the floor spoke of serious injury to the limb. If it weren't treated quickly, the woman would lose a hand, and even then, she might gain a disease and lose more than that.

Maze rolled her eyes. "Assassin, remember?"

Jaeriko stood and looked the red-haired woman in the eye. The woman's face was painted with fear.

"If Maze takes her hand out of your mouth, you have to promise me you won't scream," Jaeriko said. The woman nodded, tears leaking from her eyes.

"Why in the Nine Hells would I do that?" Maze asked angrily, turning to face Jaeriko.

"Shh—just trust me on this one," Jaeriko pleaded. "We're partners, remember? Now, remove your hand." Maze glared at her for a moment longer, then reluctantly pulled her hand from the woman's mouth and wiped it on her jerkin. The woman gasped with relief.

"Don't make me regret this," Maze said, and she stomped off to examine the boy. Jaeriko watched her go, then turned to the woman whose eyes reflected much of the terror she'd felt that day.

"You're the boy's caretaker?" Jaeriko asked. She placed one hand on the hilt of the knife, and one hand on the flesh it pinned. The woman nodded and bit her lip. Jaeriko pulled the knife out with a wet slurping sound. The woman's lip began to bleed and she swayed on her feet, but she did not cry out.

"I can't heal him," the woman said. Her voice was weak with pain.

"Shhh. No one's asking you to," Jaeriko said, stroking the torn meat of the woman's hand. The wound was deep. Even with magical healing, it would take awhile for it to regain its dexterity. "Now who are you—are you a servant of Talona?" The woman looked horrified at the thought of the goddess of disease. A good sign, Jaeriko thought.

"Ilmater, like the general is—was," the woman said. She sucked in a breath as Jaeriko dug her fingertips into the wound, her other hand clasped around her locket. "My name is Kalmia. I'm an herbalist. The general keeps me because I can't do any harm—or good—without his supplies." Kalmia closed her eyes in relief as golden swirls of healing magic coursed through Jaeriko's fingertips and puckered the woman's flesh closed. It wasn't much—it would still leave a nasty scar and it would take a couple of days for the feeling to come back, but it should be enough to keep her from disease or permanent injury. "He only gives me enough herbs to keep his son alive—never enough to cure him or to end his suffering."

"What kind of man does this to his son?" Jaeriko said, more to the world than to the red-haired woman holding her healed but still blood-drenched hand and staring at it as though it wouldn't obey her commands. The fingers twitched but refused fuller motion.

"The general does not like losing," Kalmia said, sighing and letting her hand rest, useless, by her side.

"More like he doesn't know when he's lost," Maze snapped, but her eyes held a distant softness as she beheld the stricken boy. Her hands moved almost of their own accord, wrapping the boy in his bed linens.

"Can you. . . ?" Kalmia began, looking at her hand and then up at Jaeriko, but the druid shook her head.

"Sorry. But I can take him to someone who can," Jaeriko replied. The herbalist's eyes filled with fear. "The General of Reth has nothing against the General of Arrabar's son. He sent us here to rescue him."

Kalmia's eyes closed and her head fell back to rest upon the wall. Indecision held her features taut until resolution poured over them like a soothing balm. She opened gray eyes cleared from doubt.

"Take him, then," Kalmia said. "But go quickly. It is the general's habit to check on his son after vespers and before bed."

"Way ahead of you," said Maze.

Jaeriko looked over to see that Maze had finished bundling the boy in his sheets and was carrying him to the window. If the general came in and saw his son gone, Kalmia would likely prove yet another senseless casualty of the general's misplaced loyalty. It wasn't fair. Kalmia had doubtless already suffered enough for her care of the boy.

"You should come with us," Jaeriko blurted, looking over her shoulder at Maze as she left the boy in the sheet at the window and climbed outside herself. "The general will be angry—we can protect you."

"No, I can't."

"Why?"

"I just can't!" Kalmia said, wringing her hands. Jaeriko was about to press her further, but Maze glared at her from the window. Time was running out. "He's got my brother," Kalmia whispered. "My brother . . . He's always been there for me. Protected me. Even when the war got bad, and he was called away. Now it's my turn to protect him." Her dark eyes searched Jaeriko's. "I can't just leave him."

Jaeriko softened. "Then take this." Unhooking a gnarled ivory wand from her belt, Jaeriko handed it to the trembling herbalist. Kalmia looked as though she was about to protest, so the druid added, "For self-defense."

"I won't use it," the herbalist promised, but her fingers devoured the wand's shape.

Jaeriko ran over to the window, confident the woman would use it if she had to. Maze had just dropped to the ground, and held her arms out for the boy. Bracing feet against the sides of the window, Jaeriko lowered the sheet-wrapped child into Maze's waiting arms. Then, with one look back at the herbalist and the now-empty sickroom, she, too, slipped out the window.

Ash snowed down from the charred trees around the citadel and drifted on the breeze in a gray miasma, choking their vision and their breath. The sickly green of faerie fire licked the gathering storm clouds above, heralding a tempest that had yet to be unleashed. Armed men stood still enough to be statues among the trees, their armor darkened with soot to match the forest's painted hue. The night was silent but for the trumpeting horn that echoed off the inside of the crumbling citadel.

It let them know he was coming.

Jaeriko and Maze stood by the boy they had rescued and the man they had brought him to—the General of Reth. Only one part remained to their task—the largest part of which was to stay alive. The smallest part of which was to keep the boy alive as well.

The boy, still swaddled in white linens, lay on a simple cot, lost in the oblivion of disease. His nursemaids, the blackened trees, stood all around him, and the General of Reth stood right behind him, holding a long, slender knife, like a surgeon's tool, to the boy's throat.

They waited like a drawn bow, aimed at the gate to the crumbling citadel.

The General of Arrabar burst through the gate like a lion, his ragged gold mane flying like a banner and his haunted green eyes fixed first on his son and then on the man above him. His face was haggard; his sins written as deeply upon his flesh as upon his soul. He was still dressed in the armor of Ilmater, with a white tabard emblazoned with the ribbon-threaded hands, but the white of the tabard had turned brown with dirt, and his armor bled with rust.

Twisted, pale men hung with the brassy remnants of armor poured out of the citadel and arrayed themselves around the Lion of Arrabar in a ghoulish honor guard. Upon reaching their positions, they stood still—unmoving and not breathing.

The General of Reth dipped the point of his knife in the hollow of the boy's throat and a drop of blood beaded there like sweat. The boy screamed, though whether in fevered dreams or pain, Jaeriko did not know.

"Stop! Don't kill him, Thais." The General of Arrabar's face and voice twisted in distress.

"Tell me why I shouldn't, old friend," said the General of Reth. He turned the knife to display its ruby shine. "Surely he has suffered enough."

"It's what she's been waiting for," the General of Arrabar said. "My bargain with Talona is broken the same moment as her hold on him—by death or by new life. If you kill my son, the ghouls will no longer obey me, the war will be lost, and all my suffering will be for nothing. Do you understand me? The boy's suffering will be for nothing."

The General of Arrabar stood, an arm extended as though he could stop the knife from his son's throat by will alone. Thais, the General of Reth, eyed him, as expressionless as the walking dead.

"A bargain with the Lady of Poison, Paladin of Ilmater? Sacrificing your son, and for what—another chance for Arrabar to subjugate Reth and Hlath?"

"To keep our kingdom whole," the General of Arrabar corrected. Thais shook his head.

"I wouldn't kill your son, Dominic," Thais said, and he sheathed his knife. "You were doing a fine job of that yourself."

The moment the knife ceased threatening his son, all pleading left Dominic's face.

"Now!" the leonine general commanded, dropping his arm and drawing his sword. Ghouls swarmed forward like a plague of spiders over the crumbling walls and over their brethren, murderous animation driving their limbs to inhuman speeds.

Soldiers fell out of the woods to meet them, bringing shields to bear and forming a wall of steel around the general and against the oncoming horde. At a gesture from the general, Maze and Jaeriko snapped into position; Maze guarding the body of the boy, Jaeriko farther back, clasping one of Maze's knives in a white-knuckled hand and searching frantically for ghouls who might be trying to circumnavigate their defense. Bodies splattered unhurt against the shields of the living, testing the soldiers, who held it strong. She could hear the General of Arrabar shouting orders, and in answer, pale fingers sharpening into long yellow nails gripped the tops of the shields, and ravenous eyes cleared the wall.

Thais stood with his back to Jaeriko, between her and the battle, head bowed under the ashen rain as though in mourning for the deaths to come. Soft brown hair obscured his features, and his shoulders were back. Then his hands shot out, fingers spread like talons, and clamped into the blackened bark of the trees that guarded him.

Darkness seeped out of the charred trees and out of his skin, spilling onto the ground and down his body like sap. His men cheered as the waves of night overtook them, but the ghouls skittered and keened, pulling themselves back away from the shield wall, unwilling to step into the spreading sea of glistening ebony. It overcame them anyway. Thais's head snapped back, stars burning for eyes, and the roiling shadows took flight, swirling upward in a deepening tide until everything was painted in shades of black.

Then the shield wall broke and surged forward, and the battle was joined in earnest.

An explosion of light burst from Reth's general, and for a heartbeat, even the shadows ceased to exist. Jaeriko could see soldiers in the process of impaling ghouls and ghouls with their long fingers plucking out human eyes. Maze stood in front of the boy, her long knife wet and dripping, spinning low with a leg extended at knee height. And the General of Reth dropped down from the heavens like a bird of prey, angling his burning blade at the paladin of Ilmater, who just managed to raise a sword in defense. The dark general hit the ground, and the paladin spun with the energy of the deflected blade, angling a strike at his opponent's back.

Just as it looked as though the blade would shear the General of Reth in half, he rolled backward and to his feet, slicing at Arrabar's unprotected neck, but the paladin stepped forward and bashed the hilt of his sword up into his opponent's face. The dark general's head snapped back and he stumbled, his body weaving. A well-planted kick on Reth's ribs threw the wounded general to the ground. Arrabar lunged after him, his sword poised for the killing stroke. His would-be victim cracked a smile, and an ebony tide swept over the battle, plunging the forest into darkness.

The sounds of the dying and the screams of metal on metal filled the air like a crying symphony. Blind, nearly deafened, Jaeriko felt something fly by her ear, and a stinging wetness screamed for her attention an instant later. Dropping to the ground, she felt around for a tree, a body, anything to hide behind, when a brilliant radiance blossomed again. A helmet studded the tree behind her, limned with her blood; near her feet was the head it had belonged to.

Maze screamed—a sound lost in the clamor of battle—and Jaeriko looked up. A white-fleshed ghoul scrambled up Maze's prone form. Her red-streaked hands, somehow bereft of blades, reached back toward Jaeriko, and their eyes met, equally horrified. *Help me,* Maze mouthed. Jaeriko's hand throbbed from holding onto her knife. Setting her jaw and forcing her trembling legs into action, she half ran and half stumbled across the corpse-strewn field to Maze's defense. She fell upon the ghoul in a blade-studded heap. Striking back and forth without regard to angle or point, she plied her knife against the ghoul's flesh until its white skin was rent with red gouges, and the ghoul, hissing in pain, reeled back to face this new threat. Faced with the long yellow claws herself, Jaeriko's mouth opened to scream and she dropped her knife. Then the ghoul dropped like a felled tree, with Maze wrapped around its knees, and the lithe assassin pounced up its body to cut off its head. She raised her blade, and darkness swept over the field once more.

Jaeriko felt around for her knife and recovered it, gripping it with hands sore from unexpected use. Back to back, Jaeriko and Maze huddled together, blades out, striking at anything that came near without radiating warmth. Once, twice, three times she struck at things she hoped to the gods were undead, before the clammy fingers stopped pawing in her direction. Still she crouched, blade trembling, listening for attackers so hard it hurt.

But no more came. The clashes of steel diminished until the only sounds came from a single pair of combatants. Then she felt something fly by her head, heard it thump to the ground, and all sound of combat ceased. The eerie silence was broken only by feet shuffling through leaves, and Jaeriko's heart pounding in her ears. She hoped against hope it didn't mean she and Maze were the only living things left.

Then Jaeriko gasped as a brilliant nova boomed out from Reth's general, bathing the combatants in unnatural light. The shadowy man's bare hands were wrapped around the leonine general's face, fingertips cupping the slackening flesh. Weaponless, the paladin clawed at the hands that lay almost reverently upon his cheeks, drawing blood but not moving them. Sweat glistened on the dark general's arms, and veins rose up in bruising hues under his victim's skin. They stood, locked that way, for as long as Jaeriko could hold her breath.

Then the General of Arrabar's eyes rolled back in his head, his flesh drawn and gray, and he cried out. "Mercy!" And the General of Reth removed his hands.

Upon release, Dominic of Arrabar collapsed to his knees and bowed his head. Thais put a hand on a nearby tree to steady himself, and his ribs heaved and shook. The blinding light and darkness faded, until only the eerie glow of the storm remained.

Pale corpses, weapons, and dismembered limbs littered the ground in a grotesque garden, blooming with arrows and blood. Not a single ghoul had survived the battle, and only a handful of Reth's soldiers lay fallen. They hadn't even had to kill the General of Arrabar to get his compliance—only the men he'd stolen from death's domain.

"Friend, forgive me," Dominic said, staring up into his friend's eyes. Thais looked down with pity, but the paladin's gaze had ascended farther, into the heavens. "Ilmater, forgive . . ." A bolt of lightning split the sky with a crack and coursed down straight onto the head of the kneeling general. Smoke leaked from his helmet, and his eyes stared vacantly upward. Then a second bolt struck where the first one had, and Dominic fell backward, his skin crisping inside his metal shell. A third bolt hit, and a fourth, and a fifth, shattering the sky with thunder and light and causing the little metal figure to dance, prone on the ground.

When the smoke finally cleared, a charred skeleton leered out from the General of Arrabar's helmet, and his metal armor was twisted beyond recognition of having ever belonged to Ilmater.

"Look!" said Maze, pointing to the entrance to the citadel. Standing in the doorway, wand still extended, was Kalmia. A wisp of smoke trailed from the tip of the twisted ivory. Jaeriko's wand. Thais looked up, his heavy gaze hanging on the woman in the door.

"Seize her," commanded Thais. He gestured to two of his men. The soldiers charged forward, one taking hold of her arms and the other relieving her of her wand. She did not struggle, but stared at the smoking body of her former master with hunger burning in her eyes. Thais watched his men take her.

Then two coins flashed into Thais's hands. Kneeling, he placed one in each blackened eye socket of the dead general.

"Good-bye, my friend," Thais said, and he stood. "You strived to starve out the darkness in you, but in the end, it consumed you instead." Thais shook his head and looked up from the grinning corpse. "A poor death for the last paladin of Ilmater."

Jaeriko stared at Kalmia.

"Oh, Kalmia," Jaeriko said. The woman had said she couldn't even use it for self defense. Had that all been a lie? Kalmia fixed her with a look that chilled her to the bone.

"You saw what he did to his son," Kalmia said. She lowered her gaze to the ghoulish corpses that littered the ground, then looked up again, resolution steeling her eyes. "If Reth intended on killing him, you two would have done it before we met. I could not risk him escaping justice."

Jaeriko stared at Kalmia as the soldiers bound the herbalist's hands behind her and led her off in the direction of the soldiers' caravans. The herbalist held her gaze, looking over her shoulder, until they could no longer see each other through the weave of the forest. A tug on her arm tore her attention away from the path the soldiers had taken.

"Never empathize with the enemy," Maze said softly. She pushed a pouch filled with coins into Jaeriko's hand. "Your half of the fee."

"Right," Jaeriko said. Maze looked at her for a moment, then put an arm around her shoulder and began guiding her back through the woods.

"Come on. Let's go home."

The first night on the road, the General of Reth let Kalmia go. He told her that under law he could not sanction her actions, but that he had long understood war—and justice—to be above the law. Then a strange cast had come over his storm gray eyes and he told her he was sorry to hear of her brother.

That strange look almost made her confess everything. If there was anyone who would understand her actions, surely it was he. But her fear of him kept her words in check, and she mumbled her thanks and left, heading straight back for the crumbling citadel cradled deep in the Chondalwood.

Morning had come and gone by the time she arrived back at the citadel, but she did not stop walking until she arrived at the door at the top of the white tower. Removing the shiny brass key from her pocket, she unlocked the door and stepped back. The door crashed open and the pale form of the ghoul she had trapped in the boy's bedroom scrambled toward her. Its yellow nails were filed sharp from clawing at the wood, and its body was ragged from pounding against the door, but it was animate, which was more than could be said for its fellows.

When it reached her it halted and stood too still in front of her. Then its nostrils—ragged tears in its sunken flesh—flexed. Starting with her feet, it snuffled up the length of her, pausing longest at her neck, behind her ear, where it tasted the scent of her hair without touching her. Her skin crawled, but she held still, searching its dead eyes when she could see them for some sign of the paladin's taint. She found the ghoul's eyes empty. It was free—uncontrolled by man or god.

The General of Reth must have finally managed with magic what she hadn't been able to with herbs and cured the paladin's son. Purging Talona's plague from the boy's body broke the Lady's bargain. Had he not, the ghoul she faced would still be clawing to get to his fallen master's side, as per his last orders. Orders she had prevented him from carrying out.

"Brother," Kalmia whispered. She reached her hands out but did not touch him. The ghoul regarded her, expressionless as always. Talona had warned her it would be this way. Her hands fell to her side. It was still worth it to extract her revenge. "Come with me." She could never forgive the General of Arrabar for what he had done. But neither could she destroy what he had created. Instead, she would make for herself a new life—one that included her dead sibling. "We're going home."

BLACK ARROW

Bruce R. Cordell

11 Tarsakh, the Year of the Dawndance (1095 DR)
Sarshel

Dear Madam Feor,
I have heard an account of the Last Battle for Sarshel's
Wall, and of the valor of Jotharam Feor in particular,
whose deeds proved instrumental in Sarshel's victory.
I regret to inform you your son died bravely in the line
of duty.
I know how devastating these brutal words must be
that bear news of a loss so overwhelming. But know
that I and reunited Impiltur itself thank you for your
son's precious service.
May Tyr, Torm, and Ilmater assuage the grief of your
mourning, leaving only cherished memories of your son.
May they grant you solemn dignity and peace in return
for your costly sacrifice given unasked, a sacrifice that
preserved Sarshel against its enemies, and which may
yet conclude the Kingless Years.

Yours, sincerely and respectfully,
Imphras Heltharn

A pulverized stone crunched beneath Jotharam Feor's boot as he trudged across gouged and broken ground.

Jotharam's eyes danced with anticipation. His gaze swept past the battered, chipped wall that encircled the city of Sarshel, his home. The adolescent looked without really seeing the earth scarred with months of encamped armies, swift conflicts, and spell-ignited conflagrations. Having never witnessed mass graves before, the mounds of earth dotting the far sward held no meaning for him.

Jotharam's mind was on the war, certainly. When was it not? Since the hobgoblin horde emerged from the Giantspire Mountains, anarchy had ruled the city. The goblinoid armies had overrun all the surrounding lands, but failed to sack Sarshel. Instead, they laid siege.

Only soldiers ventured beyond Sarshel's protective bastions.

But here I stride, thought Jotharam, not a soldier sworn but wearing a hauberk anyway!

He even carried a sword from the Sarshel Armory in a battered sheath. He walked beyond the wall as if on picket duty. As if he were, in truth, sworn to protect all that lay within the heavy walls.

Jotharam patted the messenger's bag slung over his right shoulder. The bag was the reason he wandered beyond the wall. It bulged with orders for the perimeter guards of the north bunker.

The adolescent grinned into the day's failing glow. The sun paused on the ragged edges of the Earthspurs as if to regard him alone. Jotharam pulled the borrowed sword from the scabbard on his belt and whirled it in the golden light. He imagined cutting down scores of desperate hobgoblin raiders.

"My blade will not be sheathed until it finds an invader's heart," he boasted. "Your days are numbered now that I have taken the field!"

Finally taken the field, he mentally appended.

His friends had been allowed to fight and defend Sarshel. Not he. It wasn't fear that prevented him from defending the city, nor any particular lack of skill. It was his mother.

A woman of noble birth and connections, his mother asked the city's soldiery to disallow his application, even when Sarshel was desperate to fill the dwindling regiments. They had obliged her request.

His fingers tightened on the hilt as he thought of his friends, who had become decorated and respected defenders while he remained safely at home with his mother.

And now the war was nearly won, without him.

Imphras, the great war captain, had come to Sarshel's rescue. Imphras was here, and with him, his legion of loyal warriors, archers, and war wizards. The man was a living legend. Tavern talk had it the force Imphras commanded had never seen defeat on the field of battle.

Jotharam's opportunity to prove his bravery for Sarshel failed before he was ever allowed a chance; Imphras broke the siege in just two days and was received into the city with adoration and fanfare.

Hope of permanently driving back the hobgoblins was born. Some said Imphras would be made king if he succeeded!

Marvelous, of course, except. . .

Imphras's arrival made Jotharam's ambition meaningless.

The boy lost his smile and kicked at a piece of masonry, burnt and broken. A smell of something strange wrinkled his nose. Brimstone, or hellfire itself, he fancied, wielded by a goblin shaman.

The odor reminded Jotharam that he stood, after all, outside the walls without his mother's knowledge or blessing. Some danger remained; no one could argue that.

He nodded to himself. Imphras's breaking of the siege hadn't completely eliminated the hobgoblin threat. Several distinct hordes ravaged the Easting Reach, and more than a few rabid goblin companies remained unaccounted for in the last reckoning. Perhaps even now they drew nigh to Sarshel to renew their siege?

The sun finally slipped completely beneath the western peaks. Coolness touched the back of his neck.

In the growing twilight, he recalled that traveling outside the wall required bravery only true warriors possessed. Warriors like him!

Jotharam's earlier delight rekindled as he ran fingers down his chain link mail.

Earlier that day, luck had deposited him in the right place at the right time. Normally, Jotharam delivered correspondence between merchant houses within the city's inmost neighborhood.

The regular garrison courier hadn't appeared that afternoon. No one else had been available to make the delivery to the edge of town on short notice. Jotharam volunteered. Despite the garrison being far beyond the boundaries set by his mother, the dispatcher gave him the message. Why not? Imphras was here!

Jotharam sprinted across Sarshel to deliver the document. He'd turned over the leather courier bag to the garrison lieutenant with such alacrity the lieutenant had immediately praised Jotharam to the garrison captain.

The captain, impressed, asked Jotharam to run the evening's orders out to the soldiers manning the north bunker. The captain was unaware of Jotharam's interdiction, and that sending Jotharam beyond the Sarshel Wall was taboo.

Jotharam didn't tell him otherwise. The young man had been issued arms and armor.

And here I am, he thought.

Would he be allowed to keep his borrowed panoply? What if—

A blistering, burning ball of flame bounded up from somewhere beyond the far trees. Slender rivulets of fire chased around the blazing sphere, like smoldering snakes eating their own tails.

All thoughts fled. Jotharam's eyes followed the blazing orb of destruction as it arced upward, slowed, then curved back toward the earth. Was it some sort of signal? A spell of warning? Maybe a—

The blazing fist smashed down, striking the city of Sarhsel's westernmost wall. Stones exploded away from the impact, and the ground shuddered.

Shrapnel clipped his cheek. Jotharam couldn't hear his own yell over the roar of flames and cracking stone.

Three more points of light popped up from beyond the trees, each arcing up and slowing, pausing as if to look down on Sarshel. As their trajectories, too, slowly curved back toward the ground, toward the wall, Jotharam finally understood.

Sarshel was under attack.

The north bunker was composed of a series of trenches that paralleled Sarshel's northernmost wall. A stone block-house squatted at the dugout's western end. The blockhouse was a small, boxlike structure, partially dug into the earth.

Jotharam sprinted along the west wall, running north toward the blockhouse, panting with more than effort. Blind fear propelled him. In the gathering gloom, he couldn't judge his true distance from the gleams twinkling through the arrow slits of the blockhouse. Was it a hundred feet, or a thousand? All his thoughts seemed brittle and fragmented.

Cruel, strident horns brayed from the west. A low rumble answered, quickly crescendoing into the combined battle scream from thousands of unseen throats. Hobgoblin throats!

A figure darted into Jotharam's desperate path. The boy tripped, and the figure shrieked. Jotharam's eyes were jerked away from their hypnotic connection with the blockhouse lights when he fell hard on his face.

He struggled back to his feet. Had he stumbled over a lost child? He turned to look back. Not a child. . .

A creature, shorter than himself and with long green ears, glared at him from a distance of three feet. A goblin, in chain mail smeared with dirt-black grease.

The goblin hissed and lunged with a short sword dark as obsidian.

Jotharam stepped back, twirled, and ran. Something patted him on his shoulder, but no pain came. He kept running.

He realized he was screaming, repeating a single word over and over: "Help!"

He ceased shouting; he needed all his breath to sprint for his life! His borrowed armor banged painfully against his limbs.

Twenty feet, forty feet. . . eighty. His breath seared his chest as he strained forward. Was the goblin right on his heels? He felt like collapsing, but instead he pushed harder.

He reached the blockhouse, despite anticipating a goblin blade in his back even in that very last moment. Without slowing, Jotharam dived headlong into the open trench in front of the blockhouse.

Soldiers milled within the trench. Sarshel infantry were

scrambling for their helms, their shields, their swords, rekindling their readiness in the aftermath of the unexpected attack. Jotharam lay dazed at their feet.

"Goblins," he cried. They ignored him.

They already knew.

Jotharam pulled himself upright on the earthen wall of the trench and glanced back the way he'd come. No hint of his long-eared pursuer was visible.

But there was movement in the direction from which he'd just come yelling into the bunker.

High up along the western wall of the city stood a lone figure in silver robes. The figure rose off the wall and into the air as if pulled up on a great hook, one hand gripping an oaken staff, the other gesticulating with purposeful vigor.

It was one of the war wizards Imphras had installed in the city! Imphras had brought them with him when he'd ended the siege. Jotharam's heart lifted with the wizard's altitude.

Before the wizard could get off a spell, a curtain of arrows with heads blazing red fire rose from the ground, too many to count. The mass of arrows arced and passed through the air where the bearded man screamed desperate magic. The wizard was wiped out of the sky as if by a club swung by a mountain giant.

A soldier near Jotharam yelled, "By Imphras's left testicle, there must be thousands!"

A voice, distorted with distance, yelled from somewhere far away, ". . . outer perimeter. . . goblins everywhere, I tell you we. . . overrun!"

A tall man exited the bunkhouse. He held a bow longer and thicker than any Jotharam had ever seen. He was clad in green and brown leathers. From his belt dangled a quiver inscribed with patterns of leaf and vine. Dozens of gold-fletched arrows nestled within, as well as four arrows each of a single color: one emerald, one scarlet, one silver, and one black.

The archer looked directly at Jotharam. He said, "Messenger! What news from inside the walls? Did Imphras send you?"

Jotharam looked dumbly down at his courier's satchel, then back up. "Uh, no. . . these orders came before the attack."

"Damn." The archer glanced east down the trench, then northeast, to give an appraising look at the detached spire called Demora Tower, which rose up just beyond bowshot.

Opposite the bunkhouse, the trench complex wound eastward, shadowing Sarshel's north wall. However, Demora Tower had no visible connection to the bunker's protecting trenchwork. It stood alone.

For the last few years, Demora Tower had languished in the hands of the hobgoblins that besieged the city.

That changed when Imphras arrived. He'd retaken the tower before he broke the siege. From its vast height, arrows and spells could be directed down on advancing enemies. More important, it was the highest point around, perfect for spying out enemy encampments.

Several more soldiers hurried from the bunkhouse, still arranging weapons and armor. The one in the lead bore the insignia of a commissioned officer in Sarshel's army. The archer grabbed the newcomer by the arm and said, "What forces were deployed in yon tower, Commander?"

"L-lord Archer," stuttered the commander, "We have a complement of twenty within—"

"Had, not have," the tall man snapped. "Otherwise they would have warned us of the hobgoblin counterattack before it was launched."

The commander stared dumbly, confusion making his

mouth slack, his eyes too large. "No, I received reports just this afternoon of a shift-change—"

"The complement in the tower was assassinated by the enemy, else we'd have had warning. Demora is held by the hobgoblins. They likely look down on us even now, watching in fiendish glee how we run about like startled fowl under their surprise attack."

The archer's features, his striking clothes, and telltale armament finally registered in Jotharam's overstimulated brain. The man was indeed who the soldier named, Imphras's own companion, the renowned Lord Archer. Jotharam gaped. The man was a legend, said to be a human foundling raised by elves in the glades of the Yuirwood, whose arrows never missed their—

The lord archer stabbed a finger at Demora Tower and said, "I must gain entry and see the shape of the battle. Imphras must know the disposition of the forces drawn up against us."

He looked at the commander and said, "For that, I need a distraction. Throw a force west, toward that bluff." The archer waved his hand at a distant outcrop. "In the meantime, I will make a break for the tower."

The commander nodded, then began to bawl out orders. Nearby soldiers started to fall into line. The lord archer grabbed the closest soldier's arm and said, "Calmora, isn't it? You're with me."

The soldier, a sandy-haired, battle-hardened woman in her late twenties, yelled, "Yes, Lord!"

The two raced east down the wide furrow of the north bunker. As they ran, the lord archer drew an arrow from his quiver, and the soldier unsheathed her sword.

Jotharam glanced at the commander gathering soldiers, looked at Demora Tower, then followed the lord archer.

Beating drums, oaths to Tyr, and brutal roars thundered

as the night's oncoming cloak smothered the day's last gleams. Here and there, that cloak was rent with flashes of red, yellow, and stranger hues. The shifting breeze brought odors of brimstone mingled with blood, but Jotharam ignored it all. He put his concentration into following the amazingly swift lord archer and warrior Calmora.

A sudden barrage of screams and brutish battle cries heralded the appearance of dozens of dark forms in black chain mail on the edge of the trench ahead. Soldiers in the dugout attempted to stop the breach with their bodies and half-drawn swords, while crossbowmen behind put a dozen bolts into the goblin foray.

The defending soldiers were too few to hold back the invaders. Ten hobgoblins, then a score more, breached the line and tumbled into the trench, weapons at the ready.

A melee broke out. Desperate torchbearers and crossbowmen alike were felled by the goblins' bloodthirsty swords.

The lord archer stopped forty paces from the fracas and began loosing arrows, audibly counting down his remaining bolts with each pull, "Ninety-nine, ninety-eight, ninety-seven. . ."

With each shot, a goblin crashed to the ground, an arrow transfixing its neck, eye, or mouth.

Calmora sped onward to the breach, her sword glimmering and the lord archer's arrows whining over her head. As she ran, a handful of other uncommitted soldiers in the trench gained heart by her example and ran after. Calmora and her fortuitous troop crashed together into the clump of goblin trespassers.

Calmora's sword was like a lightning storm over the sea of goblin heads. Jotharam marveled at the sandy-haired woman's martial skill.

The other soldiers who'd followed Calmora into the

breach likewise cut and beat at the invaders, and all the while the lord archer calmly numbered newly dead goblins, "Ninety-one, ninety, eighty-nine. . ."

The remaining goblins recognized their intrusion was failing. A few attempted a fighting retreat, but most merely broke and ran, and were cut down as they tried to scramble up and out of the trench. A couple turned and fired crossbows of their own.

A stray bolt clipped Jotharam's helm. The *clang* and following reverberation made him stumble and curse aloud like a real soldier.

When his ears ceased ringing, no goblin remained moving in the breach.

The lord archer ceased firing and dashed ahead, trampling the downed goblins as if they were mere cobblestones. Calmora fell in again at his side, and Jotharam returned to his role of trying to follow, now with a ringing in his right ear that he fancied tolled doom.

Just as Jotharam's ability to keep the two in sight neared failure, the archer and soldier paused as they drew even with Demora Tower.

A trench once connected the bunker with the base of the tower, but the hobgoblin besiegers who'd held sway beyond Sarshel filled that in long ago. A partial effort to dig the furrow anew was evident; however, the space between the new trench's endpoint and the tower stretched several hundred yards.

The lord archer and his handpicked soldier were conferring as Jotharam huffed up.

The archer was saying, ". . . or even south. Whatever the truth, it is vital we get a true assessment of their disposition. First, we must deal with the creatures that haven taken Demora Tower if we are to gain entry. It may not be easy."

His eyes left the soldier and found Jotharam. One eyebrow

rose in apparent surprise at seeing the messenger.

"I can help," Jotharam explained.

"Jotharam Feor, is that you?" interrupted the soldier. "Does your mother know you're out here?"

Jotharam started. Calmora knew who he was? Some vague recollection came to him, then, of an aunt in the militia named Calmora.

"Yes it's me; and what's it matter what she knows? I can help the lord archer!"

"How?"

"Well, uh. . . before the siege my friends and I used to sneak into Demora Tower. It was just an old watchtower, and haunted, everyone thought, so only a few sentinels ever spent any time in it. Except for me and my friends. We used to play in it—" Jotharam saw by their eyes his audience was losing patience with his explanation, so he rushed to his conclusion—"and we found a secret way to the top!"

Sandy-haired Calmora shook her head, "There's only one way in: the gate at the bottom. A single stair connects the entrance level to the observation level, where Imphras's wizards put the Wardlight. There's no room inside for secret ways in or up."

"You're wrong," protested Jotharam. "The secret way is outside the tower, up the outer wall. You can only see it once you're up close, because it's hidden by a. . . a sort of overhang that blocks it from view."

The lord archer rubbed his chin, spearing Jotharam with a searching glance. The boy's cheeks warmed under the stern regard, but he held the archer's eye.

"Let us try this path the courier knows about," decided the tall man. "But first, I must clear a route to the tower's base."

Calmora squinted over the trench wall at the tower and said, "It's too dark to see anything."

"Almost," agreed the archer, loosing an arrow. The shaft was instantly absorbed by the night. A moment later came a muffled cry and a distant, clanging thud. "Eighty-two," said the archer as he drew another arrow and loosed in the same motion. Another pregnant moment passed, which was followed by a similar brief wail and sound of a limp, armored body crashing to the ground.

"Eighty-one," he intoned, then, "Two hobgoblins were stationed just inside the tower gate. I saw Sarshel's lights reflected in their eyes."

Calmora shook her head in mock disbelief. Jotharam began to ask another question, "How did—"

"Now," interrupted the lord archer. "Run!"

Calmora grabbed Jotharam under his shoulders, and with a grunt, lifted him out of the trench. "Show us the way," she hissed.

Jotharam hesitated at the trench's lip, until he saw Calmora and the lord archer begin to pull themselves up. Satisfied he wasn't being sent alone into the night, he lit off toward the tower.

Darkness made the tower a slender gray blur. It seemed to reach down from the sky like one of Shar's own fingers.

Vague shapes on each side of his tentative dash resolved alternately as shrubs, boulders, and stands of weeds. He breathed in relief each time he drew close enough to recognize an obscure shape as a mundane object. He feared one of them would be revealed as the sneaking, grease-camouflaged goblin who had waylaid him earlier.

In the dark, Jotharam misjudged the final few feet to the tower. He slammed into one of the granite blocks that made up its massive foundation. The shock of impact bruised his forehead, and he bit his tongue.

"Pox and rot!" he muttered. All the minor hurts he had so far suffered that night were adding up.

Two shapes materialized from the darkness: Calmora and the lord archer.

"Where is your secret passage, then?" whispered his aunt.

Jotharam began sidling along the tower's base, widdershins from the main gate. Even as he moved away from the opening, he heard sudden guttural cries of surprise from within—other hobgoblins in the tower must have come down from a higher level to find their companions slain by the lord archer's deadly bow.

Ornate carvings crusted the tower's exterior, though many had worn and weathered away in the centuries since they were placed. No one remembered what prompted the long-dead wizard Demora to build so tall a tower that was at the same time so narrow that hardly any space resided within its slender width to house chambers of any consequence. Some argued that perhaps it had been constructed as a monument, not a serviceable structure. Yet in the centuries since Demora's departure, the tower had proved useful to Sarshel as a watchtower.

Indeed, it was from the tower's uppermost level that, five years ago, sentinels had seen the first hobgoblin army marching on Sarshel. Where so many other cities of the Easting Reach had fallen under sudden attack, Sarshel was able to prepare for the assault, and thus successfully held off the horde during the bitter years of the siege.

When Jotharam saw the griffon carving, he knew they were close. Another five steps, and his own initials stared back at him, shaky with childhood naiveté. Beyond that was the slender gap that seemed a natural shadowed declivity behind a relief portrait of a long-bearded dwarf.

Jotharam slipped into the narrow gap. He heard Calmora mutter, "By Tyr! Where'd the kid go?"

"In here," Jotharam whispered.

He stood in a space no more than three feet on a side; at least, so his memory told him; it was almost completely dark. He reached out and brushed the cold iron rungs his hands remembered.

"There's a ladder," Jotharam said to the archer, who was trying to fit his larger body through the narrow gap. Jotharam grasped the first rung and climbed several feet, "It goes all the way to the top!"

"Quite a climb, then," said the archer's silhouette below him.

"Yes, it is," replied Jotharam, recalling how he and his friends used to rest halfway up the vertical expanse by threading ropes through the rungs and their belts. They would tie off to hang without effort until their arms ceased aching and their breathing slowed.

He began the ascent in earnest, feeling for one cool iron rung, then the next in the stygian darkness. He was careful to find his footing each time before he pulled himself to the next rung. When he craned to look behind him, he could just make out Sarshel's lights through the narrow gap where the vertical cornice didn't quite pinch the space containing the ladder into its own perpendicular tunnel.

The quiet sounds of the lord archer and Calmora ascending floated up beneath him, ringing with the slightest echo despite their relative silence. The odor of rancid standing water also filled the crevice—rain must have found someplace to pool. He hoped he wouldn't accidentally shove his hand into a stagnant, muck-filled fissure in the tower's face.

At five stories his breath was rasping, and his arms burned. No doubt he was stronger than the last time he'd climbed the rungs as a child, but on the other hand he weighed more now than at age ten. Nor had steel armor tried to drag him off the rungs at every step with its extra weight.

Jotharam paused and rested by hanging off his rung from his armpits. Not really that comfortable, but he had no rope.

A hand brushed his foot below. He whispered, "Hold on, I have to rest."

The lord archer's voice floated up, "Time is not our ally."

The adolescent nodded, realized the archer couldn't see him, and said aloud, "Just a few moments. Otherwise I'll fall and take the lot of you with me."

"A moment, then," agreed the lord archer. Then, "Your discovery of this side route to the top could make all the difference. Tell me, son, what did Calmora say your name was?"

"Jotharam. Jotharam Feor." In the face of the archer's sudden compliment, he recalled his courtly manners, and added, "I am honored to make your acquaintance, Lord."

The man chuckled, "I'm no lord when out in the field. I'm a soldier, same as you."

The archer, not realizing Jotharam's true status, unintentionally paid him an even greater compliment. Pride opened a new reservoir of strength he'd doubted heartbeats earlier.

"I feel better now. I'm ready to go all the way to the top."

"Very good," said the lord archer.

From farther below, he heard Calmora mutter, "I needed the rest, too, Joth. But upward and onward, aye?"

Jotharam said, "There's a space at the top where we can all rest again," and renewed the climb.

Pride or no, when he finally pulled himself over the lip at the ladder's apex, the nausea of exhaustion threatened to loose the contents of his stomach.

Memory told him the ladder emptied into a chamber

some eight feet on a side, a minor sublevel immediately below the tower's main observation level above. A series of narrow steps along the inner side of the chamber led up to a trapdoor in the ceiling. He and his friends had always been too afraid to try to open it, lest their truancy so far beyond Sarshel be discovered and punished.

"Jotharam?" came a bare whisper. "Can we risk a bit of light?"

"Yes," he huffed, hoping the sound of his panting couldn't be heard in the chamber above.

A tiny blue glow appeared like twilight's first star, then swelled to the luminosity of a candle. Jotharam had to shade his eyes from the glare. The light emanated from a silver piece held by the lord archer. A hole pierced the silver disc, and a leather thong ran through it. In his other hand, the archer held a small bag from which he had apparently pulled the ensorcelled coin.

The illumination revealed a space very similar to Jotharam's memory of it, though it was smaller than he'd recalled, and the narrow stone stairs along the inner wall of the chamber were steeper, and. . . something wet dripped down from the trapdoor they led to.

"What—?"

"Blood, of your countrymen, no doubt," said the archer. "The goblins eradicated the sentinels. Let us go quietly, and pay back the goblin assassins in similar coin."

Calmora pulled her sword from the sheath at her belt as she ascended the narrow stair. Jotharam heaved himself off his hands and knees and pulled out his short sword, knowing that without training, he could contribute little.

The lord archer hung the glowing coin around his neck from its thong, then moved to stand next to Calmora. They looked up at the blood-stained trapdoor, only half a foot over their heads. The archer whispered to the soldier, "Precede me, and if you can, clear a bit of space so I can fire my bow. Tyr willing, we shall take them by surprise."

Calmora pulled back on the latch that held the panel in place, producing a slight squeal. Without waiting to see if the noise produced any reaction from above, she put both hands over her head and slammed the trapdoor open. Calmora pulled herself upward, and with a leg up from the lord archer, vaulted up and out into the observation level.

Even as the lord archer swarmed after Calmora, a guttural cry of alarm pealed from somewhere above. A shadow passed across the face of the open trapdoor, then came a metallic *clang*. Several more oafish voices shouted, and amid those cries, Jotharam could hear Calmora's voice, "For Imphras! For your deaths!"

Jotharam ran up the stairs and looked up. The lord archer stood right above, his booted toes overhanging the trapdoor. His bow delivered a steady stream of fletched death to enemies Jotharam couldn't see. With each shaft fired, he uttered its number.

When the archer turned slightly to get a better lead on his next target, Jotharam jumped and managed to get his fingers over the trapdoor's lip.

He'd have to pull himself up without help. After the grueling climb, he wondered if he had the strength to gain the observation level without help. He grunted, contracting his arms, and with a sudden lunge, got an elbow over the edge. After that, he was able to swing up a leg and scramble up out of the hole.

A great device on iron legs squatted in the very center of the observation level. It seemed composed of crystal, glass, and iron, though many of its parts were ripped from their housings and scattered on the floor. Jotharam hoped it wasn't the Wardlight Calmora had mentioned earlier in the bunker dugout, though he supposed it had to be.

Besides the Wardlight, several crumpled and broken forms lay clumped about the open-walled chamber. A few wore the uniforms of Sarshel and must have been the sentinels the hobgoblins murdered.

All the rest were dead or dying hobgoblins and goblins, many with terrible slashes still welling blood, others with arrows jutting from their chests, necks, and heads.

Several figures struggled perilously close to the edge. One was Calmora. She simultaneously struggled with three enemies, two man-sized hobgoblins and a hairy-looking beast nearly the size of an ogre.

"Seventy-three, seventy-two," said the lord archer, then, "Calmora!"

Calmora looked up even as the near-ogre dashed forward, arms to each side, its legs pumping toward a lethal speed. She tried to leap away but stumbled on a dead goblin lying behind her. Calmora's attacker smashed into her without slowing.

Both went over the edge. Even as they vanished from view, the soldier raised her sword as if to attack.

"No!" croaked Jotharam, running forward a few steps before stumbling to a helpless stop.

All was silent in Demora Tower. The lord archer lowered his bow and said, "Come away from the edge."

Utter darkness filled the air beyond the tower, and foreboding stillness seemed to leech strength straight from Jotharam's limbs. His eyes were tacky with unwept tears. He'd known the soldier so briefly. . . .

If it was true Calmora was a relative, then when he returned to Sarshel he would tell his mother the story of Calmora's bravery. She had the resources to commission a memorial for the brave warrior. A monument of black marble. . .

Jotharam wanted to wrench his mind away from the vision that played over and over, of Calmora's surprised look as she vanished off the edge, even as she hacked at the creature that pushed her off.

The boy turned from the dark expanse of sky and dark and asked, "Why isn't the Wardlight completely broken?"

The lord archer continued to tinker with the bits and pieces pulled from the strange device by the hobgoblin assassins, but he said, "Perhaps they didn't have time. Or they didn't want to create a suspicious racket by breaking the glass and shattering the crystal."

"Hmm. How does it work, then?"

The archer grunted, pulled a slender rod from a socket he'd just placed it in, turned it around, and replaced it. Then he replied, "Once each day, the Wardlight can summon a sunlike flash so potent all the surrounding land is revealed, even in darkest night. If I can get it to function, we will know the threat truly faced by Sarshel."

"I wonder how late it is?"

"Just past middark," answered the lord archer, a hint of impatience threading his tone. He picked up a glass sphere, which by some miracle hadn't rolled off the tower's open pagodalike zenith. The glowing coin hanging around his neck threw the archer's distorted, hunched shadow upon the upcurved ceiling.

"How is it coming?" Jotharam wondered.

"If you leave off interrupting me, I will likely succeed."

"Sorry," breathed the adolescent.

"Now then. . ." muttered the archer, as he made some final adjustment.

There came a *click,* and a low hum. Then, "That is it. Pray to whatever deity you revere that it proves sufficient."

The lord archer placed his hand upon an engraved palm print etched into the Wardlight's side.

The enveloping night broke wide open by a shining light that bloomed somewhere above Demora Tower. Radiance beat down from the arcane outburst to bathe the countryside. Jotharam saw all Sarshel revealed, like a toy city, in an instant. Beyond it was Lake Ashane to the east, and the battle-scarred wilderness all around, for miles in all directions. And on that plain, an army crawled forward from out of the west.

A small army to be sure, filled with black shapes mostly squat, though a few were trollish in their gangly, stoop-shouldered height. They advanced on Sarshel in a long, thin line, inching forward like the tide in a slow but unstoppable march.

A flight of burning arrows took to the sky, unleashed from the attacking line. A few fell short of Sarshel's west wall, but many scored the stone edifice, or plunged into the bunker to find the terrified flesh of defenders unlucky enough to have been standing in the trajectory of a lethal shaft.

The advancing hobgoblin line screamed and jeered. The trolls threw boulders, and goblins waved spears and torches, and sang a song of torture and woe.

Cruel horns sounded. The line surged forward, with black-gauntleted hobgoblins at the fore swinging glowing warhammers. The defenders on Sarshel's west wall answered with their own tempest of arrows, which plowed into the advancing line. Many hobgoblins fell, but many more retreated, screaming dire promises in their debased language.

The line surged forward yet again, gaining ground by increments.

However, even Jotharam's untrained eye could see the attacking army was too thin to hold the ground they gained against the still confused defense, should that defense finally firm up.

On the other hand, from the viewpoint of the defenders on the ground, the line must have seemed like the vanguard of an army of immense size. Only Demora's height revealed the line as a slender threat, scarcely wide enough to withstand even a single charge, should any dare it.

"Is that all there are?" wondered Jotharam.

"No, it is a diversionary force," said the lord archer. "Look!" He pointed east, where Lake Ashane kissed Sarshel's port district in a wide bay. Even as the Wardlight's radiance dimmed, Jotharam saw the true threat.

Hundreds of small boats, canoes, and crude rafts floated the still water of Lake Ashane, silently converging on the docks. As the commotion and clamor of the obvious attack pulled defenders to the west, the true threat to Sarshel prepared a massive onslaught from the east.

The Wardlight guttered and failed. Night returned.

"We must get word to Imphras straight away," came the lord archer's voice from behind Jotharam. The courier nodded but remained staring out into the darkness, his eyes still resting on the memory of what had just been revealed. The archer continued, "Once he knows their true strategy—oh!"

An awful hiss jerked Jotharam's gaze back into the tower cupola.

A short sword dark as obsidian protruded from the lord archer's stomach, just below his sternum. The lord archer collapsed to one knee, clutching vainly at the blood-soaked blade.

A creature with long green ears and wearing chain mail smeared with black grease stood just beyond the lord archer's reach, grinning with needle-sharp teeth.

Jotharam cried, "I know you!"

It sniggered and said in broken Common, "Good thing I follow you, little one. Very tricky, but your tricks done now. Imphras and Sarshel soon both dead."

Jotharam yelled unintelligibly and hurled himself at the foul assassin, his own sword somehow unsheathed and in his hand, stabbing, slicing, tearing . . .

The goblin evaded, dancing back. Jotharam bulled forward. His fury at seeing the lord archer so sorely wounded washed away his fear. Besides, the little cur was without its sword!

The courier landed a cut on its shoulder, but the goblin used the opportunity to slip inside Jotharam's guard. Like a performer delivering a kiss, it leaned forward and bit the boy's exposed neck.

Jotharam hooted with astonishment and dropped his sword. The goblin bit down harder. Jotharam heard it giggle through its clenched teeth. A warm spurt of blood ran down Jotharam's neck and flowed under his gambeson. Fear returned, but his rage was the stronger. A red haze fell before his eyes, and he roared.

He grabbed the clinging goblin with both hands. It would not relinquish its grip. Like a dog with its jaws around a succulent bone, the goblin clung to his neck. Jotharam's first instinct was to forcefully shove it away, but he had a sudden image of his neck being ripped out as he forced the creature off.

Instead, he started to squeeze. He clutched the creature around its throat and throttled it with all his fury-fueled strength.

The goblin maintained its grip only a few heartbeats more before its jaws loosened. It tried to gasp and squeal. Too late.

Jotharam did not relinquish his choke hold until the creature was as limp as a rag.

He threw the flaccid body to the floor, his own breath coming in great heaves. Then he remembered the goblin assassin's obsidian sword.

"Lord Archer!" Jotharam ran to the wounded man.

The archer half-reclined against the Wardlight. A still-enlarging pool of blood surrounded him. His eyes were open but glassy. He no longer clutched at his terrible wound. Instead, he struggled with his quiver.

"Lord Archer, let me help you!" Jotharam grabbed the quiver from the man's shaking hands. "Do you have a healing draught in your quiver? Is there another compartment?"

The man shook his head and said in an alarmingly breathy voice, "I have none. I left them in the bunkhouse. No—Jotharam, listen to me, now! I have something very important to tell you."

"Yes, what?"

"Reach into my quiver and pull out the black arrow."

"Yes, very well. . . I have it."

"Good, that's a good lad. Now, Jotharam, you must deliver that arrow to Imphras. He will know. . . what it means. When he sees this shaft, he will know the message comes directly from his lord archer. We worked out the signal years ago, but never had call to use it, till now. Emerald is west, scarlet south, silver north, and black. . . means the foe attacks from the west."

"I can't just leave you—"

"You can, and you will!" interrupted the archer, his voice suddenly echoing with a portion of its original strength. "Are you a sworn soldier of Sarshel? Then obey your commanding officer, a prerogative I claim now. Climb down the secret way and bring that arrow to Imphras as quick as your legs can carry you."

Unable to speak for fear he would sob, Jotharam only nodded, then saluted. The lord archer returned his salute with a shaking hand.

Jotharam turned, scrubbing at his eyes with the palm of his free hand. In the other, he clutched the lord archer's message.

He held the arrow's smooth shaft in his teeth as he hung for a moment from the trapdoor opening, then dropped onto the narrow space below.

Before he put his hands to the rungs to begin the long descent, he transferred the arrow to his empty sheath—his sword remained behind on the floor next to the strangled goblin and the dying lord archer.

He shook his head and started down the ladder. He had a duty to perform. If he didn't get the message to Imphras, more than the tall man he left behind would die tonight.

His descent through the narrow, lightless shaft was easier than the ascent. He was used to the spacing, even if he couldn't see the rungs, and he moved in the direction his heavy armor wanted to drag him.

Jotharam's foot jarred a grunt from him when he reached the shaft's bottom sooner than he expected. In the darkness of the concealed niche, he carefully removed the arrow from his sheath and held it tightly.

He peered out through the crevice, and saw Sarshel's north wall, and the bunker that ran immediately in front of it. The span was farther than he remembered.

Dark shapes obscured the wall, moving between him and sanctuary. Low, squat, misshapen figures. Goblins and hobgoblins, apparently drawn toward the base of Demora Tower by the Wardlight's night-illuminating flash. They knew they had to stop anyone from emerging from the tower if their devious plan was to succeed. He saw only a few dozen, but that was a few dozen too many. Luckily, they were converging on the tower's main entrance—they still didn't know about the secret ladder.

The image of hundreds of tiny watercraft converging toward Sarshel from the east convinced him he needed to make a break for it. How much closer were the hobgoblins to launching their ambush in the time he'd taken to climb down?

Jotharam had no more time.

He dashed from the cleft, the black arrow raised high in his right hand. He ran into the night, toward the brutish silhouettes that paused as they saw him emerge from the tower's side.

Jotharam ran toward the sanctuary of the trench, toward Sarshel's glow. He ran toward the light, whose luster was the golden dawn of judgment, in which all things find their end.

When Imphras the Great ascended the throne over reunited Impiltur in 1097 DR, hundreds journeyed to Sarshel to see the Crown of Narfell placed upon the new king's brow. The ceremony was held in an open-air amphitheatre where all could see the king mount his throne.

During the ceremony, Imphras called the attention of all present to a great monument carved of black marble.

The plaque at the memorial's base read, "Never forget these who gave their lives to save our city."

The memorial depicted three people. In the background, a woman of gallant bearing wore the arms and armor of a Sarshel soldier. To her right a tall man in filigreed leather bent a mighty bow. A quiver filled with gold-fletched arrows hung at his belt.

In the foreground a young man stood in sculpted nobility. He also wore the arms and armor of the Sarshel militia. The medal on his chest identified him as a posthumous member of Imphras's personal elite guard.

The boy's right arm rose in a confident pose straight above his head. In his right hand, he clutched one black arrow.

TOO MANY PRINCES

Ed Greenwood

The Year of the Striking Falcon (1333 DR)

Mirt gave them both the tight smile that told them he'd really rather be frowning. "Our friend the vizier? He knows of this moot?"

With his severe black brows, rugged face, and walk—an alert, muscular gait, like a wild cat on the prowl—the burly sellsword Mirt the Merciless caught the eye. The angry blaze in his eyes did rather more than that.

Yet neither of the two Amnian merchants seemed unsettled as they slipped into the turret room to face him. Behind them, Turlos, his war-leathers bristling with the usual array of blades, softly closed the door and put his back to it, folding his arms across his chest and giving Mirt the "no one lurking nearby" nod.

"Not from our telling," the Lady Helora Roselarr

said smoothly, her enormous gem-dangle earrings swaying.

Tall, large-eyed, and inscrutable, the young Amnian merchant heiress had been styled "Lady" from her cradle because her adrip-with-gold family sought to be regarded as the equal of any nobility, anywhere. Knowing what he did of nobles, that wouldn't have been something Mirt would have striven for, but then he had rather less of a burdensome weight of coins under which to stagger through life. Wealth . . . did things to people.

"He's, ah, *enjoying* the young prince," Gorus Narbridle added delicately. "We heard Elashar's screams on our way up."

The bald, heavyset man in expensive silk robes was the cruel and unscrupulous head of a merchant family that had risen very swiftly to its wealth. Which meant that Narbridle was as ruthless with himself, in controlling his drug-taking, as he was in selling various Calishite drugs and poisons to others. He looked like a grave and weary elder priest. . . but then, Mirt already knew just how clever an actor he was.

Both Amnians reached inside the breasts of their over-robes and drew forth little carved figurines that they kissed, murmured inaudible words over, and set on the table in front of Mirt.

The statuettes glowed briefly. Scrying shields of the most expensive sort, they would keep anyone outside the room from watching or overhearing what was said there.

"We shall be brief," Roselarr said crisply. "We dislike what we see unfolding here at Ombreir, and wish to depart. As swiftly as is discreetly possible. We want to get well away, out of Ongalor's reach, before our departure is discovered. We sense your uneasiness and believe we need your personal assistance to accomplish this."

"We appreciate the difficult position this will place you in," Narbridle added smoothly, "and are prepared to compensate you accordingly. Gems up front, four trade-rubies each. Plus a bond redeemable for forty thousand Waterdhavian dragons of recent minting, which we'll give to you now but sign only when we're safely out of the Dauntir."

The amount made Mirt blink and Turlos gape in astonishment. Forty thousand gold, and the same again when the escape was done!

If, of course, a certain Mirt the Merciless was still alive to accept it. Which might well not be the Amnians' intention.

"Well, now," the mercenary captain said, "the tapestries here at Ombreir aren't *that* bad, are they?"

Neither of the Amnians bothered to smile at his feeble jest. Mirt sighed and wondered what to say.

As the Year of the Striking Falcon warmed into full summer, war was raging anew, not merely in the Dauntir—the gently rolling, heavily farmed hills between the Trade Way, the River Esmel, and the mountains prosaically known as the Small Teeth—but all across Amn. Every ambitious merchant cabal that dared to enter the struggle was riding around with copious sellswords, trumpeting "royal heirs" who had seemingly been found in closets, dropped from the clouds by the gods, or stitched together in graveyards.

This throne-strife had been raging for more than half a century, and Mirt held the same opinion as most war-weary folk of Amn: that any true heirs had been slain or died of old age years ago, and the fighting still going on was but the most grimly determined merchant families of the land trying once more to openly seize the throne. Mirt wondered why anyone would want to put on a crown to so splendidly mark himself a target for all, but then. . . power did strange things to many folk.

It had done strange things to the Araunvol family, formerly a capable and haughty force to be reckoned with in gilded Athkatla, but in the end reduced to a handful of embittered nobles who walled themselves away in Ombreir, their fortified country citadel halfway between Imnescar and the Esmel— for a rider galloping arrow-straight northeast—to await their doom.

Mirt's sword had delivered that doom, for many of them, and the army he rode with had readied the others for their graves. Wherefore the Araunvols were extinct, and the Rightful Hands of Prince Elashar held the walled mansion of Ombreir. They'd buried the last bodies that very morning, in the gardens.

Across the table, the Amnians waited in silence for his response.

They had to. There was no one else they could turn to.

One of the younger sellsword captains offering his battle skills in Waterdeep, Mirt had been hired by the Durinbolds and the Hawkwinters to ride sword with the Amnian army they sponsored: the Rightful Hands. For Waterdhavian nobles, the seemingly endless war in Amn was all about coin. Rival claimants were sponsored by the Gauntyls and Gralhunds, who had also come looking to buy the services of the mercenary newly risen in reputation for his sword work in the South.

What had decided things for Mirt between the two entreaties had been the Hawkwinters. In matters of war and guardianship, they were held in the highest regard in the City of Splendors. If he served them well, any blades Mirt the Merciless commanded would entertain many offers in the years ahead.

If, that is, he survived this first hiring in the lawless cauldron Amn had become.

No noble of Waterdeep personally risked his neck in those bloody fields, for Amnians did not take kindly to outlanders meddling in their affairs. Mirt's commander these few fleeting months had been no clear-eyed Hawkwinter veteran, but a man of Amn. A tall, emerald-eyed, neatly bearded, and gently smiling ruthless murderer of a vizier, Harlo Ongalor. Mirt hated his very shadow, and strongly suspected the vizier loved him about as much.

Ongalor ruled Prince Elashar just as he did Mirt, which surprised Mirt not at all. Prince Elashar Torlath was purportedly the descendant of Prince Esmar, a son of King Imnel IV of Amn who'd long been believed to have died soon after birth.

That much, Mirt believed. What he did not believe was the rest of the tale the vizier spun so glibly whenever it seemed necessary: that all those years ago, Esmar had been spirited away to provide a royal line in hiding for Amn, "awaiting its dire hour of need."

For one thing, there was more than one Prince Elashar. Or rather, more than one man of the Rightful Hands riding with a closed helm whose seldom-seen face was identical to that of the prince. Coincidence, perhaps, but Mirt himself had bull-broad shoulders that were unusual, and doubly so in a man of his height. Such builds were more often seen in men a head taller than he—yet another man riding with the Rightful Hands looked just like Mirt. *Just* like Mirt.

Moreover, the Hands had captured several members of rival merchant families—including the Lady Helora Roselarr and Gorus Narbridle—and as he'd been alert enough to watch for all briefly-bared faces, Mirt was certain "doubles" of most of *them* were riding under the vizier's command.

Nor was Ongalor working alone. Magic aided him out of nowhere when he needed it. Which meant that his mutterings from time to time with various riders were conferences with disguised hurlers-of-magic.

Mirt's eyes might miss nothing, but he knew how to keep his mouth shut. He was, after all, being paid to do so.

So he nodded respectfully to the pretender riding with

them, and held high the princely banner: an emerald-hued human right hand clutching a horizontal dagger, point to the sinister, erupting vertically out of the top of a large, faceted emerald. Tasteless, and bad blazonry to boot, but then, Mirt wasn't being paid to be a herald, either.

There were armies riding all over Amn, some backed by wealthy traders from Tethyr or from Calimshan, and every one concealing their true natures behind this or that false heir from the various fallen royal families of Amn; ambitious—or trapped—pretenders, all.

One of those rival armies, the Just Blades, was on its way even then. A strong band of well-armed and armored butchers, sponsored by the Gauntyls and Gralhunds, and backing Prince Uldrako, a true pretender. Which was to say an ambitious young Amnian who knew full well he had no royal nor noble blood, and was passing himself off as the scion of an entirely fictitious elder branch of the royal family. His skills consisted of good looks, a complete lack of scruples, staggering indebtedness to his sponsors, and the good sense to accord them the utter loyalty of a fawning slave. Mirt happened to know that his banner (a stylized side-on crown, depicted as a black arc with five spires erupting from it, on a gold field) had been designed by the Gauntyl house limner, and Gauntyl tutors had coached "Uldrako" in his invented lineage and life story.

He had no doubt that Harlo Ongalor had done likewise with the doubles of Prince Elashar, the Amnian noble captives, and a certain Mirt the Merciless. All part of preparing for the right moment to eliminate the troublesome originals—who stubbornly persisted in having opinions and aims of their own—for replacement with their loyal-to-Ongalor duplicates.

And that right moment, Mirt suspected, had almost arrived. Why else would the vizier have ordered Mirt and only "this dozen" of his warriors to remain in Ombreir and guard "the valuable ones," with the Just Blades sweeping across the Dauntir to storm the Araunvol mansion while the main might of the Rightful Hands rode elsewhere with the doubles? The Merciless hadn't failed to notice that the vizier's chosen dozen consisted of the veterans who were most personally loyal to Mirt—and Torandral, the most inexperienced, trouble-prone youngling in the Hands.

The vizier and his wizard friends would vanish at the last possible moment, of course, once the Just Blades were at the mansion's very gates and escape was impossible. Leaving Mirt and his warriors to a bloody doom and any surviving hostages to be later spell-switched with their doubles, or magically blown apart from afar, to shatter any chances of Gauntyl and Gralhund success.

Mirt had long since become disgusted with various atrocities ordered by the vizier, as the Rightful Hands butchered their way across Amn—to say nothing of the general ruin of the fair country around the Hands—and had begun looking for a way out. Only to discover Ongalor's hidden wizards, and how closely they were watching to thwart just such desertions.

"We're trapped here," Lady Roselarr said quietly. "Are you trapped, too? Is that why you're keeping silent?"

"Or have you been enthralled by the vizier's pet wizards? Or hatching your own betrayals?" Narbridle asked, even more softly. Mirt did not have to look to know that the bald noble had drawn a little poisoned needle-dagger, under the table.

Instead, he looked to Roselarr. "To your queries: yes." Then he turned to Narbridle. "To yours: no. So put your tainted steel away."

Sighing heavily, Mirt told them truthfully, "I have no intention of betraying either of you, yet I see no road by which

I *can* aid you in any way that has even the slightest chance of achieving your freedom. Your offer tempts me even more than its amount, which is certainly what merchants in Waterdeep's poorer wards would term 'staggering.' Yet I know not how to escape Ombreir. The Just Blades—"

"Are camped the other side of yonder hill," Narbridle agreed. "While that sneering sadist Ongalor smiles, watching us all with those lazy-lidded eyes, and waits for them to close his little trap."

"We hate and fear him," Roselarr whispered. "Warrior, admit it: So do you."

"Admitting things is seldom wise for anyone in my profession," Mirt replied, "let alone someone in my current situation. That is the only reply I can give you, other than to say I understand you fully, I deeply appreciate your truly generous offer, and I shall be in touch with both of you— with utmost discretion, for all our sakes—as soon as I can. Whenever that 'soon' may be. You have my word on this."

The two Amnians sat as if frozen for a moment. Then they sighed and took up their figurines, not looking at each other. Both little carvings still glowed as they vanished once more beneath concealing clothing, signifying that their shieldings remained active.

Turlos wordlessly held open the door, and Mirt nodded the two Amnians out of the turret room, keeping his face carefully expressionless.

After the Amnians had descended the stairs out of sight, the two sellswords stood listening for a long time ere closing the door again to wall out the rest of Ombreir.

Then, leaning against it, nose to nose, Mirt and Turlos regarded each other.

"Well, now," Turlos murmured. "Well, now. . ."

Mirt shook his head grimly. "By Tempus and Tymora both, I know not what I'm going to do. This trap is intended to end in all our deaths. Things are going to get far nastier before they get better."

"Oh, yes," his trusted bodyguard replied softly, as his body shivered and shifted shape, the grim face of Turlos melting back into the sneering visage of the vizier. Ongalor was smiling a crooked smile as he warningly held up fingers that bore magic rings glowing with sudden power. "I've no doubt of that."

❖ ◉ ❖ ◉ ◉

"Another moonlit night," Deln said grimly, checking the hilts of his many blades.

"Another feast to which we're not invited," Marimbrar added, drawing on his gauntlets.

"Aye," Loraun put in sarcastically, "it seems the vizier doesn't need us to stand guard over the food this time."

"That means either he doesn't want us there to see what happens," Tauniira murmured, "and it'll probably be something fatal, to someone who's displeased Lord Most Highnosed Ongalor—or he believes his loyal wizards and bullyboys hidden among the Amnian captives can handle any trouble the rest of the Amnians might give him."

Mirt nodded. Of those hired into the Rightful Hands with him, Tauniira and Loraun were the two he most trusted, longtime veterans of his various mercenary pursuits. Not that they were much to look at. Under Tauniira's ever-present mask was a face melted into grotesquerie by the biting edge of a spell that had slain many and only just spared her, and the tall, laconic, cold-eyed Loraun was a wereserpent. Yet they missed nothing that was going on around them, and Tauniira wore literally dozens of throwing knives all over herself, many of them hidden, that had a way of swiftly sprouting in darn near everything nearby that offered her trouble. Sinister viziers, for instance.

"Before anyone asks," Mirt told his fellows, "Targrath isn't missing because he's snoring alongside our off-duty fellows. He's standing guard inside their door, on my orders. Turlos is dead."

That got their attention, instant and absolute.

"Our mutual friend the vizier," Mirt explained, "killed Turlos somewhere, and recently, and hid the body without any of us noticing. When he revealed himself to me up in South Tower earlier today, he flashed his fist, and there were rings on every last finger that glowed with magic. He did that to keep me from trying to slaughter him on the spot, but what he slew was the last vestige of any obligation I felt to him. So be not slow to blow your belt-horns, sword-comrades; Ongalor is as much our foe as the Just Blades or any friend of the Araunvols who might come calling with drawn sword and fire in their eyes. If Tymora smiles on us all, it'll be another boring night of standing sentinel, staring vigilantly at nothing. If she does not. . . well, be warned; we're at war right now."

With nods and sour grunts of acknowledgment, everyone stalked off down the darkened passages, seeking their posts. Tauniira lingered at Mirt's shoulder, watching them go.

She knew he wouldn't move until those they'd relieved—Brarn, Landyl, Elgan, Brindar, Hargra, and Torandral—came trudging back to seek their beds in the chamber Targrath was guarding. Commanders who didn't take care to mark the comings and goings of their warriors tended to lose respect instantly, warriors soon, and their own lives sooner than they'd hoped.

Some of those trudges would be long. Ombreir was a sprawling place, a massive, towering stone house rising three stately floors from the ground, with the general shape of a rider's spur connecting three towers, one to the south and a northwest-northeast pair. At the junction of the spur were a splendid sweeping stair—ornate luxury compared to the narrow, bare spirals inside the towers—and a central block of grand chambers surrounding a glass-roofed courtyard. The easternmost of those lofty rooms was a grand entry hall, for the entrance to Ombreir lay in the east. A foregate ramp approached the mansion between two ponds to reach a spired gatehouse in Ombreir's surrounding fortress wall. All around that wall was a dry ditch moat large and deep enough to swallow a man on a horse, and all around the moat were tilled fields, slopes stretching away with not a tree in sight.

Ombreir was pleasant to the eye, from its soaring stone-work to the fruit-tree shade-bower out back—enspelled to keep birds away—to the southwest, the stables to the west with their gabled servants' quarters above the stalls, and the gardens to the northwest.

Not that Mirt could gaze on those amenities just then. All he could see was the quiet luxury of the paneled, bedchamber-lined upper passage in which he and Tauniira stood. At that spot in its long, curving run, it briefly became a balcony over-looking the central courtyard. Though the sun was quite gone, its light shining through stained glass skylights had earlier dappled the yard with spectacular patterns. The courtyard held a well surrounded by three soaring darm-fruit trees—and Mirt loved darm. They looked like rose red oranges but had soft, sweet red flesh like the watermelons of the Tashalar. Five darm had vanished from those trees already. Mirt had tossed the peels down among the knee-deep mint that grew thickly along the outer wall.

Mirt looked grim. Tauniira tried to cheer him by leaning in to kiss his neck, just under his jawline. He stood as unresponsive as a statue, so she lightly patted his codpiece.

"Not now," he growled promptly.

"No?" she pouted teasingly. "Well, before morning?"

Mirt's sudden grin seemed to crack his face. "Of course."

"Yet the wheel will turn," Harlo Ongalor said smoothly, emerald eyes flashing in the candlelight as he leaned forward to smile down the glittering feast table. Nothing seemed to keep the vizier from smiling his habitual tight little smile.

"When orc hordes come, yes, war rages until one side or the other is exterminated. Yet in lands held by men, there's a time for the sword and a time when every belly wants to be full, and coins are to be made. Amn knows war well, but will not be consumed in war. Soon, now, this strife will all be over."

"*This* strife," Imril Morund drawled meaningfully. The sly, sophisticated dealer in perfumes—and, so rumor insisted firmly, poisons—wasn't quite the most sleek or handsome of the wealthy Amnians dining more or less as captives of the Rightful Hands. Yet he was undoubtedly the most urbane, glib, and confident. "It remains to be seen if any of us here will live to see another."

"Oh, but surely—" Lady Roselarr started to purr.

"Oh, but surely *nothing*," Ralaerond Galespear interrupted, lounging in his chair to strike a pose, long fingers raising his full tallglass to catch the light. He was the most handsome man in the room, and his every movement proclaimed as boldly as any herald that he knew it. A notorious womanizer, Galespear was the young and spoiled heir of a horse breeding family who owned many buildings in every city of Amn and grew ever fatter on the ceaseless flow of rents. "War claims lives," he pointed out bitterly, as if personally insulted by what he was imparting, "and we sit here in the heart of bloody war, with armies on the march all around us. If one turns this way, we can muster barely enough blades to offer them a few breaths of entertainment ere we die."

"As men of Amn," Larl Ambror snapped, "I have no doubt that we will die valiantly." The thin, dark wine merchant's face betrayed nothing, which surprised no one. Day after day it seemed carved of unchanging stone.

"Oh?" Morund asked. "Tell me now: How exactly does a valiant dying scream of agony outshine any other dying scream of agony?"

"Enough," Darmon Halandrath rumbled, his voice as deep and as oily as ever. "This is hardly fitting feast-talk." The fat, indolent, and decadent heir of a very successful family of moneylenders and city builders nodded at the three diners seated beyond him; splendidly garbed Amnians who had turned pale and leaned back from their platters, wincing or shuddering. "Amn has a bright future and is awash in rightful wealth. Talk less gloom and more of the opportunities and good things that await us all."

"Indeed," Gorus Narbridle agreed smoothly, his freshly waxed bald head gleaming in the candlelight. "I recall from my own youth the dire talk of bloodshed and doom that younglings then reveled in—and where are they now? All grown fat and rich and older, given to talking fondly— wistfully—of their youthful darings. Some doom!"

"Yet I do have a concern, Saer Ongalor," Lady Helora Roselarr said, "about remaining here in Ombreir—we few, with so many armed foes abroad in the Dauntir—after the rest of the Rightful Hands have galloped off on some mysterious mission. Why do we tarry? Are you hoping to hide here unnoticed? Or are we waiting for some meeting or other you have not yet seen fit to inform us of?"

The three Amnian heirs seated beyond Halandrath's grossly fat bulk suddenly stopped looking fearful and glared at her in unison.

Harlo Ongalor, however, spread his hands and smiled

broadly, for all the world as though Roselarr was a daughter he was deeply fond of. "I harbor no such sinister secrets, Lady Roselarr. It was in fact your safety I thought most of—though I was mindful of the importance to Amn of these other fair scions of the land around this table, too—when I sent most of the Hands a few days' ride from us, into sword-strife and bloody danger, so Prince Elashar could make himself personally known to the elder nobles of Amn who are rightfully suspicious of all so-called 'heirs' of the royal line, and so win their support. It is peril he must face, but I thought it cruel folly to hazard all the rest of you. Moreover, it will look best if I am not with him, so no one can deem me his captor or mind-master. So here we are, enjoying this excellent repast."

Narbridle quietly rose from his seat, nodding silently to the vizier.

"Fleeing from doom?" Morund asked lightly.

The bald man gave the perfumer a sour look. "The doom of an overly full bladder, yes. Not that I saw need to proclaim this. *Polite* folk do not speak of such things."

"Oh?" Imril Morund asked. "Are there 'polite folk' at this table? I thought we were all of Amn."

Surprisingly, it was Narbridle who chuckled. A moment later, the deep rumble of Darmon Halandrath's mirth began.

"Nothing," Hargra said wearily, caressing the hilt of her wicked-looking cleaver. "Yet I've got that bad feeling I get—got it strong. I'll wager none of us'll score much sleep this night."

"Then get started," Mirt said fondly, patting her shoulder. He was one of very few males—and the only human one—who could do that without the half-orc whirling to sever their offending hands. Scarred and toad faced, Hargra was both surly and *very* swift with her weapons.

Tonight, she merely grunted and ducked away, her large lower tusks gleaming as much as brown and broken fangs can. Her slap startled Tauniira almost as much as the growled words that followed it.

"He's as much on edge as I am," the half-orc told her, jerking a thumb in Mirt's direction before striding on. "Service him."

Larl Ambror's shout of horror plunged the table into startled silence. The wine merchant reeled back out of the archway that led to the garderobes, his face white—and spewed his meal violently all over the floor before fainting.

Imril Morund sprang to his feet, dagger drawn, but Ralaerond Galespear was faster, darting through the archway and reappearing again just as Morund and—surprisingly—the Lady Roselarr reached it.

"Narbridle is dead," the horse breeder told them. "Magic."

The vizier lifted a disbelieving eyebrow. "Magic? Are you an expert in the Art, Saer Galespear?"

The handsome young heir gave him a stony stare. "I don't have to be. How else but with a spell can you blast a man's head to bloody pulp, in utter silence?"

The utter silence that descended on the feast hall then was chill with foreboding.

Mirt lifted his gaze from what was left of Gorus Narbridle, his face carefully expressionless. "This would seem to be a matter best investigated by a wizard."

There was glee in the vizier's smile.

Mirt looked past Ongalor's shoulder at the three Amnians behind him. They would be the wizards, ready to blast him as they'd served Narbridle.

"I have every confidence in your abilities, Mirt of Waterdeep," the vizier said smoothly, his crooked smile broadening and making it as clear as if he'd shouted it that he knew very well the why of the murder, as well as the who and the how—and wasn't going to say.

The wave of magic was like a *creeping* in the air, an invisible tingling tension that rolled silently up to Mirt, washed over him in a moment of utter chill. . . and rolled on down the passage, as swiftly as it had come.

Mirt stood still for a long breath or two, listening hard for crashes, screams, or. . . anything.

When he heard nothing, moment after long moment, he relaxed, shrugged, and stalked on.

Seven strides later he heard an abrupt, angry whisper out of the empty air, and froze again, listening intently.

Nothing.

Slowly and warily he started walking again, frowning at what he'd heard. A woman's voice, out of the empty air, distant and yet near at hand, calm yet furious, asking: "Who *dares* to kill the Weave here?"

Mirt looked sourly around the room. "So the vizier is readying *my* neck for the noose now. I am charged to uncover Narbridle's murderer—and he and I both know he ordered the killing."

"So it's starting," Hargra growled.

At about the same time Elgan snarled, "What by the Nine Hells are we going to do?"

"Aye," Brindar spoke up. "Why don't we just sword the vizier and get *out?*"

Tauniira sighed. "At least three—likely more—of the Amnian family 'captives' are really Ongalor's wizard friends, in magical disguise. Swording the vizier, or just trying to flee, would be hurling ourselves straight into our graves."

Elgan exploded. "Then what, by the untasted charms of—"

The door boomed, driving Targrath into a sword-ready crouch beside it, as he glared at the door bar as if expecting it to spring treacherously up out of its cradle and yield passage to whoever beat his fists on the door.

"Mirt!" a young voice called, high with fear and excitement. "Mirt, open up! You're summoned! Another killing!"

Mirt sighed. "Unbar the door," he ordered Targrath with disgust. "Can't we even plot our own dooms in peace?" Striding forward, he asked calmly, "Who's dead now, Torandral?"

"Another heir! The vizier would not let me see but said the man was lying in his bed, called by the gods but without a mark on him."

"Everyone stay here," Mirt ordered. "Awake, boots back on, armed and ready. No need to go creeping anywhere. Any violence will probably soon come calling at this door."

Sword drawn, he flung the door wide. Torandral stood alone in the passage, fairly hopping in excitement.

"Just along here! In the—"

"Bedchambers, yes," Mirt said. "Get back to your post. Strangely enough, I can find my way along this passage without a guide." Then he added gruffly, "My thanks, Torandral. Diligently done."

The crestfallen young armsman smiled uncertainly, then rushed back down the passage to his post.

Watching him stumbling along, Mirt shook his head and wondered how few breaths Torandral had left in life.

Or would the jesting gods leave the young fool alive, in a day or two, when all the rest of them were dead?

Imril Morund was lying on his back, sprawled naked across the grand bed. The vizier had cast the dead man's tunic across his face, but the rest of him did indeed lack signs of violent struggle. There was a faint, sharp tang in the air, like the aftermath of a lightning storm.

Harlo Ongalor stood beside the bed, looking agitated. "Another slaying! Mirt, you must find this murderer quickly, before. . ." He waved both hands expressively.

Mirt frowned. The vizier wasn't feigning; the man was truly upset. He plucked away the tunic to lay bare the man's face.

As he'd expected, it wasn't Morund.

Mirt looked at the vizier. "A clue you wanted me to discover for myself?" he asked calmly.

Ongalor glared at him murderously for a moment, then recovered his usual smooth near smile. "But of course. This *must* be Morund—or at least the man we thought was Morund—but I don't recognize the face. Do you?"

"Yes," Mirt said, watching the vizier closely. " 'Tis the mage Klellyn. One of your longtime trading partners, I believe."

The vizier blinked, then stared at Mirt just an instant too long. Accustomed to lording it over everyone within reach, Ongalor wasn't quite the smooth actor he believed himself to be. Looking down again at the dead face, he frowned. "Is it? No, surely. . . but yes. . . *yes*, it is!"

He looked up again at Mirt as sharply as any snake. "So how do *you* know of Klellyn and my dealings with him?"

Mirt shrugged. "I was one of Klellyn's longtime trading partners, too."

The vizier's look of astonishment required no acting. "But—but he never discussed one of his, ah, associates with another."

"Didn't he?" Mirt kept his face as expressionless as the dead man's. "Well, I suppose there were those he trusted enough to talk freely with, and. . . others."

The vizier went red, then white. "You will uncover the killer of Klellyn, sellsword," he snapped, "if you want to remain ali—in my employ!"

Mirt turned away, heading for the door. "But of course," he said over his shoulder, in perfect mimicry of the vizier's own habitual, softly mocking voice.

Mirt had barely dozed off when the scream awakened him.

Tauniira tensed, bare and warm against him but awake in an instant. Mirt rolled away, growling, "You stay here, and keep the bed warm. I won't be long."

"Said the man stepping off the cliff," Tauniira hissed at him in the darkness as he buckled on his breeches and stamped his feet into his boots.

Mirt gave her a friendly growl by way of reply as he shrugged on his mail shirt and made for the door, sword in hand.

Deln and another two sentinels were waiting in the passage as he came trotting up to the row of closed bedchamber doors.

One opened momentarily, farther along, but closed again just as swiftly. It was Larl Ambror's door, though Mirt could have sworn the momentary slice of face peering out into the passage had belonged to the Lady Roselarr.

Well, such doings were none of his concern. Deln and the others stood guard over another door.

The door of Harlo Ongalor's bedchamber.

Mirt put his hand on the door ring. Locked. He leaned against the door. Barred, too.

"Begone," the vizier said curtly, from the other side of the door. "Get hence."

"You screamed," Mirt said.

"It was nothing. A nightmare."

"You've charged me to investigate two murders," Mirt replied, "and I'm doing that. Operating under Hawkwinter orders, not just yours. I insist on entering your room now, to see matters for myself. Open your door or I'll break it down— with great satisfaction."

There was a long moment of silence, then the gentle thumping of the bar being lifted could be heard, followed by the scrape of the bolt and the rattle of the lock. The door swung inward.

Deln stepped forward in perfect unison with Mirt, the points of their two swords entering the dimly lit room first. The vizier gave way before them, drenched with sweat and staring-eyed, as white as his own bed silks. . . but there was no body to be seen, nor anything disarranged in the room. Ongalor was fully dressed, and his bed had been turned open for slumber, but not slept in.

"Satisfied?" the vizier snapped, his voice thin and high with fear.

"What happened?"

Ongalor shrugged.

"You screamed," Mirt said. "What happened?"

"A nightmare," the vizier replied. "You've seen—and beheld nothing. Now go. Please."

Mirt walked slowly around the man, peering intently at

him from all sides, then turned away without a word and strode out, Deln standing as rearguard as if they were on a battlefield.

"Back to posts," Mirt ordered wearily, and the sentinels trudged away.

The moment no one else was within earshot, Deln muttered, "I saw what befell."

"You fail to surprise me," Mirt murmured. "Speak."

"Ongalor was out in the passage, creeping along like a sneak thief, listening at every door. He went past Marimbrar, then me, ignoring us like we were furniture, so we tailed him. 'Twasn't hard; he never once looked back—until he got his fright, and turned to flee. What scared him was just seeing two men, standing calmly talking to each other, away down the end of the passage."

"And these two men were. . . ?"

"Prince Elashar's double, and a *second* double. So alike you couldn't tell one from the other, but neither of them the so-called 'real' Elashar. Neither had that little scab on his cheek from where he cut himself on that hanging lamp."

Mirt nodded slowly. "They'll both have fled long since, of course. So our vizier is worried that someone *else* is playing little games in this house. Or that wizards he thought he had under control are doing what wizards always do: getting up to mischief of their own."

The strong morning sun did not seem to shine on the dust churned up by the horses trotting hastily out through the gates. Vizier Harlo Ongalor and the three Amnian heirs who did everything in unison seemed in a great hurry to be elsewhere—and Mirt suspected the sun was avoiding their dust for the same reason it couldn't reach into the stables on so bright a morning: magical barriers conjured by Ongalor's wizard allies. This one would be to keep arrows and crossbow quarrels from Ombreir striking them down from behind as they rode away, and the stables' barrier to keep anyone else from taking a horse to flee the mansion before the Just Blades came slaying.

"Good riddance," grunted Elgan, standing on the wall-walk with Mirt and everyone else, as they all watched the four horsemen dwindle over the flank of the nearest hill. "Now at least the killings will end, and we can try to decide what to do about yonder approaching army, before they butcher us all."

As he spat thoughtfully down over the wall into the moat below, a shrill scream split the air behind them—a scream that ended in a wet splattering—in the courtyard of the darm-fruit trees.

It seemed Elgan had been mistaken.

Mirt looked down at the shattered body sprawled in a puddle of blood that was still spreading. Larl Ambror, or had been. Amn now held one fewer wine merchant—or, perhaps, one fewer wine merchant's double.

Lady Roselarr had taken one look at the corpse, shrieked, and fled up the grand staircase like a whirlwind.

"Seems someone wanted her newfound love to fly," Deln muttered.

Mirt smiled sourly. "Think Ongalor's wizards did it, from afar? Some compulsion spell or other?"

Deln shrugged. "Why him? Taking *you* down would be his best strike against us."

"Oh? Wouldn't that be the best way to scare everyone into fleeing Ombreir?"

"If we can. I'm thinking they threw up barrier spells we haven't even guessed at yet, to make this place a pris—"

Deln stopped speaking in astonishment. Darmon Halandrath had mounted the stair. Gaping, everyone watched him ascend, a great rolling mound of struggling flesh surging upward.

"Tymora and Tempus preserve us," Tauniira muttered.

"Or Yurtrus gnaw our bones," Hargra added.

Panting and sweating, Halandrath reached the upper level and lurched in the direction of his bedchamber. Before he was out of view, Helora Roselarr reappeared, coming back down the stairs with her arms full of gleaming, gilded—and obviously heavy—coffers. Her face was white as bone and set hard with determination, her eyes red from the tears still streaming down her cheeks.

"Whatever," Ralaerond Galespear drawled, "are you *doing?*"

"What you should be doing," she snapped back. "Fleeing this deathtrap just as swiftly as I can!" She tried to push past him, toward the open front gates, and found herself surrounded by frowning Amnians and Mirt's warriors.

"We're going to die here, every one of us!" she cried, voice rising. "I doubt these Just Blades—if they're truly anywhere near here at all!—will find anyone left alive here in Ombreir, when they do come riding in! Someone hiding among us is butchering all the rest of us, and smiling up his sleeve all the while! I—"

Words failing her, she launched into a shriek of frustration, rammed a blinking Torandral out of her way with one of the coffers she was cradling, and shouldered her way through the rest of the warriors—who looked to Mirt for instructions. He waved a hand to indicate they should let her pass.

In her wake, Darmon Halandrath came thundering back down the stairs, clutching a leather satchel to his gigantic belly and howling for breath, sweat streaming down his nigh-purple face like a river. "M-make way!" he tried to bawl, but lacked the breath to make it more than a hoarse wheeze. "Make—"

Mirt gestured curtly, and his warriors cleared a path for the gigantic Amnian.

One or two of the other Amnians started to follow Roselarr and Halandrath in their march to the gates—only to halt in horror, and stare.

As she passed through the gatehouse, Helora Roselarr seemed to catch fire.

She shrieked, took two blazing steps, then seemed rooted to the spot, held up from falling by the sudden roaring fury of flames streaming up from her to the sky.

Blinded by sweat and trotting hard, Halandrath almost blundered into her, lurching to one side at the last moment—and bursting into flames of his own. "No!" he cried wetly, flinging his fat arms wide. *"Nooooo!"*

Mirt and the others watched in grim silence as the flames rose higher, two bright columns licking black smudges of smoke into the sky.

In mere moments Roselarr and Halandrath became ashes on bones, then bones straining to run on, then collapsing bones. One of Roselarr's coffers sagged open, spewing out a wet flood of melted gold, but the other burst with a little *pop*, sending forth an assortment of gem-adorned rings, bracelets, hairpins, and other small items that winked and glowed with magical radiances. . . that seemed to get ensnared in the air by an unseen hand or current, that sent them flying away in a common direction, along the front of the mansion wall. Faster and faster they streamed, curving to hug the wall at its every bend, and before the watchers had found time to draw more than a few breaths, they came into view again, racing along, having circumnavigated Ombreir. They sped past once more, a glittering stream, and in their wake something small and golden amid the blackened and guttering ruin that had been Darmon Halandrath rose to join them. . . followed by other. . . somethings.

"Those are magic items, aren't they?" Torandral asked.

Mirt nodded.

"Why. . . why are they circling the walls like that?"

"They're caught in the barrier Ongalor's wizards left behind," Mirt replied, "cast all around Ombreir, to trap us all inside."

As if his words had been a cue, a plume of smoke rose into the sky from the far side of a nearby hill. Up over the brow of that hill, with the swiftly thickening smoke behind them, came riding an armed and glittering host, with a banner flapping at their fore.

It was a black, five-spired crown on gold, the Crown of Prince Uldrako. The Just Blades had come at last.

❧ ❧ ❧ ❧ ❧

"They must have finished looting the Narthaen mansion, and set fire to it," Mirt mused aloud. "Which means they have every intention of sleeping here tonight."

As his warriors muttered and readied their weapons around him, Gralhund and Gauntyl banners unfurled alongside the pretender's banner, to fly openly.

Tauniira shook her head at the sight of them. "They mean to make you rue your choice of employers, Mirt."

"Won't the magical barrier protect us?" Torandral asked, fear and excitement making his voice shrill.

Mirt and his veterans shook their heads.

"It'll go down the moment they reach it," Mirt growled, "and they'll have us surrounded by then. Even if they lack a wizard with any wits about him, Ongalor and his spell hurlers are scrying us from afar. They'll take it down, and soon, now."

❧ ❧ ❧ ❧ ❧

"The barrier," Harlo Ongalor said, staring into the moving scene he could see in the sphere of glowing radiance that floated in the air in the middle of the glade. "Get ready to take it down."

The three wizards who'd conjured that sphere no longer looked like a trio of wealthy Amnians. They had been staring intently at the spell-spun scene back at Ombreir, and continued to do so, saying not a word in reply.

The vizier was not accustomed to being ignored. "Jaelryn!" he snapped, choosing the weakest mage, the one he knew was more afraid of him than the others. "Did you hear me?"

Jaelryn kept silent, and the vizier glared at him, suddenly aware that all three wizards were standing motionless, staring fixedly into the sphere as if enthralled.

"Jaelryn?" Ongalor shouted, alarmed. "Orauth? Maundark?"

"They can't hear you," a calm feminine voice announced from right behind the vizier.

He whirled, jumping back as he did so, the rings on his fingers winking into life.

A barefoot woman in the tattered, filthy remnants of a rotten but once-grand black gown stood facing him, her long, wavy silver hair coiling and lashing around her shoulders like a nest of restless snakes.

"Who are you?" Ongalor snarled, feeling the tingling that meant the greatest smiting magic of his rings was almost ready. "And what have you done to my wizards?"

The woman stared at him with open contempt in her eyes. Those eyes flared silver—and the vizier's rings exploded, taking Ongalor's fingers with them.

Gods, the *pain!*

He found himself on his knees, screaming, waving his hands violently to try to dash the pain away—and failing.

"You should tend 'your' wizards better, Vizier," the silver-haired woman sneered. "Just now, they're entranced by the Weave, and their fates depend on what I find in their thoughts. As for me. . . most folk know me as the Simbul. I serve Mystra, and the land of Aglarond. I've been watching you for a long time, Harlo Ongalor, and am quite happy to be your doom."

"My—? What did I ever do to you?" the vizier sobbed, trying to struggle to his feet and reach the wand at his belt with the bleeding ruin of his right hand.

"When I wore the guise of Alathe, you had me flogged to the bone for disputing your trade dishonesties with you in Athkatla."

The Simbul took a step closer and added calmly, "When the prettiest of the bedchamber-lasses you rented out in Murann died of her treatment at your hands—glass shards thrust into someone will do that, Ongalor—I took her place, and you promptly had me fed to your dogs."

The wand at the vizier's belt slid itself up, past his desperately grabbing hand, and turned in the air, just out of his reach, to menace him.

"And in Crimmor," the silver-haired woman continued, "when I posed as that trade envoy from Sembia and refused to be threatened into signing the deal you wanted, you had me felled in the street with a slung stone to the back of my head, and drove your wagon over me—three times, Ongalor, just to make sure you'd broken as many bones as you could. Then you laughed in my face and snatched my purse."

The Simbul bent closer and added, "Your life is so full of such cruelties that you may not recall just three slain women out of so many, yet I'm sure if I bother to give you time enough, you'll remember at least one of those slayings. Even if, just now, you can't put a. . . *finger* on it."

And she smiled at Harlo Ongalor as the wand began to glow.

It was a soft smile that held all the mercy of the grin on the face of a hungry wolf.

As the Just Blades rode down the hill, those standing ready inside the gates of Ombreir were shocked to see a dead herald hanging limply in the air at their fore, head lolling, spitted on a trio of lances.

"A herald! There'll be trouble over that," Mirt muttered.

"There will, indeed," Ralaerond Galespear said softly at his shoulder. Something in the heir's drawl made Mirt look at him—in time to see the horse breeder's handsome good looks melt away into taller, broader-shouldered, feminine beauty.

A silver-haired woman who looked somehow familiar snatched Mirt's sword out of his hand, handing him Galespear's rapier with the words, "Here. Sorry it's such a toy."

A moment later, he was missing his best dagger, too, and she was striding away through the gates.

"No one should follow me past the gatehouse," she snapped, silver hair swirling. "The barrier stands."

It shimmered around her as she spoke, but she walked through it unharmed to meet the advancing army.

"We come to parley!" one of the younger Gauntyl knights shouted. "See you not the herald?"

"There will be no parley with you, who dared to treat a herald so," the lone woman told him. "I'll grant you only one gift: swift death."

The knight sneered. "How generous! Just you, against us all?"

She shrugged. "If some of you would like to be gallant and retire while I butcher the rest, be assured I'll get to you all eventually."

"You're mad!" barked a Gralhund warrior, stalking to meet her.

"That's true enough," the woman agreed. "So, shall we?"

Reluctantly, shaking his head, the Gralhund warrior swung his axe at her—and she danced aside, sprang behind his swing to thrust steel into his armpit, and spun to slice open the throat of another warrior with her dagger.

"Doomed," Loraun murmured—but stared, jaw dropping, as the stranger with the silver hair slashed, thrust, leaped, and slew, a tireless butchery that took her into the heart of the Just Blades.

Everyone in Ombreir watched in deepening awe, waiting for her inevitable fall. . . a fall that did not come.

"Twenty or more, already," Mirt mumbled, shaking his head. He could see some sort of warding magic was turning aside hurled lances and fired arrows from the woman, but still. . .

Sheer weariness should drag her arms down soon, and they'd overwhelm her.

"I weary of this," they heard her say, through some trick of her magic—in the instant before beams of silver fire lashed out from her eyes, to blast to ashes Prince Uldrako and the senior Gauntyl and Gralhund knights riding with him. "Now begone, or I'll slay you all!"

She buried her steel in another two warriors—and the rest of the Just Blades shouted, turned, and fled, leaving more than sixty fallen on the hill.

The woman watched them go, then turned and walked back to the gates, drenched in blood not her own and leaking silver flames here and there where she'd been wounded.

"The barrier still stands," she warned those gaping at her.

"I'd not seek to depart, were I you."

She handed back Mirt's bloody sword and dagger, and told him, "I need a bath, and trust your cooking best. Make me some of that shieldfry of yours. There's still enough of Ambror left for a good meal, I think."

Mirt gave her a hard look, as men gagged or winced around him, and decided she was jesting. He hoped.

"Cook for me up in South Tower," she ordered. Then she commanded everyone else, "Where not one of you will go, until Mirt and I come down out of there."

The fire quickened. Mirt set two pans to warming over it. No need to weaken a shield when he had cookware. He laid Ombreir's best leg of lamb on the cutting board, hefted the cleaver, and set to work.

Silver hair swirled in the doorway, shedding a fine mist of water. Her bath was done already. "You know who I am, don't you?"

He nodded. That night, years ago, had just come back to him. "Dove, of the Seven," he growled. "Saw you once, dancing at the Bright Bared Battlelass, in Waterdeep."

Dove grinned. "Couldn't resist the name of that place. Pity 'tis gone. So you've seen all of me."

Mirt nodded. "Thews and thighs to out-muscle mine," he said. "So what brings a Chosen of Mystra into the endless war that is Amn?"

"Serving the goddess. In this case, hunting down Red Wizards who repeatedly offend against her wishes."

"Tell me," Mirt said, cutting up garlic. "Please."

"Klellyn, a Thayan agent. Silver fire—put my tongue in his mouth, left no mark. He cast a wildfire spell you were close enough to feel."

Mirt nodded. "Wildfire's bad?"

"He was trying to forever make magic 'go dead' in one tower here, as a trap for other mages. Lured there, a simple dagger thrust could end them. That sort of deliberate damaging of the Weave is something we Chosen are sworn to try to prevent."

Mirt set the lamb to sizzling, turned to face Dove, and asked simply, "Are you going to let me live?"

"Of course. You, I like and trust. You're no misuser of the Art."

"Was the vizier?"

"Small, puny. . . Ongalor is a vindictive fool, about half the astute schemer he thinks he is. The five wizards who work with him, though. . . Orauth is formidable, and Maundark's deadly enough."

"Why the doubles, for all of us? Why didn't he just blast us?"

"He wanted the Just Blades to slaughter all of you. The doubles obey him and can be used in many swindles. Later, he'll let others capture those doubles. When those others put forward the doubles or their remains, the five wizards will end the magical disguises on the doubles, and Ongalor's rivals will be discredited, not to be trusted by anyone in Amn."

Mirt nodded, then frowned. "Five. . . three gone with Ongalor, Klellyn dead—did you kill Ambror, too?"

"Yes. Another Thayan I was after. He'd just cast a life-draining magic that would have withered away two folk here and used their life force to allow him to mind control others at will. You're penned in with more serpents than Loraun. The fifth wizard is still here in Ombreir."

"Who?"

Dove drew Mirt's sword out of his scabbard, turned to the door and flung it wide—and drove the sword deep into Tauniira, who'd been leaning against the door listening.

Spitting blood, Tauniira staggered forward into the room.

"Behold the wizard Varessa," the Chosen said. "Ongalor's lover—and commander."

Mirt gaped at his dying comrade.

"She killed the real Tauniira months ago," Dove added. "Just as I've now killed her. After all, in war, people die."

THE SIEGE OF ZERITH HOLD

Jess Lebow

The Year of Shadows (1358 DR)

"For nearly the entire Year of Shadows, the goblin hordes of the High Peaks and the Kuldin Peaks attacked Erlkazar, laying siege to Duhlnarim for over three months. The war against King Ertyk Uhl of the Starrock goblin tribe seemed endless. . ."

—Count Gamalon Idogyr of Spellshire
A Report to Her Majesty on the State of Erlkazar

"Fire!"

Arrows vaulted over the wall of Zerith Hold. The twang of bowstrings drifted off just in time to hear the entire volley slap to the ground like a wind-driven steel rain.

"Again!" shouted Lord Purdun, the rightful ruler and keeper of Zerith Hold. His red hair and the long-healed scars on his left cheek shone bright in the afternoon sun as he stood atop the wall, looking out over the ruined battlefield.

The archers responded with another chorus of buzzing from their bows.

The half-elf, half-steel dragon ranger, Jivam Tammsel, crouched behind the crenellation, beside Purdun, winded from the fight. The ashen scales that ran down his neck, shoulders, and back slid effortlessly over one another with each gulp of air.

The two men had been inducted into Elestam's Crusaders together, and both had sworn an oath to protect the people of Erlkazar—even before there was such a thing as Erlkazar and the land had been ruled by King Alemander of Tethyr.

"How long can we keep this up?" asked Tammsel. He scratched at the thick stone with his powerful claws, dislodging a small chunk. "Korox has been gone for nearly a month, and we're running out of supplies."

"He'll be back," said Purdun. "With reinforcements from Tethyr."

"We will be lucky if he returns from Tethyr with his life," replied the half-dragon crusader, tossing the bit of stone down the archer's platform, "let alone reinforcements."

"He will return," repeated Purdun. He looked back over the wall. "We must hold out until he does."

"Do we have any other choice?"

Purdun shook his head. "None that I can see."

They had been at war with the goblin tribes for nearly a year. The surrounding villages of Furrowsrich and Saarlik had fallen tendays before. The battles in Duhlnarim had swayed back and forth for months, only to end up here at the gates to the hold—the last refuge inside a broken, nearly beaten land.

Outside, as far as the eye could see, the two groups swarmed, converging on the hills in front of Zerith Hold. Those goblins with deep yellow flesh were from the High Peaks. They generally moved on foot and were particularly good at hiding and laying ambushes. One on one, the beasts were little more than a nuisance. But by the hundreds—and thousands—they were a real danger, as the ongoing war had proved.

Though the High Peaks goblins were problematic, it was the Kuldin Peaks goblins that caused Lord Purdun more concern. They were more organized, were generally larger, and rode atop the backs of worgs—four-legged beasts that resembled huge, ferocious wolves. The goblin and its mount together were nearly a match for a single soldier, and the pairs outnumbered the denizens of Zerith Hold nearly thirty to one.

"Lord Purdun," shouted Lieutenant Beetlestone, his normal youthful enthusiasm replaced by dire seriousness. "They're forming up!"

Purdun looked out to where Beetlestone pointed. Sure enough, there in the middle of the swirling, chaotic mass of goblins, order had broken out. A large group had formed loose ranks, and they charged now for the walls of the hold.

"They've got trees!" warned the lieutenant.

Lord Purdun ran down the wall, bracing his men for another attack.

"Archers to the wall. Ready the oil," he ordered. "Take out the leaders. Don't let them inside." He stopped at the end of the defenses, pulling an arrow tight to his bowstring. "This is your home you're fighting for. I don't need to tell you what happens if Zerith Hold falls."

The goblin horde grew as it drew nearer to the walls. They had toppled some of the hundred-year-old trees from the dense wilderness surrounding Duhlnarim and carried them over their heads. The goblins had tried the trick once before. They would brace the tree, a rudimentary ladder, against the side of the hold and try to scramble up the side to get over the wall.

The result of their last attempt could be seen below. Two broken stumps lay scattered and burned, one on the ground, another in the moat. The attempt had proven unsuccessful, but they were trying it again—and with twice as many trees.

"Fire!" shouted Purdun, and he released his arrow.

The wall rumbled with the hum of bowstrings. Huge swaths of goblins were pinned to the ground by the volley. But those who held the trees were mostly sheltered from the assault—the arrows glancing off or sticking deep into the ancient wood.

"You there, on the end of the wall," shouted Purdun. "Concentrate your fire on that group there. Wait until they lift the tree. When they're uncovered, give 'em the Hells." He turned to the crusaders and guardsmen beside him. "You men, focus your fire over there, on the group with the second tree. Hold your shot until you hear my order."

The men nodded or grumbled their agreement.

The trees grew nearer, and the men pulled their bowstrings tight.

"Wait for it."

The tree rose, reaching up for the top of the wall and revealing beneath the goblins who held it aloft.

"Fire!"

Arrows rained down again, puncturing the goblins' soft bodies. They fell over, dead on impact, slumping to the ground like blades of grass under a huge foot. The tree grew unbalanced as fewer hands steadied it. It swayed sideways, then toppled over as they lost control. It rolled as it dropped to the ground, crushing the yellow-skinned goblins underneath it and exposing those who had previously enjoyed its cover.

A cheer went up from the wall as the tree fell. The goblins scrambled around beside their makeshift ladder, trying to lift it back into place, but the archers on the wall picked them to pieces.

"They're coming!" came a shout, followed by two huge thuds and the sound of wood splintering.

Turning around, Purdun's blood ran cold. Two trees had gone down under their concentrated fire, but the other two had hit home. They rested against the outside of Zerith Hold, a line of goblins climbing through their branches on their way up.

"Pour the oil!" ordered Purdun.

Four huge men made their way down the platform. They carried between them a thick log, from which hung an iron caldron bubbling over with animal fat, tree sap, and oil. They moved carefully, for the caldron had been hanging over an open fire. One misstep and they would be scorched on the slick metal—or worse, under a flood of scalding, sticky oil.

The goblins charged up the side of the trees, quickly drawing closer to the top of the wall.

"Hurry," shouted Purdun.

The caldron arrived just as the first goblin topped the tree.

Dropping his bow, Purdun pulled his long sword out of its scabbard, cutting the yellow-skinned vermin in two with his draw. Stepping up on the crenellation, he took down two more goblins, knocking them off the tree to their death far below.

"Pour it," he shouted, jumping back down to the archer's platform.

The four men lifted the log and tipped the caldron over the side. The melted fat and oil oozed out over the stone and down the side of the tree. A gush of foul broth splashed over the climbing goblins, blistering their flesh, cooking them alive. Their skin sizzled as the oil and pitch stuck to their bodies, and half a dozen goblins toppled away from the wall.

Purdun grabbed a lit torch from a nearby sconce and tossed it onto the toppled tree. The oil ignited, catching slowly at first, but then erupting into a huge blue flame.

As the flame followed the oil trail down the trunk of the tree, forcing the goblins to abandon their climb to the top, a second cheer went up along the wall.

But the celebration was cut short by the sound of swords clashing and men dying.

Goblins had reached the top of the second tree, and they poured over the crenellation onto the platform. The first few to reach the top had been cut to shreds, but their numbers quickly became overwhelming. Guardsmen thrashed about, goblins hanging from their shoulders and backs. Crusaders engaged three and four of the invaders at a time, cutting them down as quickly as they could. But they kept coming, flooding over faster than they could be killed.

A roar filled Purdun's ears as Jivam Tammsel bounded into the fray. With each swipe of his hand, he killed a goblin. With each step he took, another fell from the wall. With each breath, he bit down on another of the invaders, tearing its flesh from its bones.

The men rallied behind the half-elf, half-steel dragon, drawing strength and courage from the crusader's raw anger and power.

The goblins seemed to sense the shift in the tide of the battle. They began to scatter, running down the platform, dropping their weapons and looking for places to hide. Crusaders and guardsmen chased them down, cutting the goblins to pieces as they stopped to cower in the corners or against the stone.

Tammsel cut through three more goblins before taking a huge step and leaping over the edge of the wall. His broad shoulders disappeared from view, then the sound of goblins dying drifted over the crenellation.

Landing firmly on the leaning tree, he let out a second roar—right in the face of the oncoming invaders. A few had the courage to face the half-steel dragon, and they were rewarded with a quick, painful death, their bodies torn apart by claw, tooth, or sword.

"Throw me a rope," shouted Tammsel, bashing aside goblins as he made his way farther down the tree.

Lord Purdun obliged, finding a coiled pile of woven hemp wrapped in one of the battle boxes on the back of the archer's platform. Twisting the end into a quick knot, the crusader twirled the rope over his head and let it fly.

Tammsel grabbed the flying rope out of the air. He was about a quarter of the way down, and he dived in, disappearing among the thick branches and needles, dragging the rope with him. A moment later, he came out the other side, the rope wrapped around the trunk of the tree.

Tying it securely, Tammsel dashed back up to the wall. Behind him, the goblins filled the vacated space, not quite sure what to make of the rope. A few stopped to pick at it, but the rest clamored on, for the inside of Zerith Hold.

Leaping over the wall, Tammsel grabbed the other end of the rope and ran down the platform.

"Pull with me," he shouted.

Lord Purdun wrapped the rope around his arm and leaned back. "You men there," he ordered, "grab hold. We're going to pull the tree sideways and free it from the wall."

Archers dropped their bows. Guardsmen sheathed their swords. All of them chipped in to pull the tree away from the hold.

"One, two, three, *heave!*" shouted Tammsel.

The men added their strength to that of the two crusaders, one after another grabbing hold of the rope. They lined up along the platform, pulling the tree toward the south end of the wall, hoping to dislodge it.

All the while the goblins continued their climb.

"Pull!"

The men groaned as they struggled against the hundred-year-old tree. It was thick and heavy, and it was wedged hard against the stone wall.

"Harder!" shouted Purdun.

The tree lurched a few feet, shaking loose a handful of goblins.

"Again!"

The goblin climbers reached the top of the tree and dropped inside. Swarms more approached the top, and behind them, a hundred others. Gone were the deep green needles of the ancient tree—replaced by a sea of yellow, sloshing up the crude bridge.

"If you want to live to see another day, then pull, damn you!" shouted Lord Purdun.

The rope creaked under the strain. The men gasped and wailed, giving everything they had, pulling with all of their might. Purdun's knuckles grew white, his face red, his legs wobbling from the strain.

There was a deep, hollow grinding sound, and the men all fell backward, the rope going slack as the tree tore loose. They could hear the goblins scream as they plummeted to the ground.

Then the rope went taut again as the falling tree continued on.

"Let go! Let go!" shouted Tammsel.

The men did as ordered, releasing their grip on the rope and letting it slide away.

The rope slithered down the platform, picking up speed as it went. Its tail whipped back and forth, snapping and tearing at the flesh of the guardsmen and crusaders as it sailed past.

A coil at the end wrapped itself around a soldier's leg, binding then dragging him along. The poor man let out a shout of surprise, then he was gone, pulled over the side by the weight of the ancient tree crashing to the ground.

Lord Purdun got to his feet, charging into the thirty or so goblins who had managed to make it to the platform before their crude ladder was pulled sideways. His sword and bow lying somewhere on the ground, he had little choice but to fight with his fists.

Balling up one hand, he punched the first goblin he encountered right in his crooked, pointy nose. The little yellow beast squealed as it was knocked backward onto its rump.

"Sword!" shouted Tammsel.

Lord Purdun turned around to see a polished steel long sword flying through the air. Grabbing it out of the sky, he turned back to slash down two more goblins—one on each side of him.

The other crusaders and guardsmen had gotten themselves up off the floor and were wading into the fray as well. The half-steel dragon joined in, and they pushed the invaders back. Step by step they cleared the archer's platform, tossing the bodies over the side and into the moat as they went.

When the final goblin had been dispatched, Purdun dropped to one knee to catch his breath. He rested his hand on the hilt of his sword and brushed his sweat-drenched hair out of his eyes with his other.

Tammsel handed him a sheepskin full of water.

Purdun nodded his thanks as he looked up at his long-time friend. They had been in a lot of fights together. Most of them had involved defending then-Baron Valon Morkann from the Duke of Dusk and the agents of Tethyr. The crusaders had stopped four attempts on Valon's life. They had kept him around long enough to see him become king of the newest nation in Faerûn—Erlkazar.

Now here they were, defending their new country from deep inside its borders.

Purdun poured the cool liquid over his face and into his mouth. It mixed with the dirt and perspiration, turning it salty.

"Do you think we'll ever see the end to the fighting in Erlkazar?" he asked, handing the skin back to Tammsel.

The half-steel dragon shrugged. "Maybe not in our lifetime." He took a drink of water. "It's hard starting a new country, and the Baron Valon—"

"He's *King* Valon now," corrected Purdun.

"Ah, yes," replied Tammsel, "I've called him 'baron' for so long, I still haven't taught myself to make the change."

"Just don't let him hear you say that."

Tammsel smiled. "He hasn't had the title even a year. I suspect he sometimes makes the mistake himself."

"They're coming over the back wall!" shouted a messenger in the courtyard.

Lord Purdun jumped to his feet and grabbed Tammsel by the arm. "Come on."

The two crusaders ran down the steps, through the courtyard, and directly into the center of Zerith Hold. The interior was quiet and unoccupied. The grand halls and ornately appointed dining rooms had been left as they were before the goblin army had reached the gates. It felt odd, seeing the tables set for dinner and the tapestries neatly hanging on the walls, while outside a war raged.

Through the reception areas, Purdun and Tammsel ran for the other end of the hold, toward the armory and barracks. The doors to all the officers' quarters were open with no one inside. The sound of fighting echoed down the stone hallway as they closed in on the back gate.

Through the stables, the two men burst out into the mustering grounds. One of their fellow crusaders, Rysodyl Boughstrong—the most muscular elf Purdun had ever encountered—was leading the defense. He had a sword in each hand, and pointed one at an oncoming goblin, then lopped its head off with the other.

The mustering grounds were used exclusively by Lord Purdun's army. Mounted units gathered there before heading out on patrols. It had been added onto Zerith Hold when it became clear that the army was going to outgrow the two-hundred-year-old keep's existing barracks.

The gate was heavily guarded, but the wall wasn't as high there as it was at the portcullis off the main courtyard, or the rest of the hold. The original, higher wall was where the stables emptied out and was a fallback point in case the mustering grounds were overrun—and that time was at hand.

Goblins rolled over the wall at two points, dropping down in front of the blades of the troops waiting below. So far, they hadn't managed to get more than a few of their number over at any one time, and Boughstrong had the situation well in hand. He stood beside the other men, slicing up the goblins one at a time as they came.

"How are they getting over the wall?" shouted Purdun, his voice competing with the squealing of a dying goblin. "The tree ladders again?"

Boughstrong shook his head. "No. They're forming goblin pyramids, kneeling atop each other's backs to let others climb over. It's not happening everywhere yet, but only because the main force hasn't figured out they can get in this way."

"How many are out there?"

"Maybe a hundred. Half are stacked up on top of one another," replied the elf. "I can handle this. I'll send a runner if we need—"

Boughstrong's words were cut short as he was knocked to the ground by a four-legged black beast.

"Worgs!" came the cry.

But it was too late. Boughstrong already had one atop his chest.

Purdun swung down on the rider—a red-skinned Kuldin Peaks goblin. His sword was intercepted by the worg, its teeth biting down on the blade with a *clang*.

Purdun pulled back, slipping the sword out of the beast's jaws and cutting a huge gash in its foul gums as he did. The creature yelped and snapped its teeth, but the crusader dodged away, just barely getting out from under its fangs as they clamped down.

With a hiss, Tammsel leaped on the worg, wrapping his arms around the mount's neck and tackling it to the ground. The rider was thrown from its back, as the half-steel dragon and the filthy beast rolled across the dusty flagstones. The worg howled, its teeth making a loud snapping each time it tried to bite into the man on its back.

Purdun quickly dispatched the downed goblin, cutting its body in two with a mighty cleave. Then he helped Boughstrong to his feet.

"Ready to fight?"

The elf nodded and picked up his swords.

Three more worgs bounded over the wall, leaping over the crusaders' heads deeper into the mustering grounds.

Purdun and Boughstrong turned to face them. The man and the elf had their backs to the outer wall. The worgs' leap had put them close to the open doors to Zerith Hold—closer than Purdun and Boughstrong. Nothing stood between the invaders and the undefended inside of the hold.

"We can't let them get inside," shouted Purdun, and he flung himself at the first rider.

The soldiers at the wall followed his lead, spreading out around the worgs.

On the ground, Tammsel continued to wrestle. Fur flew, and blood splashed. They traded claw blows and snapped at each other's throats. It was a fight to the death, two primal forces struggling for survival.

Boughstrong swept around to the right of Purdun to circle behind the closest worg rider. The move confused the hulking mount, because it snapped at the air, first toward one crusader and then the other. The goblin on its back tried to control it, but it was no use; the beast, not the rider, was in charge.

The worg lunged at Boughstrong, and Purdun slashed its tail from behind. The creature let out a yelp and spun around, growling. But that's all it had time for. The elf's flanking move had worked, and he came down on the beast with his blades, severing both hind legs.

The worg's rear end dropped to the ground, little more than a bloody stump, and the creature curled up on itself. It yowled, a helpless moaning wail, and pulled itself in circles with its front legs. Confused and desperate, it flailed on the ground, trying to salve its wounds. In the process, the worg pinned its goblin rider to the ground, smashing it to a pulp with its heavy, hairy frame as it squirmed in agony.

Another yelp echoed through the mustering grounds, overtopping all the other sounds of fighting. Tammsel got to his feet, the worg he had been wrestling gripped in one hand—his dragonlike claws buried in its throat. The creature pawed weakly at his arms, struggling to breathe. Gashes in its sides wept blood and pus, and its tail stuck out straight from its body.

The yelping stopped as the worg expired. Its body fell limp, hanging from Tammsel's claws like a freshly slaughtered cow on a meat hook.

The other soldiers had dispatched one of the final two worgs when the last one turned and made a break for the open door to Zerith Hold.

"You men," shouted Purdun, pointing to half a dozen soldiers close to the door, "after him!"

But his order was drowned out by the growls of five more worgs as they came leaping over the wall. Two men were caught off guard, torn to shreds by a frenzy of claws and teeth.

Purdun looked out at the mustering grounds. They weren't making any progress. The goblins would continue to get over the wall, and eventually more of them would get into the open back door. They really didn't need to hold that part of the keep. It just wasn't smart to stay there.

"Fall back!" he ordered. "Everyone inside the hold. We're ceding the mustering grounds."

The men did as they were told, disengaging from the goblin riders and bolting for the heavy doors at the back of Zerith Hold. Purdun, Boughstrong, and Tammsel took up the rear, covering the retreat. They stood side by side, fighting slowly back, as the worgs and their goblin riders stalked forward, trying to get past and into the hold.

"Inside, now!" Purdun bolted for the opening.

The elf and the half-dragon followed suit, dashing into the waiting door, the goblin riders right on their heels.

The cry went up among the men: "Shut it!"

It moved slowly as they shoved. The heavy wood and iron door had been designed to be difficult to open and as a result was also difficult to close. The old iron hinges creaked and complained as they went, and the worgs clawed at the opening, their fang-filled snouts reaching inside for whatever they could grab hold of.

Soldiers stabbed at the snapping beasts and their riders. When one would retreat, another would take its place, blocking the door from fully closing.

"Put your back into it!" shouted Purdun. He squatted down and pushed with all his might, his shoulders pressed against the heavy wood and iron bands.

The door moved farther, banging into the worgs. They growled, tearing at the wood with their claws and fangs.

Their riders jabbed their swords into the opening, creating a further barrier to getting it closed.

"All together!" shouted Tammsel. "One, two, three—*now!*"

Everyone who wasn't pushing the door lunged at the opening with their weapons. Blades scissored over one another into the gap. Eyes were gouged out, teeth cut loose, and paws torn to shreds. The soldiers' collective attack forced the worgs back, and the last few inches of the gap were cleared out.

"Push!"

The men groaned, straining with all they had, and the door slammed closed.

The sound of the heavy wooden crossbeam sliding into place brought a wave of relief washing through Purdun, and he took a huge gulp of air. It felt good to rest, his back leaning against the solid old wood of the door. But there was still a battle to be fought, and a worg loose inside his home.

Pushing himself away from the door, he took off into the hold.

"Half of you stay here. The rest follow me." He waved the men after him as he bounded away, Boughstrong, Tammsel, and a host of soldiers right behind.

Moving down the stone hallway, the men peeled off one at a time, searching the rooms as they went. As they cleared them, they rejoined the group. It didn't take them long to search the entire army wing of the hold, and they continued on.

Reaching the entry, they found what they were looking for.

The worg stood its ground, growling at half a dozen pikemen who had it cornered in one of the formal dining rooms. The large table in the center had been turned over, and the dishes were in shards on the floor. The worg's goblin rider had been unseated and stood beside it, waving a short sword frantically back and forth.

The pikemen closed in on the pair slowly, backing them up against the wall. When the worg realized it was cornered, it panicked and leaped at the closest soldier, only to be gutted from throat to belly by the head of a pike.

Seeing its mount fall to the ground, its chest open wide, the goblin tried to skitter under the overturned table. It clawed at the cloth and detritus on the floor, but there was no room, and it too received a belly full of steel.

"I guess that takes care of that," said Purdun. "Well done, men."

Slipping his sword into its sheath, he took one last look at the ruined dining room, then headed out to take stock of the situation in the courtyard.

Outside, things had reached a relative calm. Archers on the wall occasionally lobbed arrows down on the goblins. Soldiers hurried back and forth on the lower level, tending to the wounded and collecting supplies. Bundles of bread and buckets of water were being passed around, as everyone took advantage of the break in the fighting to prepare for more of the same.

Purdun took a loaf of bread, tore it in thirds, and handed a piece to Tammsel and Boughstrong. "I wonder how long this will last."

Tammsel bit into the warm bread. "The food or the calm?"

The relative silence was broken by the sound of a thousand goblins talking all at once. Their voices rose to an excited frenzy. Then all went quiet.

Rysodyl Boughstrong bounded up the stairs to the archer's platform. He glanced down over the edge, then turned around, cupping his hands to his mouth.

"The goblin king has arrived!"

Lord Purdun hurried to the stairs, his half-steel dragon companion right behind him. Reaching the top of the crenellated wall, he looked down into the sea of goblins surrounding his keep. From the west, the goblin king approached, working his way down the road.

Easily three times the size of the second largest goblin on the battlefield, he shuffled to the top of the hill, seemingly in no hurry. In one massive fist he dragged behind him what looked like the throwing arm from a ruined trebuchet. It still had the basket attached to one end—a souvenir from a previous battle.

Even for a goblin, he was an ugly creature. His greenish skin stretched tight over rippling forearms and shoulders. He wore a collection of ragged furs, draped haphazardly over his chest and back. In some cases it looked as if the brute had done little more than bash a skunk over the head and tie its tail in with the rest of the refuse hanging from his body.

Warts covered his arms and forehead. His nose grew out from his face crooked and cocked, as if it had been broken and broken again, each time pushing out in a new direction. And a mop of stringy, greasy hair hung from the top of his head, flopping down his back, cascading over his shoulders, and getting caught under his feet as he trundled forward.

Over the hair, the goblin king sported a tarnished, twisted, and broken copper crown. It looked as if it may have at one time been the wheel of an elaborate coach. Whatever it had been in a previous life, it had seen a lot of fighting and had suffered for it.

A host of red-skinned guards rode beside him atop their worgs. They shoved aside the other goblins, clearing the way for their king. Those goblins that didn't move quickly enough were trampled underfoot or snapped to pieces in the mighty jaws of the worgs.

"So that's the famed King Ertyk Uhl," said Purdun, sizing up his opponent.

He'd heard much about the goblin king. Ertyk Uhl was the first to unite the goblins of both the Kuldin and High Peaks. The resulting union had created the Starrock tribe, the group Purdun and the crusaders had been fighting in Duhlnarim for months. The war had gone on for nearly an entire year, but never before had the goblin king appeared in person.

When Ertyk Uhl reached the top of the hill, he stopped and turned to face his collected army. The goblin king raised his battle club high, then swung it toward Zerith Hold, the loose trebuchet basket flopping over and thudding to the ground in front of him.

The silence suddenly ended as the goblins all started chattering again at the same time. Large groups formed, each working intently on some collective goal. What that was remained to be seen.

Whatever they were doing, it wasn't attacking Zerith Hold, and it gave the crusaders another rare moment to stop and think. Heading back down into the courtyard, Purdun, Tammsel, and Boughstrong sat on the edge of a low stone wall to talk.

"This is never going to stop," started Purdun. "Now that their king is here, they are going to pound us day and night. They have the numbers to rest in shifts and keep us on the defensive until we break."

"I am glad to see that you have finally come to your senses," replied Tammsel. "It is time we abandon Zerith Hold. We have put up a good fight, but there is no sense in giving up lives here. We can live to fight another day, when we have more resources and on our own terms."

"I am not suggesting that we flee," replied Purdun. "There are too many of them, and they have us completely surrounded. Even if we were to make it out alive, where would we go? Back to Tethyr? We fought long and hard to separate ourselves from their rule, and now you want to simply go back and ask if we can return to their bosom?"

"Of course not," replied Tammsel. "We are a free nation, and I intend to keep it that way."

"Good." Purdun slapped the ranger on the shoulder, smiling.

"If you're not suggesting escape, then what are you suggesting?" asked Boughstrong.

"I am suggesting that we go on the offensive."

"On the offensive? Are you crazy?" denounced the elf. "The only advantage we have is this keep. These walls are all that has held back that nearly inexhaustible army of vermin. Why would we give that up?"

"We have to kill their king," defended Purdun. "Without him, they will break. They fear him. They push on to their deaths because we are less frightening than he. But if we kill him, if they see him fall in battle, they will fear us. They will lose their nerve and their discipline, and they will break and run." Purdun looked to his fellow crusaders. "We cannot kill them all. And if we try to wait them out, then I suspect we will not make it through the night. We have no choice. King Ertyk Uhl must die."

The elf and the half-steel dragon looked at each other, then at Lord Purdun.

"We are with you," they said in unison.

"Here it comes!"

The men in the courtyard scattered, running for cover.

Over the wall, the objects flew, screeching as they came. They smelled of rotten flesh and fungus.

The projectiles came crashing to the ground in the center of Zerith Hold—piles of High Peaks goblins. They had been hurled over the wall, swords in hand.

Purdun ran back to the archer's platform. There on the edge of the large hill, the goblins had managed to construct a pair of rickety catapults. They were loading batches of goblins onto the lever arm and hurling them over the wall.

Purdun turned away and ran back down the stairs. "To the portcullis!" he shouted.

The goblins had been tied together for their voyage over the defenses of Zerith Hold. When they landed, those on top had survived the crushing impact. Those who had been unlucky enough to end up on the bottom were little more than squished piles of flesh and broken bones.

The survivors cut themselves free and ran to the portcullis and the cranking mechanism that operated the doors and drawbridge. They swarmed over the handful of soldiers standing beside the door, knocking them down and beating them into the ground—their screeches echoing off the stone walls.

Purdun and Tammsel arrived first, diving into the pile of squirming goblins—Purdun with his long sword, Tammsel with his silvery claws. The blood of their enemies flowed from the ends of their weapons, but for every goblin they cut down, two more came hurling over the wall.

"We've got to go now," said Purdun, turning and cutting the head from another goblin. "They can waste half their number throwing them over the wall, and we will still lose this fight." He came back again, cutting down two more goblins with a long, wide swing. "Eventually more are going to get inside, and all will be lost." He spun, slashing a yellow goblin across the chest, then turning and kicking another right in the groin, sending it to the ground, face first. "We have no choice. We need to surprise them. We need to kill their king, and we need to go now!"

Tammsel clawed his way through four goblins, one after the other, as he listened to his friend. Then he nodded. "I'm with you."

Purdun looked over the courtyard and spotted Boughstrong near the center, scissoring goblins to pieces before they could untangle themselves from their squished counterparts.

"We're going." Purdun motioned to the door. "Ready your men."

The elf simply nodded, finishing his gruesome work, then turning to speak with the soldiers standing nearby.

Purdun disengaged, taking two huge steps back. The goblins hissed at him, crouching and glaring. When he didn't make a move to attack, they skulked toward the portcullis and went about getting it open. Purdun let them do their work.

"Crusaders! Guardsmen! With me!" he shouted.

The goblins turned the huge wooden crank that rolled up the chain holding the portcullis. The massive iron gate began to grind open, lifting from the ground and exposing the heavy spikes on its bottom edge.

Purdun waited until it was high enough for him to duck underneath, then he made his move, leaving the relatively safe confines of Zerith Hold to take the fight to his enemy.

The drawbridge wasn't even all the way down before he and his men swarmed over. The unholy sea of goblins seethed below, waiting for the opportunity to flood into Zerith Hold. Their eyes grew large as they saw the lord of the keep come swooping down on them, riding the drawbridge like a mount into battle.

There was no time for Purdun to consider what he had gotten himself into. There was no room here for fear. As he came to the ground, he shouted a battle cry.

"For *Erlkazar!*"

And the killing began in earnest.

Purdun waded in, his sword blazing a trail through goblins and worgs alike. His men followed him into battle, screaming at the top of their lungs as they fell upon their victims. The ground before the drawbridge grew damp with blood, and the offensive surged forward.

So eager were the goblins to get inside the hold, that they pressed against one another, pushing and shoving to be the first in line—the first to be cut down. They filled the battlefield for as far as the eye could see. They stomped down the bushes and the small trees, covered up the stones and dirt on the ground, turning what seemed the whole world into a blur of yellow and red.

Archers on the platform high above rained down arrows, softening up the milling mob of goblins. Soldiers on the ground cut their way through the pressed flesh. All the while Purdun, Tammsel, and Boughstrong led the way.

They pushed out off the drawbridge, slowly working to the center of the goblin army. Worg riders swept in behind them, closing the circle and surrounding the advancing force as they had Zerith Hold.

They were cut off from any form of retreat, but that didn't matter. Retreat had never been an option.

King Ertyk Uhl bellowed something in his garbled, inarticulate language that incited his troops into a frenzy. The goblins surged forward, those in the back stampeding over those in the front. Their frenetic push hit the front line of human and elf soldiers, and they buckled, dividing them into two unequal groups. Purdun, Tammsel, and the bulk of the force remained intact, but Boughstrong was cut off, separated from the larger army with a much smaller band of soldiers.

Goblins filled the gap like a wedge, further separating the two groups. There was no time to try to regroup, no room to maneuver. There was only fighting.

Purdun and Tammsel stood side by side at the front of the pack. Goblins came at them two and four at a time, and the crusaders took them apart. They fought for their lives, fought for their home. But the goblin army was a nearly insurmountable force. They simply had the numbers, and though they died by the dozens, more and more piled into the empty spaces.

The men behind them grew tired. Their swords moved slower as their arms ran out of strength. As well trained as they were, there was a limit to how much any one man could take, and they were quickly getting to the threshold.

The ring of goblins around the soldiers constricted, and Purdun was forced back a step. A blade slipped in under his defenses, catching him just below his arm, right between the plates of his armor. He hissed and grabbed at his side. Blood covered his fingers, but there was little more to do than shake it off and continue fighting.

Beside him, Tammsel too was bleeding. He'd taken several wounds along the arms and had a good gash on the left side of his face. There may have been other wounds, but Purdun couldn't see them through the goblin flesh dripping from the half-steel dragon's claws.

Surrounded, outnumbered, outside the walls of Zerith Hold, and not making any progress toward their goal, things were looking grim. Then out of the corner of his eye, Purdun caught sight of Boughstrong. He and his men had managed to slip out from the middle of the mob, and they approached the top of the large hill—and King Ertyk Uhl.

"Up there," shouted Purdun, hoping that the sight of the elf nearing the goal would rally his troops. "It's Boughstrong." He pointed over the heads of the goblins at the crusader and his men.

A cheer went up behind Purdun and Tammsel as a renewed surge of vigor swept through them.

Boughstrong's men had lost half their own number, but they had reached the goblin king. With military precision, they cut through Ertyk Uhl's worg rider retinue, clearing a path to their target.

Boughstrong himself stepped up to the goblin king, his blades poised, ready to strike. From a distance, the green-skinned leader of the Starrock tribe looked quite large. But standing next to the muscular elf, Ertyk Uhl looked absolutely huge.

Boughstrong cut into the hulking goblin with four quick attacks. His blades struck the king dead center in the chest, sending chunks of foul fur flying in all directions. Ertyk Uhl looked down on the elf with his goopy, half-closed eyes, as if he'd just noticed a fly buzzing around his nose. Then, with a sigh and a heave, the goblin king came down on Boughstrong with his war club. The basket of the ruined trebuchet picked up speed as it came over the goblin's enormous shoulder, and catapulted over the top of the lever arm, hitting its target.

Boughstrong's head disappeared between his shoulders, pounded down through his neck and into his chest. The elf's arms went limp, and his whole body fell sideways—he was killed instantly from the impact. The goblin king kicked the corpse down the hill, watching it roll into a pile of dead worgs.

Purdun felt his stomach seize up, then drop. He could sense the energy and vigor draining from the men, watching their friend—and their best hope for success—fail and fall.

Behind him, the call went up: "Zerith Hold has fallen!"

Purdun turned to see the portcullis all the way up and the drawbridge covered with scurrying red and yellow bodies. He could see into the courtyard to the doors beyond. The goblins had reached the entry and filled the hallways. His home was lost. All he had fought for was gone.

A sharp pain brought him back to the battle—a worg clamping down on his arm. With the hilt of his sword, Purdun smashed the beast in the back of the head, pounding the heavy metal against the creature's skull. Then another bit down on his leg. Growling and snapping, it tore at his shin and calf.

Tammsel appeared out of the fray, grabbing hold of both

worgs with his powerful claws and trying to pry them loose. But the more they struggled, the more the creatures' fangs dug past Purdun's armor and into his flesh. He thrashed from side to side, trying to break free of the worgs. Then his ears were filled with a jarring snap. His body shuddered in pain and his vision went white.

A calm settled over the Lord of Zerith Hold, and he felt his fatigued body slip backward. His leg was broken, his shoulder dislocated, and he bled from several dozen teeth wounds. He could hear the screams of the people inside Zerith Hold as the entire goblin army rushed through the gates.

He looked up at Tammsel. His friend had a look of utter determination on his face. Nothing was going to stop him. If anyone was going to make it out of this alive, it would be Jivam Tammsel. Purdun considered himself lucky to have counted the half-steel dragon among his friends.

As he fell onto his back, the worgs let go. Tammsel managed to pull them away, tossing one back into the thinning press of goblins—and tearing the other to shreds with his bare hands. Everything seemed to slow, and the battle swirling around Zerith Hold came almost to a standstill.

In the near distance, trumpets sounded. Purdun wasn't sure if they were really there or if he'd imagined them as he drifted off into unconsciousness. Turning his head he looked up the hill to see horses riding into view.

Atop the lead horse, Purdun recognized a familiar face, and hope returned him from the brink.

"Korox!" he breathed, sitting up and holding his torn shoulder against his body with his good arm.

King Valon Morkann and his crusader son Korox had returned, riding triumphantly at the head of fifty men. But it was not the men who were going to save Zerith Hold. It was the five-hundred Shieldbreaker Ogres who marched behind them.

Each ogre was easily the same size as the goblin king. Filthy, ugly creatures, they wore tattered cow hides and bits of scavenged metal with improvised spikes jutting out at odd angles. Many carried broken tree trunks or large rocks in their massive hands. Others wielded the bones of dead animals or the occasional rusty steel sword.

"To the hold!" shouted King Valon, and the men rode into battle, their unlikely allies right behind.

Mass panic broke out among the goblin raiders. King Ertyk Uhl let out what sounded like a strangled wail, then he fled the battlefield, lumbering off the same way he had come. A dozen ogres padded after him, their footfalls shaking the ground as they chased the goblin king.

Spotting Purdun and Tammsel on the ground, Korox kicked his horse and pounded into the fray. He swung his sword like a mallet, in long, looping circles, taking the heads from three goblins as he made his way to the crusaders.

Reaching his friends, he leaped from his horse, sending the goblins and worgs scattering.

"No luck in Tethyr, I gather?" asked Tammsel, eyeing the fifty riders making their way to the drawbridge. "At least you got away with your life."

Korox shook his head. "We didn't go to Tethyr," replied the newest prince of Erlkazar. "My father managed to negotiate help a little closer to home."

The battle wasn't over, but it was clear the tide had changed. Without their king, the goblins were in disarray, and they scattered before the ogre forces.

Korox and Tammsel helped lift Purdun back to his feet, hefting his weight between the two of them.

"How did you manage to get the ogres to agree to an alliance?" asked Purdun, wincing from the pain in his shoulder.

"Turns out they hate the goblins even more than we do,"

replied Korox. "Come on. This fight's not over yet, and we need to get you fixed up before it is."

And the men left the battlefield to begin preparations for retaking Zerith Hold.

MERCY'S REWARD

Mark Sehestedt

The Year of the Serpent (1359 DR)

"Wake."

The side of Gethred's face stung, and there was a high-pitched ringing in his ears.

"Wake."

He felt it on the other cheek this time. Someone slapped him. Hard.

"Open your eyes or I cut the lids off. Now."

The voice was deep and had the precise pronunciation of one not used to speaking Common.

Gethred opened his eyes and winced. A meager gray light suffused the gloom, but even that was enough to stab through to the center of his head. He groaned and tried to reach for his forehead. His hands didn't move, so he tried harder, and he felt the bite of rope cutting into his arms.

Massive hands grabbed him by the shoulders,

hauled him into a sitting position, then let go. Gethred fell back, and his head bounced off a stone wall. He cried out and squeezed his eyes shut.

"I said open your eyes."

Gritting his teeth, Gethred forced his eyes to open.

The gray light wrapped around the edges of a massive figure standing before him. In the gloom, the man seemed as tall as an ogre. Standing between Gethred and the source of light, the man's features were hidden, but he could make out a great mass of hair, though where it ended and the man's clothes began, Gethred could not tell. The man dressed all in skins and furs. Most wise. So near the edge of the open steppe at the base of the mountains, the winter cold could kill quicker than the Horde.

Around the massive man Gethred could see what only the most magnanimous man ever born would have graced to call a hovel. It was a cave, dry but far from clean, with only the barest signs of human habitation—a few hide blankets, a pack, and a smattering of bones. Bits of flesh still clung to one wolf skull.

The man nudged Gethred with his boot and said, "Who are you?"

"Just a starving, half-frozen traveler," said Gethred.

The man crouched, and the sound he made sounded half sigh and half growl. "You're a liar. You're no Rashemi, and Westerners don't wander these foothills with no supplies. But you're no Thayan by your coloring. You're a mystery. A mystery I don't care to solve. You robbed my trap. Why?"

"The wolf was suffering."

"So were you."

"I only wanted to show another creature a little kindness before I lay down to die."

"Hmph. You had your first wish. I'll grant your second." A moment's silence, then, "You don't know them, then?"

"Them?"

The man just crouched there, watching. Gethred squinted and tried to make out the man's features. He could not. But the stench he emitted said enough.

"If you lie," said the man, "I'll hurt you before you die. Hurt you a long time."

"Lie?" said Gethred. "About what? I . . . don't understand."

The man took a deep breath through his nose. "You hold your tongue, but I can sense you're hiding something. I smell it. But you don't hold the stink of the *shen gusen*. And you're a man. Magic, then?"

"Magic?"

"The *shen gusen* are cunning. Powerful. You *could* be a spy."

Gethred swallowed. His throat hurt. "I don't know what you're talking about. I don't know what a *shen gusen* is. I swear."

"You swear to your gods?"

"Yes."

"Good," said the man. "Let's send you to them."

The man stood, reached behind his back, and when his hand reappeared Gethred saw the light glinting off the edge of a huge dagger. The blade was almost as wide as Gethred's palm. It looked more like a cleaver with a point, and when the man turned it, brandishing the blade, Gethred saw runes carved into the metal—sharp etchings that he could not read but which nevertheless made the back of his eyelids itch.

"Please—"

"Please what?" said the man.

"I'm no spy," said Gethred. "I swear. Please."

"But you are a robber. And it *pleases* me to give you justice."

Gethred tried to scramble away, but ropes bound his ankles, knees, and thighs, and he could do little more than wiggle like a stiff caterpillar. He only succeeded in sliding farther along the back wall of the cave.

"Nowhere to go." The man laughed and snatched the ropes around Gethred's ankles. He pulled his legs up and planted the point of his dagger in Gethred's crotch. "Think your gods will mind if you come to them less than a man?"

"Please!"

Gethred closed his eyes and stiffened his entire body. The agony in his head was forgotten as he lay there, panting and waiting for the steel to pierce.

Nothing. Gethred opened his eyes. The man stood over him, still as stone, head cocked as if listening. He didn't even seem to be breathing.

In the sudden silence Gethred heard it too. Horses approaching. Not at a gallop, but there was no mistaking the slow, careful approach of several horses.

Growling, the man dropped Gethred's legs and turned away. Blinding light filled the cave as he opened the thick matt of sticks and twigs that served as a door. He looked over his shoulder once—his eyes were still deep in the shadow of his great tangle of hair—then left the cave, slamming the rickety door behind him.

❧ ❧ ❧ ❧ ❧

In the gloom of the cave Gethred lay listening, straining to hear beyond the sound of his own panicked breathing.

The first words he heard were in one of the Tuigan dialects, calling from a near distance.

Then the voice of the massive man—"Speak a tongue a man's ears can bear to hear, not your slathering steppe speech."

The other speaker replied in hesitant Rashemi, "We ride from the horde of the Yamun Khahan. We ride from victory at the Citadel Rashemar. For five days we ride, hunting spies of the west who escaped the vengeance of the Yamun Khahan. Two days before now, we caught them. We fought. Three of our warriors died killing the spies. But one escaped. We followed his trail to a valley a few miles from here. Then we followed larger tracks. Yours, I believe, now that I see you."

"And what is this to me?" said the man. "I have no hospitality for beggars off the steppe. Go back to your Khahan."

"We do not ask for your hospitality. We seek the spy."

"Why?"

"We will take him back to the Yamun Khahan. Our lords wish to question him."

There was a long silence. Gethred thought he might have heard a horse whicker, then stomp the snow. The man spoke again. "I know of no spy. I have only one thief. And he is mine."

"This thief," said the Tuigan, still speaking a hesitant Rashemi, "our spy he might be."

"*Your* spy? You have nothing but those nags upon which you sit and the stink that follows you."

A longer silence followed. Gethred wondered how many Tuigan were out there. It couldn't be too many for one man to speak so boldly to them.

"We ask that you let us see this thief," said the Tuigan.

"No."

"The Yamun Khahan asks you to let us see this thief."

"Then let him come and ask me himself."

"We ask in his name."

"After my meal tonight I will piss your Khahan's name in the snow."

Shouts—two that seemed genuinely surprised at the man's effrontery, then many raised in anger—followed by the sounds of hoofbeats. No careful approach this time.

This was a charge. Gethred could feel the ground shaking beneath him.

He thought he heard a brief shout of surprise, fear even, then a roar so loud that dust fell from the cave ceiling. After that, the din was so deafening and so many sounds mixed together that Gethred could not separate them—the cries of men, the all-too-humanlike sound of a dying horse, bodies running, and over it all the roaring of some great animal.

The clamor slackened, then died off into a deafening silence, the only sound that of dirt and grit raining down upon Gethred. Then something else. He actually felt the approach of footsteps before he heard them.

The door was wrenched back so hard that one of the hinges tore free. Two Tuigan, both holding swords, one bloodied, slunk into the cave. Their eyes were wide with fear and their skin flushed with exertion. The one with the unbloodied sword pointed it at Gethred and said something in his native tongue. Gethred could not understand their speech, save for one word: "Cormyrean."

The Tuigan dragged Gethred from the cave. The bright light of midafternoon blazed off the snow pocketing the valley. He winced but forced his eyes to stay open to survey the scene.

The cave pierced the base of one of the hills that ringed the feet of the Sunrise Mountains. Many boulders had been strewn about through the ages, and pines blanketed the slopes. The past night's snowfall lay heavy everywhere except under the boughs, making the world a blinding white—except for the bodies.

A horse lay sprawled not fifty feet from the cave, its head hanging on by only a few strips of flesh. Blood had fountained out ten feet in every direction. Three Tuigan warriors lay nearby. Two were missing limbs, and one seemed to have run a good forty feet before death took him. His entrails were spread the final twenty feet behind him. More Tuigan—half a dozen at least, all mounted—milled around, two of them holding spare horses. Of the massive man who had held Gethred captive, there was no sign.

The two Tuigan dragged Gethred over the ground, heedless of the stones cutting him and the snow seeming to find every crevice and gap through his clothes. They threw him over a spare horse, not even bothering to cut his bonds, and in moments the entire troop was galloping east for the open steppe.

By the time they stopped, Gethred could no longer feel his face. They'd fled at full gallop for what seemed like a dozen miles at least, with Gethred tied lengthwise and facedown over the back of a horse. Had he eaten anything over the past three days, he surely would have lost every bit of it. The Tuigan horses had a smooth gait, but the land so near the mountains was rough and broken by many gulches that would fill with water come spring. Gethred was jostled, shaken, and seemingly beaten over every mile, and the ropes holding him into the saddle bit into his skin. But the Tuigan did not slow, and the wind flowing over his exposed face froze his skin to numbness. He felt sure that the only thing holding the frostbite out of his nose and ears was the thick heat given off by the horse.

Their leader called a halt as the sun slipped behind the mountains and the snow-covered steppe took on the flower-petal blue of evening. They made camp in a wide gully that ran north to south and would protect them from the wind off the mountains.

As the rest of the Tuigan made camp, one of them—Gethred recognized him as the one who had come in the cave bearing the unbloodied sword—came to the horse, loosened the ropes binding Gethred to the saddle, and threw him to the ground. He led the horse away, leaving Gethred bound in the snow. Something hard—a rock or an old root—jabbed between his shoulders, but he was too exhausted and sore to move.

The Tuigan warrior returned with another. They grabbed the ropes binding Gethred's ankles and dragged him to the nearest fire. The warriors had lit only three, and they took Gethred to the smallest.

The two warriors stood over Gethred, glowering down. Both had knives in their hands. Gethred heard footsteps crunching through the snow, then a third warrior came into view. He was taller than the other two, and two braids descended from his fur cap. His features were younger and leaner than his companions', and Gethred thought he saw the last curls of a tattoo protruding from the collar of his wool *kalat,* the large knee-length tunic worn by many of the Tuigan.

This third warrior knelt and spoke in Common. "I am Holwan, of the Khassidi. My brothers here are of the Oigur. They do not know these lands, nor your tongue. I speak for us."

Not knowing what else to say, Gethred said, "Brothers?"

One of the two Oigur said something to Holwan. It sounded harsh, and Holwan flinched. He returned his attention to Gethred and said, "Since the coming of Yamun Khahan, it is said that all Tuigan are brothers."

"Do you say this?"

Holwan's scowl deepened and he said, "How did you come to be in the house of the *shu t'met?*"

Gethred swallowed. His mouth felt dry as windswept rock. He said, "Shootemet?"

"The large man in whose house we found you."

A shudder began in Gethred's chest and spread outward till his teeth were chattering. "H-he . . . captured me. Y-yesterday, I think."

"Captured?"

"Please," said Gethred. "Water."

Gethred had fled the sack of Citadel Rashemar with four others, all Cormyreans sent by King Azoun himself, for word of the gathering Horde had reached even Cormyr. Melloren had died before they were out of sight of the citadel, a Tuigan arrow lodged in his eye. The survivors fled. But all of that Gethred left out of his tale. Likely Holwan and his companions knew or suspected much of it already. True or not, Gethred wasn't going to confess. He had little doubt he was a dead man. If not today, then certainly when this lot returned him to the Horde. But he would not betray the memory of his companions, nor their mission. He would not stand before Mielikki in the afterlife a traitor and coward.

Two days ago, this very band had caught up with Gethred and his companions. Gethred had been the only one to escape alive. He'd fled north, hugging the foothills of the Sunrise Mountains. East was only the open steppe and certain death. He'd hoped that he might be able to find some outlying Rashemi settlement and beg for shelter and supplies, perhaps even find another pass westward through the mountains. This, too, he did not tell.

Cormyr had winters, and Gethred had often traveled into the north for king and country. He knew the ways of the wild, even in the darkest days of winter. But he'd never experienced anything like the Hordelands, even though he was only skirting the edges of it. The only water to be found was snow and ice, and he knew that eating the snow would only cause him to freeze faster. He'd eaten well the night before the attack but had nothing since then. He'd been lucky to escape the sacking of the citadel with warm clothes, a good coat and cloak, his knife, and his life, but there'd been no time for supplies.

Still, the cold and thirst were worse than the hunger. Since the night their fire had led the Tuigan to them, he'd dared not light one, and so yesterday as the day drew on, despair had set in. When all your life is cold, thirst, and mile after endless mile of hard country buried in snow, when all your friends are dead, when an army lies between you and home, and you know you are being hunted, it's damned hard to hold on to hope. Although an experienced woodsman like Gethred knew he could survive many more days without food, he also knew that cold or thirst would soon claim him—that or the Tuigan still hunting him.

Holwan did not smile at that part in Gethred's tale. Gethred thought one of his countrymen would have, had he crouched where the Khassidi crouched just then, but Holwan's face was a mask, bereft of emotion.

And so Gethred decided to let the cold kill him. His grandfather had always said that the build-up to freezing to death was the worst. Death itself came painlessly, even warmly, as the body fell at first to sleep, then the endless sleep. Gethred had often wondered how even wilderness-wise men like his grandfather could have known such things. Did they call a priest to speak to their frozen friends? If so, Gethred could have thought of something better to ask the dead than, "How was it?" But Gethred's grandfather had not been the type of man to ask such questions.

Faced with the choice of allowing the cold or the Tuigan to kill him, Gethred had chosen the cold. Not so much out of fear—though that was certainly a consideration—but out of plain spite. He did not want to give his enemies the satisfaction of taking him down. Better to find a nice place to lie down and fall into Mielikki's embrace.

These had been his thoughts as he'd made his way down a valley between two long arms of the Sunrise Mountains. Trees filled the valley, and he'd figured that at the very least he could have a little shelter before he lay down to die.

He'd just made it to the bottom of the valley when he heard something—the sound of struggling beyond a stand of nearby bracken. Drawing his knife, he'd crept forward.

Pushing his way through the thick green of a holly bush, the first thing he'd seen was the body of a wolf, fur a pale gray, but the corpse had been gutted, the entrails strewn about. Cruelest of all, the jaw had been pulled open till it broke and the skin tore. Simple wanton cruelty that tightened Gethred's stomach. But the strangest thing was a large rune—all wicked angles and sharp spurs—that had been branded onto the wolf's side. In the crisp air, Gethred thought he could still smell the singed fur.

The sudden shaking of brush had turned Gethred's head, and nearby he saw another wolf, still very much alive, its throat wrapped in a snare. The line drew up to a thick branch that pulled the wolf to the height of its front legs, and with each movement the knotted loop round its neck tightened. One look, and Gethred knew it was only a matter of time before the animal's struggles would choke it to death.

Gethred's first thought was to wait for the hunter to come along so that he might beg for food and shelter, but the thought shamed him and he prayed to Mielikki to forgive him. Besides, seeing the cruel way the other wolf had been slaughtered—whether as bait or the first kill, he could not tell—and reflecting upon the rune burned there, Gethred decided he'd rather not meet this hunter. Something about the rune bothered him even more than the malice evident in the slaughter.

Gethred sheathed his knife and removed his cloak. Freeing a wolf from a snare was no easy task, even for a team of men. Moved to panic, the wolf would try to kill anyone who came near. His one hope would be to cover the animal's head long enough to cut the snare. After that, he hoped the wolf would be more concerned about getting away than ripping his throat out. If not . . . well, it spared him the choice between death by cold or death from the Tuigan warriors.

Holding his cloak spread out before him, Gethred approached, nice and slow, making no sudden movements.

The wolf's lips peeled back, revealing long teeth. The foam around the wolf's black lips was flecked with blood. Another step, and the wolf growled and lunged. But it only succeeded in pulling the noose tighter, and its growl broke off into a choked whine. Gethred took the opportunity to dive forward, throwing his thick cloak over the wolf's head and grabbing it in a tight hug. He was probably twice the wolf's weight, but still its desperate thrashing nearly threw him off. Had it not been for the tight line around its neck, Gethred knew it would have thrown him and gone for his throat.

Keeping his right arm around the wolf's neck so that the cloak enveloped its head like a hood, he made a quick grab for his knife, brought it out, and swiped at the line. The blade caught and slipped, and for one panicked moment Gethred almost dropped it. The line seemed to have been braided from some sort of tendon, and it was as strong as wire. Gethred tightened his grip and brought the blade down again.

The line snapped, and the branch holding it shot upward, shattering winter dry branches. Suddenly freed from the tension of the snare, the wolf twisted beneath Gethred and raked him with its back paws. Had it not been for his canvas coat and the leather vest beneath it, the wolf would have disemboweled him.

Gethred let go, tucked his chin to his chest, and covered his head with his arms. He knew that if the wolf came for him, it would go for the neck. If it got his throat, he could take a while to die, but the creature could snap the back of his neck with one crunch of its jaws, and he'd likely be dead before the breath left his body.

But no bite came.

Nice and slow, Gethred rolled to his side and looked up. The wolf stood at the far end of the clearing. The severed snare was still around its neck, but the tension was gone, and the line hung loose. The creature just stood there, the play of light and shadow through the boughs dappling its fur as it watched Gethred. Its gaze unnerved him. But then, wolves' eyes always had. He'd tracked, hunted, and even tamed many beasts in his life, and he'd always thought that a wolf's eyes seemed the most human.

Then something happened. At first he thought a breeze had come up, setting the boughs to swaying and moving the shadows beneath. But there was no breeze. The light around the wolf seemed to be breaking and bending, and the minuscule shadows in its fur rippled as if alive. The wolf's shape twisted and distorted, and when the shimmering of light and shadow slowed and cleared, the wolf was gone. Where the wolf had been stood a young woman, her skin and hair only a shade darker than the snow. She stood naked and barefoot in the frost, but the cold did not seem to bother her. Her gaze was fixed on Gethred, and he saw by the slight cant of her eyes and the line of her jaw that she resembled an elf more than a human.

With one hand she took the loose bit of snare from around her neck, pulled it over her head, and tossed it aside. She said something, a word or two only, in a language that Gethred had never before heard.

Dumbstruck, Gethred said, "I—"

The woman cocked her head as if listening. Though the rest of her body hadn't moved, Gethred could see every muscle was taut and tense.

"What—?" Gethred began, but the woman turned and ran away. There was a brief rustling in the brush, a soft whisper as snow fell from a dislodged branch, and she was gone.

Then Gethred heard it, too. Something approaching from the way he had come through the thick holly. Something big.

But Gethred was too tired, too hungry, and too stunned to run. He was done with running.

He was reaching for his knife, which had fallen a few paces away, when the largest man Gethred had ever seen lumbered out of the brush. The man was dressed all in skins and furs, and his beard and head of hair stood out in a great tangle. Seeing the empty snare and Gethred beside it reaching for a knife, the man let loose a bellow that rebounded off the mountainside. He descended upon Gethred.

Holwan said nothing at first, just maintained his easy crouch and watched Gethred. Finally he stood and spoke at length to his two companions in their own language. They conversed back and forth, the fire crackling beside them, then Holwan knelt again so that he faced Gethred eye to eye.

"The girl you said you saw . . . she was one of the Rashemi witches?"

"I don't know who she was."

"But you are from Cormyr."

Gethred held Holwan's gaze and said, "I'd like some more water, please."

"What is your name?" Holwan asked.

He thought a moment before deciding there was no harm in this answer. "Gethred," he said.

Holwan nodded, and something in his gaze hardened. "Gethred Cormyrean, heed my words. I am going to cut your bonds. At first light, we need you to ride. The man who had you was a *shu t'met*, a fell spirit of great power. He killed three of our company before escaping. You robbed him of his prey. Foolish. Your only hope is to stay with us. Close. If the *shu t'met* finds you, he'll kill you."

"And you won't?"

"Our khan ordered us to capture the spies from Cormyr who escaped Citadel Rashemar. Alive, he will be pleased. Dead he will be . . . less pleased. Your comrades are dead. For now, it pleases us to keep you alive."

"And your Khahan?"

"That is up to him. But I would suggest that you find a way to loosen your tongue before meeting him. In mercy, Yamun Khahan is most generous. In wrath . . . well, loosen your tongue. You are a long way from Cormyr."

That night, after being fed for the first time in days—though he was a little afraid to ask what the meat was he was eating—Gethred slept in a thick blanket beside a warm fire. He almost thanked the gods for his captivity. If the Khahan had him killed in a few days, at least tonight he was warm and fed. *For now, that is enough,* he thought as he drifted off to sleep.

How long he'd been drifting he didn't know, but when he woke it was still dark, the sky a blue darker than the sea, and every star seemed a diamond reflecting distant fire. What had woken him?

Then he heard it. Howling. Far away, he thought, but in

the winter-hardened air of the steppe, sound traveled far, and the plaintive sound seemed very clear.

Gethred sat up. The fire still crackled, but it had burned low, only a few tiny tongues of blue flame licked the dried dung the Tuigan used for fuel.

The howling came again, and the picketed horses whickered and stamped their feet. The howls seemed closer. Somewhere off to the east.

A dark shape moved on the other side of the fire. "You rest," said Holwan. "We ride hard and fast at first light."

"I hear wolves," said Gethred.

"Among my people, it is said that the sight of a wolf on a journey is a good omen."

"And what do your people say that *hearing* a wolf portends?"

"Of that, we say nothing."

Gethred lay down again. Another series of howls wafted over the camp as he settled back into his blankets and closed his eyes. Sleep took him, and in his dreams he saw the pale girl, standing between shadow and snow.

❂ ❂ ❂ ❂ ❂

Gethred's rest did not last. He woke to Holwan's boot in his ribs. Gethred started and looked up. The Khassidi stood over him, a bow in hand with an arrow nocked.

Holwan spared a quick glance down at Gethred and said, "Up. We ride."

Gethred sat up and looked around. It was still dark, but the eastern sky had begun to pale. The camp was a bustle of activity: two Tuigan packing, two others preparing the horses, and another standing on the other side of the camp with a spear.

"What's wrong?" asked Gethred.

"One of the sentries has not returned," said Holwan. "He does not respond to our call. Dayan and Kobed went to find him. They have not returned. We ride."

Gethred had little to pack. He rolled his blanket and donned his cloak—he'd slept in his coat. That done, he stood ready.

"Come," said Holwan, and he led the way to the horses.

Before they'd made it half the distance, Holwan stopped and looked east. Gethred heard it as well—another horse approaching at full gallop.

"Dayan!" one of the Tuigan called.

A rider thundered into camp, spraying snow over one of the smoldering fires. He pulled his horse to halt, but still the animal fought the reins, side-stepping, eyes rolling. The rider fell from the saddle. Two of the Oigur lunged for the animal, but they were too late. Released from the tight bit, the horse's hooves caught the snow, and it was gone.

One of the Oigur started for another horse, but he stopped after two steps. Gethred followed his gaze to the fallen rider. Blood drenched the man from the waist down, and liberal amounts of it streaked him above that. The man clutched his midsection, and Gethred saw something pale between the man's fingers. The man was using one hand to hold in his own entrails.

Holwan opened his mouth to speak, but a voice from the near distance cut him off. It spoke in Rashemi.

"Horse lovers! You attacked Vurzhad's home and robbed him of his robber! Leave the wretch by your dead fires, ride away, and the rest of you will live long enough to return to your mongrel horde!"

Gethred recognized the voice as the massive man whose trap he had robbed and who had taken him captive and threatened to geld him. He couldn't tell how far away the man was, but he sounded close.

One of the Oigur whispered something harshly in his own tongue, and the Tuigan made for the horses.

Gethred followed. He looked to Holwan and said, "I take it that you aren't accepting his offer?"

"Stay close," said Holwan.

"You don't have t—"

One of the Oigur nearing the horses jerked and flew through the air. He slid through the snow and came to a rest near Gethred's feet. A spear protruded from his chest. The light was still not strong enough to be certain, but Gethred thought he could see runes burned into the haft of the spear.

Gethred heard something whisper through the air, then another Oigur fell, a massive—and familiar—dagger lodged in his throat.

The horses screamed and pulled at their picket lines. Someone shouted, and Gethred looked to the lip of the gully. A shape stood silhouetted against the lightening eastern sky. A massive form that blotted out the fading stars.

Gethred heard the *twang* of bows—one of them Holwan's—but Vurzhad simply waved a hand, and three arrows shattered in the air before him.

The massive man stood looking down on them and said, "Now you have my spear and dagger as well as my robber. Leave them and those of you still breathing can go. This is my last mercy."

Gethred saw two of the Tuigan warriors reaching for another arrow, but beside him Holwan took his free hand and reached inside his *kalat*. Something hung on a leather braid around the Khassidi's neck, and he held it aloft. In the gloom of predawn Gethred thought he could see a twisted mass of bone, twigs, and either feather or tufts of fur.

Above them, Vurzhad snarled. "You caught me by surprise earlier," he said. "Before my own home you bested me, little shaman, because I was not ready for you. I am ready now."

Vurzhad's deep voice dropped even further, and he spoke words that even Gethred's untrained ears recognized as arcane. The man threw his head back, and his form seemed to ripple and twist and grow all at the same time. Even as the other Tuigan drew their arrows to their cheeks, Vurzhad transformed into a huge bear.

The Tuigan released their bowstrings. Their arrows struck the gigantic bear, but it did not even slow. The bear dropped to all fours and leaped into the gully, an avalanche of fur and claws that shook the ground beneath Gethred's feet.

Terrified, the Tuigans' horses reared and broke their picket lines. They jostled, bumping into one another in their haste to be away, then scattered in all directions. One of the Tuigan warriors tried to jump aside, but he was too late and the horse trampled him into the snow.

Holwan was quicker. He lunged as the horse shot past him. Throwing his bow aside, the Khassidi latched onto the horse's long mane and pulled himself into the saddle. He grabbed the reins and pulled the fighting horse around.

Another arrow stuck in the bear's side, but still it came on. It slowed long enough to swipe one of the Tuigans to the ground. Gethred winced at the sound of ripping leather and breaking bone, then a horse was thundering up on him. He looked up in time to see Holwan leaning down from the saddle, one arm reaching down.

Without thinking Gethred grabbed Holwan's arm, pulled himself onto the horse's rump behind the saddle, and they were off, leaving the camp behind and following the course of the gully.

Holwan let the horse have its lead for the first few twists of the gully, then he forced it up a shallow incline back onto the open steppe. As they crested the rise, Gethred shouted, "What about the others?"

"The *shu t'met* comes for you," said Holwan. "He will follow. Pray for us, not my brothers."

Gethred did.

Tuigan horses are not large. In fact, most people west of the Sunrise Mountains called them ponies, though Gethred knew that was a misconception. Shorter than western horses the Tuigan mounts were, but they were also heartier and more suited to life in the Hordelands. Still, hearty as they were, the beast was not suited to bearing two riders at full gallop for long, and before they had made it past two shallow hills, Gethred could hear the ragged edge to their mount's breathing.

Still, the horse's terror lent it strength, and Holwan drove the beast hard.

Gethred risked a glance back. The eastern sky was a glowing pale curtain, and the only stars still visible rode the top of the Sunrise Mountains to their right. The lightening sky shone brightly off the snowfields, and what Gethred saw lurched his stomach into a tight knot.

Their mount left a wake of flying snow behind them, but another cloud—much larger than the one they made—erupted from the snow behind them. Before it was a massive, dark shape. The bear. And it was gaining on them.

"Holwan, faster!" Gethred screamed.

The Khassidi kicked the horse's flanks, and it managed another burst of speed. Hope lit in Gethred's heart, and he looked over his shoulder—

—in time to see a claw as large as a pikeman's shield swiping at the horse's hind legs.

He opened his mouth to scream, but the horse's shriek cut him off, and both Holwan and his mount crashed beneath him. They went down in a great cloud of frost.

Gethred slid—on ice at first, but the force of his fall ground him through weeks' worth of snow, and soon his face scraped soil and rock.

Struggling to force air back into his bruised chest, Gethred forced himself to his feet. He coughed and spat, hoping to rid his mouth and throat of snow and dirt, but a fair amount of blood and at least two teeth came out with them. He scraped the snow and mud from his face and looked up.

The bear had the horse's neck in its jaws. The poor creature was kicking and screaming. The bear threw its head up and to the side, the horse's neck broke with a *snap*, and the pitiful scream stopped.

The bear dropped the carcass into the snow and turned its attention to Gethred. Its face was incapable of smiling, of course, but Gethred could see the all-too-human look of gleeful malice in its eyes.

A tottering form stepped forward from behind Gethred: Holwan. The man held a knife in one hand, but in the other he held his holy symbol high. Gethred could hear the Khassidi chanting something in his own language. Gethred couldn't understand a word of it, but he could hear the fear in the man's tone.

Fury lit the bear's eyes, and it growled low and deep, like tumbling river stones. It approached, but pain tinged the fury in its gaze. The bear did not like whatever Holwan was doing. Still it advanced, snarling. It came in slowly, each step forced and deliberate. Soon it would be in striking distance.

"Holwan—?" said Gethred, and he took a step back.

The bear lunged. One paw raked out—Gethred felt the wind of its passage—and Holwan went down.

A shudder shook the bear, and it returned its attention to Gethred. He could feel its growl shaking the earth beneath his feet.

But then something else—

Above the bear's growl, coming down from the hill behind them, was the howling of wolves. Many wolves.

The bear looked up, and Gethred followed its gaze. Wolves—dozens at least—stood at the rim of the hills.

The bear circled, looking around. More wolves. They were surrounded.

Three wolves—one of them as tall as a wolfhound but much more muscular—came down the slope at an easy run. They stopped ten paces away.

Gethred watched as the wolves' forms rippled and blurred, like mist passing over moonlight on the water. As the first light of dawn broke over the eastern horizon and hit the hollow, three elves stood before them. They were the strangest elves Gethred had ever seen. Like the woman he'd seen in the wood, they stood naked, their pale skin seemingly unbothered by the frigid air. Unlike the woman, their skin was crisscrossed with many scars, some from battles and some in such patterns that they were obviously intentional. Stylized patterns had been set into their skin with ink.

The tallest of them stood where the massive wolf had been only moments before. His snow white hair fell well past his waist, and his entire body from brow to feet was a maze of black tattoos marred by old wounds. Runes that seemed the color of wet blood in the dawn sunlight lined his arms and chest. Three deep scars marred his skin from scalp to cheek to chin, leaving empty tracks through his eyebrows. Beneath those brows his eyes stood out like frosty jewels.

He looked on the bear without fear and said, "Wear your true form before me, Vurzhad."

So transfixed was Gethred by the sight of these newcomers that he'd forgotten the bear. He wrenched his gaze away and looked back. The bear was gone and in its place stood the massive man who had trapped the wolf-girl, who had taken

Gethred captive, and who had slaughtered the Tuigan.

"Haerul," said Vurzhad. "Why are you here? This is not your hunt."

The tall elf glanced at Gethred. "This one saved my son's daughter from one of your snares, and she returned to tell me that you slaughtered one of the Vil Adanrath for bait."

Vurzhad looked at Gethred, and Gethred saw something in the man's eyes. The last thing he'd expected to see. It was fear. No, not fear. Sheer terror. Vurzhad was terrified of the naked elf, even though he was twice the elf's size at least.

"So . . . you wish me to let you have this robber?" said Vurzhad. "I let him go, and you let me go. Is that it?"

"You presume too much," said Haerul. "You snared my son's daughter. You drew the blood of my people. You think because you hide near the mountains that you are beyond my reach? You have seen your last sunrise, Vurzhad. *No one* harms my family. My son's daughter will sleep in your skin tonight."

Vurzhad screamed in defiance, and the scream became a roar—the roar of a massive bear. Gethred fell to his knees beside the still form of Holwan and covered his ears. But he could not cover the sounds of the roaring and howling.

It was over. Gethred sat in the snow, looking down upon the cold corpse of the Khassidi who had been his enemy days before and his captor for less than a day. He doubted that he would ever remember Holwan as a friend, but still . . . Gethred was sorry he was dead. Holwan had saved his life and stood beside him till the very end. Whether out of any concern for Gethred or simply to fulfill his oath to his khan . . . either way, Holwan had shown courage and upheld his honor.

Gethred sat on the other side of the hill from where Vurzhad had . . . died. *Died* did not seem the proper word for it. Gethred had only seen a little of what the wolves had done to the bear, and even that brief sight had caused every bit of his last meal to come back up.

He heard footsteps. Not the crunch of heavy feet breaking through snow, but the light tread that—damn it all—reminded him of nothing but the careful pace of a wolf. But this wolf walked on two legs.

The elf crouched in the snow on the other side of Holwan's corpse. Gethred looked up. It was not the tall one who had challenged Vurzhad. But it was one of the others who had accompanied him. The elf wore clothes now—all leather, skins, and fur, simple but expertly crafted. Where he'd come by them, Gethred did not know.

"I am called Leren," said the elf.

Gethred swallowed and said, "Gethred."

"Gethred, you saved the life of my daughter. I am in your debt. Thank you."

Gethred did not know what to say, so he simply nodded.

"Are you hurt?" asked the elf. "Your face . . ."

"Just scraped and bruised, I think."

"We will see to your injuries. You are hungry?"

Gethred's throat burned, and his mouth still tasted of bile. "No."

The elf nodded then looked down on Holwan. "This one was your friend?"

Gethred almost said, "No," but he thought better of it and said, "He died defending me."

"We will honor his body as you wish."

"Thank you." The thought of a funeral made Gethred realize he had no idea how the Khassidi dealt with their dead. Burial? A pyre? A tomb? He had no idea. Then he remembered something else. "There may be . . . others."

"Others?"

"Like this one. Tuigan. They are. . . not my friends."

The elf's brows knit together in confusion. "You mean the other horsemen?"

Gethred nodded.

"They were not your friends?"

"No."

Leren's scowl deepened.

"It is a long story," said Gethred.

"The horsemen," said the elf, "several died, as did their horses. A few survived. When last our people saw them, they were headed east into the steppe as if the Beastlord himself nipped their heels. Does this please you?"

Gethred shrugged.

"Are you well, Gethred?"

"What is going to happen to me?"

"Happen?"

"What do you plan to do with me?"

"Do?" The elf cocked his head, and a grin seemed to be trying to break out on his mouth.

"Those . . . horsemen. They were my captors."

"Those horsemen are gone," said Leren. "It is as I said: You saved my only daughter. I am in your debt. We will see to your needs, then lead you on your way. At the very least. The Vil Adanrath honor our debts. The son of the *omah nin* will do no less."

"*Omah . . . ?*"

"The chief of my people," said Leren. "The chief of chiefs. My father."

"So you are . . . a prince?"

Leren's grin finally broke. "Something like that."

"Where is"—a sudden shudder shook Gethred so hard that his teeth rattled—"the *omah nin?*"

"When last I saw him he was ordering our warriors to gather enough of Vurzhad's hide to make a blanket."

"A blanket?"

"The *omah nin* swore that my daughter would sleep in Vurzhad's skin tonight, but in the fight . . . his anger got the better of him."

"He's really making the bearskin into a blanket? I thought that was only a boast."

Leren's face became very grave. "The *omah nin* does not give empty boasts. What he says, he does."

"Gods," said Gethred. "I want to go home."

The author would like to thank Teresa Tsimmu Marino for her gracious assistance in answering his many questions on the best way to free an injured wolf from a snare. Be sure to check out her website at www.wolftown.org.

REDEMPTION

Elaine Cunningham

The Year of the Banner (1368 DR)

The night was quiet but for the distant murmur of the sea and the faint chorus of snores rising from the second floor of Kirgard Manor. What had once been fine bedchambers filled with the trappings of a noble household now held a garrison of Tethyrian soldiers, sleeping nearly shoulder to shoulder on thin pallets. Officers slept on the third floor in tiny rooms that once housed the manor's servants. These chambers offered but two luxuries: a narrow bed and privacy. A clever man with coins to spare could make do with that.

Judging from the gleam in his eyes and the smirk half hidden beneath his thick black mustache, Captain Lamphor considered himself a clever man. Who but he, his expression demanded, could have managed to have a Calishite courtesan smuggled into the garrison?

The courtesan allowed herself a hard, fleeting smile. Who indeed?

She brushed back her veil, revealing a skillfully painted face framed by a turban of autumn-colored silks. Coyly she turned away, eying him over one slowly bared shoulder as she dropped her outer robe to the floor. As she spun back toward him, translucent silk swirled around her slender brown body.

"Take that off," Lamphor said in a thick voice.

The courtesan gathered up a handful of the filmy cloth as she swayed toward him. "These silks are as soft as a maiden's sigh," she assured him in a sultry whisper. "They hide nothing, and add much."

Lamphor reached for her. As they tumbled together onto the cot, he snatched off her turban.

For a moment he lay staring down at her. His chuckle started low in his belly, shaking them both with his quiet, unpleasant mirth.

"I'm a suspicious man," he said softly, "and thought the turban might be hiding a knife. But a green elf whore?" He tugged none too gently at a pointed ear. "This I did not expect."

The elf twisted beneath him, a serpent-quick movement that surprised Lamphor and tipped him off the narrow cot. He rolled aside and managed to get to his knees before she leaped onto his back. One small hand fisted in his hair and jerked his head back, the other swept a bone knife across his throat, hard and fast and deep.

The elf known to her people as Ferret rose to her feet, still gripping the dying man's hair. She pulled his head back and captured his swiftly fading gaze with a cold, fierce glare.

"You were wrong about the whore," Ferret whispered, "but right about the knife."

She spat into his face and shoved him to the floor. Moving

quickly, she shed her filmy garment and tugged on the dark shirt and leggings she'd tucked into the lining of her robe. She draped a dark scarf over her head and put Lamphor's cap over it. The cap was too big, but it lent her dark clothes the illusion of the "uniform" worn by the new queen's ragtag army. And Tethyr's soldiers often wore head scarves to shade their faces and necks from the southern sun. If glimpsed from a distance, she could pass.

Ferret was pulling on her boots when the man's last gurgling breath faded into silence. She allowed herself a moment of quiet triumph. Captain Lamphor was the last of Bunlap's mercenaries.

For nearly four years, she had hunted humans who'd sought to enrich themselves through the slaughter of the Wealdath's great trees and the destruction of the elves who lived among them. Four years of plots and lies, four years of quietly shed blood.

Four years of forgetting what it was to be *sy Tel'Quessir*, so that her people could keep the memory alive.

Foxfire, the tribe's battle leader, would not approve of Ferret's sacrifice. Even her brother Rhothomir, who had little use for humans, would be appalled if he knew what she did when she slipped away from the forest. They all remembered what had followed the accidental death of Tethyr's King Errilam, some ninety years ago. Errilam died in the Wealdath, and many humans had refused to believe the *sy Tel'Quessir* played no part in his death. The last three kings of Tethyr had sanctioned the slaughter of the forest elves. Ferret expected no better from Zaranda, the latest would-be monarch. Even if she managed to hold her throne and proved to be an honorable ruler, her subjects were accustomed to regarding elves with suspicion and taking brutal retribution for wrongs real and imagined. Ferret well knew the price her people would pay if her private war came to light.

The narrow corridor beyond Lamphor's room was dark and silent. The elf crept down the back stairs to the second floor. Here the halls were wider, with faded Calishite carpets on the floor and a few candles burning in tarnished wall sconces. At its midpoint, the hall opened into a circular balcony, half of which overhung the grand hall—now employed as an armory—and half overlooking the back garden. The doors to the outer balcony had been left open to let in the cool night air.

Ferret slipped out into the darkness. She grimaced at the sight of two large men sprawled near the door, snoring lustily. Never before had she seen guards posted on the balcony. Most likely they'd brought their pallets out into the night breeze. She stepped over them carefully. The rhythm of their breathing did not falter.

As she started forward, one of them grabbed her ankle with a suddenness that sent her pitching forward.

Ferret managed to catch herself with her hands, but still her forehead met the tile hard enough to send white sparks shooting through her vision. Rough hands seized her and dragged her to her feet.

Her back slammed into a broad, hard chest. Long, sinewy arms held her fast. Ferret quickly abandoned the idea of struggle. Her captor was tall—her toes barely met the floor, and he had her arms clamped firmly to her sides. She sagged forward, her head lolling in defeat.

Her apparent surrender had the desired effect; the man holding her loosened his grip. Not much, Ferret noted with grudging respect, but enough for her purposes.

"Another damn deserter," the second soldier muttered as he rose to his feet. "That's three this tenday."

Ferret's captor was big, but the man facing her probably outweighed him by half. He knocked the cap from her head and thrust his face close to hers. His eyes widened in surprise.

"What have we here?" he murmured. Taking the elf's chin in one massive hand, he tipped her face up to catch the moonlight.

Ferret struck like her feral namesake, her teeth sinking deep into his neck. She wrapped her legs around his body and clung like a leach for as long as it took.

It didn't take long.

The man holding Ferret flung her away and caught his dying companion. As he staggered under the big man's weight, Ferret spat out a mouthful of blood and pulled a slim, curved knife from her boot. She couldn't reach the smaller man's throat, so she thrust her blade hilt-deep into his eye. Before he could cry out, she wrenched the hilt hard to one side and gave the knife a sharp, brutal turn, as if cranking a winch. The man was dead before he and his comrade hit the floor.

Ferret's lips firmed into a grim line as she regarded the entangled bodies. This was not good. No one was likely to seek out Lamphor before morning, but these men might be seen by any soldier who happened to pass by.

She hurried to the balcony's edge, following the heady scent of franchillia blossoms. Nimbly she climbed the rail and scrambled down the thick, flowering vines. As soon as her feet touched the ground, she started running for all she was worth.

Ferret skirted the mile-long path leading to the Trade Road, following a jagged course among the hillocks and rocky outcrops that characterized the land east of the sea cliffs. Soon she had the Trade Road in sight, and beyond it, the sweep of grasses and brush leading into the forest. She was almost to the road when a horn's blast split the still night air.

The baying of dogs answered the call.

Fear skimmed along the elf's spine, chilling her like a ghoul's caress. Tethyrian hounds were fearful creatures, long-legged and barrel-chested. Bred from mastiffs and racing dogs, they were fleet enough to run down deer, and so fierce that two of them could pull down a bugbear.

Ferret darted across the road and into the brush, twisting and turning as she ran. The belling cries of the hounds changed to excited barking, a sure sign that they'd found her trail and were closing in fast.

The trees were too small and far apart for the elf to escape into the canopy. Once she climbed, she'd be trapped—beyond the teeth of the hounds, yes, but easy prey for the men coming behind them.

Clouds parted, and moonbeams stabbed deep into a stand of young duskwood trees. Ferret caught a glimpse of reflective eyes near the upturned roots of a fallen elder tree. Only a moment passed before the lights disappeared into the tiny root-cave, but the elf's keen eyes registered a silvery coat and a long, plumy tail. It was a wolf, and a large one, perhaps preternaturally so.

She had only a moment to decide.

The crash of brush announced that the dogs were well past the Trade Road. Ferret ran directly toward the wolf's den. If she was wrong, she was dead.

At least the wolf would be quicker and kinder than the dogs.

Elaith Craulnober could not remember when he'd last felt so content, so at peace with himself and the world. Nor could he think of another place in all Faerûn he'd rather be. The garden behind Danilo Thann's Waterdeep townhouse filled him with nostalgia for Evermeet, and for once, those memories were untainted with shame or regret.

In this walled haven grew plants unique to Evermeet: tiny sapphire-hued grapes, delicate white "welcome trumpets" so sensitive to heat they would turn toward anyone entering the garden, uniquely fragrant herbs, and even some of the sky blue roses associated with the royal moon elves. How Danilo had persuaded the elves of that reclusive island kingdom to part with such treasures was beyond Elaith's powers of imagination.

But the moon elf's favorite part of the garden was the tree-lined alee set aside for sword practice. Elaith had a fine elven weapon in his hand, a skilled sparring partner, and a worthy task before him. Life was good indeed.

His opponent, a tall half-elf female, came at him in a running attack. Elaith caught her sword with his and spun their enjoined blades down and around in a circular parry, turning as he went. The move brought them face to face, swords crossed and pointing upward.

The half-elf leaned in and delivered a straight-armed jab over their crossed swords. Elaith caught her fist with his free hand.

"A bold move, Princess Arilyn, but a risky one. You could lose your dagger hand that way."

She shook him off and stepped back. "Don't call me that. But you're right about the risk. It was a stupid move. I meant to press your sword down and back while I struck—"

"But you could not," Elaith finished. "You haven't the strength."

Arilyn grimaced. "Not yet."

She came in again. Elaith parried two quick thrusts and a lunge with easy economy of motion. Their swords slid apart with a metallic hiss as Arilyn fell back.

As they circled each other, Elaith took a moment to study his opponent. As always, that meant forcing his way past the half-elf's resemblance to Amnestria, a princess of Evermeet.

His princess.

The task at hand, Elaith reminded himself, was seeing

Amnestria's daughter back to fighting form.

The half-elf's too-familiar face was set in determined lines, but it was drawn and thin, and far too pale. Pain darkened her blue eyes, and her hair, which had been as smooth and glossy as a raven's wing when they'd first crossed swords, had sprung up into an unruly mass of damp black curls.

Her mother's hair had been nearly as dark, but it was that rarest shade of moon elf blue—the color of fine sapphires, the midnight blue of a star-filled night. . .

Elaith shook off the image.

"You move as fast as ever," he told Arilyn, "but your attacks lack power and your grip is unreliable."

To demonstrate, he feinted low. The half-elf easily parried. Before she could disengage, Elaith stomped on her sword—an unconventional move that caught her by surprise and tore the hilt from her grasp.

Her practice sword had not yet hit the ground when Arilyn pivoted on her back foot and delivered a kick that landed several strategic inches south of Elaith's sword belt.

The moon elf staggered back, resisting the temptation to fall to the ground and curl up in agony.

Maybe, he conceded, his attack had not been quite so unexpected as he'd thought.

"Well countered," he managed to say, "but street fighting tactics are unworthy of a princess."

"Next time I see a princess, I'll be sure to pass that along," Arilyn assured him. "It'd be a good thing for her to know. If a tactic is 'unworthy,' it's probably also unexpected."

"Indeed."

The half-elf hooked the toe of one boot under her fallen sword, flicked it up, and caught it by the hilt. When Elaith moved into guard position, Arilyn shook her head and slid her practice sword into the sheath that had, until recently, held her moonblade.

"Thanks for the match."

Elaith's silver brows rose. "We've only been sparring since dawn. No more than two bells have rung since we began."

"You just don't want to quit when you're behind," she teased him.

The moon elf shook his head. "Princess, if you hope to wield your ancestral blade again, you must rebuild your strength."

The smile fell from Arilyn's face. "If you call me 'princess' one more time," she said softly, "I won't need the thrice-damned moonblade. I'll just tear out your liver with my fingernails."

She spun away and shouldered her way past the tall, fair-haired man just entering the practice grounds. Danilo Thann, one of the few humans Elaith counted among his friends, watched the half-elf stalk toward the garden's back gate.

"Where is she going?"

"To have her nails tended, I expect," Elaith said dryly.

Danilo blinked. After a moment he shook himself free of that puzzling vision. "We will have visitors very shortly. I received a sending—an amazing bit of magic, by the way—requesting that permission to enter this garden be granted to Shalana O Rhothomir, sister to the Wealdath's elf chieftain, Ganemede, a lythari."

"A lythari," Elaith echoed incredulously. He'd only half believed the race of wolf-natured, shapeshifting elves existed. "In Waterdeep?"

"Oh, it wouldn't be the first time. Ganemede and Arilyn are old friends. He can open a magical gate nearly anywhere, using her moonblade as a focus."

Elaith's gaze shifted to the weapons rack, where hung an ancient elven long sword. Eight runes marked its shining length, and the blue-white moonstone in the hilt fairly glowed with magic. Just a tenday past, it had turned on its half-elf wielder rather than shed the blood of a moon elf who'd thought himself long past redemption.

"I wonder if the princess will ever wield it again," he said softly.

A faint smile touched the corners of Danilo's lips. "You're lucky she didn't hear you call her that. As to the other thing, Arilyn knew what might happen when she challenged you. She figured taking the sword's backlash was the quickest, surest way to convince the forest elves to fight under your command and alongside your men."

"A form of persuasion that nearly cost her her life."

"Arilyn thought the cause worthy, and she thought you were worth the risk. Considering the response of her moonblade, it appears she was right about you."

"Imagine my surprise," the elf murmured, "especially considering my own moonblade was decidedly less optimistic."

The air near the weapons rack changed, taking on a subtle shimmering that might easily be mistaken for rising heat. If not for an elf's innate knack for perceiving magical gates, Elaith might not have seen it at all. Danilo was less prepared, and his eyes widened when two elves suddenly appeared in the garden.

Elaith recognized the female as one of the forest elves who'd recently come to Waterdeep and fought under his command. Ferret, she called herself. The male resembled no forest elf Elaith had ever seen. In fact, his coloring was similar to Elaith's: silvery hair, amber eyes. Like Elaith, he was tall for an elf, long of leg and broad through the shoulders. Had Elaith not known otherwise, he might have mistaken the lythari for kin.

"There is trouble in the Wealdath," the female said without preamble.

Danilo's shoulders rose and fell in a sigh of resignation. "I'll get Arilyn."

"Not the half-elf, not this time," Ferret said. She nodded toward Elaith. "It's him we need."

The sun hung low over the city's western walls when Elaith returned to Danilo's elven garden. Gathering supplies and information, making the necessary contacts, readying spells—such things took time.

A shimmering halo rose around the lythari. Ferret impatiently seized Elaith's hand and pulled him toward it. The three elves stepped through into the deep green shade of an ancient forest.

One step—the journey was that quick, that smooth and simple.

Elaith inclined his head to Ganemede in a gesture of respect. "I have traveled magic's silver paths many times, but never so skillfully managed."

The lythari nodded acknowledgment. "Meet me here at nightfall."

"It's a brisk walk to Suldanessellar, but we can be back before dusk," Ferret said. Without waiting for a reply, she circled the trunk of an enormous oak and started down a faint path.

Elaith soon found that keeping pace with a forest elf was no easy task. Before long Ferret veered off the path and headed for a thicket of thorny bushes—formidable thorns, Elaith noted, each as long as his thumb.

"Stay close behind me," Ferret instructed. She paused, cocked her head, and considered. "Better yet, keep a hand on my shoulder. The thorns might not recognize you otherwise."

There was magic here, subtle but powerful, quite different from anything Elaith knew. Curious, he did as Ferret bid.

The branches parted to let them pass. It seemed to the moon elf that the guardian thicket begrudged his presence, for the branches slid back into place behind him with an ominous hiss, close enough for the thorns to scrape against his travel leathers, but not quite hard enough to pierce them.

Finally they stepped out of the thicket into a tree-ringed forest glade. Stones had been piled into a shoulder-high cairn in the center of the glade and crowned with a platform of rune-carved wood. On it rested a low-sided casket topped with a rounded glass lid. Within lay an elf female of middle years, clad in armor of a style not seen in five centuries. Still as the grave she lay, untouched by death's corruption. Magic lingered in the air like incense, and so did something rarer and more wondrous: a sense of legend. Elaith went to one knee to honor a story he had not yet heard.

"Zoastria's tomb," Ferret said.

Memory stirred. Elaith knew that name. His heart quickened as he rose and stepped closer. The entombed elf's face seemed familiar to him, and her long, braided hair held the distinctive black-sapphire shade Elaith thought of as Moonflower blue. More than fifty years ago, an elf who looked very like that sleeping warrior had come to Evermeet. Thasitalia Moonflower had been kin to the royal family of Evermeet, and she named Princess Amnestria as her blade heir. Elaith had been captain of the king's guard then, betrothed to Amnestria and full of hope for the future they planned to share.

"Zoastria Moonflower, a friend to the forest folk," Ferret said, confirming Elaith's suspicions. "She was slain in battle some four years past."

Elaith whirled toward her. Anger, sudden and inexplicable, filled his heart and blazed from his amber eyes.

"That's impossible. Zoastria was the fourth moonfighter in her line. She lived and died long before you were born."

"The first time, yes," Ferret agreed, unperturbed by the moon elf's ire. "But every moonfighter adds another magic to the sword, is that not true? The elf who passed the sword to Zoastria ensured that as long as her moonblade's magic endures, a hero will return when the need is great. Arilyn is of this line. When she placed the sword in her ancestor's uncorrupted hands, Zoastria became a living elf."

Deathless sleep . . . the first of her line . . . a hero will return . . . her line . . . will return . . . a living elf.

Ferret's words tumbled through Elaith's mind, staggering in their implications.

Amnestria was the seventh in Zoastria's line.

It was possible. Somehow he'd always known it. When he'd caught his first glimpse of Arilyn nearly six years ago, for a moment he'd thought her Amnestria reborn. Such things were not unknown in Faerûn, even among the elves. But except for that one scalding moment of hope, Elaith had never really expected Amnestria to return.

But what if she could? What if she did?

"This place troubles you?" asked Ferret.

"Perhaps we should reconsider the plan."

That was not what Elaith had expected to say, but the words seemed right to him. He'd been so busy arranging the usual web of primary, secondary, and contingency plans that he'd neglected to weigh these arrangements on any sort of moral scale. In all candor, he was not in the habit of doing so. But if he'd been spared by Amnestria's moonblade to play some part in her return, he'd damn well better get into the habit!

The forest elf's face fell slack with astonishment. "Abandon the plan? Whatever for? It is a good plan."

"But not an honorable one."

"And for that, all gods be thanked," she said tartly. "Any honorable course would bring reprisals against my people."

She brushed a lock of hair off her forehead with a quick, impatient hand. "Why these doubts? You are a fine battle leader. Foxfire has been singing your praises since he returned from Waterdeep."

"Foxfire is a competent battle leader himself—more than competent, and he knows this forest far better than I do. Perhaps he could devise—"

"No." Ferret cut him off abruptly and decisively. "Foxfire is too pure of heart to do what must be done. Why else would I have come for you?"

Her words stung Elaith more than they should have. "These are strange words to speak over Zoastria's tomb."

"If I'd known how you would respond to this place, I would have spoken them elsewhere."

"Then why did you bring me here?"

"It is traditional for the *sy Tel'Quessir* to honor ancestors before a battle." Ferret pointed to the Craulnober moonblade on Elaith's hip, sheathed and peacebound. Bringing it had been an act of impulse. The symbolism was important to Elaith, even though he could not wield the sword.

"I do not know the places sacred to your line," Ferret went on, "so I brought you here to honor another moonfighter's legacy."

Something in Elaith's face made her falter. "Did I do wrong?"

"No," he said in a dull, soft tone. "You did not do wrong." *You did not,* he repeated silently, *but it appears that I must.* And just like that, his decision was made.

Some men called Elaith impulsive, though usually not to his face. That wasn't quite true. Elaith believed in destiny.

There was a reason the Craulnober moonblade rejected him, a reason Amnestria's moonblade had spared his ill-spent life. There was a reason he was thrice-pledged to the Moonflower family: raised by the elf queen, trained by her warrior king and made captain of the royal guard, betrothed to the youngest princess. And the reason for a life entwined with the royal family seemed suddenly, bleakly evident.

He could do things they could not.

Amnestria had been pledged to the service of the forest elves. It was strangely fitting that Elaith take her legacy upon himself. There was a great need in the Wealdath, but this time, the forest people did not need a hero.

They needed *him*.

Thanks to Ganemede's magic, five elves stepped into the shadows of the Mytharan Woods, a place that was old and strange even by the standards of this ancient forest. The small band included the lythari and two recruits Ferret had brought back from the elven settlement Suldanessellar. One was Kivessin Sultaasar, an elf of the Suldusk tribe. The other, to Elaith's astonishment, was Captain Uevareth Korianthil, a moon elf from Evermeet. Apparently Queen Amlaruil had sent representatives to the Wealdath four years ago, after the forest elves fought off an incursion of human mercenaries. She'd made it known to Tethyr's humans that another such attempt against her forest kin would not go unanswered.

That raised the stakes considerably.

Elaith turned to Captain Korianthil. "Are you certain you wish to be a part of this?"

The moon elf nodded, his face grim. "The Lady Shalana is right; the humans who followed her into the forest cannot carry tales of an elven assassin. There would be reprisals, and Queen Amlaruil would honor her promise. I will not see Evermeet dragged into Tethyr's so-called Reclamation War.

"And I have other reasons," Korianthil continued softly.

"You were my first commanding officer. It is an honor to serve under your command once again."

Elaith's brows rose. "Even in such a task?"

"Even so."

"We all have our reasons for killing humans," growled the Suldusk elf. "Should we hire a bard to set them all to music, or should we just get on with it?"

Elaith found himself liking the gruff warrior. "You're the expert on the Wealdath's ogres," he told Kivessin. "We'll follow you."

The elf headed off into a deep stand of ferns. Soon they heard the murmur of running water. A small creek wound its way through the forest floor. As they followed it north, the ground became rockier and the creek deeper and swifter. They walked without talking, keeping close watch on the forest around them.

Elaith could smell the ogre camp long before it came into sight. The humid forest air held the scent of campfire, seared meat, and the sharp, musky odor of the creatures themselves.

He raised one hand to indicate a halt. He took an amulet from his bag and looped it around his wrist. The world shifted weirdly, and suddenly he was looking down at his companions from a great height. The four elves staring up at him wore identical expressions of astonishment and revulsion.

"Green, I take it, is not a good color for me?" He spoke lightly, but his voice came out as a deep-throated growl.

"I'm serving under an ogre," Captain Korianthil muttered. "This just keeps getting better and better."

Elaith sent him a tusk-filled grin and turned toward the camp.

Three ogres left to guard the camp; the others were out hunting. The guards were busily arguing over a game of dice, so Elaith had no problem creeping into the younglings' den.

There were a half-score of the creatures, some huddled together like a pile of hideous puppies, others scattered around the small cave. A scrawny runt off to the side looked to be about Ferret's height and size. Elaith quickly cast a charm spell over the young ogre. The creature twitched as if trying to brush off the magical disturbance, but after a moment it rose, yawning. Elaith beckoned for the ogre to follow. The creature absently lifted its loincloth—*his* loincloth, Elaith could not help but note—and scratched himself rudely. He yawned again before following Elaith out of the cave.

The ogre guards glanced up and went back to their game. So far, so good, Elaith noted with relief. He'd feared such spells might not function well so close to the twisted remnants of an ancient elven mythal.

Suddenly the young ogre's heavy-lidded eyes widened. He looked around frantically, like a sleepwalker who'd suddenly been jarred from sleep.

Cursing under his breath, Elaith thrust a wadded gag into the ogre's mouth. He swept the creature up, slung him over his shoulder, and ran.

When they were a reasonable distance from the camp, Elaith tossed the young ogre to the ground and yanked the amulet from his wrist. The return to his own size and shape was so abrupt that for a moment he felt as if he were falling.

An almost comical look of astonishment flooded the young ogre's face. His cowed submission to an older member of the tribe gave way to rage. He leaped at Elaith, his hands reaching for the elf's throat.

Ferret dropped from the tree above, taking the creature down in mid-leap. He hissed at her like a cat and raked the talons of one hand across her face. She raised one fist to retaliate; Kivessin seized it and jerked her away.

The lythari and the moon elf emerged from the bushes.

Each of the four elves with Elaith took hold of one of the ogre's wrists or ankles, and together they bore the struggling, cursing creature to the prepared site.

Fortunately, the elves did not have far to go. A few hundred paces took them to a place where the forest bordered a nightmare realm.

Skeletal night birds winged silently though swirling mists, kept aloft by some fell magic. The trees were twisted and charred as if by fire, but their branches *moved*, twining sinuously against the cloud-tossed moon. Black roots groped their way along the forest floor as if seeking prey. The only apparently living thing was the abundance of dark ivy that threaded its way among the roots. The vines were studded with purple and red flowers—lovely, but for the scent of rotting flesh that rose from them.

The lythari shook his head sadly. "The price for such magic is too high."

Elaith could not disagree. This was the remains of a corrupted mythal, a powerful magic cast in a long-vanished elven city. As a result of that twisted magic, every creature that died within the magic-blasted landscape rose as undead. No elves could enter it without becoming deathly ill—or without alerting Mallin, the undead wizard who had ruled over the grim realm for more than six centuries.

"Drop the beast here," Elaith directed, pointing to the moss under a large duskwood tree.

Kivessin and Ferret quickly bound the struggling creature, then tied him to a rope dangling from a high branch. The other three elves hoisted the ogre whelp off the ground and tied off the rope. Kivessin yanked away the ogre's gag pulled him back toward the tree, and let him swing toward the mythal-cursed ground.

It took a couple more pushes to get the ogre swinging high enough. When Elaith judged the distance to be right, he cut the rope. The ogre whelp flew free, howling in rage and fear. He landed hard and rolled to the very edge of the poisoned forest. The creature began to shriek in earnest, writhing as if in terrible pain.

The elves took to the trees. In moments the three adult ogres crashed into the clearing. The whelp's cries had subsided. His struggles were weaker, and his small, red eyes were glassy and staring.

"Stupid elves," one of them sneered. "Got too close. Got sick. Probably off puking up their guts."

The other two did not appear convinced. They turned this way and that, peering into the forest, weapons raised and ready.

"We watch, you untie Gloove," one of them growled.

The three advanced toward the young ogre, two of them backing slowly toward the blackened realm, their small eyes sweeping the forest.

Suddenly the foremost ogre stopped. Its green face twisted into a puzzled scowl. For no obvious reason, the creature stumbled and fell. There was a sharp cracking sound. Blood poured from a wound on the ogre's twisted shin, and a jagged edge of bone thrust out of the wound.

"Run!" it shrieked.

Before the guards could react, the thud of crossbows resounded through the forest. Four large arrows streaked down from the nearby trees, trailing thin ropes. Each arrow sank deep into an ogre's chest and punched through the other side. The ogres fell, twitching.

The elves slid down from the trees. Elaith made a quick, sharp gesture with one hand. The illusion he'd painstakingly cast disappeared, and the boundary between healthy forest and cursed land shifted a dozen paces closer to the elves. Black roots and carrion flowers appeared in the place where the ogres had fallen, replacing the illusion of green moss and living plants. The ogres, accepting Elaith's illusion as real, had walked right into the cursed ground.

"Tie off the ropes, quickly," Elaith snapped. "They must be pulled out as soon as they're dead. An undead ogre under Mallin's control is no use to us."

The four elves seized the ropes attached to the impaling arrows and tied each one to the tall, slender saplings they'd prepared earlier. Four of these trees had been carefully bent until their uppermost branches brushed the ground, then tied in place.

"I never thought the day would come when I'd use a crossbow," the moon elf captain murmured.

"Did you ever suppose," Elaith said coolly, "the day might come when you'd have to shoot an arrow that size with enough force to send it all the way through an ogre's chest?"

"A longbow arrow, well shot, would have killed them just as surely," the Suldusk elf put in.

"True," Elaith said. He took hold of one of the taut ropes and gave it a brutal tug. When the arrowhead slammed back into the dying ogre's ribcage, the point sprung apart into four hooks.

"Civilized arrows would have pulled free when we yank the ogres out," Elaith said. "These will not."

The elves waited in grim silence until the ogres' death throes ended. When Elaith gave the signal, the elves cut the lines and the young trees strung upright, jerking the ogres well away from the mythal-cursed ground.

The creatures stirred and rose, their red eyes dull and staring.

Captain Korianthil stared at the undead ogres with open revulsion. "I never thought to find myself in league with such creatures."

"If they weren't dead, they'd probably feel much the same about us," Elaith said shortly. He took several amulets from his bag and handed them to the moon elf. "Put these on them, and you wear the blue one. That will allow you to command their movements."

The moon elf stared at the amulets for a moment, then raised troubled eyes to Elaith's face. "This is. . . necromancy."

"Do you know a better way to command the undead?"

A short, rueful laugh burst from Korianthil. "In all candor, Lord Craulnober, I have never given the matter much thought."

Elaith responded with a thin smile. "That's why I'm here."

Koranthil lifted the amulets. "Will the magic hold? Even though the charm spell you cast on the ogre faltered?"

"They will hold. The necromancer who fashioned them takes pride in his evil deeds—and charges accordingly," Elaith said with a wry smile.

"I see. And that would also explain how you maintained an illusion on the very borders of Myth Rhynn?"

Elaith's smile dropped away. "You do not wish to know the origin of that spell. Trust me on this."

"Forgive me," Korianthil said hesitantly, "but if you are willing to learn and use such magic, why did you not simply slay the ogres and animate them yourself?"

"I would have, if I'd been able to cast that spell," Elaith said bluntly. "I've never learned it. For some strange reason, I'd thought such magic beneath me."

"Of course," the moon elf said immediately. "Forgive me for asking."

"Tell me, captain, do you always ask so many questions of your commanding officer?"

"If you'll permit me one more, may I ask why you don't command the ogres yourself?"

In response, Elaith held up the amulet of ogre-shape. "I'll be busy."

❂ ❂ ❂ ❂ ❂

The battle that followed was hardly worthy of the name. It was a slaughter, plain and simple.

Before it began, Elaith selected the sole survivor: the youngest soldier among the party sent into the forest to track the unknown assassin.

Wearing the illusion of an ogre warrior, Elaith crept into the camp and seized the young soldier's ears. The lad awoke with a start to find himself staring into red eyes and wicked, curving tusks. Before he could cry out, Elaith jerked his head up and slammed it back into the ground. The soldier's eyes rolled back and his body went limp.

Elaith placed huge, talon-tipped fingers against the lad's throat. Yes, the soft leap of blood continued, faint but steady. The lad would awaken to a nightmare, and carry word back to his garrison. He would survive the solitary trek through the forest; the forest elves would see to that.

The disguised moon elf rose and joined the undead ogres in the slaughter.

When it was over, Elaith took the soldiers' weapons—many of them as yet unsheathed—and hacked the undead ogres into final death. When the young soldier awakened, he would believe that his comrades had fought bravely and well.

Elaith reclaimed his amulets from the ogres, and as a final touch, placed Captain Lamphor's cap on the ogre whelp's disembodied head.

"An ogre assassin," murmured Kivessin. "Do you think the humans will believe such a creature infiltrated their garrison?"

"I plan to make sure they do." Elaith raised his eyes to Ferret. "One thing remains."

The forest elf nodded and turned to her comrades. "You go ahead. This is nothing any of you need to see."

The elves regarded each other in silence. Finally Captain Korianthil touched his fist to his forehead and then his heart, a gesture of respect for an elflord. Then the three guardians of the forest elves—Evermeet captain, Suldusk warrior, and lythari—disappeared into a shimmering circle.

"There are spells that will bind the spirits of the men you killed so that they cannot identify their killer," Elaith said. "It's much easier to cast these spells on the corpses. I know a spell that will mask the killer, but it is not pleasant."

Ferret shrugged impatiently. "Get on with it."

"I'll need blood."

The forest elf didn't even glance at the gore-drenched campsite. She held out her forearm, ready for his knife.

"This is necromancy," Elaith warned her.

"Yes."

"Some would consider such magic evil."

Ferret's smile was both sad and terrible. "I think we're both past such considerations. Do what needs to be done."

And because it was his destiny, Elaith did precisely that.

CHANGING TIDES

– **Mel Odom**

Flamerule, the Year of the Gauntlet (1369 DR)

1

I still say ye're a fool to go out there in this storm, Rytagir! Better to stay on the ship where ye'll be safe whilst this maelstrom descends upon us! That shipwreck's been there fer hundreds of years! It'll be there awhile longer yet!"

"Duly noted, Captain," Rytagir Volak replied as he gazed out at the heaving swells of the Sea of Fallen Stars. There was no denying the anticipation that filled him. It had been nearly a year getting that far. "If that treasure ship would see fit to come up off the bottom of the sea and sail into port by itself, why, our lives would be even better, wouldn't they?"

Captain Zahban scowled. "Ye don't even know if *Peilam's Nose* is down there," he squalled back through the gale.

Rytagir held a hand up in the wind and spattering

rain and said, "I believe you're right. Better we should wait for a more hospitable day."

The ship's captain was a broad, burly man in a modest shirt and coat. His pants and boots had seen better days. A heavy-bladed cutlass hung at his side. A queue held back his gray-streaked black hair. More gray stained his curly black beard. The years hadn't been overly kind to Zahban, but he had all his limbs. For a man who had sailed the Sea of Fallen Stars all his life and always against those that flew a pirate's flag, it was a considerable accomplishment.

"Now I wasn't sayin' that." Zahban knotted his fingers in his beard. His broad hat shadowed his craggy face and the dark storm clouds overhead further obscured his features. "Them books what ye found this location in, there's other scholars what could cipher that out, ain't there?"

"Any man that can read and cares enough to look, Captain," Rytagir replied. He enjoyed toying with the captain's conflicted feelings of greed and worry for his charge.

The ship's crew, a loose but hungry-eyed gathering of seadogs that had faced years of the sea's cruel affections without any of her fortunes, listened anxiously.

"Well," Zahban said, "we can't be dilly-dallyin' about this treasure hunt none neither." He paused, then finished, "If there be treasure to be had down there at all."

Rytagir grinned at the man. "There's only one way to find out." He peered over the ship's side. *Azure Kestrel*, a cog named much prettier than she was and so called because of her light blue sails, strained at her leash. So far the anchor held on the sea bottom.

According to the ship's quartermaster, the bottom was a hundred and ten feet below. *Peilam's Nose* sat somewhere in the general vicinity.

If you figured those charts and currents right, Rytagir reminded himself. Sea currents, especially two hundred and seventy-eight years of them, were hard to figure.

Rytagir was of medium height and wide-shouldered, arms and legs sleek with muscle and bronzed from years of swimming, diving, and salvaging in rivers and oceans. Good leather armor covered his body. He carried a long sword at his hip and a pair of knives in his knee-high boots. He wore his yellow-gold hair cut so short it wasn't long enough to lie down.

His eyes were the gray-green of the sea. A past lover had told him that his eyes were so much that color that it seemed as though part of the sea had seeped into him and claimed him forever.

Rytagir supposed that could have been true. Lovers never stayed long. They preferred men who could at least be distracted from their other passions more than a few hours or a day. Rytagir's whole life had been about his studies, and about the things he'd found. He'd learned everything his father, a ranger in Cormyr, could teach him of the wild. But it was the seas of Faerûn—not the forests, to his father's eternal dismay—that called out to him.

Quickly, Rytagir spoke a few arcane words, then drew a symbol in the air. Power quivered through him. He vaulted over the cog's side toward the sea breaking against the wooden hull.

The crew rushed over to peer down at him.

Instead of crashing through the waves, Rytagir stopped only a mere inch or two above the water, held there by the magic he had worked. He flexed his knees to absorb the shock and remained standing, though it was a near thing because the sea was so rough. The water-walking spell kept him on top of the ocean, but the waves still provided an uneven surface.

With a flourish—and he freely admitted that he often adored attention far too much than was good for him, which his father had never been happy about because he'd always been a modest man himself—Rytagir turned and bowed to the ship's crew.

They crouched along the starboard side of the ship in fearful dread. The storm had unnerved many of them. Normally the storms were over by summer, and any squall that blew up after that tended to be disastrous. There was already talk of this being a cursed wind. Bad waters and bad winds had taken ships to the bottom over the years.

Rytagir walked precisely one hundred thirty-two strides north, northeast of *Azure Kestrel*'s position. He'd gotten the cog's precise position from the stars the night before. The sea harbored her secrets well, and the seeker who went there had to know where to look to find them. Then he ended the spell and sank like a stone beneath the waves.

2

The cold sea leached the warmth from Rytagir's body as he sank. He felt the pressure growing as he slid unimpeded toward the bottom a hundred and ten feet below. Fish swam around him, but there were no sharks. Small fish swimming freely in the area was a good sign because it meant there were no large predators around.

He reached under his leather breastplate and took out the small silk bag that rested on a necklace. A pearl, a simple white ball no larger than the nail of his little finger, mounted on a plain white gold chain rested inside. He took the necklace out and slipped it over his head.

When the necklace was in place, the pearl gleamed with spun moonlight for just a moment, and Rytagir opened his mouth and breathed. Instead of the sea, he breathed in air magically extracted from the sea. He no longer dropped toward the ocean bottom either. He hung suspended, free to make any move he wanted to.

The pearl was a gift from a sirine he'd met while exploring the Dragon Reach near Ravens Bluff in Impiltur. Most sirines tended to be destructive and often led sailors onto rocks and reefs while teasing them with their nearly naked, beautiful bodies and heartbreaking songs.

This one had been different. She'd been scared and helpless against the slavers that had taken her captive. Then, as now, Rytagir had been searching for a legendary ship taken to the bottom.

That time, he hadn't found his prize. However, he had managed to rescue the sirine from her captors. As a gift for rescuing his daughter, her father had given Rytagir the enchanted pearl to aid in his diving.

For a time, he'd dwelt among them. In the end, as always, he'd had to leave to find the next mystery, the next nearly forgotten thing. It was his life and he was sure it would be until the day he died.

A horrible death, probably, he reminded himself as he hung weightless in the sea.

Even those bad thoughts didn't weigh him down. The pearl's magic also allowed him to move however he wished in the water with no regard to depth or natural buoyancy. Without the spell, his leather armor would have dragged him to his doom if he couldn't shed himself of it in time, though the armor was enchanted as well. The armor's enchantment protected the leather from the damaging effects of seawater and also allowed him to free it from his body at a word—which was something he was loath to do because it was a very expensive and hard to replace garment.

He fanned his arms and legs as though swimming. When he'd pointed himself downward, he swam down into the darkness of the sea.

Peilam's Nose lay mired in sand on the ocean bottom on her port side. She was a large cargo ship that had sailed from the Old Empires to the Dragonmere to trade with Cormyr. Her home port had been Skuld, along the Mulhorandi coastline.

According to the texts Rytagir had read—a ship's log, a merchant's journal, and two reports dictated to the Skuld merchantmen's guild because some of the cargo aboard the lost ship had belonged to the king and an accounting had had to be made—*Peilam's Nose* had been attacked by a sahuagin raiding party.

The ship's mage and a contingent of guardsmen aboard hadn't stood a chance against the sea devils. The sailors were slain to a man, and the ship's mage gutted and flown from a cross timber of the main mast. Most of the crew had been eaten by the sahuagin.

After that, *Peilam's Nose* had been scuttled and sent to the bottom more than eight hundred miles away. It had taken Rytagir almost a month to plot her probable course once she'd gone under.

One of the old bardic songs that had fallen out of favor in the Inner Sea also contained a germ of truth about the attack. Rytagir's interest had first been caught by that song while in the Tattered Sails Tavern in Milvarune in Thesk almost a year earlier. He had been there researching some of the villages that had been left in ruins by the Tuigan Horde.

From that germ of the tale carried in the bard's sad, lilting voice, Rytagir had spent a tenday researching *Peilam's Nose*. And what her cargo manifest might have included.

When an explorer—which was how Rytagir thought of himself—didn't have a vessel and he needed one to recover lost artifacts from a shipwreck, he learned to find the details that would encourage others to invest in his knowledge and experience. In this case, he'd put together a probable manifest of the ship's cargo to tempt Captain Zahban into becoming his partner and lending his ship to the effort.

❂ ❂ ❂ ❂ ❂

Rytagir stopped his descent only a few feet above the ship-wreck. Despite the magic woven into the pearl, his vision wasn't able to penetrate much of the gloom at that depth.

He swam slowly and surveyed *Peilam's Nose* from the broken keel to the distinctive prow that named her. She'd been christened for the man who'd built her, a dwarf woodworker who'd forsaken the forge for a lathe in a lumberyard.

Even half-buried, the prow showed the fierce profile of a dwarf. His blunt nose projected well ahead of the rest of his features. The eye that Rytagir could see looked undaunted. Peilam's beard showed in the scalloped trim that flowed back over the prow until it gradually faded into the hull on both sides.

The ship was unmistakably the one Rytagir had come for. He reached into the waterproof shoulder pack he'd brought with him and extracted the journal he'd dedicated to compiling all information about *Peilam's Nose*.

Protected by the pearl's magic, Rytagir hung cross-legged in the sea and quickly sketched the ship as it lay on the sea bottom. The salvage was going to be easier than he'd expected.

More times than not, the hull—especially on a scuttled vessel—shattered and emptied her guts across the sea floor. The trail of lost cargo could last for miles.

So immersed was Rytagir in the task of recording the image for the papers or book he would write on the ship that he didn't notice he was no longer alone on the ocean floor. At least, not until he noticed the shadow that slid over his.

3

Almost casually, Rytagir closed the journal and slipped it back into the shoulder bag. His hand closed over the plain hilt of his long sword and yanked the blade free. He spun around to face the observer and raised the sword between them.

With the shadow being human-shaped, his first impression was that he was being spied upon by a sahuagin. But he knew the chances of that were small.

Sahuagin had brought an end to *Peilam's Nose*, but the murderous sea devils no longer freely traveled the currents of the Inner Sea. The aquatic predators had been sealed within the Alamber Sea behind the massive Sharksbane Wall. The defensive structure was a hundred miles long, sixty feet tall, and a hundred feet thick. Legend had it that sea elves and other creatures manned the wall to prevent the sahuagin from invading the Sea of Fallen Stars.

But his observer wasn't a sahuagin. It was a sea elf. A beautiful sea elf. Her clothing consisted of clam shells that covered her pert breasts, a triangle of silverweave armor that barely concealed her modesty, and silverweave legging armor. Her pale blue skin had white patches that were natural camouflage many sea creatures shared.

As with other denizens of the deep, she was darker on her back—her dorsal side—than her front. The bifurcation of colors was the sea's primary gift to her creatures. Dark on top, they couldn't be seen from above. Light on bottom, they were hard to see against the brightness of the surface.

She was a rare beauty, even among the *alu Tel'Quessir*, as the sea elves called themselves, because she possessed flashing silver eyes and a long, vibrant mane of red hair that swirled down to her generous hips. Neither of those colors occurred very often among the *alu Tel'Quessir*.

Her gaze held both displeasure and defiance. One hand wrapped the haft of a trident made of chipped obsidian. A silverweave net rode on her left hip, and she had an obsidian knife strapped to her lower right leg.

She wasn't alone. A dozen other sea elves floated behind her, males and females. All of them were armed. Half a dozen dolphins circled the area. The dolphins were companions to the rangers among the sea elves.

Not exactly a welcoming committee, Rytagir thought as he looked over the sea elves.

"You are human," the sea elf woman accused.

Rytagir sheathed his long sword. "I am. My name is Rytagir."

One of the younger male sea elves spoke to the woman in their native tongue. Rytagir spoke that language as well, but didn't see the need to reveal that as yet.

"*I have heard of him, lady,*" the young warrior said. His green eyes never left Rytagir. "*He's a seeker among the humans. They say he means no harm to undersea folk.*"

Rytagir was aware of his good reputation. He'd worked to have it and to keep it.

"What are you doing here?" the sea elf woman demanded.

"I'm a scholar, lady." Rytagir pointed at the shipwreck. "I've come to document the final days of that vessel."

She arched an eyebrow. "It was attacked by sahuagin and sunk. Surely your people knew that."

"We did. But we didn't know where the cargo had gone."

"If you surface dwellers were more careful with your things," one of the male elves snarled, "then you wouldn't be fouling our waters with your unwanted refuse and things you have lost."

"Not all the things that have been lost have been unwanted," Rytagir pointed out. But it was true that ships that were no longer serviceable were scuttled. Refuse from cities also poured out into the sea from rivers and from garbage scows. "I'm here today representing people who want this thing back."

The elf swam to within inches of Rytagir. "Once something is down here, human, it belongs to us. Even the gold aboard that ship. You can't have it back unless we decide that you can. Or unless you pay us to release it."

Rytagir knew that was true. Though the *alu Tel'Quessir* didn't value gold the same way the dry world did, gold still had value on the sea floor as building materials. Stories were often told in taverns of entire sea elf cities made of gold.

"I'm willing to negotiate," Rytagir said.

The male swam around Rytagir contemptuously. "We're not fools, human. We know the worth of gold in the surface world."

"I'm not here for the gold."

"Then what are you here for, human?" the female elf asked.

"For the story. To let the families of these men know what happened to them."

Mocking doubt showed on the young elf woman's face. "Three hundred years after the ship went down?" She shook her head and her beautiful tresses floated out into the water. "I doubt there are any left alive who care. Your people tend to be as shortsighted as you are short-lived."

"There are important documents aboard."

"You came for those documents? Not for the gold?"

"I came for the documents. The captain of the ship above came for the gold. That was my deal with him."

"And you claim none of this gold for yourself?" Her raised eyebrows indicated how doubtful she was at that.

"I'm going to take my share of gold. I'd be a fool not to. And expeditions like this one aren't free."

The *alu Tel'Quessir* around them laughed at that.

"What if we chose to take a share of that gold?" the elf woman asked.

Rytagir glanced at them all. "Perhaps we could come to an amenable agreement."

4

"I don't see why we have to share," the sea elf male snarled. "If we choose to, we can sink their ship and drown them all." He glared at Rytagir. "Unless you choose to run."

"Greedy surface dwellers don't run," another male stated.

Rytagir hardened his voice. "There is a ship's mage aboard the vessel. And he has an apprentice. Both of them stand prepared to defend the ship as well. They've sworn their life's blood to do that."

The *alu Tel'Quessir* knew about ships' mages. Charged with caring for the crew and the ship, all of them knew how to repair minor damage done to the ship and preserve wood, but some of them could quell storms, hurl fireballs, and summon the wind. Others, at least so Rytagir had heard, could call down lightning strikes, summon whirlpools, and raise tidal waves that could smash ships on rocks.

The sea elves had a healthy respect for magic. Still, they could be damn stubborn. Rytagir hoped to make negotiating more attractive to them.

"What bargain would you strike, human?" the female asked.

"I want the salvage from this ship."

"I would not see this ship moved," she replied. "It has become home to many sea creatures."

Rytagir understood the woman's feelings. His father tended to believe, after the same fashion, that change, unless natural, was not a thing to ascribe to. Disruption of an environment was never to be tolerated.

"I've sworn to protect the land and the seas that have been assigned to me," the sea elf woman said.

"I'm not here for the ship," he said. "All I want is the cargo, and the documents if I can find them."

"What would we get in return?" the male asked.

"If you simply allow this, I'll give you ten percent of what we recover."

"Never expect a fair deal from a surface dweller," one of the other elves muttered.

"I'll give a fair deal," Rytagir countered. "But I'm not going to let you rob me. If you help me with the transport of the goods to the ship above, I can make your share thirty percent."

"So you would want us to be your pack animals?" The male grimaced.

"Let me speak, Rasche," the woman said.

Reluctantly, Rasche backed down.

"We want fifty percent," she told Rytagir.

Rytagir smiled coldly. "We have to transport and arrange payment for salvage. That takes more time and effort. And more investment. We'll take sixty percent. That's as generous as I can be."

"Except you," the sea elf said. "If you find the document you seek, you still stand to make a profit. I know that wizards often pay well for spellbooks, and collectors pay for unique pieces of writing or art."

"Lady, I swear to you by all I hold holy that I'm not here for that kind of profit. I seek only papers and documents that will reveal more of the lost histories of some of the lands around this place."

The maid smiled. "Then I will pray for Deep Sashelas's pleasure that we will all find something worthwhile."

Deep Sashelas was the god of the undersea elves. He was known as the Knowledgeable One and the Master of Dolphins. Many undersea folk, and even some human sailors, worshiped him. Rytagir had a more than passing acquaintance with the altars dedicated to the Dolphin Prince.

He looked into those silver eyes and asked, "May I have your name, Lady?"

"Don't you dare transgress, human!" Rasche said, and shoved his spear toward Rytagir's face.

5

With blinding speed, Rytagir drew his long sword and slapped Rasche's spear aside. The blow knocked the sea elf off-balance and spun him around in the water.

Obviously embarrassed, Rasche whirled and twisted in the water to come back around almost immediately. His fingers and toes splayed to allow the webbing between them to better grasp the water as he hurled himself back at his chosen opponent.

"Rasche," the woman spoke in an authoritative tone. "Stand down."

Immediately, Rasche broke off his attack. Cruel invective in his native tongue filled the sea.

Rytagir didn't sheathe his sword. He held ready the spells that he knew. They weren't much, but they would have to serve. He knew he couldn't swim to the surface before the elves overtook him.

"Deep Sashelas preserve us from males and their warring ways," the woman said. She glared at Rasche and Rytagir alike. "Surely between the two of you there are more brains than a prawn has. If not, then this is not to be done today."

After a moment, Rytagir let out a tense breath and put his long sword away. He took his gaze from Rasche and looked at the woman.

"If I offended you, Lady, please know that I had no intention of doing so."

"I know that. It's just that these men have been entrusted to take care of me." She shot Rasche a quick glare. "They're acting on my father's orders. Much to my annoyance." Her silver eyes cut back to Rytagir. "I'm called Irdinmai."

The name meant nothing to Rytagir. But he could tell by her tone of voice that it meant something somewhere. He nodded. "Thank you, Lady. Then, with your leave, we'll inspect the ship."

"Of course. The sooner we deal with this, the better."

Rytagir walked through the water, deliberately setting himself apart from the *alu Tel'Quessir* who swam ahead of him. It was bad luck that he'd crossed paths with the sea elves. Captain Zahban wasn't going to be happy about the situation either. Rytagir fully expected to have the same argument with the ship's captain as he'd had with the sea elf woman. For the moment he chose to delay that confrontation.

At the entrance to the forward hold, Rytagir reached into his shoulder bag and took out a foot-long length of lucent coral. He unwrapped the heavy cloth that kept the pale blue light trapped inside.

With the coral, he could see several feet, but his vision was still blunted by the depth of the water. He fisted the coral and stepped through the cargo hold.

Many barrels floated against the opposite side of the hull. Most of those, according to the manifest, had been precious oils intended for use in perfumes and cooking. They were lighter than the water and floated as a result. Nearly all of the metal parts on the ship—and there were few—had rusted away. What remained wasn't worth salvaging.

The timbers, however, were a different matter. Most of them, if not all, had been preserved in the cold water. Also, most of the wood was precious. Peilam hadn't stinted on the construction of his vessel.

"What are you thinking?" Irdinmai asked.

"The salvage profits would be raised a lot if we could get the ship back to the surface." Rytagir rubbed a hand on the smooth wood.

Irdinmai shook her head. "I won't have this place destroyed. Or moved. It has become part of the sea now."

"These timbers are quite expensive," Rytagir pointed out. "If we were to salvage them, the profits from this shipwreck—"

"If we were to salvage these timbers," the maid said, "then

the creatures that have chosen to live and spawn here would lose their safe homes. The sea is cruel. Only the smartest and the quickest survive. This has been a home to these creatures for many generations. We're not going to move it."

Rytagir nodded. He knew Captain Zahban wouldn't care for the decision, but there was no choice. Not unless they wanted to fight the sea elves.

One of the elves called out in an excited voice, "Lady Irdinmai, please come see this."

6

Irdinmai pushed herself up from the ship's side and swam back toward the stern. Rytagir trailed in her wake.

Only a short distance farther on, he reached the midships. Cargo had to be carefully planned and balanced by the quartermaster so it would ride comfortably during a voyage. It stood to reason that the gold would have been placed amidships.

Thick yellow bars of gold had spilled across the other side of the hull. The pale blue light of the lucent coral brought the dull shine to life.

Perhaps there wasn't enough of it to build a house, not even a small one, but there was enough to make them all wealthy for a short while.

Irdinmai looked at Rytagir. "When we begin taking this gold to the surface," she asked, "will we be able to trust that captain and crew?"

"Yes," Rytagir answered.

The sea elf maid regarded him coolly. "The *alu Tel'Quessir* know greed, not like the Lolth-loving *Sser'tel'quessir,* but we know it. We also know it is far stronger in surface dwellers."

"That captain and those men will stand firm by the bargain they have with me." Rytagir met her direct gaze full measure.

Irdinmai was silent for a moment. "And you'll be held accountable for them."

"I thought ye'd drownt," Zahban grumbled when Rytagir heaved himself aboard *Azure Kestrel*. "Either that or taken up residence with some sea hag what would have ye."

"Shame on ye to even say such a thing," Dorlon admonished. He was lean and gray, far from his youth but a good man to have as quartermaster. "If ye haven't a care, ye'll call down all manner of bad things up on our heads."

Zahban laughed at the other man. "Ye're turning into an old woman, ye are."

Dorlon cursed the captain good-naturedly.

As he stood on the deck, Rytagir studied the dark sky. He had to squint through the sheets of rain that swamped the ship's deck. Night was still hours away, but it was hard to tell given the storm. It was almost as dark as night already.

"Well," Zahban asked, "do we be rich men or poor men?"

Rytagir couldn't help grinning. He liked being right in his projects. "She was down there, captain. And so was the gold."

The crew cheered enthusiastically.

"The bad news is that we're going to be sharing the salvage. The good news is that getting it up from the sea floor is going to be a lot easier than I thought."

"What do ye mean by—?" Zahban clamped his big mouth shut as Irdinmai caught hold of the ship's side and hauled herself aboard.

"So this is yer bad news?" Zahban asked.

Irdinmai glanced at him with sharp disdain. She favored Rytagir with the same. "I've never been referred to in that manner."

"I guess she speaks our tongue," Zahban said sheepishly.

"Quite well, actually," Irdinmai replied. "And we're not any happier about the arrangement than you are, captain."

"I reckon not, Lady." The captain's tone was respectful. "Well then, let's just make the best of this." He rolled an eye at Rytagir. "I just hope ye left us some profit to be made."

"There's enough." But Rytagir knew that every man aboard was thinking about how there could have been more.

7

After the relay was set up, everything went easier. Rytagir stayed below and supervised the salvage. The sea elf warriors didn't have much experience at working shipwrecks, but they learned quickly.

The gold was taken up first. They placed the ingots in nets and swam the loads to the surface. Zahban's men stored the salvaged goods in *Azure Kestrel*'s hold. Irdinmai stationed guards aboard ship to ensure it didn't depart unexpectedly.

Fatigue chafed Rytagir mentally and physically, but he kept himself working. Once he had the hold salvage squared away, he turned his attention to the captain's quarters.

He found the captain's log easily enough, but the papers he was looking for—the ones he'd heard about and read about in the research he'd done regarding the peace treaties—weren't there. At least, not within ready sight.

Then he started looking for secret places where documents, contraband, and the captain's personal fortune might be kept.

"Maybe those documents aren't here."

Walling away the frustration he felt, Rytagir turned to face Irdinmai. "If they're here, I'll find them," he promised.

"What's so important about those papers?"

"They'll provide a better understanding of the events that were taking place in this region three hundred years ago."

"And that's important?"

"Our histories tend to be more volatile than yours, Lady," he said. "Every time two cultures, two cities, or two nations fight, something of both is lost. If more than two are involved, even more is lost. The document I'm looking for was a peace accord. An early draft. It would be interesting to match it against the peace accord that was actually negotiated."

"Will that change anything?"

"I doubt it. But for those of us who really want the whole story and not part of one, these documents are a necessity."

"You really care more about finding this than the gold, don't you?"

"Yes. You have stories you hand down to your children, to teach them wisdom and your ways, and to teach them right from wrong."

"Of course. Every tribe does."

"Up there, few people live in tribes anymore. Many of them live in large cities."

Irdinmai bristled as if she had been insulted. "We too once lived in cities. I know what a *city* is."

"I meant no offense, lady. I only wanted to point out that cities are far larger than what you may be accustomed to down here. Many people—some of them from distant lands and different cultures—live in those cities. Thousands of them. As a result, our histories are not as pure as those among your people."

For a moment, sadness touched the silver eyes. "I've seen the ruins of cities that have fallen into Serôs," she said. "I've wandered among the buildings. I can only imagine what it might be like to live in such a place as that."

There were tales of great cities of sea elves that had vanished on the ocean floor, but no one had ever found any truth of that. Rytagir believed in the myths more than most, but even he felt they might offer hope, but not truth.

"If ever you decide you should want to see a living city, Lady, get word to me. I'll be glad to show you around one." Rytagir didn't know what prompted him to make such an offer, hadn't even known he was going to make it until the words fell out of his mouth, and he felt foolish.

Instead, she said, "If I decide to see a city, I'll do that." Then she turned and began helping with the search of the captain's quarters. "Perhaps two of us will be more clever than one."

"Thank you," Rytagir said. He strove to wall off the barrage of questions that filled his mind about whether she would take him up on his offer, and what he would do and where they would go if she did. It didn't work. She was beautiful, and there were so many places he could have shown her.

He took a dagger from his boot and used the hilt to rap against the wooden walls and floor. The thump of metal striking wood sounded different underwater.

But the sharp *crack* of smashing wood behind him drew his attention immediately. He spun, not certain what he'd heard.

Then Irdinmai called out a warning.

In the gloom barely penetrated by the lucent coral he carried, Rytagir saw a powerful figure claw through the stern windows that led to the captain's quarters. It had six limbs, and the two additional arms helped it tear through the windows.

The creature looked more fish than man. Iridescent scales covered its powerful body and gleamed under the glow of the lucent coral. Black talons curved out from its fingers. As broad as it was, it didn't look tall. But Rytagir knew from the size of the window that the creature had to be almost seven and a half feet tall.

Large, magnetic black eyes sat under a ridge of bony growth. The creature's head was hard and angular, and the jaw jutted forth. Sharp teeth filled the great, gaping mouth. Ridges carved the creature's face and gave it an inherently evil visage. Fins ran the length of the creature's arms, from its wrist nearly all the way to the shoulder.

Like the sea elves, the creature was lighter on its front than on its back. Most of the creature was teal in color, but it was uneven, stained with ragged splotches of gray and green. Great fins growing out from the sides of its head swept back to join the main dorsal fin along its back. The fins of the sahuagin of the outer sea stood out independently.

It wore a dark breechcloth of indeterminate color that hung to its first knees. The creature's legs were double-jointed, the second joint allowing the legs to bend back the other way. It carried a long club that looked like a spear. One end held a sharp-bladed point, and the other held a spiked club head. A leather harness crisscrossed its chest and held up a bag woven from underwater plants.

Rytagir had dealt with the sea devils before, each time barely escaping with his life.

"Meat," the creature shrilled in its language. It thrust the staff's blade at Irdinmai's chest.

8

Rytagir threw himself forward but knew he was going to be too late.

Irdinmai gave ground and drew her sword from her hip. The blade whisked in front of her and collided with the sahuagin's club. The club went wide of the mark.

The sahuagin snarled in angry frustration. Two more of its fellows, these with only two arms apiece, poured through the broken window.

With his feet planted, Rytagir swung his sword at the sahuagin's head. Its lower right arm flicked out and caught the blow on a bracer that covered it from wrist to almost elbow. Metal rasped on metal as Rytagir drew his weapon back.

The two other sahuagin flew across the open space. But the room inside the cabin was limited. They got in each other's way. Rytagir feinted at the head of one and ducked down as his opponent chose to bring up his club to block the perceived blow.

Crouched now, Rytagir sprang forward and slashed his sword across the sahuagin's midsection. The creature's entrails spilled out. Without thought to its dying companion, the second sahuagin grabbed the mortally wounded one's innards and began to feast.

Deep Sashelas, Rytagir swore to himself. Even though he'd heard stories about how callous the sahuagin were, he'd never seen anything like this. The sahuagin shoved its maw full and chewed and swallowed. Even the wounded one turned and snatched loose pieces of itself from the water and ate them.

Rytagir stepped around the sahuagin he'd slashed just as it convulsed like a drowning man and died. A blood cloud spewed into the water from its massive jaws.

The second sahuagin stabbed its weapon at Rytagir. After blocking the blow with his sword, Rytagir kicked the sea devil in the face. The sahuagin's face shattered under the blow and fangs drifted out into the water.

Still, the fight hadn't gone out of it. The creature regrouped at once and attacked. Rytagir blocked the spear with his left forearm the second time and thrust the long sword straight into the sea devil's neck. The blade grated on the collarbone, then sank deeply into its chest. With a quick twist, Rytagir slashed the sahuagin's throat and freed his blade at the same time.

Fearfully, he shoved the dying sahuagin from him and glanced in the direction he'd last seen Irdinmai. He felt certain she was already dead.

Instead, she bravely fought on and succeeded in blocking her opponent's attacks. Several cuts on three of the sahuagin's four arms wept crimson into the water. She was good with her weapons. She held a dagger in her left hand and as he watched, she dropped her long sword and drew yet another knife.

In a blinding display of martial arts, Irdinmai slashed her opponent from head to toe. The sahuagin flailed at her, but she blocked the blows with her elbows and forearms.

Then her right hand shoved the knife up from under the sea devil's chin. The blade was too short to reach the creature's brain, but the second knife, swept across in her left hand, sank to the hilt in the sahuagin's right temple. For good measure, to kill the reptilian brain that drove her opponent, Irdinmai cruelly twisted her blade.

The sahuagin shuddered and went still.

Calmly, Irdinmai freed her knives and put them away before reclaiming her long sword. She glanced at Rytagir.

"Are you all right?" she asked.

Rytagir nodded. "I thought you were in trouble."

"I was." She favored him with a tense smile. "We still are."

A shark invaded the captain's quarters. The fierce beast came at Rytagir with its mouth gaping. Rytagir rapped it on the nose with his sword hilt.

The shark turned tail and left, but not before it managed to grab one of the dead sahuagin by the leg and haul it back out into the open water. Before it had gone far, another shark zoomed in to rip one of the dead sea devil's arms off.

"Move," Irdinmai ordered.

Rytagir started for the door, then he saw a crack in the wall behind the elf maid. The hidden space there held several pouches and a waterproof wooden document box that just fit the description Rytagir had read about. He forced his way past Irdinmai and shoved all the contents into his shoulder bag.

Irdinmai led the way through the door. Rytagir paused just long enough to grab the lucent coral he'd dropped.

Though he couldn't see very far in any direction, Rytagir saw that the ship was overrun with sahuagin. The sea devils were locked in mortal combat with the sea elves.

"*Merciful Sashelas,*" Irdinmai whispered in her tongue, "*keep us in your benevolent sight.*"

"*We've got to swim for the ship,*" Rytagir said. He spoke in her tongue so she would effortlessly understand his words. "*We need to join forces while we're still able.*"

Irdinmai glanced at him in surprise. "The ship? On the surface?"

Rytagir knew the sea elves would be loath to leave the sea. "It's the only chance we have," he insisted. "You'll be out of place aboard, but so will the sahuagin. We can fight them off there."

Before Irdinmai could reply, two sahuagin shot out of the darkness into the lucent coral's pale blue globe. The sea elf maid knocked Rytagir aside. Sahuagin claws slashed across Rytagir's leather armor and the blow knocked him farther back.

The sea devils came around. Both grinned maliciously as they drew back their spears.

"Meat!" one of them shouted.

A dolphin swam like an arrow and struck the sahuagin before it could defend itself. The *crack* made by the spine shattering was loud in the water. Still, the sahuagin refused to die so easily. Even with its head on its shoulder, it fought to swim toward Irdinmai and Rytagir.

"Block him!" Irdinmai shouted.

9

Instinctively, Rytagir lifted his sword and turned aside the sahuagin's thrust as Irdinmai stepped toward it. Her blade sank deeply into the sahuagin's midsection. She used his spine as a fulcrum and cut through the side of the sea devil's body. Blood filled the water.

Mortally wounded, the sahuagin drew back and gave vent to a full-throated blast of rage. Rytagir's ears ached from the pain of the assault.

He swam back and pulled at Irdinmai's arm by hooking his wrist inside her elbow. The glow from the lucent coral shifted and threw shadows of her body over everything.

"We have to go."

She turned and swam after him. The sahuagin outnumbered the sea elves. Corpses of both hung in the water. Dying warriors managed only feeble movements. Both were prey for the sharks.

"Get your people together," Rytagir ordered. "Get them out of the battle."

Irdinmai sheathed her sword and smashed her bracelets in quick syncopation. Evidently the ringing tone created, or the pattern of the sounds, was unique to Irdinmai. At once the sea elves swam to their mistress's side and set up a defensive perimeter.

"Take them to the ship," Rytagir said in the sea elf tongue so everyone would know. *"We can better hold them there."*

The sea elves hesitated. Irdinmai gazed at Rytagir.

"Now!" Rytagir roared as a line of dolphins intercepted the sahuagin and sharks that came at them. *"Now, if you want to live."*

Irdinmai gave the order and the sea elves swam for the surface.

Rytagir pricked his finger with a knifepoint and spoke a string of eldritch words. Nearly all of the sharks and sahuagin turned on the ones next to them and started rending and tearing with fangs, claws, and weapons. Death spread throughout the water. Only a few of the sahuagin escaped the spell's effect.

"What did you do?" Irdinmai asked.

"A spell," Rytagir explained as he swam up to meet her.

"Magic?" She looked appalled. "You're a *wizard?*"

"Only part of my studies, Lady. I don't know many spells. That one is small." Rytagir glanced over his shoulder. The sahuagin still fought each other and the sharks. "The spell puts blood spoor into the water and encourages predators into a blood frenzy."

"We should attack them while they're confused," Rasche said.

"No. That spell won't last long. Swim if you would live. I've got one more trick up my sleeve."

There were a few muttered oaths, but the sea elves swam together.

When he whirled in the water, Rytagir saw that the sahuagin had once again taken up pursuit. He was no longer dependent on the lucent coral alone to see them. Pale gray light from the sky above penetrated the water too.

He reached into his shoulder bag and took out a small bag of sharks' teeth. Then he waited as a score of sahuagin swam at him. Many of them suffered wounds from the hands of their fellows.

"Rytagir!" Irdinmai shouted.

When he knew he could wait no more, Rytagir spoke the words sharply, traced a sigil in the water, and shoved the bag forward. Heat nearly scorched his palm as the spell consumed the bag of sharks' teeth.

A silvery ripple shot through the water and spread out, eight feet wide and almost forty feet down. The enchanted water shredded the sahuagin like sharks' teeth. Bloody gobbets of flesh, limbs, heads, and torsos floated limply in the water after the spell exhausted itself.

The sea elves cursed again, and Rytagir knew they would never trust him again.

"Swim," Irdinmai ordered.

⊗ ⊗ ⊗ ⊗ ⊗

Captain Zahban and his sailors had their hands full repelling the sahuagin. The sea devils tried to board the ship, but the crew fought them off.

"Captain," Rytagir shouted as he broke the surface, "permission to come aboard!"

"Come ahead with ye then," Zahban shouted back. He yelled out orders to his crew, and eager hands swept down to pull Rytagir and the sea elves from the water.

Archers stood to arms and feathered as many of the sahuagin as they could.

"You're a fool for staying," Rytagir said.

"Ain't ever been one to cut an' run," Zahban replied as he cleaved a sahuagin's skull with his cutlass. Blood and brain matter splattered the deck. "But I wasn't gonna give ye much more time, I'll warrant ye that."

The sea elves fell into place with the ship's crew. Together, they fought to keep the sahuagin from the deck.

"Where'd ye bring them beasties up from?" Zahban asked.

"They came up on us unawares," Rytagir shouted. He thrust his long sword through the throat of a sahuagin that had climbed up the side of the ship. Then he kicked it off his blade and back into the ocean.

"From where?" asked the captain.

"I don't know."

"I've never seen so many in these waters."

"There appear to be more coming." Irdinmai pointed to the east.

After booting another sahuagin in the face, Rytagir looked in that direction. There, on the crests of the sea, he saw four strange vessels making for them.

The vessels, mantas, were almost eighty feet across and two hundred feet long. They looked like a shambles, pieced-together craft from several wrecks. As Rytagir watched, several of the sahuagin aboard revealed glow lamps, glass globes stuffed with the luminous entrails of sea creatures.

10

"We can't stay here," Rytagir yelled as he hacked at another sahuagin.

"We're not." Zahban shifted his attention to Irdinmai. "Lady, can ye an' yer warriors hold these animals off while we make ready the ship?"

"Yes."

"Then we'll leave ye to it." Zahban yelled orders to his crew and they broke off from the defense to raise sails. "Mystra watch over us."

Rytagir remained with the elves. His arm grew tired from the constant attacks. The elf next to him went down and a sahuagin crawled triumphantly onto the deck. Rytagir sank below his opponent's sweeping blow and hacked at the sea devil's legs. His effort severed one of them and bit deeply into the other.

In the next instant, Rasche planted his trident in the center of the sahuagin's chest. Rytagir rose and planted his shoulder into the sea devil's midsection and shoved him from the ship with the sea elf's assistance.

Rasche crowed in victory and clapped Rytagir on the back. Rytagir responded in kind, and they turned back to the battle.

Azure Kestrel rocked as canvas dropped and filled her 'yards. She heeled over so hard once in the crosswinds that Rytagir thought the ship was going to tip over. For a moment they were almost face to face with the sahuagin.

Then the ship righted.

"Bring them sheets about!" Zahban ordered. "Let her run, lads! *Let her run!*"

The ship leaped forward as the sails caught the wind. The elves kept fighting, aided by the ship's archers. Gradually, then faster, *Azure Kestrel* broke free of the sahuagin.

But the mantas, powered by oars wielded by the sahuagin, surged after them in quick pursuit.

"We can't outrun them," Irdinmai said.

"We ain't gonna outrun 'em," Zahban roared from the stern castle. "Fortrag and his apprentice have got a thing or two to show 'em."

Rytagir raced up the sterncastle steps and joined the sea captain. The ship's mage and his apprentice stood on the rear deck. Ancient Fortrag, gray beard whipping in the wind, yelled incantations and held out his hand. Flames gathered there, growing larger and larger.

The four sahuagin mantas had closed the distance to less than eighty yards. Their oars dug relentlessly into the sea.

When the whirling fireball stood almost as tall as a man and the heat was so intense it drove back those near the wizards, Fortrag flung the fireball. It arced across the water and split into four separate fireballs. Three of the four hit their targets and the mantas disappeared in a maelstrom of flames.

Fortrag called out again. Rytagir felt the wind accelerate around him. A moment later, a waterspout rose from the sea and danced toward the last manta. Despite the sahuagins' attempt to steer clear, the waterspout overtook them and broke the vessel to pieces.

The ship's crew and the *alu Tel'Quessir* cheered, then they turned their efforts to saving those among the wounded that could be saved.

Two days later, *Azure Kestrel* put into port at Mordulkin. Rytagir was nearly exhausted. In addition to helping tend the wounded and taking turns at keeping watch, he'd documented everything he could of the attack. He reproduced from memory the sigils the sahuagin had been wearing, as well as those of the sailors and the sea elves.

The whole port was in upheaval when they arrived. They quickly learned that theirs hadn't been the only ship attacked. In fact, *Azure Kestrel* was one of the few to make port safely. Several others remained unaccounted for.

Zahban found himself buried in several offers of employment to get perishable goods across the Sea of Fallen Stars, but only foolish men were putting to sea at the moment.

Irdinmai was in a hurry to get back to her family, but her foremost thought had been to get medical help for those of her group that had been injured during the attack. Almost a third of the elves had died, and nearly the same number of Zahban's sailors.

After he'd helped the clerics tend the wounded and squared away the cargo, Rytagir tracked Irdinmai down. She remained with her warriors.

"Lady," Rytagir said.

When she looked up at him, he could see how tired and hurt she was. Rytagir knew the look from other captains of ships and guardsmen he'd talked to over the years who had lost men in battle. The pain was more spiritual than physical, and it would be years—if ever—in the healing.

"Yes," she replied.

"I've gotten word from some of the other captains," Rytagir said. "The Sea of Fallen Stars is filling with sahuagin. They've been freed from the Alamber Sea."

"I know," Irdinmai replied. "I've talked with other *alu Tel'Quessir* that have arrived here. Many were chased from their homes." She paused, and fear touched her silver eyes. "There is a being called Iakhovas who shattered the Sharksbane Wall and called forth the sahuagin. He plans to take all of Serôs as his domain."

Stunned, Rytagir sat beneath the canvas stretched over the litters of wounded elves. As he watched, dwarves and humans helped dump buckets of saltwater from the sea onto the injured *alu Tel'Quessir*. The old distrust that had existed between the races along the Inner Sea was set aside.

At least for now.

Rytagir turned to Irdinmai. "I'm going to talk to Zahban. He's not unreasonable. The split of the salvaged cargo is going to be fifty-fifty. Your people have shed as much blood, if not more, than ours have."

"We had an agreement before this happened. You don't have to set that a—"

"I didn't set it aside, Lady. The sahuagin did." Rytagir looked out to sea and remembered all the stories of wars that he'd read about and researched. "What lies before us isn't going to be quick or easy. If the sahuagin are truly free of the Sharksbane Wall, it's going to take everything we have to hold them back."

"I know."

Men hurried along the dock as yet another ship—showing obvious scars from recent battle—limped back into port.

Rytagir looked into Irdinmai's silver eyes. "The old fears and distrust the surface dwellers have had of the sea folk are going to have to change. And your people will have to change, too. If we hope to survive this, we have to forge new friendships."

"I know," Irdinmai agreed. "The word has already started to spread among my people."

"I'm spreading it among mine. I've already drafted letters and have sent them out to scholars and merchant guildsmen whose ears I have. It will take time."

"Then let us hope it doesn't take too much time." Irdinmai reached out for his hand and took it gently in hers. She pulled him close to her. "I'm tired, and I don't want to be alone. Do you mind?"

"Not at all, Lady." Rytagir felt her lean against him as they sat with their backs to a crate. After a time she slept and he felt her breath, feather-soft against his arm.

As he sat there, Rytagir knew things were going to change. Some things would be better and others would be worse. War always brought those changes, and he had no doubt that war was coming to the Sea of Fallen Stars.

CHASE THE DARK

Jaleigh Johnson

Charlatan. Trickster. Blasphemer.
In Amn, the only thing worse than hurling magic
is pretending to hurl it. They laughed at me, said
I'd never be worth spit to my people. Then the
monsters came. When the ogres marched on the
cities, I was the one whistling the merry tune. I
had a purpose again. If you don't have it in you
to live an honest life, the least you can do is plan
a heroic death.

—From the memoirs of Devlen Torthil
11 Hammer, the Year of the Tankard (1370 DR)

"Ten in coin says I make a pikeman drop his stick! Who'll take an honest wager?"

Devlen Torthil smiled, raking his long brown hair out of his eyes. He rolled up his dirty sleeves and surveyed the line of men guarding the camp. Easy plucking.

A plain-faced sentry named Kelsn stepped forward. "I'll take that bet."

"Splendid, man, come here, then! The problem is distraction, see?" Flipping his palm to the torchlight, Dev flourished a red scrap of cloth in the sentry's face.

"Is that blood?" The sentry was tall, his blond hair thin under his helmet. Warily, he clutched his pike against his collarbone. Behind him, the foothills of the Small Teeth rose in a jumbled wreck, purple with the setting sun.

"Not a bit, not. . . a. . . bit. Ogre tears, that's what they are." Dev wadded the red cloth into a ball, completely encasing it in his right fist. Twisting his wrist, he came up under the sentry's nose, fingers waggling above an empty palm. The scrap of cloth had disappeared.

"Wizardry." The sentry spat on the ground, dark already with mud.

Like a good soldier of Amn, Dev thought, and bit back his sharp smile. He looked up and wiped rain from the bridge of his blunt nose.

Thunder rolled across the plain, a guttural, urgent murmur that seemed to carry words into the camp and had the sentry turning north on a muttered prayer. More of the wizardry Amn feared.

Dev sighed. Wasn't right, stealing a man's audience.

"Look here, Kelsn, pay attention. You think I'd be hanging around with this bunch if I had even a breath of wizardry?" Dev waggled his fingers again. The sentry reluctantly tore his gaze from the horizon. "The problem was you were looking at my hand. You should have been putting your eyes elsewhere."

The sentry snorted. "Where then, down yer breeches?"

"Later, sunshine." This time it was Dev who spat. "Watch this first."

Dev drew a knife from his belt and laid the bare blade against his own right thumb. He held it up so Kelsn could see.

"Oh, Dev, don't be playing at that. You know we lost our holy man in the last raid—"

The torchlight flickered and succumbed to the rain, taking the sentry's words with it. In the instant before the light died, he saw Devlen cleanly sever the tip of his thumb. The appendage fell to the ground.

"Godsdamnit, I knew you were some sick bastard!" The sentry took a jerking step back from the severed digit, as if it might leap up and bite him. His pike slipped and sank, forgotten in the mud.

Dev howled with laughter. The commotion drew the attention of Breck, head of the night watch.

"Shut yer flapping mouths, the both of you!" He squatted in the mud and fished out the thumb. Angrily, he plucked up the sentry's pike and slapped the muddy weapon against the man's chest, nearly throwing the sentry off balance. "It's a fake, you idiot! I saw him do the same trick to Fareth two nights ago."

Dev tried to contain his laughter while the sentry examined the fake digit. He pulled the red cloth from the hollow end where it had been hidden all along. Comprehension wormed its way slowly over his face.

Dev waited for the rest. Anger? Wonder? Without fail, folk had one or the other reaction to his tricks.

"Rotten cheat," the sentry growled. Dev was entirely unsurprised. "I'm not putting up good coin for trickster's wizardry—"

"Part the way!"

The shouts came from beyond the perimeter of the camp. The remaining torches snapped up, illuminating a trio of men striding slowly up the hill. They carried a litter among them. In their wake, figures scuttled across the plain, bodies riding low to the ground.

Moves like an animal, Dev thought, except the beasts carried swords, and their eyes gleamed with feral cunning.

"Kobolds!" The blond sentry hefted his pike in one hand. With the other, he drew a short blade from his belt. He tossed it at Dev. "Move, trickster!"

Breck intercepted the toss. He spun the blade and planted it in the mud. "Lady Morla's orders. No weapons for this one. You know that, Kelsn, you damn fool!"

Reprimanded, the sentry jerked his head in acknowledgment and sprinted down the hill, where guards were already assembling a line to meet the charging creatures.

The litter bearers crossed into the relative safety of the camp. Their faces were drawn with exhaustion. The man draped across the litter was dying. Dev could tell by the pallor of his skin and the steaming trail he left on the cold ground. Dev didn't know his name, but he knew the man was a scout.

A cold, sharp thrill went through Devlen's body. That meant it was time for him to shine again.

On the hill, the raiding party slammed into the Amnian defenders, their hairy bodies impaled and wriggling on the pikes. Squeals of dying animals shivered through the night air. Hearing the sound, the kobolds in the back of the party broke ranks and fled.

Dev observed the whole spectacle with detached curiosity. Weaponless, he trailed behind the litter up the hill to the commander's tent. His mind was too busy to be disturbed by the screams. He was already planning his next trick.

I work alone. That's the only rule. When you have more than one mouth along on a mission, it doubles your chances of slipping the charade. And whatever you do, never pair up with a priest in war, unless he swears by his god to heal you first and even then, I've never seen anyone so twitchy as a priest on a battlefield.

—From the memoirs of Devlen Torthil

Morla was field commander of the Amnian Watch Tower Guard, affectionately named for their mission in the Small Teeth.

Morla's task had been to reclaim the watch towers being garrisoned by the monster army, led by the ogre mages Sythillis and Cyrvisnea. With those precious eyes in the foothills, Syth and Cyr could see armies marching across the land, to say nothing of what scrying spells might reveal of such a force. Armed with superior reconnaissance, the monster army had stalled or thwarted outright Amn's attempts to relieve the besieged city of Murann on the coast. Amn needed her towers back, and it was for Morla, a lone woman on the darker side of fifty, to do.

Dev might have admired her gall, if he didn't despise the old hag personally.

He lifted the tent flap and immediately regretted disturbing the air. Hot, fresh blood and the stench of burning herbs wafted liberally from the tent. Dev put a hand over his mouth.

"Where's the priest?" He coughed, trying to see into the smoky interior. "The poor devil's running out of prayer time."

Three pairs of eyes lifted from the dying scout's pallet to regard Devlen. They watched him walk among them as one might an insect that had wandered onto a lord's feasting table. Morla was the only one who spoke.

"Be welcome, Scout Devlen." She gestured for Dev to stand in the corner of the tent. Her dull gray hair was pulled tightly back, revealing a broad, wrinkled forehead. Her nose was too long for her face; she had never been a beauty, so the men whispered, but her eyes were stinging bright. It was rumored that her vision was so keen at night she could see the pinpricks of light from a kobold's eyes, miles away in the hills.

Morla's single guard stood at her left hand. Opposite the pallet squatted a short, compact figure. His robes were filthy around the knees. Silently, he fed the reeking herbs into a brazier hanging from one of the tent poles near the scout's body.

"Why the quiet, priest?" Dev asked. He wiped his streaming nose. "Aren't you supposed to be sending him to his god?"

"My name is Gerond," the priest replied without looking up. He pressed a handful of the herbs to the scout's chest, but the man was too far gone to be bothered by the stench. "The lad wanted to smell the herbs of the Wealdath, the land of his birth." The priest pointed to the brazier. "What I have is a poor substitute, but I burn them in his honor."

"Wonderful way to die," Dev muttered.

"The scout made his last report," Morla cut in. She narrowed her hawkish eyes on Dev. "I have another mission for you, charlatan."

"Sending me off again, are you? Will you miss me, Morla my love, when I'm traipsing through the dark and wet, risking death for you?"

Morla's voice was flat. "On the contrary, charlatan, the only time I think of you at all is when I'm feeding information to the enemy regarding your whereabouts."

Devlen laughed. "What sweet thoughts they are, I'm sure."

He tried to sound derisive, but inwardly he thrilled to this latest challenge. He may not have possessed Morla's cold dignity or the priest's piety, but then, he'd never needed either. Deception was his arena. He was Amn's decoy, sent to play the fiddle of Syth and Cyr. He knew the song and dance better than anyone.

Morla pointed to a map spread across a long, wooden table. "This is the route I want you to take." She pointed to the camp's current position. "Northwest across this plain—after you've gone, I'll spread the word to their spies that a courier has been dispatched to try to round up our scattered forces. You'll leave tonight and be at your destination before dawn, or you'll be dead from their archers when the light breaks and you're seen from the towers."

"What a prospect," Dev murmured. "Why that route? A shorter path and tree cover lie straight north."

"Because that ground," Morla traced a swathe of flat land with her dagger blade, "if you fail to recall, is where this army fought two days ago. We lost over four hundred souls on that plain, more than half our remaining strength. That's the route they'll expect you to take to search for survivors."

Devlen recalled the battle, but he hadn't fought in it, as Morla knew well. She would not allow a wizard—even a charlatan wizard—the honor of fighting in her army.

"So you want me to cross an open field, sweetly seasoned with the dead and dying, in clear sight of any goblins, kobolds, or ogres that might still be lingering? You know I'll do it, Morla my light, but it'll be a short walk, I can tell you that, and meanwhile your real courier won't have much of a head start getting your message through."

That was Amn's bane, of course: communication. Syth and Cyr had arcane means to carry their whispers between their forces. Battle after battle had splintered Morla's army into smaller bands that wandered like aimless, beheaded chickens. Foot traffic and brave—or stupid—couriers were the only means of exchanging information. More often than not, Amn's couriers had met with bloody disaster on these missions, until Dev had stepped in and offered his services. Now there were two messengers: the man who carried the truth, and Devlen the charlatan, with his well-oiled fiddle. Dev didn't mind being the decoy. It was his gift. He would lend it to Amn, in return for a favor to be collected later.

"You'll have company," Morla was saying, "so perhaps you'll last until the dawn."

Absorbed in his thoughts, Dev snapped to attention quick enough on hearing this last. "That's not part of the arrangement, Morla dear. This is my show."

"Not this night," Morla said. She handed him a stack of parchment, folded neatly and warmed by fresh wax. The papers bore the commander's personal seal. "Follow the route I showed you. In the center of the battlefield there is an overturned statue. Find it, and you'll know you're on the right path. Chieva, Lady Sorrow, is her name. She was planted in the field by Chauntea's faithful, in hopes of a better harvest. Can you remember this, charlatan? When you find her, break the seal on my instructions. They'll tell you where to lead the enemy. Once the trail is laid, get back here. You'll have to hurry. As it is, you'll be chasing the dark the entire journey."

"Maybe you didn't hear me." He was straying dangerously close to defiance, but Dev didn't care. "On his best day, every man in this camp moves slower than me, and makes a lot more noise."

"But they will fight to their deaths, even to protect a charlatan," Morla said. "So you'll take two and be silent about it, or I will have you beaten silent. I imagine that will slow you down enough."

Tension sat thickly in the stinking tent. The blunt-faced charlatan and a commander who'd lost half her army stared each other down. Finally, Morla lifted her left hand, the one she always clutched around her sword hilt. As soon as it left the steel, the hand began to tremble violently, a thing apart from the rest of her rigid body. Dev saw Morla's guard avert his eyes, in pity or disgust.

She clamped the hand on Dev's shoulder, where it steadied into a claw. Forcibly, she turned him to face the back of the tent. Her voice rasped in his ear, setting his teeth on edge. "There is the first of your companions, charlatan. Do you think he moves with more quiet than you?"

Dev blinked. He'd had no idea there was anyone else in the tent. But a figure stepped from the shadows, a large, hulking shape Dev recognized immediately.

"Resch," he said. He glanced at Morla. "You're sending him with me?"

"I am."

Resch, "The Silent," came to stand next to the priest. He was tall, with well-defined muscles and no tunic to hide them. His shaved head bore a wormlike scar behind his right ear. He was called The Silent because he never spoke a word to anyone. He never spoke a word to anyone because an ogre had ripped out his tongue in the initial attack on Murann, in the early days of the war.

Resch, by his manner, was still holding a grudge. Dev couldn't blame him.

"Gerond will go along as well." Morla offered the fat priest her right hand to help him to his feet. Her left had returned to its place at her sword hilt. "As you know, we recently lost our priest, Hallis. Gerond tells us he was a colleague of his," Morla said.

"Then why don't you keep him here, seeing as he's your only holy man now?" Dev asked.

Morla smiled thinly. "You're wasting time, charlatan. Dawn is waiting." She gestured to the guard, who turned and lifted the lid on an ornate, brass-handled trunk. He removed a bow and full quiver of arrows and handed them to Dev.

"You will return them, Scout, when your mission is complete," Morla said, "according to our bargain."

"How could I forget," Dev said, and this time he couldn't keep the bitterness out of his voice.

So you know what I said about priests, yet there I was, shackled up to one, and it didn't make me feel that much better, having the healer along. You know, I once asked a boy who'd survived battle if he thought his god had saved him. The boy said he didn't remember his own name out on that field, said he was pissin' blood he was so scared and didn't think any god could make it better. Some things a healing won't cure.

—From the memoirs of Devlen Torthil

The bodies weren't two days cold on the ground, and the field already had a name. Chieva's Sorrow, it was called, for the pile of ruins that used to be the centerpiece of a fallow farming ground. Chieva, the Stone Lady, hadn't lasted the season. Her vacant eyes would be staring up at the night sky, just another body in the ripening pile. Dev had to find her, somewhere in the dark.

Their unlikely trio crouched in the shadow of a clump of trees bordering the bare edges of the field. They could hear sounds: murmurings and the suggestion of movement out in the darkness.

"They were supposed to be dead," Gerond whispered. His pudgy face flooded white in the shallow moonlight. "It's been two days."

"Thought your kind wasn't squeamy around the dying," Dev said. He never took his eyes off the penetrating darkness. Beside him, he heard a soft whistle. Resch was impatient to be on the move.

The priest's eyes narrowed. "So what's your plan, Torthil?"

"Good start would be to shut yer mouth while I'm thinking," Dev said mildly. He turned to Resch. "You think you could bring down a couple of these stout branches without making too much noise?"

Resch rose from his haunches and went to the nearest tree. He shimmied up the trunk with a grace that defied his size. He disappeared into the foliage. A moment later, two branches dropped from the leaves. Dev caught them and handed one off to the priest.

"Shave the leaves, then give me your outer robe."

"What?" the priest sputtered, forgetting to be quiet.

Dev pressed a dirty finger to his lips. "We need to make a litter, and I want your holy symbol swingin' free. Any watching eyes, we want 'em to think we're out collecting the wounded."

Resch dropped soundlessly from the tree, landing next to Dev.

"Resch here, he's going to be our invalid," Dev explained. "He'll be on the litter, waiting to pop up if we get detained."

"But shouldn't we save the litter for the actual wounded?" the priest asked.

"We're not planning any stops on this trek. You heard Morla; this is a grand charade, not a rescue mission. All we've got to get us across that plain is foot speed, and every breath we waste on prayers slows us down. You understand, holy man?"

"You can't expect me to ignore that there are wounded men on that field," the priest said. "Gods, you can *hear* them.

Think how many could be healed. They could join us. If the purpose of this mission is to find more men—"

"The purpose of this mission is to reunite an army that can make a run at the towers," Dev said. "The few stragglers we can pluck off this ground won't be worth anything to Morla, not in their condition." He took the thick outer robe from the priest and knotted both ends around the poles.

"You think very highly of your comrades," Gerond sneered, "but I tell you I could restore a pair of men, maybe more, to full fighting strength."

Dev chuckled, truly amused. "You think that'll solve our problems, do you? You wave your digits and we've got a pile of whole men ready and eager to fight on? " 'Cept maybe,"—he tapped his temple—"they aren't quite whole, eh?" He pointed at the litter. "Try it out, big man, and let's hope your tongue bore the worst of your weight."

He heard the priest catch his breath in alarm, but Resch merely made a rude gesture and lay back on the litter. Dev saw the scarred man tuck his mace in the dangling folds of cloth.

Dev looked again across the field. He guessed they had at least two miles of open ground to cover, carrying corpse-weight all the while. The bulky priest would slow them to a crawl. Dev cursed. It would be a miracle if they cleared the field before midday.

"Up and out," he said, and they were moving, hauling the litter over the rough pile of stones that marked the border of the field.

In truth, Dev had no idea if his plan would buy them any degree of safety. His best hope was that any passing patrols would see a pair of desperate humans collecting their dead, not worth the effort of returning to a field where so many of their own lay rotting.

Dead grass crunched under Dev's boots. For a long time, it was the only sound in the party. When the desolate earth gave way to oddly formed lumps and piles, Dev fixed his gaze firmly on the horizon.

He let his boots fumble aside the bodies, wincing when the soft suede came away wet and, in some cases, still warm.

The smell was harder to ignore. Sweet, sickly wafts of rot and human waste hit his nose. Dev gagged and swallowed back the bile that rose in his throat. If he'd had any sense, he'd have fashioned a mask for his nose and mouth. He glanced back at Resch and saw the man's chest heaving.

"Get it under control," he hissed between clenched teeth. "Better they think you've expired already, makes us less of a threat. What say, priest?" he asked. "Can your god clear this air for us, or does he only believe in the reeking herbs?"

"Fair punishment, for leaving these men behind," Gerond said. The priest's voice was strained from the load he carried. His face shone bright red, his cheeks sucking in and out on each breath. Every few feet, he hesitated, casting furtive glances all around in the dark.

"Keep moving!" Dev snapped. "I told you these men are no use to us."

"What are you talking about? You're a damn fool if you think I can't help them!"

On the litter, Resch made a soft clicking sound with his teeth. A warning.

"You're injured. Play the part," Dev barked, but he lowered his voice.

He glanced back at Gerond to pry the man's attention from the field. "Do you know why Morla's hand shakes, holy man?"

"No," Gerond admitted. "I have not had the opportunity to treat the commander, but I assumed the ailment stemmed from some sort of palsy. Age, I expect. What does that have to do with anything?"

Resch clicked his teeth again, fast and low, an eerily perfect parody of amusement.

"Her first engagement, Morla got herself stuck in the gut with a spear," Dev said. "Not one of them sleek sentry's blades, either, I'm saying barbed teeth, a goblin weapon wielded with an animal's brute strength." Dev heaved aside another body. A cloud of flies stirred up by the motion drifted lazily in front of his face. Dev spat at the air, but the insects buzzed relentlessly around his hair and ears. "Well, Hallis the holy man wasn't anywhere nearby at the time, so what's she going to do? Gut wound won't kill you quick, and Morla, she'd rather slit her own throat than lay out in the sun with an open wound, so what'd she do? No bandages, no time to make 'em, so she just balls up her left fist and sticks it in the wound to stop the blood."

"Merciful gods," Gerond murmured.

"Not so merciful, as it turned out," Dev said cheerfully. "The men lost sight of her. Eventually, they found old Morla wandering the battlefield as the fighting was winding down. She was half dead with fever and infection, but it took Hallis the longest time to get her to sit down and take her hand out of her own entrails. Turns out, she'd pressed that fist so hard in her wound she'd made it twice as painful as it could have been." That pain was something Dev didn't want to contemplate. "But Hallis treated her in time, knitted that wound up smart with his prayers and beseeching to his god. Didn't even leave a scar on her lovely, wrinkled belly. But that left hand, you can't make it forget. Unless she minds it with her whole strength, that hand trembles. No priest or prayer in this whole world going to fix that. The only cure's in Morla's mind, and she hasn't rooted it out yet."

Dev had turned away, his eyes back on the horizon, but he could feel Gerond watching him.

"All men are not created the same," the priest said after a moment. "Most would rather live than die. Most would prefer to walk off this battlefield alive, if not whole."

"Better they'd died."

"Then why do you serve Morla?" Gerond demanded. "Won't a similar fate await you?"

Dev shrugged. "I serve Amn any way I can, holy man, any way they'll let me—for a price."

"Whatever gold you receive won't be enough, if you die out here," the priest said.

"Is that so?" Dev asked, his voice rich with scorn. "Who said I wanted gold?"

"Then what?"

Dev halted and gestured for Gerond to lower the litter. "Shut it, now. We're here."

"How do you know?"

"Because I just busted a shin trying to move this body here," Dev said.

He pointed to the ground. A large stone statue lay across their path. Like a lass sleeping in moonlight, Chieva had her serene face turned to the stars. Moss and curling weeds twined around her solid arms, which were raised in supplication to the goddess.

Dev motioned for Resch to remain on the litter. He and the priest took cover at the base of the statue. Leaning against the stone, Dev took out Morla's instructions and broke the wax seal. He folded back the parchment and began to read.

There was quiet on the field for a long time after that.

Dev didn't know how much time passed, but suddenly, someone was shaking him insistently. He looked up into Resch's wide, shadowed face. He hadn't registered the man's presence.

"What's wrong with him?" he heard Gerond whisper. Resch motioned for the priest to be quiet. His gaze moved between the parchment and Dev's face. The question was obvious, and abruptly, Dev realized that Resch the Silent probably couldn't read.

Dev handed the parchment to the priest. "Tell 'im," he said. Gerond took the instructions and read aloud:

"Scout Devlen, if you are reading this, you have reached Lady Chieva, and here your true task begins. You will not be leading a decoy mission this night. Instead you carry vital missives to be distributed to our fractured camps throughout the foothills of the Small Teeth. My own men are leading the kobold and goblin patrols astray so you may move among the enemy. Your skills in the wild will be put to the ultimate test in this, as will your tactics of deception. Good fortune to you, charlatan, and I trust you'll forgive me my own deception—"

He stopped reading when Dev wheeled around and vomited on the statue.

Mouth burning, Dev emptied the contents of his stomach. The field around him wavered, seeming to take on an unreal quality. Resch and the priest were far away. He was alone, drifting in the land of the dead, with only Chieva for company. The arms of the statue dug into his chest. Chauntea's emissary was holding him up in sympathy, Dev thought. He almost felt ashamed for fouling her with his terror.

Then, in a rush, the world returned to normal pace. The priest was speaking, too loud. The priest was always speaking, Dev thought. He wanted to cave in the man's skull.

"I didn't understand before," Gerond said, shaking his head in wonder. "I thought you a mercenary, but now I know better. Amn hates you for pretending wizardry. The only way for you to salvage any honor at all is to die a hero's death, in service to the land that shuns you."

"Hard to do out here, chasing the dark with a couple of mouthy hangers-on," Dev muttered, but he hadn't recovered his dignity. He wiped his dripping chin.

Gerond chuckled. "But you *wanted* to die alone out here, didn't you? Playing the part of the reckless decoy, responsible for nothing and no one except yourself. It doesn't matter that no one's here to see. You have Morla, a respected commander, to relate the tale of your deeds once you're gone. That's your price." The priest leaned in close and dropped his voice. "But now everything's fouled up, isn't it? Foul as your wet breath. Lives other than your own have been placed in your hands and you're terrified you'll fail them. Then no one will ever speak well of you."

Dev hurled himself at the priest, but Resch stepped between them, catching him with an immovable arm against his chest. With the other, he shoved Gerond back. He shot the priest a fierce glare when Gerond opened his mouth to speak.

Slowly, Dev relaxed. Things had spun wildly out of control. The deceiver had finally been deceived, and look how he'd fallen apart because of it. He shook his head. A mess, Dev, that's what you've always been. That's what they've always told you.

"We have to move," he said, gathering himself. He shook his head when Resch went to the litter. "No more time for that, pretty face. You weigh too much, and speed is our only chance now." He took his bow off his shoulder and nocked an arrow from the quiver. The fletching felt soft against his fingers, his muscles comfortably tight as he drew the string. "Let's go," he said.

He concentrated on putting one foot in front of the other, his mind whirling with the implications of the mission Morla had given him.

Was it a punishment? Did she expect him to fail? Dev had a hard time believing the old woman could be so cruel, but then, he'd been wrong before about her.

Dev stepped around the sprawled body of an ogre with a line of arrows bristling from its spine. Goblins and kobolds lay in similar frozen agony, the blood crusting their muzzles. Dev averted his eyes. His stomach felt wrung out, twisted with stale nausea. He breathed through his teeth until his tongue ached and he couldn't stand it.

Testing the air a moment later, he was surprised to find it fresher, so much so he thought he could breathe without fear of retching. Even the clouds of flies had dissipated. For an instant Dev was relieved, then he felt a wave of fresh terror course through his body.

The air shouldn't be so pure, not with all the dead monsters lying in piles. It should be foul with rotting ogre flesh.

Unless some of the monsters were still breathing.

Dev kept walking, trusting his companions to be behind him. He could hear the priest huffing along to his left. He heard nothing to his right, but he could smell Resch's faint odor. A swift night breeze at his neck told him the way was clear directly behind him. Just ahead and to the east, he saw the mangled remains of a dead horse and her rider. They'd collapsed together on the field. Amn's banner fluttered slackly from the rider's hand. It was no sort of fortification, Dev thought, but it was close enough. He headed straight for the banner, motioning for his companions to follow.

A fine mess, Dev, and that's the truth, he berated himself. You should have seen this ambush coming before you put your foot in it.

When he could see Amn's colors, Dev spun, drew his bowstring taut, and released.

The arrow whistled past Resch's shoulder, but the big man didn't flinch. He dropped flat to his stomach behind the dead horse and yanked the priest down with him. In the distance, the arrow thudded into a dead ogre's neck.

"What in the Nine Hells is he doing!" hissed Gerond. "Have you gone completely mad?"

When there was no response, no break in the night air,

Dev honestly wondered if he *had* gone insane. But he waited, his own eyesight as keen as Morla's in the dark, and where his arrow met gray ogre flesh, he saw a core of blood well up, overflow like a fountain, and bubble down the monster's neck. The ogre had only been playing dead, but Dev had made it true.

Resch shouted a garbled warning. Automatically, Dev pivoted and fired a second shot, aiming at what might have been a drifting shadow. Arrow thudded again into flesh, and this time an animal cry broke out across the battlefield. It was the worst sound Dev had ever heard.

Gods keep us, he thought, we're already surrounded.

"Stay down!" he bellowed. Resch and Gerond scrambled to make room for him as Dev rolled over the dead horse's flank. Viciously, he twisted the animal's legs out of the way to make room for his quiver.

Two more creatures leaped up from their death poses. Dev laid his bow across the saddle and fired, clipping a kobold's haunch. To his right, Resch swung his barbed mace, caving in the skull of the second kobold as he crawled over the makeshift wall to get at them. When the creature stopped twitching, Resch hauled its body up next to the rider's, but the cover still felt pitifully inadequate.

The priest chanted a low, monotone prayer, and touched Resch on the shoulder. Green light shone through his fingers, casting hollow, eldritch shadows on the vacant-eyed horse. Then the spell drained away, and Resch's flesh seemed darker, healthier, his movements more precise. The priest then turned to Dev, but Dev waved him off.

"Save it," he snapped. "Keep them back. If they get close enough, they'll rip us apart!"

Grimly, Dev thought that seemed precisely the monsters' plan. More bodies became animate from the field, until five stood between them and freedom.

Dev took bowshots at random, more to keep the monsters

at bay than with any real aim. He planted a stack of arrows in the mud at his knees, determined to keep shooting until they were too close to pick off.

The priest raised his holy symbol. His eyes were closed, so Dev couldn't tell if he was frightened or merely concentrating. The monotone chant sounded again. Dev thought he must be seeing things. He could actually *see* the spell cloud seeping from the priest's lips, a white fog that had no scent, and no more consistency than pipeweed smoke. The divine magic drifted past Dev's cheek, numbing him with cold. Dev recoiled, and his next shot went wild.

The monsters took the distraction and scurried closer, using the bodies of their own slain companions to absorb Dev's shots.

"Get that mace ready, sharp tongue!" Dev cried. "They're coming in for a visit!"

He grabbed the silent man by the shoulder, but Resch didn't move. He was doubled over, his forehead against the ground. He clutched his stomach, his mouth slack in soundless pain. Dev couldn't see the wound, but the way Resch's body convulsed told him it was bad. It had happened so fast, the attack, and now they would be overrun. He hadn't even broken a sweat.

Furious, defeated, Dev fired blindly into the night. He didn't care if he ran out of arrows. He'd take some of the bastards down with him. Damn them and damn Morla for trusting a charlatan.

Resch had managed to maim one of the kobolds before he went down. The creature limped away, clutching a ruined leg. Dev took one more in the eye when it looked out from its hiding place. There were still three left, too many for himself and the worthless priest.

Dev hooked the bow on the slanted saddle horn. He'd never been skilled enough to wield a sword, but his fists would serve. He was about to vault over the horse when he felt the vibration.

He wasn't able to identify the source at first. But then the white mist came again, this time emanating from the dead horse's mouth.

Atrophied muscles contracted, and the beast's bent legs jerked weirdly back into their proper alignment. Dev fell back on his elbows, too frightened to put up a defense against the advancing monsters. His mouth hung open, horrified at the sight of the dead horse rising up before him, dragging her limp rider across her back.

The animal got to its feet in time to block the final advance of an ogre and its kobold minions. The creatures hesitated, as stunned as Dev by the animated horse. The beast's black mane was pressed to its back by dried blood. A long sword slash cut across its neck, exposing musculature and white bone.

Shaking itself, the horse reared. It turned on the closest kobold, spewing white vapor and with its dead rider in tow. Rotting hooves came down, trampling the creature before it could run. Horse screams joined the dying kobold's pitiful wailing.

The remaining kobold and ogre fled. Dev could hear the priest casting another spell. He turned in time to see a cluster of black shadows hanging in midair. The lifeless forms shaped into the outline of some kind of mallet or hammer.

Dev watched it spin through the air, slamming into and through the back of the retreating ogre's skull. Shadows and blood exploded in the air, and a second hammer followed the first. Dev waited for it to find the skull of the fleeing, screaming kobold, wondering if the creature would feel the same numbing chill Dev had tasted when the priest's magic touched him.

Then the shadows were spinning toward him, blocking out the moon. Dev didn't realize the hammer was meant for his skull until it was almost too late. He ducked, but the spectral weapon clipped him on the side of the head.

Dev thought he felt his eardrum shatter. He fell sideways, one arm crushed under him, his body hitting the ground like a limp doll's—or a dead horse, he thought. He appreciated the irony for a breath until he lost consciousness.

I know what yer thinking, and it's absolutely right. He could have killed us at any time. He had something a little more painful in mind.

—From the memoirs of Devlen Torthil

"Don't worry," Gerond said, "your friend won't be in pain much longer. The poison will soon run its course."

For an interminable amount of time since he'd regained consciousness, Dev had been watching Resch squirm and convulse on the ground. Every muscle in his body stretched taut, it looked like the man would rip himself apart before it was over. Sweat poured down Resch's face, but he never made a sound. The silence was the worst part. Dev thought he could have handled it better if the dying man had been screaming obscenities.

"The spell is an interesting twist on traditional invigoration magic," Gerond explained, as if Dev was curious. "For a brief time, it strengthens the target immeasurably, but at the cost of disintegrating many of the vital functions of the body. That part of the process takes a bit more time."

"Cyric preach that one to all his followers, or just the fat ones?" Dev asked. His head throbbed, and his muscles were stiff where the priest had tied his arms. Taunts were the only weapons he had left.

"To think I almost killed you while you were sleeping," Gerond said. He knelt next to Dev and twisted his head around by the hair. "Lucky for you, I wanted one last conversation."

Pain flooded Dev's skull, and he whimpered involuntarily at the sight of the shadowy hammer floating in midair above the Cyricist's shoulder. He forced a laugh, though his jaw was locked with pain.

"No wonder your herbs reeked," he murmured. "And they call me the blasphemer."

Gerond smiled faintly. "You don't know what a relief it is not to have to play the charade any longer. Or do you? Do you ever grow tired of being the deceiver, Devlen?"

Dev would have shrugged, if the pain of it hadn't threatened to put him out again. "All I know," he said, his eyes straying to the dead kobolds lying nearby, "is you killed your companions."

"True, but like you, they're not very reliable." Gerond leaned forward, flipping Dev onto his stomach with a casual hand.

He's stronger than I thought, Dev realized sickly. His breath quickened, thinking the priest was going to cave in his skull after all, but instead he felt the priest clasp one of his bound hands.

"Why are you out here, fighting for Amn?" Gerond asked. "What is between you and the commander? I might be able to use it later, but either way, it will satisfy my curiosity."

Dev didn't answer. The pain was swirling in his head. He wondered if the sensation was blood, filling up his skull. If he were truly lucky, he would die before the bastard had a chance to be done with him.

"Suddenly you're not all mouth," the priest murmured. "But I hope you can still appreciate a good jest."

Dev heard the clink of steel as Gerond drew a knife from

his belt. Still holding Dev's hands, the priest peeled one of his thumbs back. Dev felt the blade against his skin.

"What is between you and Morla?" Gerond repeated the question calmly. When Dev still didn't answer, he pressed the blade into Dev's thumb, neatly severing it below the nail.

Dev howled, curling automatically into a fetal position. The priest held onto his hands, slick now with blood. He thrashed and screamed over and over, the cries turning finally to frenzied laughter. He couldn't seem to stop, even when the Cyricist's dark prayers sealed over his wound, leaving an empty stump that was cleaner than any magician's trick.

The watching gods are going to slay me with irony. Dev beat his head against the hard-packed earth until his vision swam. Darkness cheerfully claimed him, but he knew that when he awoke he would still be maimed, and he would have to tell the priest everything.

When you're a soldier, there's nothing more valuable than the trust of the man—or woman—fighting next to you. If that trust is broken, the whole army suffers. To be a good soldier, or a good commander, you have to understand this. Even if it ruins a life.

—From the memoirs of Devlen Torthil

"I was in the militia, Esmeltaran," Dev said. "This was years before your friends came to drive us out."

Dev was dimly aware of the priest, standing somewhere behind him, probably watching for more patrols. He could hear Resch farther away, in the last throes of the poison. If sound was any indication, the man was throwing up blood and gods knew what else.

The animated horse trudged the field in slow circles, a spell-locked trance from which it couldn't escape. Dev remembered a time in his home village, when he'd seen a lame foal shuffling around its paddock, just before a farmer put a knife across its throat.

"Step and drag . . . step and drag you here to me . . . hush you little pony . . . hush you goodnight," the farmer sang.

"Go on," the priest said. "Did you know Morla then?"

"We were on the wall together," Dev said. "Morla and I had the best eyes. Esmeltaran's militia is small. We all knew each other."

"You were friends," Gerond said, surprised. "I hear it in your voice. What happened?"

"One night, I saw something from the wall, something Morla didn't see." Dev stopped speaking, but he knew it wouldn't be enough to satisfy the priest.

"What did you see?" Gerond asked.

"Nothing, as it turned out," Dev said, "a trick of my eyes, a shadow. If I could have bitten my tongue, my life might have turned out a little differently than it has."

"I don't understand," the priest said. Dev could hear the impatience in his voice. He shifted, and managed to roll onto his back so he could look the priest in the eyes.

"I was scared, see? I was young, and I didn't trust my instincts—that what was out there wasn't a threat to me or Morla. My heart was thumping like to leap out of my chest, and then my whole body started to shake. It had to be sure. It *needed* to see that there was nothing out there. They say that's what happens with sorcery, and those that can juggle it. The need overwhelms any common sense. Suddenly, a person can do things, things that no soldier of Amn has a right to do. Like send a shaft of light—bright as sunshine—across a city wall to pierce shadows that hold. . . nothing."

Dev's head had started up a pounding again. He closed his eyes until the pain became bearable.

"So you touched the Weave, completely unaware, and the city—Morla—expelled you from the militia," Gerond said. He almost sounded sympathetic. It made Dev's skin crawl. "Was it then you became the charlatan?" the priest wanted to know. "Or have you always been the deceiver, Torthil, and just didn't know it?"

"You've had enough of my stories," Dev snapped. His eyes offered a challenge. "Time for sleep."

"As you wish," Gerond said. "No more deceptions, no more decoys."

He moved forward, and Dev braced himself. Thank the gods the story of my life is a short tale, Dev thought, or poor Resch might have died in the middle.

"The problem is distraction, see?" Dev said, and gasping, sobbing, the dying warrior that had once been Resch the Silent, heaved his body up from the ground, using muscles, bones, and bowels that had ceased to obey him. But somehow, he got to his feet and slammed his body into the priest's back.

They hit the dirt hard, but Resch was already dead. His weight pinned the priest long enough for Dev to lunge onto his back.

Wrapping his bound hands around the priest's neck, Dev thrust back, clumsily, using his heels. The rope bit into fleshy folds and lodged somewhere beneath Gerond's chin. There it would stay, or Dev knew he would be as dead as Resch.

"No prayers, no thoughts." Dev pushed down, grinding the priest's hands into the ground when he would have reached for his holy symbol. "Hush, little pony, hush."

Convulsions wracked the priest's body, but Dev kept his grip. He waited until the bloated body flopped once then lay still on the field. Only then did Dev roll away.

A dull thud sounded nearby. Dev snapped around, tense at the thought of more enemies, but it was only the horse. Freed from the Cyricist's hold, the beast crumpled in a heap of ungainly legs next to Resch's body.

Dev closed the scarred man's eyes, then went to find the priest's knife for his bonds. He tried to ignore the blood staining the blade.

Not quite the hero's grand tale. Me on my belly with an insane priest lopping off all my precious appendages. I was too damn scared to do anything, and all the while there's Resch, thrashing and bleeding out poison, trying to hold onto what was left of his body long enough to help me. I wouldn't have blamed him for rolling over and calling it done, but I didn't understand. I didn't realize how long he'd been waiting to get back at someone for the way he'd been violated. Death wasn't going to take precedence over revenge, not for Resch. Never underestimate the power of trauma to bring on clarity.

—From the memoirs of Devlen Torthil

"I read your account of what happened. You did well. More than well."

Morla stood at the opening of the tent. She'd sent her guard away. They were alone. When she turned, finally, to look at Dev, her face was the color of brittle bone.

"By Lady Selûne, I swear I didn't know about Gerond." Morla looked sick. "How could I have known?"

"How could you?" Dev echoed. He thought she seemed small, somehow, without her guard and armor. An old warrior woman. Tired. "You know I forgive you, Morla my light." The words came out hollow, with none of the usual bluster.

"Do you?" Morla was watching him, with her keen vision that missed nothing. "Do you know why I acted as I did?"

"You always do what you think is best for your people."

"For Amn. Your home."

Dev inclined his head. "Your people, as I said."

"Without stability, without trust, Devlen, everything falls apart. Amn will not—"

"Amn doesn't need to think of me as being more than a charlatan, Morla," Dev interrupted. "I see that now. Comes to it, I'd rather be the decoy."

"You have the potential to be so much more."

He looked at her through narrowed eyes. "That was a long time ago. What do you want from me now, Morla? Absolution? I gave it. Your army? I carried out your mission. I'm finished now."

"You can still serve Amn. You wanted to die a hero," Morla said. "I want you to live as one. My penance, if you want it that way." Her hand shook minutely, though she still clutched her blade. "Please consider it."

A hero. That's the best bait to dangle, and Morla knew I'd wanted it bad. When I walked off Chieva's Sorrow that dawn, I had to leave Resch's body behind. Resch was a hero, but he'd had to die in agony for it, and the only thing folk would ever truly remember about him was that he'd lost a tongue in battle. At least he'd repaid one of the bastards in kind. So I walked off that field to become a war hero—better than dying, but somehow it didn't have the fire I expected. I was still a charlatan; that's what folk would always remember about me. A charlatan with a cap off his thumb. But I still played the best game in Amn. I was the trickster who could fool the monsters. Maybe they'll remember that too. Or maybe all of this is a load of piss, and I never did anything heroic. Maybe I just wrote that I did. That's the point, see? You never know when someone's playin' yer fiddle. You just never know.

—From the memoirs of Devlen Torthil

BONES AND STONES

R.A. Salvatore

The Year of the Tankard (1370 DR)

An uneasiness accompanied Thibbledorf Pwent out of Mithral Hall that late afternoon. With the hordes of King Obould pressing so closely on the west and north, Bruenor had declared that none could venture out to those reaches. Pragmatism and simple wisdom surely seemed to side with Bruenor.

It wasn't often that the battlerager, an officer of Bruenor's court, went against the edicts of his beloved King Bruenor. But this was an extraordinary circumstance, Pwent had told himself—though in language less filled with multisyllable words: "Needs gettin' done."

Still, there remained the weight of going against his beloved king, and the cognitive dissonance of that pressed on him. As if reflecting his pall, the gray sky hung low, thick, and ominous, promising rain.

Rain that would fall upon Gendray Hardhatter, and so every drop would ping painfully against Thibbledorf Pwent's heart.

It wasn't that Gendray had been killed in battle—oh no, not that! Such a fate was accepted, even expected by every member of the ferocious Gutbuster Brigade as willingly as it was by their leader, Thibbledorf Pwent. When Gendray had joined only a few short months before, Pwent had told his father, Honcklebart, a dear friend of many decades, that he most certainly could not guarantee the safety of Gendray.

"But me heart's knowin' that he'll die for a good reason," Honcklebart had said to Pwent, both of them deep in flagons of mead.

"For kin and kind, for king and clan," Pwent had appropriately toasted, and Honcklebart had tapped his cup with enthusiasm, for indeed, what dwarf could ever ask for more?

And so on a windy day atop the cliffs north of Keeper's Dale, the western porch of Mithral Hall, against the charge of an orc horde, the expectations for Gendray had come to pass, and for never a better reason had a Battlehammer dwarf fallen.

As he neared that fateful site, Pwent could almost hear the tumult of battle again. Never had he been so proud of his Gutbusters. He had led them into the heart of the orc charge. Outnumbered many times over by King Obould's most ferocious warriors, the Gutbusters hadn't flinched, hadn't hesitated. Many dwarves had fallen that day but had fallen on the bodies of many, many more orcs.

Pwent, too, had expected to die in that seemingly suicidal encounter, but somehow, and with the support of heroic friends and a clever gnome, he and some of the Gutbusters had found their way to the cliffs and down to Mithral Hall's western doors. It had been a victory bitterly won through honorable and acceptable sacrifice.

Despite that truth, Thibbledorf Pwent had carried with him the echoes of the second part of Honcklebart Hardhatter's toast, when he had hoisted his flagon proudly again and declared, "And I'm knowin' that dead or hurt, Thibbledorf Pwent'd not be leavin' me boy behind."

Tapping that flagon in toast had been no hard promise for Pwent. "If a dragon's eatin' him, then I'll cut a hole in its belly and pull out his bones!" he had heartily promised, and had meant every word.

But Gendray, dead Gendray, hadn't come home that day.

"Ye left me boy," Honcklebart had said back in the halls after the fight. There was no malice in his voice, no accusation. It was just a statement of fact, by a dwarf whose heart had broken.

Pwent almost wished his old friend had just punched him in the nose, because though Honcklebart was known to have a smashing right cross, it wouldn't have hurt the battlerager nearly as much as that simple statement of fact.

"Ye left me boy."

I look upon the hillside, quiet now except for the birds. That's all there is. The birds, cawing and cackling and poking their beaks into unseeing eyeballs. Crows do not circle before they alight on a field strewn with the dead. They fly as the bee to a flower, straight for their goal, with so great a feast before them. They are the cleaners, along with the crawling insects and the rain and the unending wind.

And the passage of time. There is always that. The turn of the day, of the season, of the year.

G'nurk winced when he came in sight of the torn mountain ridge. How glorious had been the charge! The minions of Obould, proud orc warriors, had swept up the rocky slope against the fortified dwarven position.

G'nurk had been there, in the front lines, one of only a very few who had survived that charge. But despite their losses in the forward ranks, G'nurk and his companions had cleared the path, had taken the orc army to the dwarven camp.

Absolute victory hovered before them, within easy reach, so it had seemed.

Then, somehow, through some dwarven trick or devilish magic, the mountain ridge exploded, and like a field of grain in a strong wind, the orc masses coming in support had been mowed flat. Most of them were still there, lying dead where they had stood proud.

Tinguinguay, G'nurk's beloved daughter, was still there.

He worked his way around the boulders, the air still thick with dust from the amazing blast that had reformed the entire area. The many ridges and rocks and chunks of blasted stone seemed to G'nurk like a giant carcass, as if that stretch of land, like some sentient behemoth, had itself been killed.

G'nurk paused and leaned on a boulder. He brought his dirty hand up to wipe the moisture from his eyes, took a deep breath, and reminded himself that he served Tinguinguay with honor and pride, or he honored her not at all.

He pushed away from the stone, denied its offer to serve as a crutch, and pressed along. Soon he came past the nearest of his dead companions, or pieces of them, at least. Those in the west, nearest the ridge, had been mutilated by a shock wave full of flying stones.

The stench filled his nostrils. A throng of black beetles,

the first living things he'd seen in the area, swarmed around the guts of a torso cut in half.

He thought of bugs eating his dead little girl, his daughter who in the distant past had so often used her batting eyes and pouting lips to coerce from him an extra bit of food. On one occasion, G'nurk had missed a required drill because of Tinguinguay, when she'd thoroughly manipulated out of him a visit to a nearby swimming hole. Obould hadn't noticed his absence, thank Gruumsh!

That memory brought a chuckle from G'nurk, but that laugh melted fast into a sob.

Again he leaned on a rock, needing the support. Again he scolded himself about honor and duty, and doing proud by Tinguinguay.

He climbed up on the rock to better survey the battlefield. Many years before, Obould had led an expedition to a volcano, believing the resonating explosions to be a call from Gruumsh. There, where the side of the mountain had blown off into a forest, G'nurk had seen the multitude of toppled trees, all foliage gone, all branches blasted away. The great logs lay in rows, neatly ordered, and it had seemed so surreal to G'nurk that such a natural calamity as a volcanic eruption, the very definition of chaos, could create such a sense of order and purpose.

So it seemed to the orc warrior as he stood upon that rock and looked out across the rocky slope that had marked the end of the horde's charge, for the bodies lay neatly in rows—too neatly.

So many bodies.

"Tinguinguay," G'nurk whispered.

He had to find her. He needed to see her again, and knew that it had to be there and then if it was to be ever—before the birds, the beetles, and the maggots did their work.

When it is done, all that is left are the bones and the stones. The screams are gone; the smell is gone. The blood is washed away. The fattened birds take with them in their departing flights all that identified those fallen warriors as individuals.

Leaving the bones and the stones to mingle and to mix, as the wind or the rain break apart the skeletons and filter them together, as the passage of time buries some, what is left becomes indistinguishable to all but the most careful of observers.

A rock shuffled under his foot, but Pwent didn't hear it. As he scrambled over the last rise along the cliff face, up onto the high ground from which the dwarves had made their stand before retreating into Mithral Hall, a small tumble of rocks cascaded down behind him—and again, he didn't hear it.

He heard the screams and cries, of glory and of pain, of determination against overwhelming odds, and of support for friends who were surely doomed.

He heard the ring of metal on metal, the crunch of a skull under the weight of his heavy, spiked gauntlets, and the sucking sound of his helmet spike driving through the belly of one more orc.

His mind was back in battle as he came over that ridge and looked at the long and stony descent, still littered with the corpses of scores of dwarves and hundreds and hundreds of orcs. The orc charge had come there. The boulders rolling down against them, the giant-manned catapults throwing boulders at him from the side mountain ridge—he remembered vividly that moment of desperation, when only the Gutbusters, *his* Gutbusters, could intervene. He'd led that counter-charge down the slope and headlong, furiously, into the orc horde. Punching and kicking, slashing and tearing, crying for Moradin and Clanggeddin and Dumathoin, yelling for King Bruenor and Clan Battlehammer and Mithral Hall. No fear had they shown, no hesitance in their charge, though not one expected to get off that ridge alive.

And so it was with a determined stride and an expression of both pride and lament that Thibbledorf Pwent walked down that slope once more, pausing only now and again to lift a rock and peg it at a nearby bird that was intent to feast upon the carcass of a friend.

He spotted the place where his brigade had made their valiant stand, and saw the dwarf bodies intermingled with walls of dead orcs—walls and walls, piled waist deep and even higher. How well the Gutbusters had fought!

He hoped that no birds had pecked out Gendray's eyes. Honcklebart deserved to see his son's eyes again.

Pwent ambled over and began flinging orc bodies out of the way, growling with every throw. He was too angry to notice the stiffness, even when one arm broke off and remained in his grasp. He just chucked it after the body, spitting curses.

He came to his first soldier, and winced in recognition of Tooliddle Ironfist, who had been one of the longest-serving of the Gutbuster Brigade.

Pwent paused to offer a prayer for Tooliddle to Moradin, but in the middle of that prayer, he paused more profoundly and considered the task before him. It wouldn't be difficult, taking Gendray home, but leaving all the rest of them out there. . .

How could he do that?

The battlerager stepped back and kicked a dead orc hard in the face. He put his hands on his hips and considered the scene before him, trying to figure out how many trips and how many companions he would need to bring all those boys home. For it became obvious to him that he couldn't leave them, any of them, out there for the birds and the beetles.

Big numbers confused Thibbledorf Pwent, particularly when he was wearing his boots, and particularly when, as on this occasion, he became distracted.

Something moved to the northwest of him.

At first, he thought it a large bird or some other carrion animal, but then it hit him, and hit him hard.

It was an orc—a lone orc, slipping through the maze of blasted stone and blasted bodies, and apparently oblivious to Pwent.

He should have slipped down to the ground and pretended to be among the fallen. That was the preferred strategy, obviously, a ready-made ambush right out of the Gutbusters' practiced tactics.

Pwent thought of Gendray, of Tooliddle, and all the others. He pictured a bird poking out Gendray's eyes, or a swarm of beetles crunching on his rotting intestines. He smelled the fight again and heard the cries, remembering vividly the desperate and heroic stand.

He should have slipped down to the ground and feigned death among the corpses, but instead he spat, he roared, and he charged.

Who will remember those who died here, and what have they gained to compensate for all that they, on both sides, lost?

The look upon a dwarf's face when battle is upon him would argue, surely, that the price is worth the effort, that warfare, when it comes to a dwarven clan, is a noble cause. Nothing to a dwarf is more revered than fighting to help a friend. Theirs is a community bound tightly by loyalty, by blood shared and blood spilled.

And so, in the life of an individual, perhaps this is a good way to die, a worthy end to a life lived honorably, or even to a life made worthy by this last ultimate sacrifice.

G'nurk could hardly believe his ears, or his eyes, and as the sight registered fully—a lone dwarf rushing down the slope at him—a smile curled on his face.

Gruumsh had delivered this, he knew, as an outlet for his rage, a way to chase away the demons of despair over Tinguinguay's fall.

G'nurk shied from no combat. He feared no dwarf, surely, and so while the charge of the heavily armored beast—all knee spikes, elbow spikes, head spikes, and black armor so devilishly ridged that it could flay the hide off an umber hulk—would have weakened the knees of most, for G'nurk it came as a beautiful and welcome sight.

Still grinning, the orc pulled the heavy spear off his back and brought it around, twirling it slowly so that he could take a better measure of its balance. It was no missile. G'nurk had weighted its back end with an iron ball.

The dwarf rambled on, slowing not at all at the sight of the formidable weapon. He crashed through a pair of dead orcs, sending them bouncing aside, and he continued his single-noted roar, a bellow of absolute rage and. . . pain?

G'nurk thought of Tinguinguay and surely recognized pain, and he too began to growl and let it develop into a defiant roar.

He kept his spear horizontally before him until the last moment, then stabbed out the point and dropped the weighted end to the ground, stamping it in with his foot to fully set the weapon.

He thought he had the dwarf easily skewered, but this one

was not quite as out of control as he appeared. The dwarf flung himself to the side in a fast turn and reached out with his leading left arm as he came around, managing to smack aside G'nurk's shifting spear.

The dwarf charged in along the shaft.

But G'nurk reversed and kicked up the ball, stepping out the other way and heaving with all his strength to send the back end of the weapon up fast and hard against the dwarf's chest, and with such force as to stop the furious warrior in his tracks, even knock him back a bouncing step.

G'nurk rushed out farther to the dwarf's left, working his spear cleverly to bring it end over end. As soon as he completed the weapon's turn, he went right back in, stabbing hard, thinking again to score a fast kill.

"For Tinguinguay!" he cried in Dwarvish, because he wanted his enemy to know that name, to hear that name as the last thing he ever heard!

The dwarf fell flat; the spear thrust fast above him, hitting nothing but air.

With amazing agility for one so armored and so stocky, the dwarf tucked his legs and came up fast, his helmet spike slicing up beside the spear, and he rolled his head, perfectly parrying G'nurk's strike.

He kept rolling his head, turning the spear under the helmet spike. He hopped back and bent low, driving the spear low and getting his belly behind the tip. And, amazingly, he rolled again, turning the spear!

Almost babbling with disbelief, G'nurk tried to thrust forward on one of those turns, hoping to impale the little wretch.

But the dwarf had anticipated just that, had invited just that, and as soon as the thrust began, the dwarf turned sidelong and slapped his hand against the spear shaft.

"I'm taking out both yer eyes for a dead friend," he said, and

G'nurk understood him well enough, though his command of Dwarvish was far from perfect.

The dwarf was inside his weapon's reach, and his grip proved surprisingly strong and resilient against G'nurk's attempt to break his weapon free.

So the orc surprised his opponent. He balled up his trailing, mailed fist, and slugged the grinning dwarf right in the face, a blow that would have knocked almost any orc or any dwarf flat to the ground.

I cannot help but wonder, though, in the larger context, what of the overall? What of the price, the worth, the gain? Will Obould accomplish anything worth the hundreds, perhaps thousands, of his dead? Will he gain anything long-lasting? Will the dwarven stand made out on that high cliff bring Bruenor's people anything worthwhile? Could they not have slipped into Mithral Hall, to tunnels so much more easily defended?

And a hundred years from now, when there remain only the bones and the stones, will anyone care?

I wonder what fuels the fires that burn images of glorious battle in the hearts of so many of the sentient races, my own paramount among them. I look at the carnage on the slope and I see the inevitable sight of emptiness. I imagine the cries of pain. I hear in my head the calls for loved ones when the dying warrior knows his last moment is upon him. I see a tower fall with my dearest friend atop it. Surely the tangible remnants, the rubble and the bones, are hardly worth the moment of battle. But is there, I wonder, something less tangible there, something of a greater place? Or is there, perhaps—and this is my fear—something of a delusion to it all that drives us to war again and again?

Along that latter line of thought, is it within us all, when the memories of war have faded, to so want to be a part of something great that we throw aside the quiet, the calm, the mundane, the peace itself? Do we collectively come to equate peace with boredom and complacency? Perhaps we hold these embers of war within us, dulled only by sharp memories of the pain and the loss, and when that smothering blanket dissipates with the passage of healing time, those fires flare again to life. I saw this within myself, to a smaller extent, when I realized and admitted to myself that I was not a being of comforts and complacency, that only by the wind on my face, the trails beneath my feet and the adventure along the road could I truly be happy.

I'll walk those trails indeed, but it seems to me that it is another thing altogether to carry an army along beside me, as Obould has done. For there is the consideration of a larger morality here, shown so starkly in the bones among the stones. We rush to the call of arms, to the rally, to the glory, but what of those caught in the path of this thirst for greatness?

Thibbledorf Pwent wasn't just any dwarf. He knew that his posture, and his need to speak and grin, would allow the punch, but indeed, that was how the battlerager preferred to start every tavern brawl.

He saw the mailed fist flying for his face—in truth, he might have been able to partially deflect it had he tried.

He didn't want to.

He felt his nose crunch as his head snapped back, felt the blood gushing forth.

He was still smiling.

"My turn," he promised.

But instead of throwing himself at the orc, he yanked the spear shaft in tight against his side, then hopped and rolled over the weapon, grabbing it with his second hand as well as he went. That's when he came back to his feet, he had the spear in both hands and up across his shoulders behind his neck.

He scrambled back and forth, and turned wildly in circles until at last the orc relinquished the spear.

Pwent hopped to face him. The dwarf twisted his face into a mask of rage as the orc reached for a heavy stone, and with a growl, he flipped both his arms up over the spear, then drove them down.

The weapon snapped and Pwent caught both ends and tossed them out to the side.

The rock slammed against his chest, knocking him back a step.

"Oh, but yerself's gonna hurt," the battlerager promised.

He leaped forward, fists flying, knees pumping, and head swinging, so that his helmet spike whipped back and forth right before the orc's face.

The orc leaned back, back, and stumbled and seemed to topple, and Pwent howled and lowered his head and burst forward. He felt his helmet spike punch through chain links and leather batting, slide through orc flesh, crunch through orc bone, a sensation the battlerager had felt so many times in his war-rich history.

Pwent snapped upright, taking his victim with him, lifting the bouncing orc right atop his head, impaled on the long spike.

Surprisingly, though, Pwent found himself facing his opponent. Only as the orc stepped forward, sword extended, did the battlerager understand the ruse. The orc had feigned the fall and had propped up one of the corpses in his place (and had retrieved a sword from the ground in the same move), and the victim weighing down on Pwent's head had been dead for many days.

And now the real opponent seemed to have an open charge and thrust to Thibbledorf Pwent's heart.

The next few moments went by in a blur. Stabs and swats traded purely on reflex. Pwent got slugged and gave a couple out in return. The sword nicked his arm, drawing blood on his black armor, but in that move, the battlerager was able to drive the weapon out wider than the orc had anticipated, and step in for a series of short and heavy punches. As the orc finally managed to back out, he did manage a left cross that stung Pwent's jaw, and before the battlerager could give chase, that sword came back in line.

This one's good—very good for an orc—Pwent thought.

Another vicious flurry had them dancing around each other, growling and punching, stabbing and dodging. All the time, Pwent carried nearly three hundred pounds of dead orc atop his head. It couldn't last, the dwarf knew. Not like this.

A sword slash nearly took out his gut as he just managed to suck in his belly and throw back his hips in time to avoid. Then he used the overbalance, his head, bearing the weight of the dead orc, too far out in front of his hips, to propel him forward suddenly.

He came up launching a wild left hook, but to his surprise, the orc dropped into a deep crouch and his fist whipped overhead. Improvisation alone saved the stumbling Pwent, for rather than try to halt the swing, as instinct told him, he followed through even farther, turning and lifting his right foot as he came around.

He kicked out. He needed to connect and he did, sending the orc stumbling back another couple of steps.

But Pwent, too, the corpse rolling around his helmet spike, fell off balance. He couldn't hope to recover fast enough to counter the next assault.

The orc saw it, too, and he planted his back foot and rushed forward for the kill.

Pwent couldn't stop him.

But the orc's eyes widened suddenly as something to the side apparently caught his attention. Before he could finish the strike, the battlerager, never one to question a lucky break, tightened every muscle in his body, then snapped his head forward powerfully, extricating the impaled orc, launching the corpse right into his opponent.

The orc stumbled back a step and issued a strange wail. But Pwent didn't hesitate, rushing forward and leaping in a twisting somersault right over the corpse and the living orc. As he came around, rolling over his opponent's shoulder, the battlerager slapped his forearm hard under the orc's chin while slapping his other hand across its face the other way, catching a grip on hair and leather helm. When he landed on his feet, behind the orc, Pwent had the battle won. With the orc's head twisted out far to the left and the warrior off-balance—surely to fall, except that Pwent held him aloft—and unable to do anything about it.

A simple jerk with one hand, while driving his forearm back the other way, would snap the orc's neck, while Pwent's ridged bracer, already drawing blood on the orc's throat, would tear out the creature's windpipe.

Pwent set himself to do just that, but something about the orc's expression, a detachment, a profound wound, gave him pause.

"Why'd ye stop?" the battlerager demanded, loosening his grip just enough to allow a reply, and certain that he could execute the orc at any time.

The orc didn't answer, and Pwent jostled its head painfully.

"Ye said 'for' something," Pwent pressed. "For what?"

When the orc didn't immediately respond, he gave a painful tug.

"You do not deserve to know her name," the orc grunted with what little breath he could find.

"Her?" Pwent asked. "Ye got a lover out here, do ye? Ye ready to join her, are ye?"

The orc growled and tried futilely to struggle, as if Pwent had hit a nerve.

"Well?" he whispered.

"My daughter," the orc said, and to Pwent's surprise, he seemed to just give up, then. Pwent felt him go limp below his grasp.

"Yer girl? What do ye mean? What're ye doing out here?"

Again, the orc paused, and Pwent jostled him viciously. "Tell me!"

"My daughter," the orc said, or started to say, for his voice cracked and he couldn't get through the word.

"Yer daughter died out here?" Pwent asked. "In the fight? Ye lost yer girl?"

The orc didn't answer, but Pwent saw the truth of his every question right there on the broken warrior's face.

Pwent followed the orc's hollow gaze to the side, to where several more corpses lay. "That's her, ain't it?" he asked.

"Tinguinguay," the orc mouthed, almost silently, and Pwent could hardly believe it when he noted a tear running from the orc's eye.

Pwent swallowed hard. It wasn't supposed to be like this.

He tightened his grip, telling himself to just be done with it.

To his own surprise, he hoisted the orc up to its feet and threw it forward.

"Just get her and get out o' here," the battlerager said past the lump in his throat.

Who will remember those who died here, and what have they gained to compensate for all that they, on both sides, lost?

Whenever we lose a loved one, we resolve, inevitably, to never forget, to remember that dear person for all our living days. But we the living contend with the present, and the present often commands all of our attention. And so as the years pass, we do not remember those who have gone before us every day, or even every week. Then comes the guilt, for if I am not remembering Zaknafein—my father, my mentor who sacrificed himself for me—then who is? And if no one is, then perhaps he really is gone. As the years pass, the guilt will lessen, because we forget more consistently and the pendulum turns in our self-serving thoughts to applaud ourselves on those increasingly rare occasions when we do remember! There is always the guilt, perhaps, because we are self-centered creatures to the last. It is the truth of individuality that cannot be denied.

In the end, we, all of us, see the world through our own, personal eyes.

G'nurk broke his momentum and swung around to face the surprising dwarf. "You would let me leave?" he asked in Dwarvish.

"Take yer girl and get out o' here."

"Why would you. . . ?"

"Just *get!*" Pwent growled. "I got no time for ye, ye dog. Ye came here for yer girl, and good enough for her and for yerself! So take her and get out o' here!"

G'nurk understood almost every word, certainly enough to comprehend what had just happened.

He looked over at his girl—his dear, dead girl—then

glanced back at the dwarf and asked, "Who did you lose?"

"Shut yer mouth, dog," Pwent barked at him. "And get ye gone afore I change me mind."

The tone spoke volumes to G'nurk. The pain behind the growl rang out clearly to the orc, who carried so similar a combination of hate and grief.

He looked back to Tinguinguay. Out of the corner of his eye, he saw the dwarf lower his head and turn to go.

G'nurk was no average orc warrior. He had served in Obould's elite guard for years, and as a trainer for those who had followed him into that coveted position. The dwarf had beaten him—through a trick, to be sure—and to G'nurk that was no small thing; never had he expected to be defeated in such a manner.

But now he knew better.

He covered the ground between himself and the dwarf with two leaps, and as the dwarf spun to meet the charge, G'nurk hit him with a series of quick slaps and shortened stabs to keep him, most of all, from gaining any balance.

He kept pressing, pushing, and prodding, never allowing a counter, never allowing the dwarf to set any defense.

He pushed the dwarf back, almost over, but the stubborn bearded creature came forward.

G'nurk sidestepped and crashed the pommel of his sword against the back of the dwarf's shoulder, forcing the dwarf to overbalance forward even more. When he reached up to grab at G'nurk, to use the orc as leverage, G'nurk ducked under that arm, catching it as he went so that when he came up fast behind the arm, he had it twisted such that the dwarf had no choice but to fall headlong.

The dwarf wound up flat on his back, G'nurk standing over him, the sword in tight against his throat.

I have heard parents express their fears of their own mortality soon after the birth of a child. It is a fear that stays with a parent, to a great extent, through the first dozen years of a child's life. It is not for the child that they fear, should they die—though surely there is that worry, as well—but rather for themselves. What father would accept his death before his child was truly old enough to remember him?

For who better to put a face to the bones among the stones? Who better to remember the sparkle in an eye before the crow comes a'calling?

"Bah, ye murderin' treacherous dog!" Thibbledorf Pwent yelled. "Ye got no honor, nor did yer daugh—" He bit the word off as G'nurk pressed the blade in tighter.

"Never speak of her," the orc warned, and he backed off the sword just a bit.

"Ye're thinking this honorable, are ye?"

G'nurk nodded.

Pwent nearly spat with disbelief. "Ye dog! How can ye?"

G'nurk stepped back, taking the sword with him. "Because now you know that I hold gratitude for your mercy, dwarf," he explained. "Now you know in your heart that you made the right choice. You carry with you from this field no burden of guilt for your mercy. Do not think this anything more than it is: a good deed repaid. If we meet in the lines, Obould against Bruenor, then know I will serve my king."

"And meself, me own!" Pwent proclaimed as he pulled himself to his feet.

"But you are not my enemy, dwarf," the orc added, and he stepped back, bowed and walked away.

"I ain't yer durned friend, neither!"

G'nurk turned and smiled, though whether in agreement

or in thinking that he knew otherwise, Pwent could not discern.

It had been a strange day.

I wish the crows would circle and the wind would carry them away, and the faces would remain forever to remind us of the pain. When the clarion call to glory sounds, before the armies anew trample the bones among the stones, let the faces of the dead remind us of the cost.

It is a sobering sight before me, the red-splashed stones.

It is a striking warning in my ears, the cawing of the crows.

—Drizzt Do'Urden

SECOND CHANCE

Richard Lee Byers

29 Flamerule, the Year of Risen Elfkin (1375 DR)

The autharch's soldiers tied Kemas's hands together and pulled the rope over a tree limb so that only his toes touched the ground. Then they beat his naked back, shoulders, and ribs with a cane.

The boy tried clenching his jaw so he wouldn't cry out, but that didn't work. Then he tried not to hear anything the autharch, alternately cajoling and screaming as the mood took him, had to say. If he didn't understand the questions, he couldn't answer them and so betray his comrades and his faith a second time.

Preventing that was the most important thing in the world, but he could already feel that it wouldn't always be. The jolting pain would go on and on until stopping it was all that mattered. Then he'd tell the autharch whatever he wanted to know.

So why not give in now, if surrender was inevitable in any case? He struggled to push the tempting thought out of his head.

Then one of the legionnaires said, "Someone's here to see you, Autharch. An officer from Umratharos." The beating stopped as everyone turned to regard the newcomer.

The stranger possessed the thin, long-limbed frame of a Mulan aristocrat, like the autharch, or Kemas himself, for that matter, but contrary to custom, didn't shave his scalp. Straw-colored hair framed a face that might have been pleasant if it weren't so haggard and severe. The blond man bowed slightly, as if the autharch might conceivably outrank him but not by much, and proffered sheets of parchment with green wax seals adhering to them. He wore a massive gold and emerald ring on his middle finger, and Kemas sensed he was displaying that to his fellow noble as well.

Broad-shouldered and coarse-featured for a Mulan and possessed of mean, pouchy eyes, the autharch scanned the documents, then grunted. "A tour of inspection."

"Yes," the blond man said in a rich baritone voice. "Our master"—Kemas assumed he referred to Invarri Metron, tharchion of Delhumide—"wants to make sure every noble in his dominions is loyal to Szass Tam and making ready for war."

The autharch peered about. "But where is your retinue, Lord Uupret? Surely such an important official isn't traveling alone."

"For the moment, yes. My men fell ill, and rather than stay with them and risk catching the sickness myself, I rode on alone. My business is too important to delay."

The autharch blinked. "Yes. I'm sure."

"Then I hope you'll be kind enough to explain what's going on. Why are you and your troops encamped in this field?"

"To further the northern cause, I assure you. Just east of us stands a temple of Kossuth. Obviously, I won't allow a bastion of His Omnipotence's enemies to exist on my own lands, especially when it's positioned to threaten traffic on the Sur Road. I'm going to take the place, kill the fire worshipers, and then my wizards will raise them as zombies to serve our overlords."

The blond man nodded. "That sounds reasonable. But what about the boy?" Kemas flinched.

The autharch chuckled. "Oh, him. I attacked the temple last night, but we didn't make it inside the walls. Which was fine. I didn't expect to on the first try. I was really just feeling out the enemy. Anyway, after we fell back, this little rat evidently decided he doesn't like fighting very much. He sneaked out of the shrine and tried to run away, and our sentries caught him. Now we're persuading him to tell us everything he knows about the temple's defenses."

"He looks about ready." The blond noble advanced on Kemas and gripped his raw, welted shoulder. Kemas gasped and stiffened at the resulting stab of pain.

"Be sensible," the newcomer said. "Spare yourself any further unpleasantness. Give the autharch what he wants."

Kemas felt lightheaded. He thought he was fainting or dying, and would have welcomed either. But the sensation passed, and he started talking.

It shamed him. He wept even as he spoke. But he couldn't stop.

When he finished, the autharch said, "That's that, then. He'll make a scrawny excuse for a zombie, but at least he won't be chickenhearted anymore."

"My lord," the blond man said, "I would regard it as a favor if you'd give the lad to me. As you say, he wouldn't be all that impressive an undead, and I confess, I'm fond of certain pleasures. Seeing him like this, teary-eyed, barebacked, and bloody, reminds me that I haven't had the opportunity to enjoy them since I set forth on my journey."

Kemas had imagined he couldn't feel any more wretched,

but he was wrong. He shuddered, and his stomach churned. He wondered if his further torment, whatever it turned out to be, would be Kossuth's punishment for his treachery.

The autharch cocked his head. "Since the boy isn't fit to travel, I take it that you plan to bide with me for a while."

"With your permission. It's a stroke of luck that I have the chance to watch you and your men actually fight a battle. It will give me a better idea of your capabilities than anything else could."

"Well, I'm delighted to offer you my hospitality, especially if it will lead to you carrying a good report of me to Tharchion Metron." The autharch shifted his gaze to one of the soldiers. "See to Lord Uupret's horse and provide him with a tent."

"You can toss the boy inside it," the blond man said. "It will be convenient to have him close at hand."

The legionnaire didn't literally toss Kemas, but he shoved him. The push sent a fresh burst of pain through the boy's back and sent him staggering. He fell, and with his hands tied behind him, could do nothing to catch himself. He slammed down on his belly, then rolled over on his side to peer up at the tharchion's emissary. He was afraid to look at him, but afraid not to, also.

The blond man's face was as cold as before, but revealed none of the gloating lust or cruelty his prisoner had expected. The officer sang something, crooning so softly that Kemas couldn't make out the words, then darkness swallowed everything.

When Kemas woke, a pang of fear froze him in place until he remembered what had befallen him and that, in fact, he ought to be afraid. Hoping to take stock of his situation without revealing that he'd regained consciousness, he opened his eyes just a little.

Night had fallen, and the wavering yellow light of a single lantern pushed the deepest shadows into the corners of the tent. The flaps were closed, but the blond man sat on a camp stool facing them anyway, as if he could still see out. He slumped forward with his left hand supporting his forehead, seemingly weary or disconsolate.

Which was to say, he had his back to Kemas, and scarcely seemed alert. He had, moreover, untied his captive's hands.

Kemas cast about. He didn't see any actual weapons within easy reach, but a wine bottle sat on a little folding table. Trying to be silent, he pushed back his blanket, rose from the cot, picked up the bottle, and tiptoed toward the man on the stool. He swung his makeshift bludgeon down at his captor's head.

The blond man jerked his upper body to the side, and the bottle only clipped him on the shoulder. Kemas jerked it up for another blow, but twisting around, his captor grabbed his forearm and immobilized it. Then he jumped up, hooked his leg behind Kemas's, and dumped him onto his back. Still gripping the boy's arm, twisting it, he planted his foot in the center of Kemas's chest.

"I don't want to hurt you," the blond man said.

Kemas kept struggling, but the only result was to grind pain through his shoulder joint.

"It's true," the blond man said. "If I were your enemy, why would I untie you or lay you on the cot? Why would I use my songs to heal you? You did notice that someone tended your wounds, didn't you? Otherwise you wouldn't have the strength to play tricks."

Kemas hadn't noticed, but recalling the beating he'd taken, he realized it must be so. "All right. I yield."

The blond man gave him an appraising stare, then released him. He moved to the tent flaps, pulled them slightly apart to make a peephole, and peered out. "Good. It doesn't look like anyone heard us scuffling."

Keeping hold of the bottle—not that it had done him much good before—Kemas clambered to his feet. "I don't understand any of this."

The blond man waved for him to sit down on the cot and dropped back onto the stool. "Then let me explain, starting with the basics. Are you aware that the zulkirs have gone to war with one another?"

"I heard you and the autharch say something about a war, but I couldn't take it all in."

"Well, here's the nub of it: Szass Tam wants to make himself supreme ruler of Thay, and the other archwizards refuse to accept him as their overlord. By and large, Delhumide and the other northern tharchs stand with the pretender, while the southern provinces support the rest of the council."

"But what does that have to do with the temple? Why did the autharch attack us?"

"The Church of Kossuth stands with the council, as well it should. Szass Tam betrayed and murdered scores of your priests and monks. The news just hadn't reached you in this remote location. But it did reach your autharch, and he decided to wipe out your enclave before you could strike at him or his masters."

"Judging from the way you talk, you're against Szass Tam, too."

"Yes. My real name is Bareris Anskuld, and I serve in the Griffon Legion of Pyarados. I'm on a scouting mission to find out what Szass Tam's forces are up to in Delhumide and who still stands against them. I ran into the real Lord Uupret on the trail, and when I realized I could use his ring and documents to examine Szass Tam's troops and fortresses up close, I killed him and assumed his identity."

"Didn't he have a company of guards protecting him, like the autharch asked about?"

"Yes, but I had my griffon, my magic, and a formidable comrade who dogs my steps whenever I'm not pretending to be somebody else."

Even so, fighting an important noble's retinue sounded

liked a desperate undertaking. "Aren't you afraid of meeting someone who knew the real Lord Uupret?"

Bareris shrugged.

"And if you want people to think you're just an ordinary noble in the service of the tharchion, wouldn't it be wise to shave your head? So you don't look. . . peculiar?"

"I'm a bard. If I offer an explanation for my hair, I can make people believe it, just as I made the autharch think it reasonable that one of his master's chief deputies is traveling alone."

"I suppose." But it seemed clear that Bareris was taking risks that no prudent spy would have chanced, as if some self-destructive part of him wanted his enemies to penetrate his disguise.

The blond man scowled. "That's enough blather about me. The night won't last forever, and we need to talk about how to save your temple."

Kemas swallowed. "Do you think it can be saved? I. . . I told the autharch the truth. I told him everything."

"I know. I laid a charm on you to compel you."

"What?"

"Keep your voice down!"

"Why would you do that if you're really the autharch's enemy?"

"Because I judged that you were going to talk eventually in any case. Was I wrong?"

Kemas wanted to deny it, but the words wouldn't come. Instead, his eyes stung, and he squeezed them shut to hold in tears. "No," he whispered.

"You don't need to be ashamed. Torture breaks nearly everyone in the end."

"Well, you should have let it break me!" Kemas didn't know why that would have been preferable, but he felt it nonetheless.

"Had it gone on much longer, it might have injured you badly enough that I couldn't heal you, and that wouldn't do. I have a task for you."

Kemas took a deep breath. "What?"

"After you gave the autharch what he wanted, he convened a council of war and made a battle plan. I used my influence to keep it from being as cunning a strategy as it might have been, though it's possible I didn't need to." For just an instant, Bareris's lips twitched up at the corners. Kemas realized it was the only time he'd seen the bard display any semblance of a smile. "Contrary to his own opinion, the autharch isn't a subtle man. If he were, he would have realized that your temple likely hadn't heard the tidings from the south and tried first to take the place by trickery."

"So the battle plan is worthless?"

"No. My magic couldn't accomplish that much. It simply isn't as good as it could be. But here's the real point. I now know exactly what resources the autharch commands, and precisely how he intends to employ them. It's information the temple's defenders can put to good use, once you carry it to them."

Kemas stared at him. "Me? I'm a prisoner!"

"It's dark, and I pilfered a legionnaire's cloak and tunic for you to wear. You should be able to sneak out of camp and back to the shrine."

"But you can cast spells. Your chances are better than mine. Why don't you do it?"

"I'm needed here. The autharch's troops aren't elite warriors, but they look fairly capable, they outnumber your temple guards, and they have a couple of necromancers to lend magical support. I can improve your chances by lurking in their midst and then lashing out at the right moment. I'll kill the wizards and proceed from there."

Once again, Kemas could only infer that his companion

had little regard for his own safety. "Is protecting our little shrine so important that it makes sense for you to run such a risk?"

"Anything that hinders Szass Tam's forces for even an instant is worthwhile. I wrote down the autharch's plan while you slept. Are you ready to take the parchment and go?"

Kemas swallowed. "No."

Bareris frowned. "Do you think I'm trying to trick you?"

"No, I believe what you told me. It's. . . you heard what the autharch said about me. I'm a deserter."

"And so?"

"I'm afraid of all this! I want to get away from the danger, not put myself back in the middle of it."

"Yet the temple means something to you, or you wouldn't have resisted torture for as long as you did."

"I suppose."

"How long did you serve there?"

"Nearly my whole life. My family's Mulan, but we don't have much land or money, either, and I'm a younger son. My father enlisted me in the Order of the Fire Drake—the sworn protectors of Kossuth's holy shrines and relics—thinking it would make a good life for me."

"Did it?"

"Yes. I made friends, and I liked the masters and teachers." He sneered. "I even liked the martial training and thought I was becoming a fine warrior. I imagined I'd do well if I ever had to fight a real battle."

"But until the autharch came, you never did."

"No. The temple's in the middle of settled territory and has walls like a real fortress. Nobody's bothered it for generations. The garrison was mainly there for the sake of tradition."

"Tell me what happened during the battle."

"I was on the wall with my bow. I was about to start shooting, and then an arrow flew up from below and hit

Abrihando—the fellow next to me—in the chest. He fell down, thrashed, and screamed for me to help him. But I'm no healer. I couldn't do anything. I just stared at him until he stopped moving.

"Afterward, I wanted to crouch down behind a merlon and stay there so an arrow wouldn't hit me, too. Still, I made myself shoot a few times. Then zombies ran toward the foot of the wall with ladders. Our shafts couldn't stop them."

"No," Bareris said, "you generally have to cut them to pieces."

"People scurried to shove the ladders over backward, but some of the zombies made it onto the top of the wall anyway. They smelled rotten, and their eyes shined yellow. They swung their axes, and more of our folk fell, some shrieking, some already dead.

"I put down my bow and drew my sword. I really did mean to go and help. But then something even more horrible than a zombie climbed over the top of the wall. It was a dead man, too, but with its belly ripped open and lengths of gut hanging out and waving around like snakes. They even had mouths full of fangs."

Bareris nodded. "A vilewight."

"I just couldn't make myself go near it. Not even when it caught my friend Madivik with its gut-arms. He screamed for my help, too, but I stood frozen while the poison of the thing's bites shriveled him away. It turned toward me next and would have had me too, but one of the temple priests cast a blast of fire at it. I don't think he destroyed it, but he knocked it back over the wall.

"After that, I was done. I scurried down off the wall walk and hid in the stable until the autharch broke off the attack. Later on, I sneaked out one of the posterns."

Bareris nodded. "It was your first real battle, and fear got the better of you. It happens to many untried warriors, especially if facing nasty foes like undead. You'll do better next time."

"I don't want there to be a next time."

"Deep down, you do. You'd grieve to see your comrades and your temple destroyed. It's evident in every word you say."

"You don't understand. When I ran away, I broke my vows. Even if I did manage to get back inside the temple, the other Fire Drakes would kill me themselves."

"Maybe not. If you consider them your friends, they're likely fond of you as well. Perhaps enough to show mercy, particularly considering that you'll have brought them useful information, and if not, at least you'll die knowing you've redeemed your honor."

"That's all that matters to you, isn't it? You don't care at all about staying alive, but I do!"

Bareris hesitated, then said, "I won't argue that you're mistaken. But I've taken your measure, too, and I can see that if you let it, shame will blight the rest of your life. Whatever else happens to you, in your own estimation you'll be the coward and oathbreaker forevermore. But it doesn't have to be that way, because you have what I never will: a second chance to make things right."

Kemas took a long breath. "All right. I'll try."

"Good." Bareris sprang to his feet, grabbed a pair of folded garments, and tossed them to the boy. "I have a sword for you as well."

When Kemas had donned his disguise, tucked Bareris's message inside the tunic, and hung his new baldric over his shoulder, he and the spy proceeded to the tent flaps. Bareris peeked out, then said, "Go on."

Kemas reached to pull the hanging cloths apart, then faltered.

"I can sing a song to bolster your courage," Bareris said. "I will if you need it. But I'm afraid that if I do, afterward you'll worry that you only acted bravely because you were drunk on magic."

"I'm all right," Kemas said. Trying not to think or feel, just move, he forced himself out into the open.

No one was up and about anywhere close at hand. Kemas headed north, past officers' tents and the snoring mounds that were common soldiers asleep in their bedrolls on the ground. He averted his eyes from the dying campfires lest they rob him of his night vision and resisted the urge to tiptoe like a thief in a pantomime. Better to move as if he had nothing to fear and trust his stolen garments to protect him.

A figure emerged from the darkness. The soldier peered at Kemas, and he held his breath. Finally the legionnaire raised a casual hand, Kemas returned the wave, and the man turned and trudged away.

Another twenty paces brought Kemas to the edge of the camp. Now was the time to creep, so the sentries wouldn't spot him sneaking away. Even if they believed he was one of their own, slipping out of camp to engage in some sort of mischief, they'd still try to stop him.

Mouth as dry as desert sand, heart thumping, he kept low and skulked from shadow to shadow. Perhaps his dark mantle and wiry frame helped to hide him, or maybe the tired men on watch weren't exceptionally vigilant. For no one spotted him, and eventually he peered back and judged that he'd left the camp a long bowshot behind.

Now he could turn his steps toward the temple, and until he drew near to the ring of pickets surrounding it, give more thought to haste and less to stealth. If that was what he really wanted to do.

Did he? At that moment, he was free. Safe. He needn't face the autharch's soldiers and undead horrors again, nor scorn and possible punishment from his own comrades. He could avoid it all simply by running away.

But he wouldn't avoid the guilt that would come as a result. Bareris, damn him, had warned that it would weigh on him like a curse till the end of his days.

Kemas made sure his broadsword was loose in the scabbard, then he headed east.

Stands of apple and cherry trees rose among the fields surrounding the temple. As Kemas had already discovered to his cost, the autharch's pickets were lurking in the groves, taking advantage of the cover, and no doubt eating the ripening fruit. Unfortunately, even knowing they were there, Kemas saw little choice but to skulk through the orchards himself. The only other option would be to attempt his entire approach to the shrine over open ground.

He made it far enough to spy the limestone wall of the temple complex between the trees. Then a soldier pounced down in front of him, or at least it startled Kemas so badly that it felt as if a wild beast had plunged out of nowhere to bar his path. In reality, the legionnaire had simply slipped down from the crotch of the tree where he'd been perching, his form obscured by the night.

"Who are you?" the picket asked.

Kemas reminded himself that it was dark. He was, moreover, wearing the uniform of the autharch's guards and coming from the direction of the noble's camp, not the temple. Maybe he could talk his way out of this. He took a breath and said, "The officers decided you could use a few more men standing watch up here."

"Did they send you without a bow?"

Kemas shrugged as if to convey disgust at the idiocy of the men in charge.

"Come talk to the sergeant," the picket said. "He'll tell you what to do."

No, Kemas thought, he'll recognize me. He had too good a look at me when you bastards caught me before.

He wanted to turn tail, but if he fled now, he'd never reach the temple. He smiled and said, "All right." As soon as the soldier turned his back to lead the way, he'd draw and cut the fellow down from behind.

But he was no accomplished deceiver like Bareris, and something in his tone or manner must have put the legionnaire on his guard, because the man frowned and gripped the hilt of his own blade. "Tell me the name of the person who ordered you here," he said.

Kemas whipped out his sword and ran at the picket, hoping to kill his adversary before the other man's weapon cleared the scabbard. But the soldier scrambled backward, and that gave him time to draw. He beat Kemas's blade out of line and extended his own, but fortunately, his aim was off by a hair. Otherwise, Kemas's own all-out charge would have flung him onto the point.

He hurtled past the picket, knew the man was surely pivoting to strike at him from behind, managed to arrest his forward momentum, and lurched back around. The guard's sword flashed at his neck, and he parried it.

The jolt stung his fingers but didn't quite loosen his grip. He riposted, and trained reflex guided his arm through one of the moves his teachers had drilled into him. He feinted to the flank, disengaged, and cut to the head. His sword split the left side of the picket's face from brow to chin and crunched into the bone beneath. The soldier's knees buckled and he dropped, dragging the blade down with him.

His feelings a tangle of relief, incredulity, and queasiness, Kemas stared down at the other swordsman. Shouts and the thuds of running footsteps jarred him from his daze. The legionnaire's comrades had plainly heard the ringing of blade on blade, and they were rushing to investigate.

Kemas yanked his sword free and sprinted onto the clear ground between the grove and the temple wall. When he'd covered half the distance, arrows started flying after him. He couldn't see them, but some came close enough that he heard them whisper past his body.

He fetched up in front of one of the sally ports. The light of the torches on the battlements shined down over him, and he realized that, even though he'd distanced himself from the tress, he was likely a better target than before. He pounded on the sturdy oak panel. "It's me, Kemas! Let me in!"

With a *crack*, an arrow plunged into the door. Kemas threw himself flat and continued to shout. Other arrows clattered against the entry. Some rebounded and fell on his back and legs.

Then he caught the groan of bars sliding in their brackets. He looked around, and the postern opened just enough to admit a single person. He jumped up, scurried through, and the small gate slammed behind him.

With the arrows streaking at him, he hadn't been able to think of anything else, and felt a giddy elation at escaping them unscathed. Then, however, he observed his rescuers' glowering faces and the naked weapons in their hands.

"Surrender your sword," Zorithar said. With his long, narrow face and broken nose, he was one of the senior Fire Drakes and notorious for the harsh discipline he imposed on the youths in training. His expression and tone were like cold iron.

Kemas gave him the weapon hilt first. "I need to talk to Master Rathoth-De. It's important."

"Don't worry about that," Zorithar said. "He'll want to talk to you, too."

Kemas's new captors marched him to the hall where the high priest administered the temple in times of peace, and where he still sat in the place of honor at the head of the council table. But he had no martial expertise, and thus it was Rathoth-De who was actually directing the defense.

The commander of the Fire Drakes looked too old and frail for that duty, or any responsibility more taxing than drowsing by the hearth. But his pale gray eyes were clear and sharp beneath his scraggly white brows, and he carried the weight of his yellow-and-orange plate armor as if it weighed no more than wool.

He studied Kemas's face for a time, then said, "It was a crime to run away and folly to return."

"He ran afoul of the autharch's men," Zorithar said. "They were chasing him, and apparently he had nowhere else to run."

Kemas swallowed. "With respect, Masters, that isn't true. I mean, it is, but there's more to it. I came back to bring you this." He proffered Bareris's letter.

Rathoth-De muttered and ran his finger under the words as he read them. His scowl deepened with every line. "It says here that the autharch knows everything about the temple, including which section of the north wall has fallen into disrepair."

Kemas took a deep breath. "Yes, Master. He tortured me, and I told him." He might have explained that at the end it was a charm of coercion that had actually forced him to talk, but somehow that seemed a contemptible evasion.

Zorithar sneered. "No surprise there. You'd already proved yourself a coward." He turned his gaze on Rathoth-De. "Maybe we can reinforce the wall."

"Master," Kemas said, "if you read on, you'll see that the scout from the Griffon Legion believes that our best hope is to let the autharch execute the plan he's devised and then turn it around on him."

Rathoth-De skimmed to the end, then grunted. "This does suggest possibilities." He explained Bareris's idea.

Zorithar frowned. "We've never even heard of this Anskuld person, and we don't know that we can believe a word he says. This could be a ruse."

"If I may speak, sir," a warrior said. "I have to say, I don't think so. I was watching from the wall when Kemas ran to the temple. The archers were doing their best to hit him. Which they wouldn't, if the autharch wanted him to deliver a false message."

"I agree," said Rathoth-De, "and even if I weren't convinced, the autharch has the numbers to overwhelm our little garrison eventually. We need to try something both bold and clever to have any hope of defeating him."

Zorithar shook his head. "So that's your decision? To gamble everything on this one throw?"

"I think we must." The old man turned his gaze on Kemas. "The only question remaining is what to do with the lad."

"He forsook his comrades and broke his vows to the god," Zorithar said. "Drown him as the rules of the order decree."

"Even though he risked his life to return and make amends?"

"I'm not convinced that he did it out of remorse," Zorithar said, "or devotion, or of his own volition. But it doesn't matter anyway. The rule is the rule."

"Masters," Kemas said, "I know the punishment for what I did, and I'll accept if you say I must. But let me fight for the temple first. You can use every sword."

"Not yours," Zorithar said. "You'll shrink from the foe as you did before, and leave your brothers in the lurch."

"You may be right," said Rathoth-De, "but surely the boy has given us some reason to think he's found his courage. Enough, I think, to warrant putting the matter to a test. Are you willing, apprentice?"

Kemas drew himself up straighter. "Yes."

"Then approach Kossuth's altar."

The altar was a polished slab of red marble with inlaid golden runes. Tongues of yellow flame leaped and hissed from the bowl set in the top. Such devotional fires burned all around the temple complex, and Kemas had long since grown accustomed to their heat. But as he came closer, it seemed to beat at him, because he knew and dreaded what was to come.

"Place your hand over the flames," said Rathoth-De.

Kemas pulled up his sleeve to make sure it wouldn't catch fire, then did as his master had commanded. For a moment, it didn't hurt, then the hot pain flowered in his palm and the undersides of his fingers. It grew keener with every heartbeat.

It occurred to Kemas that it shouldn't be this way. He was pledged to Kossuth, and his god and fire were one. But he wasn't a priest, just a glorified temple guard, unable to reach the ecstasy and empowerment presumably waiting inside the torment.

He told himself the ordeal surely wouldn't last for long, for unlike Zorithar, Rathoth-De wasn't cruel by nature. But it did last. The pain stretched on, and the old man kept silent.

By the burning chain, did Kemas smell himself? Was his hand *cooking*?

It was brutally hard to know that he could snatch it back whenever he chose, and no matter what else might follow, this particular agony would subside. He clenched his will and muscles to fight the urge.

Until hands gripped him and heaved him back from the flames. He peered about and saw that two of his fellow warriors had wrestled him away.

"I told you that you could stop," said Rathoth-De, "but you were concentrating so hard on keeping still that you didn't hear me."

Kemas took a breath. His hand throbbed. "Then I passed the test?"

"Yes." Rathoth-De shifted his gaze to Zorithar. "Wouldn't you agree?"

Zorithar grimaced and gestured in grudging acquiescence.

Steeling himself, Kemas inspected his hand. It wasn't

the blackened claw he'd feared to see, but it was a patchwork of raw, red flesh and blisters. "I put my off hand over the fire, so I can still use a sword. But I won't be able to manage a bow."

"Don't be so sure," said the high priest. "If there's one thing a cleric of Kossuth learns to do well, it's tending burns."

The priest chanted prayers over Kemas's hand, smeared it with pungent ointment, and wrapped it in linen bandages. The next day, though the extremity still gave its owner an occasional pang, it was well enough for him to aid in the preparations for the struggle to come.

To his relief, the other Fire Drakes accepted his presence among them without offering insults or objections. Evidently the majority believed him fit to resume his place.

He wondered if they were right. He'd fought and killed the picket, but it had taken only an instant, and desperation and his training had seen him through. He'd endured the fire, but realized now that that too had only taken a few moments, even if it had seemed an eternity at the time. It didn't necessarily mean he'd found the courage to stand his ground while a true battle raged on and on.

As Bareris had warned they would, the autharch's force approached the walls after sunset. Across the temple complex, horns blew the alarm, and Kemas rushed up the stairs to his assigned place on the wall walk.

When he squinted out over the parapet, it certainly appeared as if the autharch's entire company stood in battle array before the main gate. Supposedly the noble's mages had cast subtle illusions to foster that impression, and the darkness likely aided as well.

In any case, it steadied Kemas to know that he was looking out at a diversion, not a committed assault. A hurtling arrow could still kill him just as dead, but still, for the moment at least, the danger seemed limited and endurable. He strung his bow, nocked a shaft, picked out a murky figure on the ground below, and let fly.

He continued that way for a while, shooting steadily and ducking down behind a merlon whenever it seemed that an archer or crossbowman on the ground was making a concerted effort to hit him. Twice, scaling ladders thumped against the parapet, but not near him, and the defenders who were closer dislodged them expeditiously.

Then, his kite shield and surcoat emblazoned with the rampant fire-breathing wyrm that was the emblem of the order, Zorithar came striding along the wall walk. He scowled at Kemas. "Rathoth-De thinks the real battle is about to begin. Find a place among those who are going to fight it."

Kemas swallowed. "Me?"

Zorithar snorted. "Of course, you. We've determined that you're a fearless hero, remember? Now, move!" He hurried on, no doubt deciding who else he could pull off the front wall without the enemy realizing that the defenders knew what was about to occur.

Kemas scurried down the stairs, ran across the temple grounds, and found a place to stand. After that he had nothing to do but wait. He strained, listening for some warning sign of what was to come.

He never heard it. Rather, the decaying section of the north wall exploded inward all at once, and men ducked and averted their faces to shield their eyes from flying gravel. By Bareris's reckoning, the autharch's wizards weren't especially powerful adepts, but even so, the crumbling stonework had been too weak to withstand them.

Beyond the breach, men howled like banshees, and charging feet pounded the ground. The autharch's troops meant to penetrate the opening before their foes could shake off their surprise and move to defend it.

It was only when the first attackers had scrambled

inside, and were attempting to find their bearings amid the darkness and choking dust, that they perceived their counterparts hadn't been surprised. The Fire Drakes had expected their enemies to enter how and where they had, and had spent the day transforming the immediate area into a killing box. Carts, benches, piles of brick, and anything else that could be incorporated into barricades shielded ranks of warriors standing poised and ready for slaughter. Archers perched on the sections of wall to each side of the breach, and on nearby rooftops.

The priests of Kossuth cast their most destructive spells, and blasts of flame ripped through the mass of the enemy. The temple bowmen shot. Kemas caught himself nocking, drawing, and releasing as fast as he could and forced himself to slow down and aim.

Though it was scarcely necessary. The autharch's men were jammed so tightly together that any arrow was likely to find a mark, and the flying shafts and bursts and sprays of fire did such grievous harm that surely the attackers' first impulse was to turn and flee.

But they couldn't. They still had comrades, oblivious to the slaughter erupting just a few yards ahead, pushing through the breach behind them and bottling them in.

Their officers and sergeants realized it, and that the only possible way out of the trap was forward. They bellowed commands and their soldiers rushed the barricades.

Kemas dropped his bow and snatched out his sword just in time to parry the thrust of a spear. The Fire Drake on his left swung his mace and bashed in the spearman's skull.

Kemas returned the favor mere moments later, dispatching an axeman who was pressing his comrade hard. Up and down the line and on all three sides of the killing box, men roared and screamed, struck, defended, and fell.

A moment came when Kemas didn't have a foe within

reach. It was then that, panting and wiping stinging sweat from his eyes, he spied Bareris.

True to his word, the bard was fighting alone in the midst of the foe. His sword was bloody from point to hilt, and a sort of haze shrouded his body. The blur no doubt made him more difficult to target and was evidence that he wasn't *entirely* suicidal. But it surely couldn't protect him from the foes driving in from every side, and Kemas was certain he was about to die.

But then the opponents in front of Bareris faltered as though abruptly afraid to engage. That too must be the result of one of his songs. He ran at the men he'd cursed, and they recoiled. The unnatural terror evidently hadn't caught hold of the soldiers to the rear and on his flanks, and they struck at him but missed. He reached one of the barricades, and recognizing him for an ally, the Fire Drakes behind it helped him clamber to the other side.

At that point, Kemas glimpsed motion from the corner of his eye and remembered that his own safety was likewise at issue. He hastily faced straight ahead and beheld the zombies shambling toward him.

From the moment the wall burst open until then, he hadn't been scared, perhaps because he hadn't had time to think. But it was as if the brief respite he'd enjoyed had given dread fresh purchase on his spirit, or maybe it was simply the withered, decaying faces of the walking dead that stabbed fear into his heart and loosened his guts.

He reminded himself of what Bareris had told him. A living warrior could defeat a zombie. He just had to cut it to pieces.

Somewhere overhead, a priest chanted a prayer, and three zombies burst into flame before they could reach the barricades. Unfortunately, the creature stalking straight at Kemas wasn't one of them.

It moved slowly, though, and that enabled him to strike

first. His sword bit deep into the zombie's neck. Had it been alive, the stroke would have killed it, but its black, slimy lips didn't even twitch, nor did it falter. Reeking of corruption, it heaved its axe over its head, then swept it down in an awkward but powerful blow. Kemas twisted aside to keep it from splitting his head in two.

He pulled on his sword and it stuck, possibly caught between two vertebrae. Its head flopping on its shoulders, the corpse-thing lifted the axe for another try. Kemas gripped the hilt with both hands, heaved with all his might, and the blade jerked free.

He cut at one of the zombie's upraised hands. His sword lopped off fingers, and the axe fell out of the dead man's grasp. He took another swing at its neck and hacked deeper. The creature toppled forward and wound up draped over the barricade. Kemas was reluctant to touch the filthy thing, but it was in the way, and so he gripped its shoulder and shoved it off onto the ground. It was only then that he felt a surge of elation at having bested it.

He started to smile. Then, hunched forward, gut-tentacles writhing and lashing, the vilewight appeared among the autharch's troops. Despite the press, the legionnaires scrambled to clear a path for it.

The undead's sunken eyes burned brighter, and its fanged mouth sneered. It extended a gnarled, long-fingered hand, and a shaft of darkness leaped from the tips of the jagged talons. It blazed across a portion of the barricade, and the men it washed over collapsed, their bodies rotting.

Priests chanted. Fire leaped up around the vilewight but guttered out instantly, leaving it unburned. Archers loosed their shafts. Some pierced the dead thing's flesh, but the creature didn't even appear to notice.

It pointed its hand again. Another flare of shadow cut into the ranks of the defenders. Meanwhile, one of the warriors slain by the previous attack lurched up onto his knees, threw his arms around the legs of a live man, and sank his teeth into his thigh. A second dead Fire Drake clambered up off the ground.

Kemas realized that if spells and missiles weren't working, someone needed to get in close to the vilewight and tear it apart. Otherwise it would keep hurling sprays of shadow, killing Fire Drakes, and transforming their corpses into undead slaves until the survivors could no longer hold the barricades. Unfortunately, it looked as if even the temple's bravest protectors feared to approach the creature.

But Kemas had forgotten the man who seemingly cared nothing for his own well-being. Bareris vaulted back over the barricade and charged the vilewight.

Had they chosen, the autharch's living soldiers could have intercepted the bard, surrounded him, and cut him down. But perhaps they too feared to come too close to the vilewight, or maybe they were simply confident of its prowess, for they chose to orient on other foes.

The vilewight cast a blaze of darkness. Bareris sprang to one side, and the leaping shadow missed. He shouted, a boom loud and startling as a thunderclap, and his cry split the undead's leprous hide and knocked it staggering. The bard rushed in and cut at its torso.

At the same moment, someone among the enemy yelled a command, and the legionnaires renewed their assault on the barricades. It seemed to Kemas that they didn't attack as fiercely as before. Now that their lord had brought his most powerful weapon into play, they expected it to turn the tide of battle, and saw no reason to take extraordinary chances while it did its work.

Still, they fought hard enough that for a while, Kemas didn't dare look at anything but the space and the foes immediately in front of him. Finally the pressure eased. He peered back at Bareris and the vilewight, and gasped.

During the first moments of the duel, it had appeared that Bareris was a match for his foe, and maybe he had been, but if so, Lady Luck had turned her face from him. He was unsteady on his feet and had switched his sword to his off hand because his dominant arm dangled torn and useless at his side. It looked as if gut-tentacles had bitten him both above and below the elbow, and he'd ripped the wounds larger by pulling free.

He'd landed more than one slash in return, but it hadn't made any difference to the lithe, pouncing manner in which his adversary circled, feinted, and struck. The bloodless cuts didn't seem to trouble it any more than the arrows hanging from its flesh like a porcupine's quills.

It sprang in, clawed hands raking, lengths of intestine striking like adders. Bareris dropped low, beneath the attacks, and tried to slice its leg out from under it. He scored but failed to cut deeply enough to make the vilewight fall. At once it twisted and stooped to threaten him anew. It caught the sword in its fingers, allowing the edge to bite in order to immobilize it, and reached for the griffon rider with its gut-tentacles. The rings of lamprey fangs gaped wide.

For an instant, Bareris strained to pull his weapon free, but his left arm wasn't strong enough. He relinquished his grip and flung himself backward to avoid the gut-serpents. As he scrambled to his feet, he snatched a dagger from his boot.

The vilewight regarded the smaller blade, and its jagged leer stretched wider. It knew Bareris no longer had any hope of defeating it. Not alone, and if any of the Fire Drakes was brave enough to go to his aid, that dauntless warrior was busy with other foes.

Obviously, no one would expect Kemas to do it. He was just an apprentice. A boy. He'd already done as much as any fair-minded person could ask.

Yet if he faltered just then, allowed fear to paralyze him once more, then everything he'd accomplished—killing the picket, holding his hand over the flame, and all the rest of it—had been for nothing. The autharch's men would slaughter the Fire Drakes and priests just as if Kemas had never found the courage to return at all, and somehow, the thought of that was insupportable.

He left his place at the barricade and scurried along behind the backs of the men who were still fighting there. He needed to put himself directly in front of Bareris and the vilewight, so he wouldn't have any other enemies in his way when he advanced.

As he climbed over the barrier, the moment felt dreamlike and unreal. Maybe that was his mind's way of trying to dampen terror.

He ran at the vilewight. It glanced in his direction, then lunged at Bareris. Apparently it hoped to finish off its wounded opponent before a new one could close the distance.

It might well have succeeded, too, because Bareris stumbled. But one of the temple priests, still alive somewhere and hoarding a measure of unexpended power, chose that moment to bring another burst of flame leaping up around the vilewight's feet. As before, the flare died without burning it, but the attack slowed the creature for an instant. Time enough for Kemas to circle around behind it.

Hoping to sever its spine, he cut at its back. He gashed its leathery hide, but that didn't keep it from starting to pivot in his direction.

He could keep trying to cut it as Bareris had already slashed and stabbed it repeatedly, but suddenly a different tactic occurred to him. He tossed his sword in the bard's direction—even wounded and with his good arm crippled, Bareris could wield it as well or better than he could—and sprang onto the vilewight's back. Up close, the carrion stench of the undead filled his nose and mouth with foulness.

He hooked his fingers into the creature's eye sockets and clawed the cold jelly away.

The vilewight stiffened, staggered, and lifted its hand. Darkness seethed around the talons. Kemas grabbed its clammy wrist to keep it from discharging a flare of shadow into his face.

But he couldn't defend against all its attacks. He didn't have enough hands. Gut-snakes twisted around to reach for him, their rings of fangs gnashing.

Bareris rushed forward with Kemas's broadsword in hand. He struck savagely, repeatedly, and the sightless vilewight couldn't block or dodge. The strokes landed to better effect than before.

Bareris cut into one of its knees. It fell forward, and Kemas scrambled clear of it. The bard hacked its skull to pieces, and it stopped moving.

Kemas felt empty and could think of nothing to do but stand, wheeze, and look at the fallen creature. Bareris, however, wheeled at once, searching for other threats.

But he needn't have bothered. While they'd fought the vilewight, their comrades had held the barricades against the rest of the autharch's servants, and it looked as though the demise of their ghastly champion had destroyed the attackers' morale. They shrank back from the ranks of Fire Drakes, and someone shouted, "Retreat!" They turned and scrambled for the breach.

The defenders didn't try to stop them. Kemas wondered if it was because everyone was too exhausted to strike a single unnecessary blow. The Great Flame knew, he was.

He was even wearier at the shank end of the night, when the priests had tended the wounded and lit the funeral pyres of the dead, the Fire Drakes had made the complex as secure as it could be with a hole in the wall, everyone had eaten a hot meal, and Rathoth-De sent for him. He was glad of his fatigue, for perhaps it was the numbing effect of it that kept him from feeling anything much as he entered his masters' hall. His arm in a sling, Bareris stood conferring with the officers of the temple.

"We won," said the high priest, an unaccustomed hint of petulance in his voice. "It doesn't seem fair that we should have to leave."

"But you must," Bareris said. "You repelled the autharch's household troops. You won't withstand a real army when Invarri Metron gets around to sending one against you."

"He's right," said Rathoth-De. "We need to pack up the relics, treasury, and sacred texts and clear out as soon as possible." He smiled. "Don't take it hard, Master. It sounds as if the Firelord has work for us in the south."

Kemas decided he'd come close enough to bow. "Sir, I'm here to face your judgment."

Bareris frowned. "Surely the boy has proved useful enough that it would be folly to punish him."

"Thank you for speaking up for me," Kemas said, "but please, no more. This is a matter for the Fire Drakes, and for my commander to decide."

Rathoth-De smiled. "So it is, and our rule says a deserter must die. But it appears to me that he already has. The god's fire burned away what was unworthy in you and purified what remained, and that's good enough for me."

Kemas sighed and felt his muscles go limp with relief. He hadn't been conscious of feeling particularly afraid, yet it was suddenly clear to him just how much he'd wanted to live.

Scouting for threats on griffon-back, Bareris, along with his ghostly comrade Mirror, accompanied the servants of Kossuth on their journey south. Kemas tried repeatedly to make a true friend of the bard but always found him taciturn and aloof. He could only pray that, just as Bareris had helped him find his way to fidelity, so too would the blond man one day discover a remedy for the spiritual sickness afflicting him.

ABOUT THE AUTHORS

Richard Lee Byers is the author of over thirty novels, including several FORGOTTEN REALMS® titles. His short fiction appears in numerous magazines and anthologies. A resident of the Tampa Bay area, he spends much of his leisure time fencing and playing poker. His current projects include the final volume in his Haunted Lands trilogy and the screenplay for the Plague Knight, a major release from Rogue Planet Pictures.

A former biopharm research tech turned game designer and author, **Bruce R. Cordell** has over sixty listed credits, including three published novels, with more on the way. Bruce lives in Seattle with his wife and a menagerie of gentle house pets. He keeps his blog at brucecordell.com.

Elaine Cunningham is a history buff and a Celtic harper, which would explain her affinity for bards. She is excessively fond of Siamese cats, which goes a long way toward explaining her preoccupation with elves. Songs & Swords, a series focusing on the adventurers of bard Danilo Thann and half-elf fighter Arilyn Moonblade, will come to an end in the upcoming novel *Reclamation* (April 2008). It does not, unfortunately, include a Siamese cat.

Ed Greenwood is the stout, bearded, jolly Canadian librarian who created the FORGOTTEN REALMS world (Elminster, the Seven Sisters, liches, long-missing elf sorceresses, and all) and unleashed them on an unsuspecting world. The world seems, hundreds of novels and game products later, to have largely forgiven him for it.

On the long road to publication, **Jaleigh Johnson** has written ad copy, gaming material, Gen Con diaries, horror fiction, science fiction, fiction for children, fiction for adults, fiction for small, furry animals and gnomes, etc. She is very happy to add the FORGOTTEN REALMS world to that list. When not writing, Jaleigh enjoys gardening, biking, gaming, and movies. Visit her online at www.jaleighjohnson.com.

Paul S. Kemp is cool, handsome, and generally rocks. Or so he tells each morning when he faces the Hell of another day in service to the Man. He is the creator of Erevis Cale and has written six novels and numerous short stories for Wizards of the Coast, all set in the FORGOTTEN REALMS world. Visit him at his weblog: http://paulskemp.livejournal.com/

Though never actually referred to as "the man of steel," **Jess Lebow** likes to think that somewhere, someone might have once used that phrase within a few hundred words of his name. He hasn't found any documented proof that this has ever happened, but if he does, you can be sure he will let you know. His fifth and most recent book, *Obsidian Ridge*, will be out in April 2008. When not writing FORGOTTEN REALMS novels, Jess is the Content Director for Flying Lab Software and the hit online PC game *Pirates of the Burning Sea*.

Susan J. Morris has been a book editor at Wizards of the Coast for three and a half years, but this is her first time writing in the Realms. Her other published works include a book on card games (co-written), *A Practical Guide to Wizardry* (upcoming), and an essay on why jellyfish are important for the continued survival of humanity.

Mel Odom is the author of dozens of books that involve fantasy, SF, TV, and movie tie-ins. His novel, *The Rover*, won the 2002 National Library Association's Alex Award. He lives in Oklahoma with his wife and children, blogs at www.melodom.blogspot.com and can be reached at mel@melodom.net.

Writer **R.A. Salvatore** is so old now that he's forgotten most of his life. He hates writing bios, for that reason.

Mark Sehestedt grew up on the high plains of eastern New Mexico. He now lives in foggy New England. He is the author of *Frostfell* in the Wizards series, as well as the upcoming *Sentinelspire* in the Citadels series. If you enjoyed this story and would like to know more about the Vil Adanrath and the Endless Wastes, be sure to check out *Frostfell*.

Lisa Smedman is the author of six FORGOTTEN REALMS novels (with more on the way), as well as a dozen DUNGEONS & DRAGONS® adventures, the majority of them set in the RAVENLOFT® and DARK SUN® worlds. She is also the author of five SHADOWRUN® novels and numerous adventures, sourcebooks, and short stories for various roleplaying games. Her original fiction includes *The Apparition Trail*, an alternative historical fantasy set in the Canadian west of 1884, and the children's novel *Creature Catchers* set in an alternative Victorian England where mythological creatures exist. Her personal website is at www.lisasmedman.topcities.com.

Editor **Philip Athans** has written a few FORGOTTEN REALMS novels himself, including *Annihilation*, the penultimate volume of R.A. Salvatore's War of the Spider Queen, which inched him onto *The New York Times* best-seller list, and The Watercourse Trilogy, which did not.

RAVENLOFT™
the covenant

RAVENLOFT'S LORDS OF DARKNESS HAVE ALWAYS WAITED FOR THE UNWARY TO FIND THEM.

From the autocratic vampire who wrote the memoirs found in *I, Strahd* to the demon lord and his son whose story is told in *Tapestry of Dark Souls*, some of the finest horror characters created by some of the most influential authors of horror and dark fantasy have found their way to RAVENLOFT, to be trapped there forever.

LAURELL K. HAMILTON
Death of a Darklord

CHRISTIE GOLDEN
Vampire of the Mists

P.N. ELROD
I, Strahd: The Memoirs of a Vampire

ANDRIA CARDARELLE
To Sleep With Evil

ELAINE BERGSTROM
Tapestry of Dark Souls

TANYA HUFF
Scholar of Decay

HEIRS OF ASH
RICH WULF

The Legacy . . . an invention
of unimaginable power.
Rumors say it could save the
world—or destroy it. The
hunt is on.

<u>Book 1</u>
VOYAGE OF THE MOURNING DAWN

<u>Book 2</u>
FLIGHT OF THE DYING SUN

<u>Book 3</u>
RISE OF THE SEVENTH MOON
November 2007

BLADE OF THE FLAME
TIM WAGGONER

Once an assassin. Now a man
of faith. One man searches
for peace in a land that knows
only blood.

<u>Book 1</u>
THIEVES OF BLOOD

<u>Book 2</u>
FORGE OF THE MINDSLAYERS

<u>Book 3</u>
SEA OF DEATH
February 2008

THE LANTERNLIGHT FILES
PARKER DEWOLF

A man on the run. A city on the watch. Magic on the loose.

<u>Book 1</u>
THE LEFT HAND OF DEATH

<u>Book 2</u>
WHEN NIGHT FALLS
March 2008

<u>Book 3</u>
DEATH COMES EASY
December 2008

Land of intrigue.
Towering cities where murder is business.
Dark forests where hunters are hunted.
Ground where the dead never rest.

To find the truth takes a special breed of hero.

THE INQUISITIVES

BOUND BY IRON
Edward Bolme
Torn by oaths to king and country, one man must
unravel a tapestry of murder and slavery.

NIGHT OF THE LONG SHADOWS
Paul Crilley
During the longest nights of the year, worshipers of the
dark rise from the depths of the City of Towers
to murder . . . and worse.

LEGACY OF WOLVES
Marsheila Rockwell
In the streets of Aruldusk, a series of grisly murders has rocked
the small city. The gruesome nature of the murders spawns
rumors of a lycanthrope in a land where the shapeshifters were
thought to have been hunted to extinction.

THE DARKWOOD MASK
Jeff LaSala
A beautiful Inquisitive teams up with a wanted vigilante to take
down a crimelord who hides behind a mask of deceit, savage
cunning, and sorcery.
November 2008